SHADOWS'
EDGE

SHADOWS' EDGE

TWO MYSTERY NOVELS BY

Wade Wright

SHADOWS DON'T BLEED

and

THE SHARP EDGE

RAMBLE HOUSE

ISBN 13: 978-1-60543-361-5

ISBN 10: 1-60543-361-6

Ramble House Edition: 2010
Cover Art: Gavin L. O'Keefe
Preparation: John Wright and Fender Tucker

SHADOWS DON'T BLEED

ONE

THE GIRL HAD been silent for the past twenty miles, staring through the windshield into the bright yellow tunnel the car's headlights gouged into the night, thinking her own private and probably frightened thoughts.

Her name was Connie March, just seventeen years young, petite, and brunette and with perhaps the biggest problem a girl her age could have. Five days ago she had left home without warning to either parents or friends. Returning from school that afternoon she'd packed a few essentials into a small suitcase, and quietly departed. A note had been left, but one which offered very little explanation of her act.

As I turned south at the State highway intersection to get back onto U.S. 99, I felt her move at my side.

"I wish—I wish I was dead," she said very softly.

I glanced to my right. "Don't. Not long from now you'll be glad you aren't."

"That's easy to say," she returned without malice, and went back to staring stiffly at the road that rushed rapidly at us.

"How—how am I going to face them?" Her voice was still quiet and distant, and when I didn't answer, she said: "I feel so ashamed—so—so dirty."

"They want you back, Connie. Why do you think they went to the expense of hiring me? It's not going to be so tough."

She moved again, and not long later I heard the gentle, shuddering sounds of sobbing.

Afraid that anything I might say would be interpreted as pity, I kept quiet, trying to concentrate on the job of driving, hoping that things were going to work out for the youngster. The blow she'd been handed would be a shattering one for a seventeen-year-old. But then others like her had somehow managed to pick up the pieces and weave them together again so that the scars didn't show too much.

When he'd discovered her note, Connie's father had made his own inquiries. Then loath to take the matter to the sheriff's office had instead approached his attorney. Hal Whitman had been the attorney. He had also been at my side during the Korean thing, and he knew the kind of business I operated from my Los Angeles office. At a meeting in Whitman's office, Ralph March briefed me on his daughter's background, whispered his fears, and emphasized that he and his wife had given her all they could. I believed him then, and Connie had later confirmed his claims.

Her trouble was far from unique. There were a lot of girls around able to tell the same kind of story. And there'd be lots more.

A boy older than her—an infatuation, and later the frightening and distressing discovery of pregnancy. In Connie's case the boy had not been tall enough to stay and pick up the tab. Without mentioning his intentions to her, he'd simply packed up and taken a job in San Francisco. Connie had found out where he was, had tried to contact him by telephone, and when that had failed, tried to get to San Francisco herself by means of busses and thumbed rides. Her father's suspicions had originated only after her quiet departure. Up until then no one had even guessed at her condition. The girl had told me that much about her troubles when I'd found her in Salinas and convinced her she'd be wiser to return home. What she hadn't told me was what she'd hoped to achieve by going after the boy. On that point she herself was still a little hazy.

At the eastern turn-off from the Central Valley Highway, she straightened up and began to fiddle with her purse. I looked her way; saw her working at her eyes with a wisp of pale cloth.

"All right now?" I asked.

"Yes . . . thank you."

The night was warm, but the few stars scattered about in the black sky shed little illumination. In the distance, the Sierras hulked darkly against the sky. The road began slanting downhill and then the twinkling of lights became visible as we rounded a bend.

We drove on in further silence.

Sensing the approaching end of the journey the girl made an attempt to tidy her clothes and repair her face.

"Do you—do you think they're going to be mad?" she asked.

"No," I told her honestly. "I think they'll be only too glad to have you home again. I think your father knows, or at least has guessed."

She made no comment.

A sign loomed up out of the darkness:

REPOSADO.
City of Contentment.
Population: 4,700. 5 miles.

Reposado, a thin sprawling line of lights looking much like a mammoth glowworm hopelessly trying to crawl away from the encroaching shadow of the mountains. I hoped for the girl's sake that her parents would help her to forget, to make the most out of what was left. She was going to need help like that.

I felt grateful the responsibilities of parenthood were not mine.

I caught only a vague glimpse of movement over on the left of the road as we drew nearer the city. But apparently the girl had seen more.

She gasped and the sound brought my foot from the accelerator to the brake. Someone had stepped out of the growth lining the road, then had quickly retreated.

"Did—did you see him?" she asked a little breathlessly.

"Only just. Why?"

"There was blood—All over his shirt there was blood!"

The brake received further pressure from my foot until the car slid to a stop at the side of the road. A few yards ahead was another sign, one that announced the city limits.

"What are you going to do?"

"I don't know." And I didn't. If there was someone bleeding it could mean help was required. It could also mean trouble. And if there was to be any of that I didn't want to leave the girl alone in the car.

"He looked hurt," she said anxiously. "He seemed to be bleeding terribly. Don't you think we should find out?"

I opened the door on my side, rolled up the window, and thumbed down the door lock. "You wait here. I'll take a look." I closed the door, making sure it was locked. The one on her side was. I'd seen to that when putting her into the car.

Out in the night everything seemed so very much quieter. A night bird twittered distantly and then went silent when a far-off scraping sound broke out of the tangled thicket lining the road. I started walking carefully back to where we had seen the figure appear, wishing now that I had not locked my gun away in the car's glove box.

There was no way now of being absolutely sure of where we had seen him. I continued up the road until I was certain that the point of his appearance was somewhere between where I stopped and where the car was parked. Nowhere was there any sign of an accident.

On the way back to the car I heard it again: a crunching noise deep in the brush. I stopped and listened and my ears began to play tricks. After a few seconds the sound echoed again, fainter now, like the noise of someone or something moving away.

I walked back to the car, unlocked the door, and got in behind the wheel.

"What was it?" Connie asked.

I shrugged. "Whoever it was has taken off again."

"He looked badly hurt," she said almost to herself. "All that blood . . ."

"I'll report it to the sheriff's office after I've delivered you," I promised, twisting the key in the ignition.

When we were moving she spoke again. "Did you see his face, Mr. Cameron?"

"Only very briefly. Why?"

"It—it looked strange, and yet familiar somehow. As if—as if I'd seen him before." She sighed wearily. "I hope he'll be all right."

"You think it might be someone you know?"

"No. I just have the peculiar feeling I've seen him before."

I felt the vibration through the seat when she shivered. Then, watching the approaching city lights, she decided to drop the subject.

"We're almost there, aren't we?"

"Almost."

"I'm afraid," she whispered.

The impulse to reach out and touch her, to tell her not to be, was checked.

A little more than a hall hour later Connie March had been welcomed home warmly, hugged and kissed by grateful parents while I stood and watched and was glad that sometimes there were moments like that in a profession that dealt mostly in dirt. The parents expressed their thanks and I prepared to leave.

Before I went, Connie reminded me of my promise. "Mr. Cameron," she ventured softly. "You won't forget, will you? About that man we saw?"

"What man?" her father wanted to know.

"I won't," I said, and left her to explain.

Hal Whitman's office would be closed and his home address was something I didn't know. It would probably be in the book, but my report, I decided, could wait until morning. I planned to stop over in town for the night anyway. The day had been long enough without adding another long drive to it.

Reposado kept no city police. The County Sheriff had his office there, and his men provided what services were required. From a Texaco station I picked up directions, drove over to the square red brick building on the corner of Delano Street, and went inside.

Except for a deputy reading a magazine behind a steel desk out in the front office, the building appeared to be deserted. He lowered the magazine and nodded a greeting without getting up.

"Something I can do for you, mister?"

I told him what I had seen and he listened attentively. When I finished, he said: "You're saying you went back to look for him but he wasn't there?" He closed the magazine and placed it carefully on the desk. It was called Batmania, or something, and looked like it had been produced on a duplicating machine. The cover looked like something I should remember.

"He was gone," I said. "From the sounds of things he was moving fairly quickly. Or clumsily. Whichever, he apparently didn't feel like waiting for help."

"But he was hurt. You're sure about that?"

"There was blood on his shirt," I supplied. "He could have been injured. Or maybe it was someone else who'd been hurt and it was their blood he was wearing. It's something to consider."

Without any enthusiasm, he asked: "Can you describe him, this guy you saw?"

"Sorry." I shook my head. "I didn't get that good a look."

The truth was that I had not even seen the blood on his clothes. I had only Connie March's word for that. But for the present I had no desire to involve her in any possible questioning.

Behind me a door opened noisily and heavy footsteps thudded against the floor. The deputy swept the magazine off the desk and into a hastily opened drawer. I turned around to see a huge man wearing a leather hip coat and a western-styled hat come into the office.

Ignoring my presence, he turned to the deputy. "Anything here?"

The deputy shook his head. "Not a thing," he answered, now wide awake and alert. "Whole town's quiet, like always. Just this fella here with a report about seeing someone hurt up on the road into town."

As if only then recognizing my presence, the big man slowly turned his gaze on me. "I'm Sheriff Mulder. Your name?"

"Paul Cameron."

"Not from here, are you, Cameron?" His voice matched his appearance perfectly. Heavy and rumbling, it was delivered from somewhere deep down in his chest. Or stomach.

"No. Los Angeles."

"Which road was this you saw it?"

I looked at the deputy, then back at him. "How many are there?"

"Two. The main road from the highway, and the old dirt one north of town."

"It would be the main road," I said.

He nodded slowly. "This man you saw . . . tell me about him."

For the second time I related the story. Smoke-gray eyes watched me out of a brown, sun-wrinkled face while he hitched the thumb of his right hand into the wide leather belt that circled his broad trunk and transferred his weight to one leg. Facing him, I was glad I was just a citizen reporting an unusual incident.

"How long ago was this?" he asked when I ended the report.

"Not more than forty minutes or so."

"Not being from here," he said quietly, "you wouldn't know who it was you saw. Right?"

"I only glimpsed him. I thought you might be interested."

"Probably there's a simple explanation," he grunted, straightening up. "I'll look into it."

The deputy asked: "Want me to put it on the air, chief?"

"No need for that. I'll ride up and take a look myself. Most likely find nothing, but I guess I better check it out."

Without anything further to either the deputy or me, he lumbered off to an office at the rear of the big room. His movements were those of a big tired bear in dusty boots.

The deputy looked up at me as if to say something when the switchboard at his left buzzed and he had to plug in a line. From the office the sheriff had entered could be heard the rumble of his voice, but nothing of what was being said.

"Know a good place to eat?"

The deputy looked up as if surprised to find me still standing before his desk.

"You could try Rosa's. It's just a little way down the street and the grub's okay for the price. Try her chili." He turned to check the rear office. "But you better hang around a bit. Sheriff may still want you."

As if in response to the warning the board buzzed once more and Mulder emerged from his office.

For a while he stood motionless, leathery face without expression, gray eyes clouded as they studied me. A freshly lit panatela was wedged between his lips, the leather belt again supporting his hand. Solemnly he said: "Thanks for the tip, Cameron. I'll check it out. You can take off now."

I said a quiet good night and took off.

Wronged girls, bleeding men and surly lawmen were things I wanted to put behind me. I'd missed lunch and was hungry enough to eat anyone's cooking.

I went in search of Rosa's.

The sun shot up early and warm the following morning, driving me out of the hotel room somewhat earlier than had been intended. I passed up breakfast, settled the bill, and after locking my bag in the car's trunk took a leisurely walk down the wide street that split the town into two uneven halves. Somewhere there was bound to be a place that sold coffee a little less muddy than that which I'd choked down at Rosa's.

There was—a long, narrow but modern and bright lunchroom operated by a husband and wife team. Over two cups of coffee I paged slowly through the thin morning edition of *The Reposado Record.* There wasn't much in it. I read through a lengthy report about a coin collection that was to be exhibited in the city the following week, and that brought the time around to eight-forty-five. About then Hal Whitman should be putting in an appearance at his office.

In an air-conditioned reception room on the second floor of what might have been a recently constructed white building, I was greeted breezily by a hennaed-haired woman with teeth that would have inspired fresh ambition in a retired orthodontist. Then quietly she apologized because Whitman had not yet arrived.

"He phoned in to say that he'd been detained," she explained, still holding the ivory smile. "But I'm sure he won't be too long, Mr. Cameron. Would you care to wait?"

She had seen me briefly only once before, and I was a little surprised that she was able to remember who I was. Mine is not the kind of face that sticks out in a crowd, and operating out of Los Angeles, a city with roughly four hundred licensed operators, it's something I've come to regard as an asset of sorts.

"Thanks," I said, "I'll wait." And went over to one of the three large chairs backed up against the wall.

I was back to the front pages of a three-day-old *Sacramento Bee* when Whitman arrived a good three quarters of an hour later. He came in quietly, greeted his receptionist, and offered me his hand when I stood up.

"Good to see you back so soon." Light glinted on even teeth, but as a smile it was strictly a mouth movement. "Shall we go in?"

He held open the door to his private office and let me in. I stood until he was around the desk and seated before lowering myself into the heavy blue client's chair. It was barely noticeable these days, but for several years Hal Whitman had limped badly because of a bullet that should have found a roost in me. Looking at him now I could momentarily smell again the earth when he'd knocked me down into the mud during the advance on Hamhung, feel his body jerk when the slug ripped into his knee instead of somewhere in my belly. That was Korea, and that was fourteen years ago when we had been little more than kids. The years since had dispatched us in separate directions. Hal back to his studies and then a lucrative practice in San Diego: me, to a number of different places and never to where the real money was. None of the years had changed him much. A little heavier perhaps, and now some gray pushing through the blond crew cut, but basically the same Hal Whitman.

He reached for a silver box on the desk and offered me a cigarette. I shook my head and went on watching him. When the cropped mat on his head had turned white women were still going to find him handsome.

"March phoned me at home last night," he said, streaming smoke through his nostrils. "There's someone you've made very happy, Paul. And you were a damned sight faster than any of us ever expected."

"I was lucky," I said, trying to understand the look in his eyes. "She's pregnant, Hal. She was trying to find the father, a kid from these parts." I gave him the details.

While I talked his eyes again flicked to the framed photograph that rested near a corner of the desk. He'd done it a couple of times since we'd come into the office. I shifted my position on the chair. "You want this in writing?"

He shook his head. "No need. March is happy that his kid is back. I don't think he'll want to keep a record of how she was found and returned."

For several long seconds he was silent, watching smoke drifting lazily up from the cigarette he held.

"Something the matter, Hal."

His head went back a little as though the question had bounced against his jaw. "The matter?"

"I've seen the signs enough times to recognize them," I said quietly. "But if it's none of my business . . ."

Stamping out the cigarette in a large ashtray that matched the silver box, he pushed back the swivel chair. Without a word he reached out and turned the picture frame so that we could both see the photograph it held.

The face of a fair-haired girl smiled at me across the expanse of polished mahogany. Somewhere in her late twenties, with the kind of beauty that tempts girls to make for Hollywood and settle for jobs serving hash until one of the legendary agents happens by.

Instead of saying anything I let my eyebrows ride up and ask the question.

He responded with one of his own. "Were you ever married, Paul?"

"Once nearly. But only nearly."

"I was," he returned. "Four years, and then suddenly, in a matter of days, it was kaput! There was someone else—someone who'd been around for nearly a year before I knew about it. It hurts to end something like that," he finished softly.

"Your ex-wife?" I asked, looking back at the photograph.

"My next, I hope." Plucking another cigarette from the box, he put it between his lips and took his time about lighting it. "Want to do another job for me?"

I uncrossed my legs. "If I can help . . ." I started, sensing something personal about to crop up.

"No, this isn't a favor I'm asking. It's a job."

"All right. Tell me what you want done."

"Find another girl for me," he said, smiling tightly as if trying to hide the discomfort of an ulcer. "Find where she is and who she's with." His gaze was back on the girl's picture, perhaps a bit more firmly focused.

"You sure you want me in on something like this?"

Nodding slowly, he turned his face back to me. The smile gone, he pulled deeply on the cigarette. "It's either talk to someone or go crazy. Already I've waited too long to satisfy the damned suspicions that have been gnawing at my guts. Her name's Bridget. Bridget Cole. A sweet kid, Paul. Or so I've always believed," he added, the cigarette taking a beating between restless fingers. "I suppose once a man has been made to look a fool he tends to become a little suspicious afterwards. Perhaps it's because he doesn't want to start something that's going to end in another big bust. When I heard the rumors that she'd been seen around with someone else I tried to ignore them. There were times, I admit, when I felt I had to ask her, just to be sure. But"—he sighed loudly and killed the smoke—"I guess I lacked the nerve."

"How much to the rumors?"

"I don't know. Twice during the past weeks she was supposed to have been seen with another man—a flashy, well-dressed creep." Sturdy fingers irritably massaged the side of his jaw. "Dammit, Paul, I could have found out, and that's what makes it so tough now. All I had to do was ask her about him, that's all. I'd have known whether or not she was lying. But I didn't. I guess it was just a case of simple cowardice—scared in case I found out the truth, and scared in case she thought I didn't trust her."

"You know who this person is, the one she's supposed to have been seen with?"

"No. I never saw him myself. Friends told me about him."

There was little I could contribute to that so I waited for him to continue.

"Every Friday she drives up to Fresno to visit friends there. She leaves after the museum closes and returns early Saturday morning so she'll be back in time for work."

"That where she works? At the museum?"

A nod of confirmation and he carried on:

"Yesterday we had lunch together and I asked that she cancel her usual arrangement and accompany me to a party last night. She said it was impossible, that her plans had already been made and couldn't be changed. I guess I became a bit irritated and we got into an argument. Before we were through eating I wound up holding the ring I'd given her only a month ago."

"Just because you asked her to break a date?" I swung my gaze back to the photograph. It told me nothing of the girl's personality.

"I suppose it went a bit deeper," he answered. "People say and do things when they're steamed up and I'm no exception to the rule. It was the first time that we'd ever argued, but it was a lulu."

"Did she go last night? To these friends, I mean."

"She went somewhere," he returned grimly. "But not to any friends in Fresno. This morning I phoned her apartment to apologize, but she wasn't home. I waited around, and when by eight she still hadn't returned I phoned her friends up there—a couple by the name of Shelton. They were expecting her all right, but she never pitched up. The first person I thought of, and God knows why, was this guy she's supposed to have been seen with." He paused long enough to brush a hand over the blond mat and to take another deep breath. "Since then I've been chasing around trying to find her. At her office, to friends—anyone who might know where she's gone."

I said: "This doesn't have to mean what you're thinking."

"No, it doesn't have to mean a thing. There could be absolutely no connection between where she's gone and the stories I've heard. The whole thing could be no more than a case of coincidence, anxiety and an overworked suspicion." As if all the talking had left him empty, he slumped down in the chair, lacing his fingers together in his lap. "But then where is she? Why hasn't she come back from wherever she's gone? If she had no intention of visiting those people in Fresno, why did she have to lie about it?"

They were not the kind of questions I could answer and I didn't try.

Very quietly he asked: "Will you help me find her?"

I'd seen Hal Whitman fight in court a few times, and in Korea I'd seen him lead men against rough odds. I'd seen him bleeding and aching without flinching, but I'd never seen him look as he did now.

"Where do we start?" I asked.

"One of the people I spoke to this morning," he said, coming forward to lean on the desk, "was a girl friend of Bridget's who owns a hobby shop here in town. She claims to have seen her yesterday afternoon on her way out to Retreat."

Again I frowned my question.

"It's the name of the Danhurst place," he explained. "The old lady happens to be Bridget's aunt. Though why she would be going there is something I can't even begin to understand. Her visits to that place have been few and far between. The old woman is a recluse, and since her niece came to live in Reposado she's never once attempted to be friendly. Nobody, I might add, is welcome at Retreat."

"Your fiancée a newcomer to town then?"

"She arrived about seven months ago. I met her the first week she was here."

"How about the aunt? Have you tried finding out if she's there?"

"I tried, but the old woman wouldn't talk to me. Her son answered the phone—told me Bridget was there last night, that she'd left a little after eight. He didn't know what she came for or where she'd gone after leaving, and he wasn't very interested in continuing the conversation."

"And that's where you want me to start? By seeing the Danhursts?"

"I'll go with you." He stood up, pushing back the heavy swivel chair with the movements of his legs. "Christine Danhurst doesn't like me, but if she knows where Bridget is, then, by God, she'll tell me."

I got up and straightened my coat. "I'm ready any time you are."

A shallow smile flashed across his smooth face. "Thanks. Give me just five minutes to cancel any appointments I might have lined up and I'll be with you."

It took only a few minutes for him to give the toothy female the instructions necessary, and then we went down to where he had parked his car. With the convertible's top down and its motion creating a cool, pleasant breeze, I thought of several things I'd rather be doing on such a morning instead of searching for trouble.

If the girl, for some reason of her own, was with her aunt, she wasn't going to welcome a visit by Whitman and friend. They would want explanations of each other's actions, and if their scrap yesterday had been bad enough for her to toss back his ring, any meeting now was bound to be stormy. But these were things I couldn't tell him, and so for something to say, I said:

"How come the move, Hal?"

He turned his head slightly to look my way just as the car's wheels bumped off the paved road and onto the stretch of hardened earth that unraveled in the direction of the mountains.

"How come what move?"

"Down in San Diego you had quite a setup. This looks like only a part of it."

"Don't I know it," he grunted, and stared silently ahead. Seconds later he again inclined his head in my direction. "You're thinking it's a step down, that it?"

"It was just a question."

"It started after my marriage folded," he went on as if I hadn't spoken. "I went a little to pieces, I guess. The bottle was my buddy those days, Paul. It took a while to snap out of it, but by the time I did, my two partners had arranged it so that I'd have no option but to sell my share of the practice. What I got out of it I used to set up an office here."

I kept quiet, watching the outline of a pink structure that had appeared against the horizon when the road started curving north.

The laugh that sounded next to me contained no mirth and was as dry as the dust that floated behind us. He said:

"The business was established long before I ever came along. All I did was move it into new offices. Its original founder retired to Santa Ana and gave me the opportunity of taking it over. The way things have worked out I'm making as much here as I did slaving down south. Reposado's no metropolis, but there's money here and a good lawyer can earn a handsome part of it." A hand left the wheel and pointed. "That's Retreat ahead. When we get there you'll appreciate the name more."

The pink building was fast growing larger. "You said the old lady wouldn't talk to you on the phone. Think she'll see us now?"

"She'll see us," he asserted firmly. "It may not be easy, but she'll see us. To her I'm just another shyster. She let me know that the second time I came out here. Both occasions I was with Bridget, and they were the longest and coldest damned hours I've ever spent anywhere." He shook his head and the laugh sounded again. "We sat there alone with her, without a drink or even the offer of one. Bridget tried hard to make conversation, but it was simply no go. Christine Danhurst made it clear that she did not enjoy visitors, no matter who they might be. In the end she turned on me. She wanted to know why I had come out there with her niece—what kind of game I was up to. Hell, she's a weirdo, I promise you. A real honest-to-god nut! She's hidden herself away from people for so long she's grown suspicious of all strangers."

"How about her husband? He the same?"

"He's dead," I was told. "Nat Danhurst died a long time ago. I never met him, but I heard he was much the same as his wife. They lived out there with just their two kids and a couple of servants and he came into town only when it was absolutely necessary, or never at all. Danhurst was worth a sizeable fortune, and with that kind of money you can buy all the privacy you imagine you need. And privacy, it would seem, is about all they ever wanted. Someone once told me why he built that monstrosity and came to live out here. Something to do with the death of their first kid, I think, but I've forgotten the details."

Before I could ask anything more about the family the road took another twist and brought us up to the front of the thing he had called a
monstrosity.

TWO

BIG AND RAMBLING, tall and pink; I thought Whitman's description of the house was slightly exaggerated. Its designer had striven for a Spanish effect, but in the process had sneaked in several ideas that had been strictly from the Deep South. It stood two storeys high, square, and wide and proud, its façade ventilated with long narrow windows fringed in simple ornamental white. Four of the upper windows each had their own open balcony. There was a certain lonely and aloof beauty in the structure, but not the kind that was easily discernible. Once, as a small boy, I had stood before a similar house and made myself one of the many promises circumstances had prevented fulfilling. So far I had never owned any kind of property. Perhaps it was the lonely, empty surroundings or the apparent need of attention that caused Whitman to think of it as he did.

Nobody watched over the high iron gate fixed into the seven-foot surrounding wall, but when I got out of the car to swing it open a heavy bell fitted into the latticed metal started to clang. Its noise would carry back to the house and was probably a lot cheaper than a full-time gateman.

I waited until Whitman had driven through, then swung the gate closed. In some way it was designed so that its weight, and perhaps offset hinges, made the task of opening and closing it fairly easy. I went around the car and got in beside Whitman, conscious of the silence and the absence of life near the house or the rows of trees that stood in the foreground.

"You'd have thought they'd have had that thing electrically controlled," I said.

"You'd have thought," he muttered.

Two cars were parked in the shade of a wide portico built to the left of the house, another docked at the bottom of the rambling steps that rose from the asphalt drive to the wide front door. We pulled in behind it and got out. Hal looked at the smart gray Mercedes as if it were familiar, but said nothing.

I was behind him on the third step when the door opened and a small man in a suit that complemented the color of the car parked in front of ours emerged from the house. In his left hand he carried a black leather bag. On his gaunt face was worn an expression of deep concern.

Whitman was the first to speak. "Hello, Myron. Someone sick?"

The little man cocked his head sharply, the beaked nose twitching. Swiftly his glance swung over to where I had stopped. I offered a smile, which he didn't bother to reciprocate.

"Paul Cameron," Hal said, nodding in my direction, sensing the need for an introduction. "Dr. Myron McGill."

As a doctor he reminded me more of a defeated undertaker. His small frame was stooped and the hair on his long head had withered and thinned so that the pale shiny pink of his scalp shone through. I put out a hand that he accepted cautiously. Under the warm flesh I could feel the outline of thin bones. He retrieved his limp hand and took another step down.

"Anyone ill?" Whitman asked again.

"No. Not really. This is just one of my usual visits." The prominent Adam's apple jumped violently when he cleared his throat. "Christine— Mrs. Danhurst—I see her regularly. Last night she was not too well." Once more he glanced my way. "You here on business?" he asked Whitman.

"Unofficial business."

The sad face suggested he didn't believe it, and for a moment I thought he was going to ask another question. But something quickly changed his mind. Nodding to each of us in turn, he said a crisp "Good morning", and descended the rest of the steps to his gray car.

We waited until he was on his way before continuing up what was left of the steps, and only when we reached the top did I notice that the front door was still partially open and that somebody had been watching us from the shadowy interior.

She stepped into view as we halted at the door. A tall woman with striking black hair tied tightly to the back of her head. Bright eyes shone in a dark and stolid face while she appraised us. Her Spanish ancestry was evident, but not in her speech.

She said: "Good morning, Mr. Whitman."

Hal waited until the clanging of the gate bell stopped. "Hello, Luisa," he greeted. "I'd like to have a few words with Mrs. Danhurst, if she's up."

"She is," the woman called Luisa answered calmly. "But you well know, Mr. Whitman, that she never receives visitors without prior consent to an appointment."

"Just let her know I'm here, Luisa. Tell her I want to talk about her niece. Inform her it's important that I do."

Very slowly she wagged her head. "I would rather not, sir. May I suggest you telephone—later? Mrs. Danhurst has just seen her doctor and I know she will have no wish for visitors." Her shiny eyes had focused accusingly upon me.

I looked back into the face that was both young and old and wondered how she would react if I told her two inches of her blue slip was showing.

"Luisa," Hal said a little impatiently, moving closer to her, "either you tell her I'm here or I'm going in unannounced. Which is it to be?"

The bell on the gate sounded again.

"Please wait." She remained unruffled by his threat, but moved back inside, closing the door on us.

While he paced about nervously I used the time to look over the grounds. They were large and in need of a steady gardener. Over the wall and far off in the distance from which we had come I could see a dust cloud floating behind the doctor's car.

Luisa's voice startled me when soundlessly she re-opened the door.

"Please come in," she announced, disapproval making her words nothing but hollow sounds.

She shut the door then led us down a dim arched hallway to another open door on the right. After ushering us in she quietly faded from sight.

The room was massive, crowded with furniture and adornments on the walls that ranged from original oils to the mounted head of a doleful buffalo over the great stone fireplace. The air was thick and sickly sweet, and not unlike that of a museum. In an upholstered rocking chair near the fireplace and a wide-screen TV set, someone sat completely motionless.

"Mrs. Danhurst?" Whitman said, moving between a matched pair of weighty chairs to get nearer to the fat woman.

"You said you wanted to talk about Bridget Cole," she snapped back at him. "You told Luisa your business was important." Her voice was like the shuffling of wet gravel.

"It is," he said, stopping before her.

A concert grand piano stood like a multiple coffin at my left. I used it as a resting place for my elbow while waiting for the outcome of Hal's intended questions, and studied the paintings.

"Who is he?" the scratchy voice queried.

"A friend," he told her, impatience blunting his tone. "About Bridget, Mrs. Danhurst . . ."

"Another lawyer?" she demanded to know. "What do you want of me, Whitman? What is the meaning of bringing uninvited strangers into my home?"

"Paul's a friend, not a lawyer, and my business here is personal—and important."

She looked across to where I lounged against the piano, dark eyes fiery with anger or something that could have been no more than a glare of suspicion. They seemed to penetrate and succeed in making me feel uneasy.

"You. What is your business? What do you want?"

I stared back at the huge mound of pallid flesh that looked like spoiled dough stuffed into the white sleeveless dress, and hesitated with my answer.

Hal saved me the trouble of a lie. "Mr. Cameron is a private investigator."

"A *what?*"

"A private detective."

"I know what you said!" she rasped loudly. "What I want to know is your reason for bringing such a person into my home."

"Paul's helping me. We're trying to find Bridget. I tried to talk to you on the phone this morning, but—"

"I am fully aware of what transpires in my home, Mr. Whitman." She heaved a heavy, tired sigh that rocked her bountiful chest. "What about Bridget? What do you mean you're trying to find her?" Her voice had grown more subdued, but it was the kind that could never be entirely soft even when she tried.

Hal told her about the girl and while he talked I went on looking at the pictures on the walls.

One was of a distinguished middle-aged man dressed in the fashion of nearly thirty years past. I thought I knew who he might be. Another was of a girl who would have been one of the beauties of her day. Blonde, slim and smiling warmly. I wondered where she fitted into the Danhurst history. Or if she did.

The old woman was talking again when I lost interest in the picture.

"Bridget was here last night. Gerry told you that, did he not? He also told you what time she left. Was that not sufficient for you? Do you doubt his word?"

"I'm not doubting anyone," Hal returned loudly. "All I'm trying to do is find her. Dammit, she's your niece, isn't she? Aren't you at least interested enough to try help me find her?"

The room gathered a tomb-like silence when she failed to provide an immediate reply.

"Surely she must have said something of where she was going?" he insisted, his voice revealing some signs of strain.

"I've already told you she said nothing to me of her intentions."

"Then why did she come here, Mrs. Danhurst? What did she want?"

"Money." The eyes in the lumpy face grew glassy and cold. Icily she said: "She wanted to borrow five hundred dollars."

"Five hundred . . .! Why? For what? What did she want with that kind of money?"

"I thought," the massive woman returned coldly, "that my niece was engaged to you? Wouldn't you be in a far better position to answer that question?"

Hal's head shook slowly, bewilderedly. "Why didn't she ask me . . .?"

"Didn't she?"

"The money," he said, ignoring her question. "You—gave it to her?"

"I do not make a habit of lending money," she told him, pudgy fingers fiddling nervously with something in her ample lap. "There are banks for that sort of thing. On this occasion, however, I broke one of my cardinal rules."

"You gave it to her? You gave her five hundred dollars?" It was impossible for him to keep the astonishment from his voice, and as I listened I could feel the start of trouble creeping in on us.

I began to wish that I'd driven back to L.A. instead of staying the night in town.

"Did I not say so?" she demanded irritably, then drew a deep breath. "Now . . . if you have done with your questions, Mr. Whitman, I wish to rest. I did not have a good night and my doctor has administered a sedative, the effects of which I am beginning to feel."

"But surely she must have said why she needed the money? She must have told you something!"

She glared at him, pale lips tightening.

"Mrs. Danhurst, if Bridget's in any sort of trouble, for God's sake tell me so that I can help her."

"She told me nothing. Absolutely nothing. I gave her the money because she appeared to be desperate for it. What she wanted it for, and if she was in any kind of trouble, are things I do not know." Under her bulk the chair began to rock. Eyelids drooped sleepily. "I have answered your questions, now will you be good enough to take your friend and go away? I am very tired." The eyes closed completely and the rocking chair gathered momentum.

"Mrs. Danhurst . . .?"

"If you do not leave," she said, eyes still shut, "I will be forced to ring for my son and have you forcibly removed." In her lap thick fingers toyed with a small square gadget and the TV screen came to life. "Goodbye, Mr. Whitman," she said.

I walked up behind him as sounds of other voices began to fill the room, touched his arm and motioned him to the door. He pulled angrily at the collar of his shirt, but followed.

The woman named Luisa was waiting in the hall and led us quickly to the front door. As she opened it the bell on the gate began to clang. Luisa froze with her hand on the big brass doorknob but let us move past her.

We were on our way down the steps when the car crawled up the drive.

"For someone who doesn't welcome or encourage visitors," I said, "the lady of the house is getting enough of them this morning."

Whitman didn't comment. Like me, he was watching the car that had pulled to a stop behind his convertible. A blue ranch wagon that carried County markings.

The sheriff scrambled out from behind the wheel, slammed the door shut and looked to where we stood.

This morning he was dressed in neat suntans, without the leather jacket. The broad-brimmed hat was tilted comfortably to the back of his head.

Recognizing us, he stopped at the front of his car and waited until we were down the steps.

"Morning," he greeted somberly. "Been trying to find you, Counselor. Your girl at the office said you'd gone out, but she didn't know where. Hadn't figured on finding you here though."

"Something you wanted?" Whitman asked.

"Just a few questions," Mulder replied, his gaze shifting to me. "Thought you'd have been back in Riot Town by now, Cameron. Something holding you here?"

I smiled back. "Something."

"Mr. Cameron is working for me," Whitman informed him, a slight edge to his words.

"Oh?" Mulder's surprise appeared to be real. "Personal work, counselor?"

"Yes, Sheriff. Very personal." He started to walk past the gleaming six-pointed star.

"A minute." Mulder put out a restraining hand. "I said I had a few questions."

Almost angrily the lawyer brushed away the hand. It left me wondering what existed between them.

"Miss Cole. Bridget Cole," Mulder said, brown face like old leather, as if Whitman's act of irritation had not been noticed. "She's your fiancée or something, right?"

"What about her? Where is she, Mulder?"

"How about I ask my questions first?" He grinned thinly. "That be okay by you?" He waited a moment or two, and when Whitman made no reply, asked: "When last did you see her, Counselor?"

"Yesterday—at lunch. Look, if—"

"How about last night?"

"Mulder, if she's done something, for God's sake stop playing around with me and say so!"

"She hasn't done a thing, Whitman," the sheriff told him, voice softer by shades. "That the last time you saw her?"

"Isn't that what I just said? Look, Sheriff, if Miss Cole is—"

"Easy, Whitman, easy." He unhooked his left thumb from his belt and pulled his huge frame up to full height. "I'm just doing my job, and these questions are part of it." He glanced up at the sun, frowned, looked at me, and then back to where Whitman waited impatiently. "I've got tough news for you, Counselor. The girl's dead."

Whitman stiffened and it was a while before he made any sound. "No . . ."

Mulder took off his hat, rubbed the heel of his hand across his forehead, at sweat that wasn't there. "You didn't know?"

For a very long moment the stunned look on Hal Whitman's face stayed rigid. His mouth twitched soundlessly and then at last the one word—dull and flat, like an echo of the sheriff's statement. *"Dead . . ."* Hands went up to cover his face and he turned quickly away from our stares.

"She was killed," Mulder announced to no particular listener, sticking the hat back onto his head.

I reached into my pocket for cigarettes while high overhead the sun seemed to have gone suddenly cold.

THREE

WATCHING WHITMAN LEANING on the tail end of the convertible, his back to us, the sheriff appeared to have lost all interest in me. I dropped my cigarette to the ground and stepped on it.

"What happened?"

At the sound of my voice he turned but did not answer. "You okay?" he asked Whitman.

Whitman stepped away from the car, brushed at his hair, and came around. Nodding mutely he took the two steps that brought him back to where we waited.

"What happened to her?"

"Don't know for certain, but it wasn't nice. She was beaten up pretty bad. We've got her down at the morgue where Doc. Hamilton will do what's necessary." Mulder paused just long enough for the information to sink in before asking: "Think you're up to making identification?"

"Yes," Whitman told him dully.

"Came here to tell the old lady, seeing as she's the nearest kin. Though I wasn't too hopeful about getting her to identify her niece. Her son could do it, I suppose. But seeing as you're—"

"I *said* I'd do it!"

"Sure, sure," Mulder said placatingly. "There're some more questions I'll need to ask you as well. But first I'd better break the news to the old girl. You'll stick around here for me?"

Without waiting for agreement, he started up to the house.

"Want me to go along with you?" I asked Whitman when we were alone.

"Please," he said. Then: "Paul, will you stay here for a while? I'll pay for your time."

"There isn't any need for that. I'll stay the rest of the weekend at least."

"Thanks." His hand touched my arm and the fingers squeezed tightly. "Why, Paul? Why her?"

"That's what the sheriff will try to find out," I answered, watching Mulder standing at the front door, talking to Luisa. Turning back to Whitman, I said: "Let's go and wait in the car."

I was opening the door on the passenger's side when I spotted a movement upstairs in the pink house. Like a sad-faced Juliet of modem times, a girl stood on one of the small balconies and looked round-eyed down at us. I had only one quick glimpse before she turned and disappeared back into the house. Her hair had been long and as black as a raven's breast, and she'd been pretty. But in that one short glimpse I had witnessed something else. Perhaps it was only my imagination, or the news the sheriff had brought, but in her face I had seen the shadows of grief.

I got in beside Whitman and shut the door. The expression on his face was much the same as the girl had been wearing. She'd probably been listening while we'd talked, I decided. It had been a subject of sorrow.

"Will you do me a favor?" Whitman asked quietly. "Will you forget what you heard about the five hundred dollars?"

"The sheriff's with her now," I reminded him. "Won't she tell him?"

"Perhaps. But if she doesn't, will you keep it to yourself?"

"If that's what you want."

"I want to hire you."

"Hal, forget it. I don't especially go for Mulder, and I've a feeling you don't either. But he'll find the person responsible. You don't need me for something like this."

"I still want you to work for me. If you will. It—it's all I can do for her now. But I was thinking of other things. Not just of who—who killed her." He choked on the last words, then coughed hurriedly to cover his embarrassment. "I want to know why she needed money, why she didn't come to me for it."

"Is there any point in that now? What do you hope to prove?"

"Prove?" he asked listlessly, gripping the steering wheel so tightly his knuckles showed white. "Nothing. I'm not trying to prove a thing. All I want to know is who killed her and why she needed money. I want to know what kind of trouble she was in." He stopped talking to stare intently through the windshield, as if the answers he sought might be there among the trees. "I want to know these things before Mulder does."

"Am I permitted to know why?"

"Her name," he said softly. "Mulder won't care how much dirt he lets the papers get hold of." He shook his head as if trying to dislodge the thought. "I don't want her private life dragged through the papers, Paul. That much I can still do for her."

"The trouble she had could have been the cause of this," I said. "If it was, I don't think I'm going to be of much help to you."

"But we can try. We have to."

"You have any ideas about it?"

"None. She never once hinted about trouble. That's another reason why I must do what I can now. She must have had a reason for not telling me about it." He sighed and dropped his hands from the wheel. "I knew there was this other party—the one I told you about," he said, and turned his head so he could look at me. "Paul, you don't think he . . .?"

I shrugged. "I don't know. No one could at this stage." I waited before asking: "Are you going to tell Mulder about him?"

"No."

At the house a door closed.

"Time to go," I announced, seeing the sheriff on the steps.

Mulder got into his car, started the engine and pulled in at our side.

"Follow me into town. We'll go straight to the hospital."

Whitman mumbled something too soft to hear, but organized himself behind the wheel and reached for the key sticking out of the dash.

As we started after the ranch wagon I took a last look up at the balconies of the big house. They were empty. I thought about the girl, and then once more about the thing I'd been thinking about ever since Mulder had delivered his grim tidings. Nothing had been mentioned of where the killing had occurred, but last night Connie March had said a man was bleeding. It was not a thought to pass on to Whitman, so I kept silent and settled back to swallow the dust of the car ahead.

With fresh paint and much gleaming glass, the sprawling single storey building of the Reposado District Hospital gave the impression of having totally outlawed death. Until you drove around the circular gravel drive to the shadowed rear and saw the painted sign that pointed in the direction of the morgue.

Mulder led the way; spoke briefly to the attendant inside, then pushed open the white vinyl-clad swing doors.

"In here," he instructed.

Over at a washbasin a tall, unhealthy-looking man in white smock and red rubber apron was pulling the same colored gloves over long fingers. At the sound of our arrival and apparent recognition of Mulder, he gave a mute signal and walked over to the table in the center of the cold tiled floor, and waited.

Whitman stopped abruptly and sucked in his breath at the sight of the sheet-covered thing positioned on the stainless steel table. Mulder went to stand on the other side, beside the man in the apron. Pretending the stink of formaldehyde was non-existent, I took Whitman's elbow, eased him forward.

"Ready, Whitman?" Mulder asked.

"Let me see," he croaked back.

The sheet was drawn slowly away until what was left of the girl's face was revealed. Whitman choked back a painful sound and quickly turned away. I left him, took a step closer for a better look at the pathetic upturned face.

It was badly bruised and dirty with sand and blood, but not ugly to look at, nor difficult to recognize. The one in the smock and apron covered it up, said to Mulder:

"I was just about to start when you came in. Shouldn't take too long, this one."

"How about it, Counselor?" Mulder asked.

"Yes," Whitman mumbled. "It—it's her." Then disregarding the rest of us, broke for the exit.

The sheriff came quickly around the table and pushed past me. I followed him out.

"Think you can stand a few questions?" he asked when we caught up with Whitman.

"Can't it wait?" I asked him. "He's been through enough this morning as it is."

"Sure," Mulder grunted. "If he insists it can wait. But if I'm going to find the one who did that back there,"—he poked his thumb at the room we had left—"the sooner we get it done with the better."

From his pocket Whitman pulled a handkerchief and brushed it roughly across his eyes. "I'm all right," he said. "I'll answer your damned questions. Ask them."

"Not here. We can do it over at my office." Mulder's gaze swung sharply at me. "You'd better come along also. There're one or two things I want to ask you as well."

Outside I took the keys of the convertible from Whitman and drove him to the sheriff's office. Another man was on duty at the outer desk, and while Mulder questioned Hal Whitman inside his office, I sat on a hard bench and watched the deputy trying to act busy.

They were inside a long time before the door finally opened and the sheriff called my name. I got up and went to him. Whitman came out of the office as I got there, looking as if he'd been crawling around in hell.

"I'll wait for you," he said quietly. "I'll wait out in the car for you."

I nodded and entered the spacious office where Mulder motioned to a still-warm chair before shutting the door.

Behind the desk he folded thick arms, leaned back heavily in the chair and let his gray eyes glint accusingly. For nearly a minute I sat quiet, as though confronted by a two hundred pound snake intent on hypnotizing me.

I said: "I've been through this sort of thing before, Sheriff. Why don't we just get down to the reason for having me here?"

"How's that again?"

"The frozen eye treatment. I've had it before. It wastes a hell of a lot of time."

Letting his breath hiss out loudly he unfolded his arms and flattened the palms of his big hands on the desktop.

"You disappoint me, Cameron. I guess I had you sized up all wrong. I didn't take you for a snot-nose. Maybe I forgot for a minute that you're a big shot private dick from down south. Probably you're too used to dealing with the big city cops and making fancy money out of digging the dirt for all them movie and TV people. Here I was thinking that you're just a private ticket who wants only to keep his nose clean—especially after coming out of your way here last night to turn in a report like a square citizen. Now you want to make me a liar by proving I had you pegged wrong, that you're nothing but a wise guy who thinks I'm just a dumb and stupid small time cop."

I didn't bother to correct his impression of the kind of work I usually did or the type of people who generally hired me. It wasn't worth the time.

"How long you been in the game, Cameron?"

"Sometimes it seems too long."

"Yeah, I know what you mean."

"Then you probably know that a snot-nose doesn't get to be a big shot. Not in my business."

"Forget it," he grinned, and waved a hand magnanimously. "I've got a homicide on my hands, and those we don't have too often in these parts. A girl's been killed and it means there's a killer loose somewhere in my county. It's my job to find him, and find him fast. And that means that if you've got something that's going to help the investigation, you're going to tell me about it, regardless of any personal commitments."

"The first time I saw the girl was in the morgue," I told him. "I know nothing that's going to help you. Sorry."

"How about me being the judge of that, huh? Whitman said he had you working for him. What's he hired you to do?"

"Didn't he tell you?"

"Yeah, he told me. Only this time I'm asking you."

I dug into my pockets until locating the crumpled packet of Camels I'd been carrying around for three days, and lit one. The way Mulder's mood continually changed was enough to make anyone uncomfortable.

"He wanted me to find out where Miss Cole had gone," I told him. "Last night she was supposed to visit friends in Fresno, but she never arrived there. This morning when she hadn't returned he became concerned enough to ask me to find her."

Softly his broad right hand patted the desk. "That doesn't sound like much sense to me. So what if she wasn't home this ayem? You don't throw a fit and hire a private cop for something like that. Or do you?"

"He was in love with the girl. It should explain his actions. And now that she's been found dead it doesn't sound so senseless to me."

"Okay, okay," he conceded. "He was in love with her so he hires you because he's scared something might've happened. That right?"

"Something like that."

"You mean he was worried about something happening to her— something like what has happened?"

"No, I don't think so. He only wanted me to find where she had gone, if not to Fresno."

"That, according to him," Mulder said slowly, "was this morning. Only you happened to be in town last night. And last night she wasn't considered missing, was she?"

"I'd been doing other work for him," I said, and pulled on the cigarette. "My presence here today prompted him to ask for help."

"This other work concern the girl?"

"No."

"Tell me about it."

"I can't. You'll have to ask Whitman about that. But it had nothing to do with Miss Cole. Whitman hired me on behalf of one of his clients, and the two jobs are not even remotely connected." I blew smoke at the desk corner where it broke up into feathery fragments. Like my thoughts. "Last night," I said, "I reported seeing a man up on the road. Did you find him?"

Removing his hands from the desk he leaned back in the swivel chair and closed his eyes. "I was wondering how long it would take you to get around to that. As a matter of fact he wasn't found."

"Pity. You might have had a closed case on your hands by now."

"Think so?" One eye opened. "I went personally looking for this bleeding character you say you saw. And you know what I found? Nothing! That's right, nothing! No trace of blood, any sign of an accident— nothing. You claimed to have seen him on the new road, right?"

I nodded.

"Know where the girl was killed, don't you?" he inquired casually, and opened the other eye.

"No, you haven't mentioned it yet." If the question had been designed to trick me into an admission of some kind, he showed no disappointment at its failure.

"There's another road leading here to Reposado, an old one that's seldom ever used these days. This morning one of my men out on routine patrol found the car, and her lying in front of it. That's where it happened, and that road's about two miles straight from the new one—the place where you're supposed to've seen this guy with all the blood piddling out of him."

"Two miles isn't very far if you're running from a killing," I suggested.

"In the kind of condition you described?"

"Perhaps he wasn't hurt that bad after all," I said, and asked if a time of death had had yet been estimated.

"Last night sometime, but it's going to be hard to pin-point it on the nose."

"Motive?"

"Robbery. Maybe even rape. Maybe both. Her clothes were torn up pretty bad and her purse was empty when we found her." He held up a hand, fingers stiff and parted. "She was carrying five hundred bucks with her last night."

I killed my cigarette and tried not to look surprised.

"Her aunt gave it to her, and the same aunt tells me she wanted the money because she was in some kind of trouble. The money was gone when we got to her." He came forward in his chair and pointed a thick finger at me. "How's it figure to you now?"

"Robbery?"

The finger went away.

"How about her dying being the result of the trouble she was in?"

"Perhaps. But I'd still like to know who it was I saw on the road last night, and where I could find him."

"You'd be wasting your time. Look—just supposing you did see someone, and supposing he was bleeding like you said. How'd he get hurt? By the girl?" He shook his head. "Uh-uh. There was nothing around her that could've hurt anyone like that. Besides, we found no trace of blood near where the body was discovered, and nowhere else around there for that matter."

"All right," I said, getting up. "I only reported what I saw. Don't blame me for it."

"You got me wrong, Cameron. I appreciate what you did. But let's face it. You can't give me a description of the person you saw, can you? What do you want I should do? Go chasing phantoms?"

"Her killer would have to have stopped her car, wouldn't he?" I asked as he rose almost reluctantly from his chair. "You said she was killed outside of it."

"Yeah, but that's easily explained. The car had a flat. She must've stopped to fix it, but instead of just pulling on the hand brake, she let the car run back until it got fouled up in the brush. It was half off the road when we found it." He picked up his hat from the cabinet behind the desk and positioned it carefully on his head. "The way it ran back she'd have had a sweet time trying to get the wheel changed." Rounding the desk he got a hand on the doorknob but made no move to open it. "Anything you got to tell me now?"

I gave him another headshake.

Mulder sighed and I could feel his breath on my face. "Going back home now, I suppose?"

"No. I'll be here a while yet."

"Oh?" This time there was no surprise. "Still working for Whitman then?"

"Working for him," I affirmed, "but on your side, Sheriff."

"I hope so, Cameron. I hope so. I've been sheriff here for a long time without any trouble from private cops. I hope you're not going to give me any now. I hope you're not one of those smart TV-type monkeys that go around holding out on the law."

"Anything I might turn up you'll hear about," I promised.

"What makes Whitman think he should hire you to try and find her killer?"

"As I said before, he was in love with the girl."

"Yeah. Like you said before." He turned the knob and opened the door.

"I'll be in touch," I said by way of a parting bid.

"If you don't you can be sure I will," he grinned. "And, remember what I said about her trouble maybe being the reason for her having to die?"

I said nothing, waiting for the bit he had been saving for a punch line.

"Her car was chock full of suitcases and stuff, nearly every damned thing she probably owned. To me it looks like she was on her way out of Reposado for good. Another thing is she never even bothered to quit her job. So . . . maybe the trouble she had was right here in town, and she was running from it, wouldn't you say?"

In Whitman's apartment he poured himself a stiff dose of bourbon and found a cold beer for me. Tilting the glass he downed most of the contents and swore loudly.

"Damn him! Damn him to hell!"

I sipped some of the beer while he voiced a few more vociferous maledictions.

"If you didn't do it," I said cautiously, "why bother about Mulder? You're letting him get to you, Hal."

"You heard what he said about her clothes? You said he told you about all the stuff she had in the car." He finished off the drink and tossed the glass violently against the couch cushions. It bounced and rolled off onto the carpet. "Mulder'd love to pin something like this on me. My God, how he'd enjoy that!"

"What makes you so sure?"

"He as much as said so, that's why. Oh no, not in so many words. But I'm not so stupid I couldn't read the inference in what he had to say. He thinks Bridget was running from trouble, that I was that trouble." Picking up the glass from the floor he carried it back to the miniature bar for a refill.

"What's between you and the sheriff, Hal?"

Before answering he disposed of half of the fresh drink.

"You noticed, did you?"

"I noticed something, and it wasn't love."

"Up here I don't touch criminal cases, Paul. There wouldn't be enough in it to feed me if I went back to that line of practice. But a few months ago I was asked to defend a young Mexican kid who'd been booked for illegal entry with intent to rob. It was a favor for a certain client, and I did it. The kid claimed Mulder roughed him up while under arrest, and he still had marks on his body to support the charge. I made a point of that in my defense, but Mulder produced witnesses to prove that the kid had tried to break away while being taken to jail, that he'd been hurt during the course of his recapture. I lost the case and the boy got a year at Chino. But the press played it up a bit, especially about the beating Mulder was alleged to have handed out. Election was near then and that kind of publicity didn't do our sheriff very much good.

"Oh, he won, but with not the kind of majority he was used to. And that," he ended, killing the rest of the bourbon, "is what exists between Walt Mulder and me." For a few moments he studied the empty glass he held before looking back to me. "Now do you think he wouldn't enjoy seeing me saddled with the blame for what's happened?"

"Did Mulder rough up the kid?"

"The boy maintained so. I had only his word. Anyway, the papers pounced upon it. It made good reading."

I swallowed some more of the beer while he poured himself yet another shot. He was headed for a bender and I wanted to be away from there before it really got going.

I said: "Hal, I want to ask you something, and I want you to answer truthfully. Is there anything about this business that you haven't told me?"

"No, I've told you everything, and that's the gospel. I know nothing—nothing about it. And that—that's . . ." Without finishing he flopped down on the couch, carefully deposited the glass at his feet and cradled his head between his hands. "She was in trouble and I—I was the guy she was going to marry. But she couldn't come to me with it. I couldn't even see that she might have had a problem. All the time I—I . . ."

I finished my beer and took the glass back to the bar.

"All the time what, Hal?"

"I thought—I thought the funny way she was acting had to do with—with this guy she'd been seen with." His shoulders began to heave and I didn't have to be told what was happening. The anger Mulder had sparked off was rapidly being quenched under the flood of memories, regrets and the realization of loss that the alcohol had turned loose.

I went to the door and opened it.

He looked up. "Where are you going?"

"To Fresno. It's a place to start."

He nodded, drew the back of his hand across the dampness that stained his eyes and tried to smile.

FOUR

IT WAS CLOSE to four, the sun already starting to stretch the shadows, when I arrived in Fresno and picked up directions to the address Whitman had given me.

The house was middle-class, but recently built, and the paint and front yard had been treated well. A powder blue Chevy was parked in the short drive, while on the left-hand square of lawn a man stood and mopped sweat from his forehead as a power mower throbbed impatiently at his feet.

I climbed out of the car and crossed the grass to him. He saw me coming and put away the handkerchief.

"Mr. Shelton?"

"I'm Dan Shelton," he confirmed.

"Paul Cameron," I said, offering to shake hands.

Shelton stood an inch or so shorter than my six-two, but probably weighed quite a bit more. He had a grip that was strong, and he knew it. "Uh-huh. And what can I do for you?"

"Do you have a few minutes to talk?"

"Sure," he smiled. "Just as long as you're not here selling."

"Nothing like that, Mr. Shelton. I'm a private investigator, representing Harlan Whitman of Reposado. That mean anything to you?"

"Whitman? Sure. That's Brid's guy, ain't it?"

"The same."

"Never met him personally," Shelton said. "Matter of fact this morning was the first time I ever talked to him, and that was only on the phone." Then, as if it had only just clicked: "You did say—private investigator, didn't you?"

He bent over and shut off the mower's engine. "There's trouble?" The friendly expression slipped away from his sunburned face.

I nodded. "Whitman told you about some of it this morning, I imagine."

"You mean to tell me Brid still hasn't turned up? She's still not back home?"

"She's been found," I said. "She's dead, Mr. Shelton."

"Dead? Look, mister, if you're trying to be funny that's a hell of a—" He cut it short, shut his mouth and wiped his hands against soiled khaki slacks. "No, you're not, are you? You're serious. What—what happened? Car smash?"

"She was murdered. Last night, on her way here, I think."

Still having difficulty in absorbing what I'd given him, he shook his head.

"The sheriff's office is handling the investigation," I continued, "but Whitman's hired me to look into it on his behalf."

"Yeah," he muttered. "From what Brid used to tell us about the guy, he'd want to do something like that."

"Will you help us?"

"Of course, if I can. But hell, there's little I can tell you that'll be of any use."

"She was a friend of yours, wasn't she?"

"Sure. Though more of the wife's than mine. A few years back they worked together down in Vegas. That was before Marge and me was married. When Brid moved up to Reposado she used to come visit us every Friday. Used to stay the night here. That's how I come to be a friend of hers. She was a nice kid. A real nice kid." He fumbled in the pocket of his pants and came up with a squashed deck of Luckies, which he held out to me. I waved a hand, declining.

"How'd it happen?" he asked, once the cigarette was burning.

Using as few words and as little detail as possible, I told him.

"Geeze," he muttered, flipping the half smoked butt out onto the sidewalk, "what a lousy way for a kid like that to go."

"When she was found," I said slowly, "she had packed suitcases in her car. According to Sheriff Mulder, nearly every stitch she owned. Was she planning to move up here for good?"

"Move here? Hell, no. Of course not. Who says so?"

"Nobody, Mr. Shelton. We're simply curious about all those clothes. A girl doesn't travel with that much gear for just a one-night visit, does she?"

"No. But it doesn't have to mean she was moving here," he countered, "or that we knew anything about it."

"Do you think Mrs. Shelton would know if she was planning to take up residence elsewhere?"

After a moment's hesitation he said: "We can ask her. But I can tell you now Marge won't know. If she did she'd have told me."

"I'd welcome the opportunity of talking to your wife," I said.

Shelton turned slightly to look at the house.

"Mind if I first tell her why you're here? She ain't going to take this news too easy, and I think I'd best give it to her in private. That okay by you?"

"I'll wait out here," I told him.

As he walked slowly up to the house I began to wonder if I hadn't made a mistake. Alone inside he would have time to brief his wife on what not to say—if there happened to be anything they didn't want me to know. I shrugged away the suspicion and watched two young girls cycling up the street, exchanging rapid chatter as they passed the house. At the corner of the block they stopped to talk to three other youngsters, then together the group continued along the street, headed somewhere to take advantage of what was left of the day. A picture of Bridget Cole, bruised and bloody, cut through my thoughts like winter rain.

"Cameron?"

I turned toward the sound of the voice.

Shelton stood in the doorway, beckoning.

Inside the house he introduced me to his wife, a small, pale blonde woman who was still taking care of an attractive figure and face. Crying had already rimmed her eyes with red, but she agreed to listen to my questions.

She knew absolutely nothing, she insisted, about any plan Bridget Cole might have had of leaving Reposado. The girl had never once mentioned such a thing to her.

"When she visited you here, Mrs. Shelton, did she ever say anything that would perhaps have indicated she was in any kind of difficulty?"

The blonde head shook slowly. "Never. But I sensed something. I'm not sure what, but there was definitely something different about Brid these last few weeks."

"How different, Mrs. Shelton?"

"I don't really know," she answered. "She seemed a little . . . well, distant, I suppose. I can't really explain it. It was as though she was always busy thinking about something. Do you know what I mean?"

"I think so. Your husband tells me you and Bridget once worked together. That was in Las Vegas, was it?"

"Yes, at the Casino Crescendo." The handkerchief she'd been twisting into many shapes went back to her eyes. "Poor Brid," she whispered. "Poor Bridget."

"What sort of work did she do there, Mrs. Shelton?"

"We were both cashiers. Brid was still working there when I left."

"Do you mind me asking why you left?"

"Of course not," she answered quickly, and glanced at her husband who was seated beside her. "I met Dan there."

"I was on vacation," Shelton continued for her. "That was three years ago. I married Marge before I left and brought her back with me here to Fresno."

"Ever any trouble at the Casino?" I asked his wife.

"Not really," she replied quietly, and with a small amount of reluctance. "I don't suppose you can call guys chancing their luck with the girls trouble, can you? I mean, it's natural, isn't it?"

"Did Bridget have any special men friends down there?"

"Nothing special. She had friends, of course, but none you could call special. She was kind of funny that that way."

I said nothing, but my silence supplied the question.

"What I mean is, she never showed any interest in serious friendships with any of the men. Even when Mr. Formento would ask her to join him for dinner after work it was always a polite no thanks."

"Formento?"

"Mel Formento? He owns the Crescendo."

The name meant nothing to me.

"Would you have any idea why she appeared to avoid men? At least, avoid relationships with any?"

"I think she was trying to save money. She didn't like Vegas very much. She just wanted to make enough to get out with something to show for her time there. The pay was very good, and if a girl saved hard enough she could accumulate a nice savings real easy."

"Would you say she'd succeeded in saving something?"

It took her a little while to mull over that one. At last she said:

"Yes . . . I think she did."

"Mrs. Shelton," I began quietly, "I'm going to ask you something that may sound like a strange sort of question, but I'd appreciate your answer." I gave her a few moments to think about it before going on. "Did Bridget ever talk about trouble with Hal Whitnan?"

"That certainly is a strange question," she said, quickly wiping at a tear that had slipped loose. "Of course she never—not once. She was in love with the man; they were going to be married." Then, with suspicion creeping into her voice: "I thought you said you were working for him?"

"I am," I assured her. "Hal's more than just a client; he's a friend. And I'm glad to hear what you've told me."

I stood up, feeling I'd wasted a trip. Shelton rose also.

"There's one thing we haven't told you yet, Cameron. Me and Marge weren't sure whether we should, but I've been thinking it over, and I guess you oughta know. It can't do no harm now."

"Dan!" his wife cried, getting up to clutch his arm in her small hands.

"It's all right, honey," he told her, putting a consoling hand over hers. "It's best this way. We want to help all we can, don't we?"

Looking up at him, seemingly still uncertain, she gave a small nod and released his arm.

"One thing you'll have to promise me, Cameron. If what I tell you has got nothing to do with what's happened to Brid, you keep it to yourself."

"If it has no connection," I promised. "You have my word."

"It's just that I'd hate like hell for something like this to get back to Whitman, 'specially if it ain't important. I mean, her coming up here Fridays and everything . . . Well, there's no telling how he might take it."

"Take what, Mr. Shelton?"

"The phone call last night. Some character phoned here asking for Brid, and he got kind of rough on the line when I told him she hadn't showed. He phoned back twice afterwards. The last time he was a lot more civil, but even then I don't think he believed me."

"He by any chance leave his name or number?" I asked without much hope.

"He sure did," Shelton responded triumphantly. "I wrote it down. Wait here and I'll fetch it."

He went out of the room, leaving me alone with his wife and a slightly strained silence.

She said: "This is a terrible thing . . . I still can't believe it's really happened."

Nothing I could say would have made her feel any better, so I refrained from trying and waited for her husband.

He returned shortly and handed me a slip of paper. "That's the only name he gave."

Printed on the square of white paper was the one word: CARL. Next to it a number.

"May I keep this?"

"Sure. It's no use to me. Just sorry we can't be more help. We'd like to, believe me."

"Maybe you have," I said. "What you've told me may help a little. I don't know how much, but in this business every scrap counts."

Marge Shelton invited me to stay for a cup of coffee but I declined with thanks, shook hands with both of them, and went out to my car.

The shadows had grown considerably longer and the street was empty when I drove away.

At a flashy hamburger haven I stopped for coffee I could have had for free, collected some change and took it with me to where a phone was fitted to wall on the far side of the room. The place was crowded and the racket from the jukebox carried back to where I checked the number Shelton had provided. But it was of little importance. I wasn't about to conduct a conversation.

I dialed the number and listened to the hum.

"Silver Horn Motel," a male voice chimed melodically in my ear.

I twirled the dial so that the noise might sound as if the line had gone on the blink. Then quietly hung up.

Back with my coffee I ordered a burger and quizzed the kid behind the counter about the location of the Silver Horn.

The directions he gave sounded a little involved, but I figured I'd be able to find it without getting lost.

The Silver Horn was very different to most of the motels I had been forced to stay at from time to time. This one had grounds that were beautifully landscaped, complete with an over-size heated pool and a warmly lit restaurant adjacent to the main block. A few fun lovers still frolicked in the pool when I pulled in on the concrete parking lot.

I wasn't sure how I was going to learn the other part of Carl's name— until I entered the reception block and found an unattended desk and the register lying upon its artificial black marble top.

Making sure the clerk was not where he could spy on the desk, I spun the register around and traced a finger along the entries. Most were entered as Mr. and Mrs., and of the six weeks I covered on the five pages only one had the initial "C". It belonged to a C. Myburgh, and was one of the few single entries. Replacing the register in its correct position, I struck the silver bell.

The time it took the clerk to put in an appearance I could have covered more pages than just five. He slipped in smoothly behind the desk, apologized profusely for having kept me waiting and automatically reached for a pen.

A thin, sleek, well-polished creature who wore a built-in smile, a shiny set of plastic teeth and a perfume that wasn't very subtle.

"I'm supposed to be meeting a friend here," I informed him. "Mr. Carl Myburgh. Could you give me his room number?"

"Mr. Myburgh, sir?"

"Mr. Myburgh."

"Oh, yes." A manicured finger slipped over the register entries, and when he raised his head the smile was expanded. "Mr. Myburgh has a *suite,* sir. Shall I ring to announce you?"

"Don't bother. He's not expecting me until tomorrow. I'd prefer to surprise him. Just give me the suite number and tell me how to get there."

The number I knew, having read it from Myburgh's entry, but I didn't have a clue about finding it among the hundred-odd units at the motel.

"Perhaps I should check to make sure they're in," the clerk offered, switching off the smile. "It could save you quite a little walk if they aren't."

"No," I said, not wanting to give Myburgh an opportunity of asking what business I had with him, or perhaps telling the clerk to give me the air. "I'd prefer to spring the surprise."

He didn't believe a word of it, but he wasn't capable of refusing the request with diplomacy. I got the number and directions and left him with a dollar that failed to turn the smile on again.

What the clerk had referred to as Myburgh's suite was one of the larger units that had a view facing the swimming pool. But from the drawn curtains it appeared he wasn't much interested in views. I touched the bell, hoping I wasn't ringing a wrong number.

Almost immediately the door opened and a soft voice said: "Yeah?"

"Mr. Myburgh?"

The eyes that looked up to study my face were bloodshot, but alert. Thinning brown hair was carefully oiled down against his scalp, and in the expensive pea-green suit that swathed his light frame he looked like a tired businessman nursing a problem.

"He's gettin' himself dressed," he answered at last. "C'mon inside."

Waiting until I stepped into the small hall he pushed closed the door, then motioned towards the living room.

It was large and elaborate, comfortably furnished and arranged to justify the price of twenty-eight bucks a day I'd seen on the tariff card at the reception desk. A near dead bottle of Scotch kept company with two glasses and overflowing ashtrays on a circular coffee table, while from an open door a male voice hummed softly off-key, performing an unmusical duet with a noisy air-conditioner.

"Siddown," the green suit invited.

On one of the chairs someone had thrown a Sequoia National Park publicity pamphlet. I picked it up, sat down, and smiled at my nervous host.

He took a seat on the sofa directly opposite, looked at the bottle, back my way, then poured out the final shot. I watched while he took a plastic case from his pocket, removed a blue tablet, placed it carefully on his tongue and hurriedly reached for the drink.

With the drink downed and the plastic pillbox returned to his pocket, he leaned back. "You got a name?"

I glanced down at the penciled rings around two names on the pamphlet I held, then placed it on the arm of the chair.

"Cameron."

"Uh-huh. And I'm supposed to know you?"

"Do you?"

"Nah, and I got a hunch you don't know me neither. What's your business here?"

"Carl Myburgh."

"The business, mister, the business."

"Clam up, Joey," a new voice commanded. "I'll take it from here."

I looked sideways.

Shrugging into an expensive lightweight sports coat, a tall, smooth-skinned number with dark wavy hair and a thin moustache stepped into the room. He was handsome enough to be a movie bit-player or even a TV soap opera lover, but I doubted he was either. I stood up. "Myburgh?"

"And your name's Cameron. All right," he smiled, "now we're buddies. Surprise me."

"No surprise. Only a message."

He came closer, stuck his hands deep into his pants pockets and rocked back and forth on his heels. Self-assurance was smeared all over his pretty face.

"If you've got a message for me, friend, aren't you delaying delivery?"

"It's from Bridget Cole," I said.

The hands jumped out of his pockets and the one named Joey got up from the sofa.

"What about her?" Myburgh demanded, the pleasant smile replaced by something I couldn't read.

"Don't you know?"

Swiftly he closed the gap between us, grabbed a handful of my shirt and jerked me up against him. Apparently it had been the wrong kind of question.

I said: "Let go or I'll cripple your love life."

He let go. But not the way I would have preferred. As his fingers untwined from my shirt he shoved and I went backward into the chair I'd been using.

Standing closer now, Joey gaped at me, eyes as round as teacups. In his hand a flat .32 automatic did some staring of its own.

"Now let's dispense with the crap," Myburgh admonished harshly. "What about the girl?"

I straightened my tie. "She couldn't make it last night."

"Cameron, I'm waiting to hear something new. I know only too goddam well she never made it."

I looked at him, and then over to where Joey was pointing his gun at me.

"What's the message?" Joey asked.

"No message," I said. "She's dead."

Quick glances passed between them. Softly Myburgh said: "Tell that again . . .?"

"She died."

"How?"

"Violently."

"Like the crap, friend, go easy with the smart repartee. I'm not in the mood. What happened to her?"

"Someone killed her, last night. I think she was headed here when it happened."

Stroking the meager growth on his upper lip, Myburgh allowed that to sink in before speaking again. And when he did his voice had lost its smooth quality.

"Okay. You've told me what happened. What you haven't told me is why you're here, how you found me."

"It wasn't hard. Last night you left your phone number with someone."

"You some kinda cop?" Joey put in.

"Some kinda."

"You a cop or aren't you?"

Returning my gaze to Myburgh, I said: "Private."

"Let's have a look."

I started to reach under my coat when he stopped me.

"Keep it right there. Joey can do it." He made a sign to Joey and relieved him of the gun.

While Joey removed the leather case from my inside pocket Myburgh kept the .32 pointing down at my face.

"He ain't carryin' no iron," Joey informed him, handing over his loot in exchange for the gun.

Myburgh opened the case, read the photostat of my license, then flipped through the other plastic sheaths and examined the cards of identification that connected me to several out-of-State organizations.

Completing the scrutiny he tossed the identification into my lap.

"You're tied to a lot of people, Cameron."

"A dollar here, a nickel there," I said, tucking away the folder.

"How are you tied to me?"

"You knew the girl."

A humorless smile pushed the moustache out of position. "So that's why all the hokum about getting to see me. You think I had something to do with it?"

I said nothing.

"You're looking in the wrong direction, friend," he said. "The people who gave you my number can tell you I was trying half the night to contact her. Three times I phoned their place. If I had anything to do with what's happened, would I waste time on something like that? Would I waste time on calls when I knew I wasn't going to reach her?"

I smiled up at him and remained silent.

"What the hell's that supposed to mean?"

"The calls could have been no more than a way of providing yourself with an alibi. It's been used before."

"Listen, you smart monkey—" He reached down for me.

Joey's voice stopped him. "How're we supposed to know this joker's dealing' it straight? How're we supposed to know he's tellin' the truth?"

"You may have something there," Myburgh murmured. "How about it, Cameron?"

"You've got a phone. Call the Reposado Sheriff's office. They'll be happy to confirm it."

He nodded. "Get our stuff together, Joey. We're pulling out."

Joey came forward, gave him the .32 and retreated soundlessly toward the door Myburgh had used.

"What's your part in the affair?" Myburgh asked.

"The obvious. I want the one who did it."

"Why? What was she to you?"

"Nothing. Its part of the dollars and nickels bit. What was she to you?"

"A broad. Just a good-looking broad."

"That all, Carl?"

"Just a broad is what I said. We were friends."

"The news of her death doesn't appear to have saddened you much."

"You think so?" He checked the time on his watch. "Joey, get the lead out in there." To me he said slowly: "Things have happened fast. There hasn't been time for emotions. Besides, I'm not exactly the type."

"And she was just a good-looking broad," I added.

"Very cute. Keep it up and you'll push me just that little bit too far."

I pointed to the room where Joey was thumping things around. "If you've nothing to be afraid of, why the run-out?"

"I'm a businessman," he said softly. "I can't afford an involvement in anything like this. Wives don't quite understand or appreciate situations in which another woman figures. In any case, we were planning to leave in the morning. After listening to you though, I've decided not to risk waiting around. There's nothing, not a thing, I could tell the police or anyone else, but it could lead to publicity . . . and that I don't want. So we're leaving a little earlier. Not running."

"You married?"

"Don't I look it?"

"About as much as Frankenstein looks sexy."

He smiled. "So much for appearances."

Joey came back lugging two heavy cases. He stopped and waited for Myburgh's instructions.

"Get them into the car, then settle the bill. We're leaving for Sacramento tonight." Then to me: "What's the make and number of your car?"

I told him.

"Repeat it."

I did, wondering about the mention of their destination

The fact that I was able to repeat the information twice without making a mistake seemed to satisfy him.

"He's got a car outside, Joey. You heard that?"

"I heard," Joey grinned back, and continued on his way with the two cases.

We listened for the closing of the door. Then Myburgh spoke:

"Who're you working for?"

"It wouldn't interest you."

"You'd be surprised what interests me. But no matter, it isn't important." The gun waggled as though to underscore what next he had to say. "Now here's something for you. It's a free tip. Call it compensation for the treatment I gave you. I don't know who you're working for, and as I said, I'm not particularly interested. You said you were trying to find the one who's killed Bridget Cole. Okay, so it will mean money for you if you do. Check?"

"If," I said. "But who says I haven't already done just that?"

He laughed and pushed the gun forward a few inches. "Don't be a kook. If it was me who'd done it you think I'd let you go on living?"

The announcement brought a small amount of relief. Until then I wasn't sure what he'd been intending.

I said: "You couldn't kill me here anyway. They know who occupied the place."

"I could take you away and do it someplace else, couldn't I? Think about it."

"I have. Also about the desk clerk who knows you and who will remember me. Not to mention the people who gave me your number."

Once again he laughed. "Well, if that doesn't prove I don't know how to go about eliminating someone, what does?"

It didn't prove a thing, not in my book. But I didn't mention it. "You know about guns," I told him idly.

"Only as a means of protecting myself. I travel a lot. When I do I prefer to be armed."

"You were going to give me a tip," I reminded him.

"Yeah, I'd almost forgotten about that. I'll give it to you, and I suggest you take it very seriously." The .32 made another small move. "If you want to find the person responsible for what's happened to the girl, go back to Reposado. She had man trouble there."

"She told you that?"

"How else would I know? Didn't I say she was a friend? Friends confide in each other when they've got troubles, don't they?"

"Supposing what you say is true. She'd have mentioned names. Got any?"

He gave a couple of slow nods. "She did. But I'm not repeating it. I don't want to become involved in this sort of thing. I can afford neither the publicity or the time."

"Why?"

"You don't listen very well, do you? Didn't you hear me tell you? Business, my friend. Business."

I let him have the butt end of a smile.

Before he could make something of it Joey returned, sweat heavy on his forehead, his breath coming in heavy pants.

"All fixed," he announced. "But I ain't feelin' so good. It's this damned bellyache again. I still think I oughta see a quack."

Myburgh ignored him.

"All right, Cameron," he said. "Let's go."

I got up from the chair.

"Know anything about the kidnapping laws of this State?"

He looked at the gun in his hand, then passed it back to the waiting Joey.

"Don't get worked up so. No one's forcing you to go anywhere. We're taking you to your car and then we're leaving. Nothing else."

"I can make a lot of noise out there."

"You'd sound pretty stupid if you did." He grinned contentedly. "What would you shout about? Assistance in apprehending us perhaps? But, why? What have we done?"

"Let's go," I sighed.

Between the two of them I walked to where I had left my car. They waited until I was in behind the wheel before Myburgh said:

"Just one small favor. Wait five minutes before leaving, will you?"

Then without any more he and Joey took off.

In the glove box was a gun that I could use to stop them. But as Myburgh had said, what for? He knew I hadn't swallowed his story, that there was more than just friendship between him and the dead girl. He knew also that there wasn't a thing I could do about it. Not right then.

I took the key from my pocket, jabbed it hastily into the ignition switch, and twisted. The engine kicked over and settled down to a steady purr. I pushed the gear lever up into reverse. One thing I could do, and that was to find out where they were going. I knew it wouldn't be Sacramento.

But as the car started backing out all the talk about its registration number started to make sense. One of the tires was flat.

I switched off the engine, got out and checked the wheels. It turned out to be the front right—flatter than a Bowery bum at sunrise.

While I stood and cursed Joey under my breath, a car pulled out of the parking lot some distance off, and turned toward the highway. It was too far away to read the number, except to see that it wore Nevada plates. While it was moving away another engine revved to life, and soon another car was swinging off the lot, moving fast. Its registration plates were only a blur in the distance.

I reached for a cigarette, lit it, took another look at the flat wheel, then started the walk back to the reception block.

FIVE

THE CLERK BOBBED out of his office behind the counter, smiling in smooth anticipation. Until he saw who it was that had rung the desk bell.

"Yes . . . sir?"

"Something tells me I was taken for a dollar," I said, and held out my hand.

Shaking his head as though he did not understand, he made a weak attempt to fix the smile back on his face. "I'm sorry, but I'm not sure that I'm with you."

I leaned on the counter. "Then let's put it this way. I was hoping to surprise somebody, but the surprise was spoilt by a telephone warning. You owe me a buck."

Staring curiously he gave up the business of trying to smile. Then seeing that my upturned palm hadn't moved, reluctantly took a small wad of bills from a back pocket of his pants and peeled off a single.

"There!"

I thanked him, folded the bill and dropped it through the slot of a metal charity box perched on the counter.

"Now what can you tell me about Carl Myburgh?"

"I thought he was a friend—or so you claimed," he submitted smugly, folding his arms across a narrow chest in an effort to look superior.

"Not a very good one. I don't particularly like people who wave guns at me and deflate the tires of my car. Nor those who shy away from police questioning."

"Guns?" The arms came lethargically undone and he stepped in closer to the desk, saturating the air between us with the warm sweetness of roses. "Are you from the police?"

"What was the little one's name?" I asked, pretending I'd not heard. "Myburgh's colleague."

"Mr. Ortell?"

I nodded. "How long have they been registered?"

"Only a few days. I could look it up to be quite sure." Eagerly he reached for the register.

I said nothing, leaving him to hastily page through the entries.

"Ah yes, here we are. C. Myburgh and J. Ortell. They've been with us for exactly three days now."

"Besides me, what visitors have they had?"

"I'm sorry, sir, I don't recall them having any."

"No female visitors?"

"Absolutely not!"

"Was Myburgh out for any length of time last night?"

"That I couldn't tell you."

'What about the little one—Ortell?"

"I'm sorry, but I can't be of assistance there—much as I would like to. Our guests are continually in and out and we have no way of keeping any sort of track of their movements. Not," he tacked on quickly, "that we would care to do such a thing. The Silver Horn is an extremely respectable establishment; our clientele is of the very best. We—"

"Sure," I said. "Now how about my car? Do you have someone who can fix the wheel?"

"Oh yes, yes I can arrange that without any trouble at all. I'm only sorry that you have had to be so inconvenienced. I can assure you *I* personally had no idea—absolutely none." Eyebrows lifted delicately. "You're positive it *was* Mr. Ortell who did it?"

"I could be mistaken."

"You—mentioned guns?"

"Also a flat wheel," I said, looking at my watch.

Back in Reposado I checked in again at the hotel, cleaned up and changed my shirt, then tried to contact Hal Whitman. The phone hummed a long time. I cradled it to go downstairs for dinner.

While waiting for the waitress to bring my coffee I gave myself a cigarette and mulled over the events of a lousy day, wondering how far the sheriff's office had progressed. The coffee arrived. I drank it, killed the cigarette and decided to call at Whitman's apartment before doing the next obvious thing.

It was dark behind the glass partitioning of the front door as I stood there prodding the bell. Its echo was loud inside, but it was the only sound. Either he had drunk himself into oblivion, or else he was out somewhere. I jabbed the bell once more, waiting a full minute before turning away toward the elevator. Nobody could be that drunk.

I drove slowly out to Retreat, trying to dream up a way of suitably framing the questions I had for Mrs. Christine Danhurst. But by the time I arrived at the iron gate I hadn't come up with any idea that would help.

I slid out of the car, unlatched the gate and swung it open, discovering that a hook on a length of chain had been provided to secure the gate in an open position, enabling a driver traveling alone to pass through without it swinging shut on the vehicle.

I was easing off the hand brake after closing the gate and returning to the car, when I saw the girl standing at the edge of the drive. She looked like a small lost ghost bathed in the beams of the headlights.

With the gate bell chiming its last dying notes I drove carefully up to where she waited, strangely afraid that any sudden movement would cause her to disappear. I stopped the car, waiting a few moments before getting out.

"Good evening."

She said: "Hello," and started to slowly turn away. "You're from Mr. Mulder, I suppose?"

"I'm not. Were you expecting one of the sheriff's men?"

It stopped her. She came around again, paused, and then came nearer.

Black as when I had first seen it, her hair just missed her shoulders, curling in at the ends to accentuate the oval of her face. Now, in the harsh light of the headlamps, there appeared a sheen of blue that complemented the deep cobalt of large, heavily lashed eyes. She was small with slightly heavy breasts and a good figure fitted trimly into a simple blue blouse and a gray denim skirt. Small scuffed leather moccasins covered her feet. Standing before me she looked unreal, like something an artist had painted upon the night as a portrayal of the fear and uncertainty of the young.

"I remember you now," she said, slowly nodding. "You were here this morning. With Mr. Whitman." It came as a flat, unemotional statement, as if the words were not hers but those of an apathetic ventriloquist concealed by the trees at her rear.

"I remember you, too." Taking a forward step I offered her my hand. "I'm Paul Cameron."

She shied back and put her hands out of sight. Her mouth opened, but it was several staggering seconds before any sound came. "I'm-I'm sorry. You startled me. I'm—I'm Sandra Danhurst." But she made no attempt to take my hand or reduce the gap that had been created between us.

"Your mother home, Sandra?"

"She's always home. But she won't see you."

I said, partly because her remoteness bothered me, and possibly because in her I saw a way of smoothing the path to the old woman: "I can try. Would you like a ride back to the house?"

She considered the offer. "No—thank you."

"The night's getting cool, Sandra. It will be warmer inside."

"You're wrong," she said softly. "It's colder. It always is."

I shrugged and moved back to the car.

"Mr. Cameron . . ."

"Yes?"

"Have you—have you come about Miss Cole?"

"Yes," I answered. "You knew her, didn't you?"

"I met her only once or twice, that's all. I never knew her. I wish I had. She seemed nice."

"Last night?" I asked.

She shook her head. The blue-black tresses swayed out of place and she had to lift a hand to tidy them. "No, not last night. I never saw her last night."

"Feel like changing your mind about going in now?"

Again she let her head signal an answer. "Why do these things have to happen?"

"Are you asking about Bridget Cole?"

"Yes." Her hand went back to her hair as she turned her eyes toward the sky. "Do you—do you believe—in a superior being?"

It was the last thing I expected to hear, and, when I looked at her face, now turned back to me, and the expectancy in those dark eyes, there was slackness in my jaw.

"If you're asking do I believe in God," I said slowly, "the answer is yes."

"I don't!" For the first time the pitch of her voice changed. "If there is a god—a God like the one I was taught to believe in, why does He permit all these awful things to happen?"

It was not the kind of question I was equipped to answer, but she needed to be answered. I tried:

"We blame Him for a lot of things, Sandra. Sometimes we tend to forget that the troubles around us are nearly all of our own creation." I waited to see if had any effect, but saw no noticeable change of expression. "I gather you're talking about the way Miss Cole died?"

In reply I was given a small nod. Then: "Yes . . . I was thinking about that. I was thinking of other things as well. Like poverty and—and sickness and . . ." The flatness had left her voice. In its place there was something that reached out and pleaded for an answer. A correct and reassuring answer.

"Sandra, I've been around for a while now, but I still haven't found half of the answers to the questions I've asked myself." I edged closer and this time she did not move. Her eyes were focused intently upon my face, waiting. "I've known of poor men who became millionaires, of athletes who became cripples, and sick men who beat their afflictions to become champions. It's part of life's strange pattern, I guess, and men play a major part in shaping their successes and disasters."

"Some people never have a chance," she retorted hotly, "to be anything but an ugly part of that pattern. How would you explain that?"

I couldn't.

"Which people are you talking about, Sandra?"

Her breasts lifted and fell heavily when a large sigh was expelled. Narrow shoulders slumped as if relieved of an invisible burden. "Just people. People who are born cripples and . . . Well, people like that, those who never have a chance to be normal."

"Will you tell me something?" I asked gently. Her eyes became wary, but she answered with another tiny nod. "Something's troubling you. That's why you're out here trying to find an answer to these things. Would you like to tell me what it is?"

For a long uncomfortable moment there was only silence while she stared up into my face. Then she said: "Everything has been bothering me. Everything in this whole stinking, rotten world we live in. It's full of rottenness and cruelty and unfairness, and God made it so. Who else could?"

Before I could attempt an answer she turned her back on me and started off for the shelter of the trees that stood not far away, like tall, misshapen priests of darkness, waiting to embrace her to their fold.

"Sandra!" I called, and went after her. A few steps and I thought better of it. I returned to the car, troubled that I hadn't been able to give her any of the help for which she'd been seeking.

Nearing the house I saw again the wide car portico at the left and the two cars parked under its cover. I saw also a familiar gray car standing at the steps of the house. I pulled up near the portico and stepped out onto asphalt.

One of the cars was a low white Triumph sports model with an erected black hood. The other, a Buick, two years old. Both cars glistened beautifully from recent polishing.

The structure housing the two cars was linked to the main building by a wall as high as its roof. I was still turned in its direction when a voice behind me asked:

"Were you looking for something?"

I came around quickly to find the tall, young-old figure of the woman called Luisa watching me. Her face was stiff with controlled anger.

"I was on the way to the house," I explained. "Good evening, Luisa."

"Minutes ago I heard the bell on the gate. You've certainly taken a long time to get here. If you have business you should come straight to the house, not wander about."

"Why?"

"This is private property."

"Okay, Luisa. I apologize for taking so long. Truth is I met someone on my way up."

"Who?" she snapped.

"A night nymph."

If it were possible, her face became even more rigid.

"Is Mrs. Danhurst up?"

"She will not see you. She is resting."

"She's seeing Dr. McGill, Luisa. That's his car, isn't it?"

"That is different. He is her doctor. Now I suggest you leave."

I shook my head. "This is important. If I can't see her now I'll be forced to go to Sheriff Mulder. Tell her that, and tell her all I want is ten minutes."

"What business is it you have?"

"With your mistress? Private."

Eyes flashed brightly in a face turned to stone. She said something in rapid Spanish that was too fast for me to even try to understand.

"Come with me," she ordered.

I followed her into the house and waited in the arched hall while she went into the room where I had first met the old woman. The door shut behind her and I couldn't hear any sound from the other side.

It was a while before the door reopened and Luisa beckoned mutely. I went into the inadequately lit room and found the small balding figure of Dr. McGill standing near the fat woman who sat in the same chair she had been occupying that morning.

" 'Evening, Doctor," I greeted. "Mrs. Danhurst."

"Hello, Cameron," McGill returned coolly. "Mrs. Danhurst was about to retire but consented to see you. It's against my advice and I must insist that any business you have be conducted within five minutes."

"Thanks. How long it will take is going to depend upon Mrs. Danhurst." I looked down at the mountain of flesh. She stared ahead at the dead TV screen as though unaware of my presence, or as if the fact that I was there was of no consequence. "Could I have a few words with you in private, Mrs. Danhurst?"

"Listen, Cameron—"

She looked up abruptly and the doctor clipped short the protest he'd started.

"It's all right, Myron. Leave us alone for a few minutes."

"Christine, I refuse to have you upset by anything this man has to say. Is that clear? It's time you were in bed and—"

"You sound as if you're expecting me to break bad news, Doctor."

"Dr. McGill knows your profession," Christine Danhurst intoned harshly. "Also that you're working for Whitman." She lifted a thick hand and waved it heavily at McGill. "Leave us, Myron."

McGill left reluctantly, slamming the door behind him.

A sherry decanter and two glasses stood on the table between the big woman's chair and the one the doctor had been using. The glass nearest to her she lifted and sipped at the reddish brown fluid. A little of it spilled over her lip and trickled down her chin like blood on the jaw of a surfeited vampire.

"Your business, Mr. Cameron," she barked, dumping the glass and wiping the back of her hand across the tier of chins.

"This morning you told us that Bridget Cole came here last night to borrow five hundred dollars: that you gave it to her."

She said nothing.

"Sheriff Mulder tells me that when his men discovered her body today there was no five hundred of anything in her purse, on her person, or in the car."

"Are you calling me a liar?" she asked, not looking at me but at the blank screen that watched her like a giant alien eye. "Are you insinuating that I fabricated that story?"

"I'm insinuating nothing, nor am I calling you names. What I'm here for is to ask again if the girl said anything about her need for that money."

"I told you she didn't. Both you and Whitman."

"You did. And that's what's bothering me. A few hours ago I spoke to some people who were her friends. They gave me to understand that she had money of her own."

"So she said," the woman grunted. "I never asked for proof. I merely gave her what she'd asked for and she left."

"If she had money of her own, Mrs. Danhurst, why would she come to you for financial assistance? Didn't it strike you as strange?"

"Naturally." With what seemed like much effort she moved her head to peer up at me. "And I asked her about it. She told me she needed the money immediately and couldn't get it out of the bank at that time of day, or cash a check of that size in town. I told you also that she sounded desperate. She wouldn't tell me anything about that, so don't ask me about it. I don't know."

"Couldn't she have asked you to cash a check for her?"

"She gave me one, Mr. Cameron. I threw it away. And if you find that difficult to believe, then don't."

"It's difficult," I said, "but I'll try. Would you tell me why you threw it away?"

"Because I did not believe it to be worth anything. Also I wanted to see the last of her. Five hundred seemed a fair price for that."

"You didn't like her very much, did you?"

"I have never made any bones about it."

"Why, Mrs. Danhurst?"

"That is none of your business."

"You're refusing to tell me?"

"I am refusing," she grated roughly, "because it is no concern of an outsider. And you are no more than that—a nosy outsider."

"Why didn't you tell us this when we were here this morning?"

"I told the sheriff. That was sufficient."

I found myself again staring at the two paintings on the wall. In particular at the slim, smiling blonde girl. Mostly to relieve the tension she was creating, I asked: "Would that"—I pointed to one of the pictures—"be Mr. Danhurst?"

She saw what I was looking at, to where I pointed, and nodded without comment.

"May I ask who the girl is?"

"It is I, Mr. Cameron. And now . . . if you have run out of questions . . ."

"I'm finished," I said, accepting the dismissal. "Good night, Mrs. Danhurst."

"Wait," she ordered in a voice that sought in vain for gentleness.

"Yes?"

"You don't believe what I've told you about the money, do you?"

"I'm trying to."

"It's the truth. Mulder could probably show you her checkbook if you asked. And if you're still wondering why I disliked the girl, I'll tell you that, too. Rightly or wrongly I believed she came here to Reposado only to ingratiate herself upon me, to try and earn herself a part of the Danhurst money. I haven't much longer to live, that should be obvious to you. Provided my children continue to abide by my wishes it will all go to them. Not to anyone else."

"Did it ever occur to you that perhaps all she wanted was your friendship, not your money?"

"I have given that thought. I could have been wrong. But I doubt it. And now—*good night*, Mr. Cameron."

I was going to say something, but just as I opened my mouth the door was thrown open and a heavy-set muscular boy strode into the room. His hair was dark and wavy and cut long; his skin smooth and richly tanned. A good-looking young buck whose appearance was spoilt by the sullenness etched deep into his features.

His eyes flashed quickly at me, then over to the old woman. "You all right?" he asked her. "McGill told me who was here."

"Everything is fine, Gerry. There is no need to get excited. Mr. Cameron was just on his way out."

Gerry glared at me. "I don't like people disturbing my mother, Cameron. I sincerely hope you haven't been doing anything like that."

"So do I," I said, and moved past him out of the room, noticing the tightly bunched fists as I went.

McGill was standing in the hall waiting for me to leave. He didn't bother to say good night. At the door Luisa also fired a cold glare, which I accepted as a silent farewell. I raised a hand to them and left. Silently.

Driving down to the gate I thought about what the old woman had said, and for some reason I couldn't explain found myself accepting her story.

I stopped at the entrance and was about to open the car door when a small figure flitted into the path of my lights and started swinging the gate open. The job done, she walked slowly around to my open window.

"Hello, Sandra. I was hoping I'd see you before I left."

"I was waiting for you. I wanted a chance to apologize for those awful things I said. I know there are some things I can't begin to understand, but I do believe there is a God, Mr. Cameron. I do believe in God. I—I just wanted you to know. I feel ashamed of myself for behaving as I did. I—I guess I am a little crazy."

"You're not crazy." I gave her what I hoped might be a reassuring smile. "You're just groping for answers even the greatest brains haven't yet uncovered. Let's just try to accept these things and make the best of them. Deal?"

She smiled back and it was a warm and pleasant thing to see. "Deal," she said softly.

For a while the look of loneliness and sorrow fled and her face belonged to a pretty woman who hadn't a care. I put a hand on the one she had resting on the window. This time she didn't draw away.

"Are you staying in town?"

I told her I was, and the name of the hotel accommodating me.

"You'll be going back to Los Angeles soon, I suppose?"

"How did you know I was from there?"

"Your car plates told me."

"Just as soon as this business is cleared up I'll be going home," I told her. "Why do you ask, Sandra?"

"I don't know. I—I just thought it might be nice to talk to you again sometime." She stepped back and dropped her gaze to the ground, a little embarrassed by her remark.

"Talking to you would be nice," I said. "Anytime."

"I—I'd better go in now," she murmured. "It is getting cool."

She moved away and raised a hand in return for my salute.

"I'll close the gate," she called, and I drove off with a vivid picture of her face dimming all the other things on my mind.

About half a mile from the big house I pulled off the road and set about waiting for the gray Mercedes. The doctor would not, I was sure, enjoy a discussion out there, but for my purpose it would save time.

Twenty minutes dragged slowly by. I had smoked halfway through a cigarette when I heard the approach of a speeding engine only seconds before the oncoming lights became visible.

Throwing away the smoke, I opened the door. But as I got out realized I had waited a little too long. The car was traveling fast and the oncoming lights were now only yards away. It would be past before I had time to step out into the road and flag it down.

In a screaming white blur that kicked up dust and small stones in my direction, it flashed on by. Not a Mercedes. A white Triumph with Gerry Danhurst behind the wheel.

Danhurst drove fast but carefully avoided extending an invitation to the Highway Patrol. There were not many other cars traveling the highway at that hour so I was able to lag a good distance behind without the risk of losing the small car's taillights. Bathed in pale moonlight, lush grazing land slipped by as the miles diminished, and soon city lights sprang up into view to the right of the highway.

I knew what lay south of Reposado and I had a hunch he wouldn't be going further than there. Following him had been sheer impulse, and watching the rear of the fast moving car now, I obeyed another impulse, took the holstered .38 Colt Agent from the glove box and clipped it to my belt.

The sports car ground down its speed when it touched city limits. I followed suit. Danhurst drove slowly and directly through the business district without having to stop and check his bearings.

I was right on his tail when he pulled up near a small saloon that had its name flashing in huge green neon near the darker fringe of the city. I double-parked, making sure he was headed across the street and inside the bar before looking around for a vacant slot in which to leave my own transport. Once out of the car the noise from the saloon rushed out to welcome me.

Men, most of them still in work clothes, thronged the long counter, and the round tables scattered about the floor provided drinking space for a mixture of rough-looking males and worn women, chattering and laughing and trying to make their voices heard above the din created by their neighbors. The sour stench of sweat was thick in an atmosphere already polluted by the familiar odor of stale, spilled booze and cigarette smoke.

I squeezed in between a couple of elbows at the bar and sighted Danhurst further down the line. His eyes were trailing the grubby apron while he shouted for service, uninterested in anyone who might have followed him in. He ordered his drink from the shelves, knocking it back so fast the barman had to perform a repeat by the time he returned with change for the five spot Danhurst had shoved at him.

The boy was on his third drink before the apron discovered there were others also waiting to be served. I ordered a beer and went back to watching. When it arrived I had reason to regret the decision. Cold army soup had been more palatable.

Singing started at one of the tables, an old hillbilly ballad that was filled with added agony by the poor harmony. Other voices joined in and no one appeared to be very much concerned with the noise. Danhurst was the exception. He sent the vocalists a withering scowl and signaled impatiently for still another drink. I went on struggling with my glass of rodent urine.

I lit a cigarette to try and kill the taste of the beer just as Danhurst knocked back the last of his drink and pushed himself away from the bar. He went out without seeing me. Pocketing my lighter I forgot about the beer and was about to go after him when from one of the tables I saw someone hastily freeing himself from his cronies.

A young Mexican draped in a dark jacket and a mauve open-collar shirt was forging a path between those who blocked his way to the door. Thick, slicked down hair ledged small ears stuck to the sides of a narrow, dark face that had somehow got in the way of something hard. His left eye was discolored and puffy, the lower lip cracked and swollen.

As he passed me I came away from the bar and gave him a few seconds before following through the door.

Danhurst was over at his car, the door open, half of him leaning into the pint-size coachwork. The rest of his body emerged after a while, a cylindrical object wrapped in brown paper clutched in his right hand. Groping in his pocket with his free hand he stood staring down at the car. Something clinked onto the ground and he swore loud enough to be heard from where I stood. Placing the parcel carefully upon the ground, he got down on his knees, hands moving along the surface of the street.

I looked around for the boy in the mauve shirt, but he had vanished. My gaze swung back to where Danhurst was getting up, the parcel tucked under his arm now. Noisily he slammed the car door, locked it and dropped the keys back into his pocket.

Patiently I smoked what was left of my cigarette and watched him start down the street on legs that were not anxious for exercise. The street lighting ended a few yards beyond the saloon, leaving the rest of the buildings there to the mercy of the long shadows. I was ready to cross over, to satisfy my curiosity, when a figure scurried across the street.

On the other side he paused while Danhurst continued to increase the distance between the two of them. Then from out of his dark jacket pocket came something that glinted evilly in the limited light. I waited while he fiddled with the article, while the seconds shrank away and a coldness slivered up my spine like a wet snake.

I dropped the cigarette, stepped on it, and as soon as he moved started off down my side of the street. The shadows became inkier and the surroundings quieter as the boy slipped along the pavement, rapidly reducing the gap between him and his quarry. He moved as if he belonged to the night.

Danhurst was approaching the entrance of an alley when the boy began to close in.

It would have been interesting to watch the rest, and to find out why, but I didn't think Danhurst was in any kind of condition to take care of himself. I jerked the .38 loose from its holster and ran across the street with as little sound as possible. But the boy heard, and he turned.

For a moment he froze rigidly, undecided, perhaps having glimpsed what was in my fist.

He turned to run, but I got in front of him and jabbed the muzzle of the gun into the hardness of his lean belly. It brought him to a swift stop. An uttering rattled in his throat and his right hand came up defiantly.

I said: "Do you want to die?"

The poised fist trembled in the air while flight wrestled with common sense. Deciding the gun wasn't an ornament, he let his arm drop heavily and raised an icy glare up to my face. I looked quickly over his shoulder. Danhurst was entering a two-storey frame house, apparently oblivious to what was happening behind him. I pushed the boy away, put out my free hand, palm up.

"Dar."

"I speak English!"

"Then you heard what I said. Give it to me."

His head tilted back sharply and a stream of spit landed at my feet.

I shook my head. "Kid, you're not so tough a stretch for attempted assault and robbery won't soften you up." I put out my hand. "The knuckles!"

Grudgingly and without haste he pulled them from his hand and gave them over.

They were homemade—a piece of an old leather belt stitched into a loop, half its circumference decorated with a hundred points of boot tacks. With that wrapped around his fist, win or lose the fight, his opponent would end up with shredded flesh. I dropped it into my coat pocket.

"What's your name?"

The dark face closed up sullenly.

With my left hand I reached into my inside coat pocket, watching him carefully as I did. I took out the leather folder, flipped it open so that he could see the photostat under the plastic. It was too dark for anyone to read much of the wording, but he appeared impressed with what he saw.

"Raul," he said. "Raul Ybarra."

I put away the I.D. case. "Ever been arrested before, Raul?"

He answered with a quick sideways wag of his head.

"You could pick up a lot of time for something like this," I informed him quietly. "Mugging carries a pretty severe rap."

"I'm no mugger!" he asserted fiercely. "I don' try rob no drunk!"

"Then why?"

Under the coat narrow shoulders moved uneasily. "I get even, thasall."

"Even for what?"

Slim fingers whisked across the injured eye and the thick lip. "The bastardo—he beat me up when I can't fight back."

"You know who he is?"

"*Si,* I know. I work for that fat cow of a mother he got. In Reposado I work there for a couple months. Then he give me this"—he caressed the damage to his face tenderly—"and throw me out without pay."

"Just like that? He beat you up and tossed you out for no reason at all?"

He recognized my skepticism "I tell the truth, damnit! He tell me I steal the vino—the wine. But he is liar! Maria, she give it to me and I hide it in garage while I am working."

"Who's Maria?"

"Maria Valpez—the cook. She too work for them."

"So Maria was the one who swiped the wine?"

He shrugged. "I forget it in garage when I go home. Then I come back to fetch it and he hear me. He say I come back in the night jus' to steal, and then he knock hell outa me!" Another stream of spit whistled over his lips. "Cerdo! Beeg people—lotsa dinero! He can fight me and I hit him and he shout for his frien' the sheriff."

"And now you figured to get even, that it? Were you expecting him to come here tonight, Raul?"

"No," he said, emphasizing the denial with another swift movement of his dark head. "I come here to look for work. I see him in the bar, drinking."

"Know where he's gone?"

"No. A woman maybe."

"All right, Raul. Now what really happened back in Reposado?"

"I tol' you what happen. Whassa matter? You don' believe?" A low whine of self-pity had crept into his voice.

"I believe you've left out a few things."

"I don' try steal nothing from him," he insisted. 'I go back for the vino and . . .'" His voice trailed off into the silence of the street. The noise back at the bar sounded distant and unreal.

"And?"

"Okay, so I'm stupid. I don' jus' get the vino and vamoose—no, I go look to see what the noise is." His eyes flicked up to mine, trying to see whether or not I was ready to believe what he had to say.

"I'm listening."

"Inside there is noise. I hear the woman shouting. I listen. Then I go look in the window by the garage. The curtain it is close and I don' see nothing. Then I hear the woman—the Señora Danhurst—shout some more. She is not inside house. It jus' sound like that when I am by the garage. She is by back of house, the place with the wall. I want to go, but I think maybe I find out first what is happening. On top of garage you can see down into yard behind wall and it is not hard for me to climb on top. What I see is him"—he jerked an erect thumb over his shoulder to where Danhurst had gone—"and he is drunk, or something. He is on ground and his mother she is there with him. She look up and see me on roof." Shoulders slumped when he sighed. "She shout and she point. I try to jump, but it is too high. I think maybe I can run away before she find out who it is. But him, Gerry, he catch me as I climb down. He has been drinking and he ask what I do there. But first he hit me," he complained with a whine. "He hit me before I can tell him about the vino. I tell him, but he don' listen. He jus' hit!"

"What was happening back there in the yard?" I asked.

"Sorry, the light is not good and I don' see so much. Jus' what I tell you. He is drunk and he falls and mama she is having the fits." A quick grin permitted a brief showing of even white teeth. 'You ask me he get up pretty damn quick to catch me."

"You're sure it was Danhurst you saw?"

Limp shoulders moved again. "Is only him and his mother and the sister. The sister, she is different. Not like him. The brother he is pig!"

"When was all this supposed to have happened?"

"*Miércoles.* Wednesday night."

I tried to visualize the bulky Christine Danhurst out of the chair, the only place I'd ever seen her. It wasn't easy. "How about the old lady? Sure it was the Señora Danhurst?"

"I am sure." He nodded slowly. "I make no mistake. You not miss *that* woman."

I thought about it, said: "All right, Raul. Scram."

"*Quê?*"

"Take off before I decide to do something about you."

"You don' arrest me?"

"Maybe next time." I put away the gun.

He backed off uncertainly. *"Mil gracias, señor . . .* thank you!"

"De nada," I mumbled.

This time he did not concern himself with stealth or noise as lean legs catapulted him up the street and into the past.

SIX

FOR NEARLY FIFTEEN minutes I stood in the dark and watched the only window that showed a light on the upper floor of the old frame house. Probably Ybarra's guess had been correct, but having invested time in tailing Danhurst from Reposado, it seemed reasonable to spend a little more in ascertaining that it was a woman he had come to visit. So I waited and watched, though I couldn't see what importance Danhurst's love life could have on the job I was supposed to be doing.

It had been a long day and I was beginning to feel tired. I looked up again at the light spilling out from the edges of a lowered roller blind and considered calling it quits and going home. Had the decision been made a minute sooner I might not have heard the screeching female voice that traveled down to where I stood.

It came as a sharp squeal of pain. I stiffened, then the voice cried again:

"No—! Gerry, no—!"

By then I was moving toward the entrance of the house and could hear no more.

Inside it was dark, but I was able to find the wooden stairs that led up in the direction of the screams. On the upper floor was a short hall in darkness, dim light showing at the base of one of the doors. I was in front of it when another door opened and the hall was suddenly washed in yellow light. A male voice growled:

"What in hell's name goes on here tonight?"

Smooth and chunky, he was dressed in broad striped pajamas that hung like a gaudy maternity smock from his protruding belly. The balding head was a little like the one made famous by Oliver Hardy, but not the irritated eyes that squinted angrily.

"It's all right," I told him. "You can go back to bed."

With his hand still poised on the light switch near the open door, he scowled at me. "You a cop?"

"Go in and shut the door. I'll take care of this."

"Ain't right for decent people to have to live under the same roof as a lousy hooker," he grumbled. "She oughta be kicked out and locked up. This ain't the first time she's made a disturbance here, I can tell you." He turned back to his room, but before shutting the door paused to throw a little more information at me. "There's a guy in there with her, and they're both stinko."

Loudly the door closed behind him, only to open again long enough for a hand to reach out and click off the light switch. Once more I was alone in the darkness, and if other eyes peeped from behind other doors, I didn't notice.

I knocked hard on the one that showed light, but except for faint, muffled sounds it was now silent on the other side. When no move was made to open up I knuckled the wood again, waited, then tried the handle. It was locked.

"Open up!" I ordered, not too loudly. "Otherwise we'll have to break it down."

Danhurst must have had his hands close to the knob for right away a key scratched in the lock and the door swung in a scant three inches.

Pushing against it, I sent him stumbling backward. A low, growling curse greeted my entry, but he did nothing to stop me from stepping inside the room and shutting the door.

On the bed, a girl who could not have been much past twenty was huddled against the headboard, a sheet bunched up over her naked body. It failed to cover very much, but with tears smearing her face and her hair a tussled blonde mess, I saw little that was appealing. The thin line of blood weeping from her mouth didn't help either.

She'd been crying, but now the tears were turned off as she watched me without excitement, wiping the blood from her mouth with a corner of the sheet.

"What the hell do you want?" Danhurst demanded from where he leaned his rump against a cheap, scarred tallboy. His coat was hooked over the back of a thinly upholstered chair, his shirt open all the way down the front and dangling out of his pants. Sweat made the smooth, hairless skin on his chest and muscled belly glisten. On the ratty bit of furniture behind him stood a bottle and a half-filled glass. Another lay on the floor next to a small pool and a balled-up piece of wrapping paper.

"Get your coat on," I told him. "We're going home."

Like someone trying to get their vision back into focus, he stared at me. "Says who?"

"I do. And I'm in a hurry. So move."

He was drunk, but struggling hard to co-ordinate his thoughts. Without comment he tucked the shirt back into his pants, not bothering to button it. I looked at his handsome, sneering face, trying to find something of his sister there, strangely pleased when I could not.

On the bed the girl moved up on to her knees. The sheet slipped down to expose a firm, rounded breast and a lot more of her body. The fact seemed not to worry her.

"Where do you think you're taking him?"

"Home."

She opened her mouth, but Danhurst beat her to the draw.

"You're no damned cop! I recognize you now. You're that stinking peeper Whitman hired!"

"Grab your coat, Gerry."

"Just a minute," the girl cut in, sliding off the bed and discarding the sheet completely. "He's not just walking out here like that! Not after what he did to me! You know what he did?"

"No. And I'm not especially interested. You look all right to me."

The words she spat out were of deep purple. "The bastard tried to beat me up and rape me! That's what he did! You heard me yell after he hit me, didn'tcha?" Defiantly she placed her hands on naked hips and puffed out a nicely formed but slightly sagging bust. "He's not getting off that easy!"

"Put your clothes on, Bonny," Danhurst grunted. "He isn't in the market for what you've got."

Hissing through clenched teeth the blonde advanced upon him, right hand drawn back to strike. Clumsily he pushed her away. She hit the bed, rolled over on to her back and used the words again.

"Okay, hot shot. You asked for it! I'll get some real cops up here. We'll see how big you are in front of them!"

I knew what she planned, but before the scream could leave her mouth I had a hand clamped over it. She toppled backward, tugging at my wrist while trying to sink her teeth into my fingers. I said:

"Get the cops up here, Bonny, and I'll be forced to tell them how you picked him up in the bar and brought him to your room. It won't look too good for you with that booze around and the both of you drunk. Now make up your mind. Are you going to behave?"

Her eyes were things on fire, her body quivering with rage. But she managed a sound I took to be a promise, and I let go, and massaged my hand. The teeth marks were deep, but she hadn't drawn blood.

"You ready?" I asked Danhurst. "Or do you want more trouble?"

Not yet quite with it, he slowly nodded. Taking his coat from the chair he pulled it awkwardly on.

"Yeah, I'm ready."

"Not quite," I said. "You did hit her. She deserves some compensation."

"What?"

"Pay her."

The glare I got questioned my sanity, but he brought out his wallet and plucked loose two twenties. Dropping the money onto the bed he prepared to pocket the wallet again, changed his mind and added another bill to those that had fallen next to the girl.

"Satisfied?"

I offered him a worthless smile and took his arm. The girl was scooping up the money as I led him to the door.

"Hey, you?" she called.

We both turned.

"What?" Danhurst asked.

"Not you, big shot. Him. What's your name?"

"Not one that's important."

"Okay, Mr. No-name, have it your way." She was on her belly, looking at us across the bed, the money clutched in a small, tight first. "I like your style. Next time you're around drop in to say hello. It won't cost you a thing."

Danhurst said something too low for either of us to hear.

"Yeah, sure." I pushed Danhurst out of the room, said: "Sleep easy," and closed the door behind us.

Going down the stairs I had to help him or otherwise he would have taken them head first in the dark.

On the street, I said: "What was that all about?"

"What's it to you?"

"You were beating her up, Gerry. Had she yelled any louder you may have had real trouble on your hands."

"So thanks for rescuing me," he mumbled, and started up the street to where we'd left our cars. He was sobering up rapidly, but I still didn't like the idea of him driving.

"I'll give you a ride home," I said.

"Like hell you will. There's nothing wrong with me and I've got my own wheels."

"So have the H.P. And they could take that buggy of yours, believe it or not."

He stopped, leaned his back against a high, broken fence. "Something's just occurred to me, " he said, fumbling in his pockets until coming up with a cigarette case and a heavy lighter. "What are you supposed to be doing here? You been following me?"

"I saw you in the bar. I also saw someone follow you out and try to jump you." I gave him a few moments to absorb it before asking: "Know a young Mex named Ybarra?"

Sticking a cigarette into his face and lighting it he delayed answering. At last, with smoke curling from his nostrils, he said:

"What about him?"

"He was the one who tried to jump you." I took out the knuckles and showed them to him. "He was wearing these when I stopped him."

Danhurst sucked deeply on the cigarette. I couldn't see much of his face behind the cupped hand and the red glow, but I knew he was studying the thing I held.

"What did he have against you, Gerry?"

"How the hell would I know? The little punk's a screwball."

I put away the lethal strap. "He said you beat him up."

"Maybe I did." He flipped the smoke out into the street where it landed in a shower of tiny sparks. "I clobbered him all right. He was stealing stuff from the house. I caught him at it the other night. He'd come back to collect something he'd swiped and hidden away." This time it was he who waited before asking: "What did he tell you?"

"Much the same. Except he added a bit about climbing onto the garage roof after hearing your mother's shouts, of seeing you lying on the ground in the walled-in back yard. Your mother, it seems, was trying to get you back onto your feet."

"The stinking little greaser!" he spat vehemently, adding a selection of profanities that applied themselves to the name of Ybarra. Then he laughed. It sounded strange after the angry outburst. "You believe him? You swallowed that crap?"

"Shouldn't I have?"

"Believe what you want. It doesn't bother me."

"Okay," I said.

"He was lying. He was busy picking up a bottle in the garage when I caught him. A bottle of wine he'd swiped from the house."

"So you beat him up."

"Why not? He was stealing. Hell, if he'd asked for it I'd have given it to him. But I hate thieves."

"Do you usually make a habit of hitting people?"

He came away from the fence. "What are you driving at?"

I tensed, expecting a fist to whistle out of the darkness. "You hit the girl," I said quietly. "What did she do to you?"

"I hit her and she asked for it. And it's none of your damned business. You offered me a ride. So why are we waiting?"

Walking the rest of the way he bumped several times into me as he swaggered uncertainly along. He was one of those somewhat fortunate people I'd come up against only a few times—those who can carry a load and still manage to speak reasonably intelligently without slurring their words.

"Want me to have your car garaged?" I asked, before shutting my car door on him.

"No, it'll be all right where it is. I'll pick it up in the morning."

It wasn't a decision I'd have made, but I didn't waste time arguing. And that was the last he said until we were a few miles from Reposado.

"You still wondering why I hit that blonde tramp?"

"Not anymore. Like you said, it's none of my business."

"Like hell you're not. I hit her because she's a damned liar. There was another guy with her just shortly before I showed up at her room. She didn't even have time to get rid of his cigarette butts. I didn't see them until it was too late, otherwise I wouldn't have stayed."

"You don't have to explain that to me."

"So all right, I didn't have to. Just don't go thinking I'm some kind of crazy kook that runs around beating up on people for kicks. There's nothing wrong with me, so straighten yourself out on that."

"Have I given you reason to think I doubted it?"

"Ah forget it," he sighed, and sank down into the seat. Then after a while: "She's not really so bad."

"Who?"

"Bonny. The blonde. She's had a rough time, that's all. I suppose I feel sorry for her really."

"See her often?"

He took his time to reply. A car coming from the opposite direction refused to dim its lights and I was forced to slow down until it passed.

Next to me he said: "Not so often. It's quite a ride down there and I don't get around that much."

"Why pick a girl so far from home then? There must be others in Reposado?"

"Sure there are. But in a hick town like that it would be all over the place in no time flat. Everybody knows everybody else's business in that dump. That's why the old man built Retreat."

"He must really have wanted privacy. I notice visitors aren't encouraged."

"They're not." For some reason he decided the remark needed further amplification. "My mother's a sick woman. She doesn't like people bothering her."

"And you, Gerry? You strike me as a boy who'd like to live it up a little. Don't you find things a bit boring there?"

"If I do, it's my business. So let's drop it."

"If you wish." We drove on in a mile of more silence. Then I asked: "Did you know Bridget Cole?"

He moved stiffly at my side.

"Did you?"

"I knew her. But not well. She was a cousin of some kind, that's all. She was also Whitman's girl. If you want to know about her, ask him."

"Given any thought to the way she was killed?"

I could feel his eyes on the side of my face when he sat upright. "No I haven't," he blurted stridently. "She visited Retreat the night she died, but that doesn't mean any of us know what kind of trouble she ran into. And while we're on the subject, I'm warning you again to stop annoying my mother with any of this. Sheriff Mulder will do what's necessary. There's no need for Whitman to hire himself a bloodhound."

"Who told you he hired me for that?"

"Drop it will you? I've no interest in the subject." Sinking back into the seat he lapsed into silence, remaining that way until I stopped in front of the big iron gate.

I thought he had been asleep, but once the car stopped he sat up straight and unlatched the door.

"No need to go in. I can walk from here." With the door open I could see him clearly in the glow of the courtesy light. By the time he was out of the car and fully on his feet he had his wallet in his hands again, taking money from it. "What do I owe you?"

"For what?"

"For the ride and what you did back there?"

"Forget it."

Two bills came loose. He leaned into the car aid laid them on the seat next to my thigh.

"I pay my way. No favors. Take it."

I picked up the money without looking at it, squeezed it into a ball and flipped it back at him while he was straightening up. It fell somewhere at his feet.

"You're a big boy, Gerry. It's time you started learning something about people."

I leaned over, pulled the door shut and reversed away from the gate. He was still standing there when I started towards the lights of town.

Reposado was quiet. Most of its citizens had tucked themselves away for the night. I entered the hotel, hoping to be able to find a cup of coffee before doing as the rest of the town had done.

The desk clerk had his nose in a glossy magazine and glanced up drowsily when I approached and asked for my key.

He unhooked it from the rack and pushed it tiredly across the counter.

"There's somebody been waiting for you, Mr. Cameron," he yawned, then went back to the magazine.

The lobby was deserted, except for a man slumped low in one of the big club chairs, his long legs stretched out in front of him, arms folded, eyes hidden by a brown hat tilted down onto the bridge of his nose. I went to him.

"You waiting for me?"

At the sound of my voice he jerked up out of the chair, pushing his hat back onto his head so that he could see who had spoken.

"Cameron . . .?"

I said it was and he produced a big bony hand, which I took. He towered over me, and unless his school coach had been blind to height, would have been a member of the basketball team. A coat in need of pressing hung loosely from his shoulders and the blue bow tie was fixed crookedly at his throat. He was one of those people who would always have trouble trying not to look sloppy.

"My name's Rudge. *Reposado Record.* Not the biggest, but we cover the entire county, and then some." His long face creased into a slow, easy smile that showed large teeth. "I was talking to the sheriff when your name came up."

"Sit down," I invited, and settled myself into another nearby chair.

Rudge got his legs into a position where they wouldn't trouble him, dredged up a slightly battered deck of Chesterfields and held them out. I said no thanks and waited until he had lit one for himself.

"Sheriff Mulder tells me you're working for Harlan Whitman. He didn't sound very pleased about it."

"He'll recover," I said. "And you? What do you want from me?"

"Anything you've got to tell me will do. Mulder's given me most of the facts, but I figured you could have something worthwhile to add."

"I don't. He knows as much as I do. Probably a whole lot more."
When he went on waiting, I asked: "Did he tell you how the girl was
killed?"

"No, I got that from Hamilton, the coroner. She was choked to death."
He sucked on the cigarette and smiled. "Surprise you?"

"A bit. I saw her at the morgue, and there it appeared as though she'd
been beaten up."

"It helped. But it wasn't what killed her. Hamilton himself was somewhat surprised to find what he did. There were marks on her throat—not
enough to help much, but enough to make him look further." Forcing
twin streams of smoke through thinly flared nostrils, he went on: "The
way they've laid it out is like this. Whoever attacked her hit and kicked
her into unconsciousness. Then he, or she, finished off the job by stran-
gulation. Pretty, no?"

"He or she?" I queried. "Has Mulder come up with something to indicate a woman might have had a hand in it?"

Rudge hitched himself forward, took a last drag on the cigarette and
squashed it out in an ashtray already almost filled with similar butts.
"Nope. That's just me being cautious. I've been too long in this game to
accept much at face value, even though Hamilton's of the opinion the
bruises on her body were made by a man's shoe." He leaned back. "Anything you can tell me, Mr. Cameron?"

"Not yet. I'm still poking around without much luck."

"How about this one then? Where can I contact Whitman?"

I tried not to look surprised. "His apartment would seem the most obvious place."

"Nope, not at home. I've been trying to reach him for a statement ever
since the two of you left Mulder's office this morning. I thought you
might know if he'd gone off somewhere."

"I don't. After our session with the sheriff I took him home and left
him there."

"Off the record, and that's not intended as a pun, I'll tell you something. It hasn't filled our sheriff with joy." He paused, seemingly uncertain about what next he should say. "I guess you know Whitman had a
scrap with the girl yesterday?"

"He told me about it. But the way I heard it, it was an argument, not a
fight."

"Whichever, someone's informed Mulder about it and he doesn't like
it. So far, with the exception of the money missing from the girl's purse,
there's no apparent motive for the killing."

"Has Mulder mentioned to you the person I reported seeing last
night?"

"He did, and I checked into it and drew a blank, same as he did. None
of the hospitals in the nearby vicinity were called on to attend such a
case. Of course, friends could be caring for the guy you say you saw.

Only Mulder's pointed out something that's inclined to rule out that possibility."

"Such as?"

"Supposing you did see someone, and supposing he was bleeding. Supposing also that he had something to do with the Cole girl's death . . . You believe that, then you have to accept that either the girl wounded him or there was someone with her who took care of it. If the girl had hurt him it would have to have been before she died, and that means the wounded guy's blood would have got onto her clothes when he throttled her. It didn't. Hamilton sent the clothes to the lab for checking and they turned up nothing. On the other hand, if the girl was not alone, if it was a friend of hers who made her attacker bleed, then ask yourself who killed Bridget Cole?" When receiving nothing from me, he said: "Personally, I don't see her having had anyone with her when it happened."

"Going to tell me why?"

Rudge grinned again. It gave his face all the qualities of a handsome horse. "Do I have to?"

"I guess not. No friend would have waited until she was already beaten up before attempting to help, not unless he or she had also been attacked. And if it was anything like that, what happened to the friend?"

"Roger! And what was used to wound the guy? Nothing was found at the scene." Except for the very smallest of frowns, he cleared his face of all expression. "This kind of thinking can get pretty complicated, can't it? Anyway, there's been nothing to suggest she wasn't alone."

I said: "And like Mulder, you don't think much of the piece about the bleeding man, do you? That's what you meant when you said Mulder's theory rules out the possibility of such a person being cared for by friends or relatives."

"Let's face it," he said, trying on a polite smile, "there's only your word for it. You're the only one who's supposed to have seen him."

I thought about Connie March, but said instead: "Right this minute I can't tell you anything that would make a better story, Rudge. And even if I could I'd have to give it to the sheriff first. But I'll make a deal with you."

"Uh-huh? What kind?" He took off his hat, scratched at tight hair that was like compacted steel wool, then stuck the lid back on to the side of his head.

"Anything I come across will be passed on to you straight after I've turned it over to Mulder."

As if the offer was the kind that had been made many times before, Rudge smiled again, knowingly. "In return for what?"

"Some background information. I'm a stranger in your town, remember?"

While he pondered the suggestion he busied himself lighting another cigarette. "Okay, shoot. What's it you want to know?"

"I heard there was some hostility between Whitman and the sheriff."

"You talking about that business over the kid who claimed he was beat up while in custody?"

"Uh-huh. That one."

"If there was I never got to hear about it. It's a possibility, though. Whitman made things look bad for the sheriff, but he couldn't prove the accusation. It fizzled out and died after the kid was sentenced. But Mulder got himself some publicity that could have cost him an election."

"How much do you know about the Danhursts?" I asked.

"That," Rudge sighed regretfully, "could take all night, and most of what I could tell you would be sheer speculation. None of us know a hell of a lot about that crazy family. The old woman's a recluse. She runs that place with an iron fist and a big purse and she's made it clear she doesn't need people. The son's a strange one. Keeps to himself mostly, especially after the last lot of trouble in town."

Again I waited with my mouth shut.

"It didn't amount to much," Rudge continued. "He was in a bar down the street and he'd been drinking rather heavily. Some drunk made a crack about his mother and Danhurst flattened him. I was there to see it, but don't ask me exactly what was said. I didn't hear. Anyway, it obviously did anything but amuse young Danhurst. Nothing ever came of the incident, but it might have. If others hadn't stepped in to break up the fight there's a chance he would have killed the drunk."

"And the daughter?"

"She's different. On one or two occasions I've been able to talk to her and she strikes me as an all right kid. Though how anyone can live a normal life stuck away in that nutty house is beyond me. But maybe that comes under the heading of their business, hmm?"

"Were the kids educated here?"

"Uh-uh. After the old man died they were sent away to school, but they returned and presently they're both pretty well settled in."

"I heard the father had money. I heard that he built the house because of something that happened in the family. Know anything about that?"

"Old Nathaniel Danhurst had loot, for sure, and plenty of it. After he died I did a story on him, based on the few facts I could dig up. But the old woman killed it. She didn't want the publicity. Matter of fact neither did Danhurst when he was alive. They both hated any kind of publicity." Flicking ash at the ashtray and missing it by inches, he inhaled deeply on the cigarette before going on with his story.

"Danhurst inherited a sizeable chunk of money when he was still a youngster, then set out turning it into a fortune through deals in California oil and real estate. Sometime in the thirties he married a girl named Christine Fuller." He stubbed out the smoke and looked inquiringly at me. "The name ring any bells?"

"Not immediately. But I did see a picture of Christine Danhurst in the house. It was painted when she was considerably younger and . . . not so large."

"Yeah . . . You wouldn't say so to look at her now, but back in the thirties Christine Fuller was a real beauty. She was also a name on Broadway in those days. Danhurst married her in New York and they came to live in San Francisco. Christine retired from the stage as soon as she learned she was pregnant. Their first kid, a boy, was born here in California. They stayed a couple of years in Frisco and then returned to New York, and that, as it happened, was a bum move for both of them. The child died of pneumonia, I believe. Whatever, it cut the old man up pretty bad. He retired from active business and elected to settle in Reposado. That was in forty-three, when this place wasn't much more than farmland. But Danhurst's decision to build a home here prompted others to follow suit. I guess they figured there was more to his move than just the desire for solitude."

"Was there?"

"Uh-uh." Before going on he gave his lungs another beating by lighting still another cigarette. "Admittedly the place has prospered. This isn't a big town, but there's money here, even if it is in control of just a few. No . . ." he drawled, "Danhurst's reason was only to get away from his former associates and the life he'd led before. They wanted to try again to raise a family in a surrounding which was supposed to be designed for just that purpose. Danhurst was crazy for kids. Or so I've heard. He did a lot for them while he lived. The children's charities could always count on him for a big donation whenever it was needed. Anyway, not long after they settled in the big house Christine fell pregnant again. Danhurst sent her to New York to have the kid. Apparently he wasn't taking any chances because she spent some months there and it must have cost him a pile. The same thing happened when the girl was born. They've lived here since and they've minded their own business and insisted that others did the same."

He took a few moments to study the cigarette he was holding, as if wondering how it had got into his hand. Then he took another pull at it and said: "If you want my opinion, and it isn't worth much, I think Danhurst and his wife blamed themselves a little for what happened to their first kid. I once spoke to the old guy and a few things he let slip gave me that impression."

He paused, inviting a question. When getting none, he said: "The winter was lousy in New York the year the kid died. They'd gone out, it seems, and the nurse who'd been hired to look after the kid neglected her duties somehow. The kid sneaked out of his room and contracted what everyone first thought was just a bad cold. It turned into pneumonia, and that was it. Danhurst reasoned that if they hadn't gone to New York and hadn't gone to a party that night, it might not have happened."

"He tell you these things himself?"

"No," he replied, dropping more ash to the floor. "He never told anybody very much about himself or his family. Most of it is what I've pieced together from little items picked up here and there, and, as I said, from things he let slip when I did have the opportunity of talking with him."

I considered what he had given me.

"I guess that's the price tag for being rich, Cameron. With money one's inclined to lead a pretty hectic life. You can hop around the world just as it suits your fancy. Just as easy as taking a bus ride down the street. Life can be a ball."

"Until the ball stops bouncing."

"Not funny, but maybe appropriate. You're right though. It stopped bouncing in New York. The boy was about four years old then—old enough to have been a personality that could be remembered and missed." Once more he lapsed into thoughtful silence. Then: "She's a screwball, the old woman, but I can't help being sorry for her. Nobody gets near her if she can help it. It's as though she's tried to lock out the entire world."

"A doctor named McGill doesn't appear to have much trouble with her."

"Myron McGill? Hell, it's natural he'd be a privileged visitor. He's been their doctor ever since Gerry was born."

He stood up and I followed. "What makes you so interested in the Danhursts?"

"Who wouldn't be? They struck me as a rather strange family. And Bridget Cole was part of it, even if just a small and distant part."

There was only an inch of his cigarette left, but he stuck it back on his lower lip and grinned down at me. 'Nothing you want to give me?"

"I can't; not now. But I'll stick to my promise."

"Sure," he grinned around the remnant of cigarette. "I can wait. Maybe then you'll tell me where you've been tonight that's kept you out so late, and why the need for a gun."

"I didn't think it showed."

"It did. But only when you stood up. Thought you private operators favored shoulder rigs?"

"Ever try wearing one?" I asked, and offered him my hand.

He shook it, plucked the fragment of a butt from his mouth and dropped it with expert aim into the overflowing ashtray. Then he thought of something and dipped his hand into an inside pocket to pull out a folded newspaper sheet.

"When I heard how the girl was supposed to have been killed I remembered something that happened a long time ago. I dug into the files and came up with this." He handed me the folded paper. "After what Hamilton turned up at the autopsy, it isn't worth a damn now, not even as an idea."

I unfolded the sheet, read the headlines of the story that had appeared in a vintage edition of his paper.

"It'll give you something to read or wrap your garbage in," he said, then turned and walked out of the hotel with a careless flap of his hand for a goodnight wave.

When he'd gone I sat down and read the newspaper page. It was dated January 1950, and carried a story about the murder of a seven-year-old girl named Marlene Leonard.

The gist of it was that the child's body had been found by her parents several hundred yards from their home. She'd been dead when discovered, beaten to death, her clothes ripped from her body. Walter Mulder had not been sheriff then, but his predecessor, a man named Hepple, had seemed to think the child had been the victim of a band of motorcycle ruffians who'd invaded the town shortly after the New Year festivities. Written at the end of the story with a red ballpoint scrawl was the one word: UNSOLVED.

I put away the paper and went to talk to the desk clerk about having some coffee sent up to my room.

After two cups of the welcome brew I stripped and then tried Whitman's number again. Once more it just went on ringing. I hung up, turned off the light and got into bed.

In between a sleep that arrived quickly, I had a brief dream of a girl with raven-black hair and tears on her cheeks.

SEVEN

A HEAVY knocking on the door got me out of the bathroom the next morning. The banging continued while I slipped into a shirt, buttoned up the front, and shoved it into my pants. The delay was short, but just long enough to make whoever was outside impatient. The door opened before I could reach it and, looking like a man who'd been forced to eat a burnt breakfast, Sheriff Walter Mulder barged into the room.

"You get up late for a working man, Cameron," he said, scowling. With a quick, careless shove he slammed the door.

"It's the seventh day. I guess I'm entitled to some extra sleep." I looked past him to the door. "Wonder why I didn't latch that thing?"

Hooking his thumbs into his wide belt he allowed his shoulders to relax a little. He looked tired and irritable and there was redness in his eyes and a growth on his face that, combined with his stance, gave the impression of an old-time gunfighter prodding for trouble. "Where's Whitman?" he grunted.

"At home, I'd suppose."

"Ditch the funny talk, fella. I've been up most of the night trying to make sense out of this damned business and this morning I'm not in the mood for your brand of humor."

"It wasn't meant to be funny," I said, picking up a tie to loop around the shirt collar. "I take it you've checked at his apartment?"

"You can take it and . . ." The rest he allowed to die a sudden death. "Where is he?"

"I've been trying to reach him myself—without any success."

"Try it again, mister. The two of you left my office together yesterday."

"You think I've got him hidden?"

"For the moment I'll keep what I'm thinking to myself." One hand loosened itself from the broad belt and rubbed at the bristles dulling his chin.

"Why the sudden anxiety?" I turned to the dresser mirror so that I could knot the tie. "What do you want with him?"

In the mirror I caught a quick reflection of movement and in the next instant felt a hand with the grip of a hydraulic grab fasten onto my shoulder and spin me roughly around. Something blurred past my face and sent me rocking back into the dresser. My jaw stung and there was the taste of salt in my mouth.

I put a hand to my mouth and glared at him. His right fist was poised for any trouble I might decide to make, but seeing I wasn't dumb enough to try a stunt like that he let it drop to his side where it lingered uncomfortably close to the holstered gun.

"Don't wise talk me, fella, and don't ever turn your back on me when I'm speaking!" he hissed through tautly drawn lips.

"I've told you once I don't know anything about Whitman's whereabouts. He wasn't home last night and nobody answered his phone. More than that I don't know."

"He's your client, isn't he?"

I took my hand away from my mouth. There was blood on it. "But not his keeper."

Mulder's eyes were no longer tired. They narrowed into hard gray slits and he moved forward.

I stepped away from him. "Don't try it. I'm not some Mexican kid you can knock around. I know enough about the law to know I don't have to take that kind of stuff from you."

It froze him.

"What the hell are you yapping about?"

From my pocket I jerked a handkerchief and dabbed at my mouth. It wasn't bleeding much and probably wasn't half as bad as it felt. I said: "Someone told me about you and that episode and how it nearly cost you an election. I could be wrong, but it occurs to me you might like to see the rap for the girl's murder fitted around Whitman's neck."

"Cameron," he growled extra deeply, "that kind of talk could cost you an expensive job of bone setting. You open your mouth like that again and s'help me I'll tear you apart and the hell with the consequences."

"I said I could be wrong."

"You couldn't be more wrong!" he fired, trying to keep a rein on a rising temper. "I'm the law in this county and I've had to rough people up now and again, but it's always been with good cause. Whitman tried to make an issue of such an instance and fell on his face. It nearly cost me the last election, that's for sure, but the day I let a thing like that influence my work I'll toss in this badge." He tapped the star on his chest then rubbed at his unshaven chin; visibly embarrassed by the speech he'd delivered.

I threw the handkerchief onto the bed. "You still sound pretty anxious to get him. Going to tell me why?"

"Some answers to some questions is why. He told you about that trouble with the greaser, but I bet he never bothered to mention he had a fight with the Cole girl at lunchtime on Friday, did he?"

"He did, but I didn't think it very important. He was sore because she wouldn't cancel a visit to Fresno so she could accompany him to a party here in town. It sounded like the kind of spat most people have at some time or other."

"He also tell you about her giving him back the ring?"

"He did."

"How about the party? He mention that he went to it—alone?"

"I don't recall asking or him telling."

"You wouldn't." He grinned suddenly, letting the lids of his eyes droop again. They killed any effect the smile might have been trying to make. "In which case you wouldn't know that he left the party early. And," he added carefully, "he didn't go home."

It was time to again stare dumbly.

"Someone at the party tried to phone him round about eleven. He wasn't there."

I had no intelligent response to that one.

"Feel like changing your mind now?"

"I don't know where he is. If I did I'd go to him. I'd like to see how he reacts to what you've said about Friday night."

The sheriff sniggered. "Know something? I think I actually believe you. I think your client offered you a sack of horse manure and you bought it at full price."

When I failed to comment he heeled about and walked to the door, opened and held it.

"On the other hand," he said, "I know the two of you were buddy-buddy way back when. Could be your job's really to try and pull him out of the mess he's made. How about that?"

I shook my head.

He grinned back at me. It was more like the snarl on the face of a bear. I could still see it even after he'd shut the door and was gone.

I finished dressing and then went downstairs to do the second thing I'd been planning to do that morning. The first had been to try and contact Whitman, but after Mulder's visit it now seemed pointless.

Several yards past an old-fashioned gas station that was doing no business at all, I found the old road that swept northwest of town. There the blacktop ended, changing abruptly into a strip of sun-baked earth wide enough for only two cars. A road-closed barricade had been set up at the start of the road. Probably by Mulder, wanting traffic kept out of the area until the girl's car could be brought back to town. They seemed to be taking a long enough time over a chore like that, but perhaps there were reasons I didn't know about.

Hoping nobody would see and raise an objection, I moved aside the obstruction and drove through. On the return to the car, after placing the barricade back into position, I paused to check whether anyone watched. But on that Sunday morning that part of town still slept soundly. I stripped off my coat, hung it over the back of the seat, got in behind the wheel and started up the slow climb. Already the sun was warming up the day and I felt in need of something cool to drink.

The ground was rough and pot-holed, the surface still powdery enough to create dust trails in the wake of the car's rear wheels. I rolled down the window and let some of the dust filter inside as perspiration started between my back and the warm leather of the seat, wondering why anybody would want to use the road unless they were in a real hurry and anxious to save a few miles.

Sunlight glinting on silver was the first sign I got of the car. I pulled up several yards behind it, killed the engine and got out. With its rear wheels rammed deep into the brush that grew at the road edge, the little car looked like a crippled beetle waiting for the sun to bake out its intestines. I thought of the girl I had looked at in the morgue, and quite suddenly there was a chill in the morning air.

Now that I was there the trip seemed like another waste of time. Mulder's men would have covered everything, and if there was anything to be found they would have found it. Mulder himself would have supervised the operation, and regardless of what my personal feelings were, I didn't regard the sheriff as just another hick cop.

The left rear wheel of the little Volkswagen was flat, the tire twisted, sand nestling in the squashed rubber. Here and there around the car were faint imprints of men's heels. I spent a few lonely minutes looking around the ground before giving it up to try the car doors. Both were locked tight.

From the highway, which I could not see, the sounds of swiftly moving vehicles began to grow louder and more frequent. I tried figuring out how far down the highway this part of the old road was located and settled for roughly two miles at most. Discarding the guesswork I glanced up at the sky, at the three jets that had zoomed into view from the direction of the Lemoore Naval Air Station.

The planes circled, then climbed high into the clear blue. Triple plumes of white smoke appeared, twisted and turned until a crazy pattern had been drawn in the sky. After a while they decided there was another place they had to go, and I went back to doing what I'd started.

In the dust were traces of the VW's tire imprints. They ran a few feet ahead of the car, then doubled back again. Mulder had told me what he thought had happened. The tracks seemed now to support his theory. In their own silent way they told a story of a car stopped, a driver slow with a hand brake, the small vehicle rolling backward until its rear had been driven into the brush.

There was nothing else to see. Huge boulders peeked through the growth and there were umpteen places where a person could have entered on a short cut to Reposado or any of the other nearby towns. With my hands in my pockets I started a slow walk up the road. At the start of a narrow curve I stopped, leaned up against a tall, jutting rock, and lit my first cigarette of the day.

Resting against the rock I looked back toward the little red bug of a car and continued my leisurely contribution to lung cancer. Over to my left I thought I heard something, listened, and picked up only the increasing traffic noises from the highway. I flicked the cigarette away into the dust. Immediately several large ants that had been racing around in all directions converged upon the butt. In no time at all they were joined by hundreds more of their tribe, rolling it about, pushing and pulling, and somehow avoiding the smoldering tip. With amused interest I continued to watch, and it was only after a few minutes of doing so that I realized part of my attention had shifted to another object in the sand.

I pushed away from the rock and went over to it. The ants scurried away from the path of my shoes. The object I'd spotted was buried in the dust, only a thin, shiny edge visible, like the ridge of a tiny gold coin. I got down onto my haunches and picked it up. A .22 caliber cartridge case, the outside surface still smooth and clean. I sniffed it but could smell nothing.

I straightened up, backed away from the ants, back to my resting place. It needed no expert eye to see that the shell held in the palm of my hand had been recently fired. And perhaps it proved that the man Connie March had seen had been bleeding, that it had not been something concocted in the imagination of a worried teenager. This was something that could make a man bleed.

I dropped the shell into a pocket of my pants and was about to start off back to my car when I heard the sound again. This time I knew it was real. And closer.

I could almost feel eyes watching as I turned slowly around, feeling large and naked and helpless.

Somebody else was there, someone very close. Without moving I strained to pick up anything that would give away his location, but all that reached my ears was the thumping of my heart. Things happened quickly after that. Across the strip of dirt there was a distinct noise, loud enough for anyone to hear. I pressed against the rock, trying to make sense of the sound. The first I'd heard had come from my left, the second emanating from the right. Either I had mistaken the first noise or there was more than just one person. Again something rattled loudly across the road.

Easing carefully away from the rock I was compelled to make small noises of my own. My car was not too far away, but to reach it I'd be forced to enter into the open, and that seemed like it might be the wrong thing to do. On the other side of the road, somewhere in the brush, there was more rattling—the sound of a stone kicked loose and rolling. I waited, sweat beading my forehead and back. The play was old. At Saturday morning matinees I must have witnessed it a hundred times. But I fell for it now, all the way. Behind me there came a sudden, quick and sharp movement. Fingers bit into the back of my neck so that I couldn't turn my head . . . and then the jets returned and dropped a package of bombs onto the back of my skull.

An ant crawling up my cheek and a surging sickness deep in my stomach finally brought me around. My head was aching and ringing to the sound of a childhood tune an off-key tenor was chanting somewhere inside: *Detective, detective, you're one hell of a detective. Detective, detective . . .* I raised myself onto my knees and let my stomach have its own way.

For a long time I sat in the sand contemplating the dust on my shoes, waiting for the flushes of hot and cold to pass, hoping for the throbbing in my skull to recede. The sun was high, warm and unfriendly.

A small eternity later I forced myself up onto my feet and felt in my pants pocket, for a handkerchief. Only when I already had it in my hand did I notice that the left hand pocket was pulled inside out. There was no need to check, but I did. The shell was gone.

Stuffing the lining back into place I stumbled clumsily over to where I had picked up the cartridge case. The ants were still there, now fooling around with the cold tube of cigarette ash. But there was nothing else to see. I felt like hell.

Making a U-turn on the narrow road was awkward, but somehow I managed it and drove back to town. Each bump threatened to shatter what was left of my skull.

At a telephone booth on a corner against which two youngsters lounged, I stopped and looked up the number of Dr. Myron McGill. He was the only one of his kind that I knew, and one seemed as good as the other.

The book gave just one address for McGill. I asked the kids holding up the wall where Bayo Street was, and waited while they appraised my disheveled appearance before condescending to give directions.

Bayo was a quiet short strip of road three blocks from, and running parallel to the wide main street. McGill's place was a large squat house painted a pale lilac. A shingle with his name and a string of letters hung from two lengths of chain suspended from a wooden gallows at the front gate. No flowers grew out front, but the squares of lawn had been recently trimmed and looked fresh and neat. I parked in front of the gate, walked up to the door and pushed a finger into the big brass button set in its center. A bell rang distantly inside.

He took a long time to answer, and when at last he opened the door I wasn't sure which of us was the most surprised.

"Cameron! What—what do you want?"

He wore slippers, a rumpled pair of blue slacks, and a white shirt that looked as if it had been slept in. His thin white hair was uncombed, his face unshaven, eyes bleary.

"Some help," I answered. "I've been hurt. Will you take a look?"

Straightening his small stooped shoulders in an effort to make himself more presentable, he took another uncertain look at me before saying: "Come in, come in."

I went in and he closed the door quietly.

We stood and studied each other in a silence that was fast becoming uncomfortable. Inside the house the air was stale and just a bit nauseat-

ing, while from the small-framed medic came a more personalized and
familiar odor.

"I'm sorry if I got you up," I offered apologetically.

The unruly white head shook vigorously. "No, no, it's quite all right,
quite in order. I—I was working late last night. I must have fallen asleep
at my desk."

I tried to smile understandingly, but it hurt.

"Will you—will you go in there, please?" He indicated a white door
leading off the entrance hall. "I shan't be long." And with that, turned
and left me alone.

Beyond the white door was a room equipped with much the same sort
of stuff seen in similar rooms. A white covered examination table was
against one wall, partially shielded by a screen. Glass-fronted cabinets, a
single chrome-plated chair and enamel-topped tables took up the rest of
the space. The Venetian blinds were closed but the room was not dark. I
sat down on the hard chair and looked at the items displayed on the
walls. Most were framed diplomas, the largest from a school of physi-
cians in San Francisco where he'd graduated as a general practitioner.
Others testified to ability in obstetrics and gynecology. Not much else in
the room bragged of success.

His soiled attire concealed under a short white coat, hair roughly
combed into place, McGill returned after a few minutes and switched on
the overhead light.

Peering down at me, he asked: "What exactly is the problem?"

"My head." I pointed to the place that hurt.

Without saying anything he glided around the chair and began fingering my scalp in a way that was not gentle. "Hmm," he mumbled to himself, "Let us see, let us see."

His breath wafted downward, on it the smell of peppermint. I smiled
at my thoughts, then winced sharply when his fingers found a soft spot to
probe.

"The skin is broken, Mr. Cameron, but there is no need for a dressing.
You have a very nasty bump, but it will go away in a few days." I felt
him step back. "How did you say this happened?"

I hadn't told him, but I did then. "Somebody slugged me. Someone
who apparently didn't want me prying into the way Bridget Cole died."

Behind me there hissed the quick intake of breath. "Oh . . .?"

"Out there where she was killed I found something." I went on. "But
someone didn't want me to keep it. I don't know who he was; I never had
a chance to see him. He got the drop on me and I got this. When I woke
up the thing I'd found was gone. So had he."

Silently McGill moved to one of the glass-door cabinets. While he
shifted things about there I gave some more thought to the person who'd
jumped me. It had been a sucker play. While he stood watching he had
only to toss a few stones over my head and across the road to draw my
attention away from where he hid. And while I concerned myself with

the noise the stones had made he'd crept up and bounced something hard off my head. The heroes of a thousand white hat westerns seen as a kid had used similar tricks numerous times, but from all of those celluloid adventures I had apparently learned nothing.

How and when he or they had got there gave me a little more to think about.

Rummaging about in another cabinet, McGill said over his shoulder: "This object you discovered . . . what it was?"

"A .22 shell," I answered slowly. "Recently fired."

A bottle dropped to the hard tiles where it smashed and sent brown liquid spreading across the tiles like an evil growth. The doctor ignored it, hastily opened a drawer and began searching inside. It took him a while to find what he wanted.

"Something wrong, Doctor?"

"Wrong? What on earth could be wrong?" Though his voice held steady, the pinkness was drained from his undertaker's face.

"You seem nervous."

"Nonsense! You surprised me, that is all. I didn't know the girl had been shot." He moved back to my rear. "I assume that is what you have been implying?"

"She wasn't shot," I said.

"Oh? Then what . . .?"

Something cold seeped through my hair and began to sting.

"I don't know. I'm still trying to find out. She was strangled, not shot. But the night she died I reported seeing a bleeding man on the road to town. Your sheriff didn't seem to believe me."

Some of the liquid trickled down my neck. With a quiet curse McGill hurriedly dabbed at it.

"I'm afraid I do not follow you. What has a bleeding man to do with the way Miss Cole died?" He stepped aside. "There. You can get up now."

The stinging had stopped, so had some of the ache. I stood up. "A spent bullet could explain why the man was bleeding. Only . . ."

"Yes?"

"Nothing," I replied, because right then I was still unable to explain much of it to myself.

Into the palm of his left hand McGill shook a few white tablets from a bottle taken from his pocket, then dropped them into a smaller plastic container and offered it to me.

"If the head still aches, take two of these every three hours. They're excellent pain-killers."

I took it to the sink and poured a glass of water. Downing two of the tablets I drank all of the water, set down the glass, and asked:

"Do you use this place much?"

"What do you mean?" His beaked nose twitched and his eyes began to assume hardness.

"A question, Doctor, that's all. You appear to have trouble finding things."

"I use it often enough to keep me busy." A thickening layer of frost coated his words.

"Sure. Besides, it's none of my business, is it?"

"Quite. Absolutely none at all."

"What do I owe you?" I asked.

With a brisk wave of his hand he brushed aside the question. "Nothing. I was glad to be of service."

I nodded, buttoned my coat.

"I trust you will report this matter to the police?"

"Just as soon as I leave." I went to the door. "You from San Francisco, Doctor?"

"What? Oh—yes. Why do you ask?"

I pointed to the framed diplomas. "I imagine you've been attending the Danhursts from the time they lived up there?"

"I doubt very much if that also is any of your concern," he snapped. "You ask a great many personal questions, Mr. Cameron. May I ask why?"

I said: "I'm trying to find a killer. In the process the Danhursts have aroused my curiosity."

"They, too—the Danhurst family—are no concern of yours," he fired angrily, nose twitching, pale face growing blotchy. "You were told once to stop annoying them, and I'm telling you again. What happened to that girl has nothing at all to do with them. Do you hear that?"

"It was impossible not to."

"Then you may leave." In spite of the heat rising in the little man the dismissal was ice cold.

"You wouldn't have recently treated a bullet wound would you, Doctor?"

"How dare you!" he blustered, stepped to the open door and made a harsh gesture. "If you do not leave immediately, my obnoxious friend, you will force me to do something you'll have cause to regret."

I stepped through the doorway. "Even a flesh wound could cause a lot of bleeding, couldn't it?"

"Get out!"

"I'm going. Thanks for the help. My head feels better already."

Leaving McGill fuming, I went out to my car and from there drove to the sheriff's office. A desk-bound deputy let me know that Mulder had gone home to catch up on some sleep. He wouldn't part with the sheriff's home address, warning of the inadvisability of trying reach him there. In turn I declined to tell him what I wanted.

Back in the car I smoked through a cigarette and thought about Dr. Myron McGill. It was while doing so that I remembered I had still to eat. Getting rid of some more of the dust my shoes had gathered while out on the old road where the girl had died, I went in search of the lunchroom I'd used the previous day.

In addition to a bunch of kids sipping soft drinks around a noisy juke-box, there were perhaps a dozen other people eating. I found a place at the counter, gave the wife part of the team my order, asking for a Coke while waiting. Halfway through it someone got onto the stool next to mine.

"Hi!" a female voice greeted quietly.

I turned and looked into the small smile of Connie March.

"Hello, Connie. Buy you something to drink?"

She considered the offer, nodded. "I was hoping I'd see you again. You know I never even said thanks for what you did?"

I said something appropriate while trying to get the attention of the woman behind the counter.

"I mean it," the girl said. "I—I suppose it may sound strange to you now, I mean after the way I acted in Salinas. But—well, I feel much better now that I'm home and Mom and Dad know about it and . . . and . . . Well, you know what I mean."

"Uh-huh. And it makes a welcome change this morning. Thanks."

The woman on the other side of the counter caught my signal, came over and took the extra order.

Leaning closer, Connie whispered confidentially: "Do you remember that person we saw? The one on the road?"

"I remember. And like I promised I reported it to the sheriff. Only he thinks I've been seeing things that weren't there. I'm told nobody answering to a description like that had checked into any of the local hospitals."

"But we both saw him!"

"I know, but I never told him about you."

"You didn't?" she asked, surprised. "Why not?"

"You had problems of your own. I didn't feel like adding to them."

"Well I did see him," she insisted. "And he was—" She broke it off when the Coke arrived, waiting until the woman departed before speaking again. "Mr. Cameron, do you think we could move into one of those booths?"

I took her arm and led her to a booth that was out of earshot from the rest in the room.

Once seated, she picked up the rest of what she had to tell me. "Remember I said he looked like someone I'd seen before?"

"Uh-huh."

"Promise you won't laugh if I tell you something?" she asked earnestly, hazel-brown eyes round and serious. "I've been thinking about it a lot and . . . Well, I'm still not sure, but I think I remember who he reminded me of."

"I won't laugh," I promised.

"You wouldn't know him, but there used to live a man in Reposado named Danhurst. He died a long time ago."

"I've heard of him."

Her head bobbed eagerly. "This is the part that's going to sound really silly. But when I saw that man, the one bleeding so much, that's who he reminded me of!"

After finishing what was left in it, I shoved aside the glass.

Connie lifted hers, took a lady-like sip, then gave me a searching look. "You haven't laughed, but you think it's pretty crazy, don't you?"

"I don't know what to think or say, Connie. You admit Nathan Danhurst is dead, so it couldn't have been him you saw."

"I didn't say it was him," she protested mildly. "Just that it reminded me of him, that's all."

"You're saying he looked like Danhurst?"

"No, I don't think it was that." Momentarily unable to provide an explanation, she shrugged her shoulders and reached for her glass. "I only saw his face for a moment. It wasn't Danhurst, I know that. I don't know who it was. I don't even know if I'd recognize that face again. I'm just telling you what I saw. I thought you might want to know." She drank some more before continuing. "Look, Mr. Cameron, I'm no great shakes at psychology, but I think it was something about the man that made me think of Mr. Danhurst. It could just have been something he was wearing or . . ." Again she shrugged. "I don't know. Perhaps I've just an overactive imagination." She glanced at her wristwatch, grabbed her glass and finished the coke. "Zow! Mom will be wondering where I've got to." She began sliding out of the booth. "I only came down to buy the Frisco and L.A. papers."

"I'll give you a ride home," I offered.

"No, please don't bother." She rose quickly. "It's only a short walk and I can use the exercise."

"Connie," I said, "what you've told me may make more sense than either of us realize. I'm glad I stopped in here."

"You mean he—that man—he might have something to do with the Danhursts?"

"Not necessarily, but it is possible. The face you saw need not have been one you know, but rather one you've seen with someone or at someplace that is familiar to you. Memory can be tricky that way. You see a face and because you feel you know its owner and can't put a name to it, it worries you. A possible explanation is that the face is only a small part of a larger scene, and it's that entire scene which is locked away in your memory, which you cannot consciously recall."

"I think I understand," she said thoughtfully.

"It's quite possible you have seen the person before, and quite likely in the company of one of the Danhursts, or at a place associated with them."

"You're right," she nodded thoughtfully. "I know it couldn't have been the old man because he's dead, and besides, I never ever saw him in the flesh. He died when I was still a baby, but I did see several pictures of him Daddy had in a big scrapbook he used to keep clippings of any big event that took place here. He told me who it was and quite a lot about the family. It always seemed terribly sad to me. Often I used to look at the pictures and imagine all kinds of romantic and sinister things about the people who live in that big house. There weren't many pictures, but I remember them all well. In most he had been photographed with people, and there were even one or two of him and his wife before they were married." She stopped to catch her breath. "You think it might have been one of those people I saw in the pictures that made me think of old Mr. Danhurst?"

I unfolded myself from the booth. "Does your father still have that scrap book?"

"No, unfortunately. Mommy got rid of it last year, along with a lot of other junk. That was the last time I looked through it."

"Do you know any of the family, Connie?"

"I've seen them and I know who they are and what they look like. That is, except Mrs. Danhurst. Few people here in town have actually seen her. Once I spoke with Sandra Danhurst, and a number of times I've seen her brother Gerry." A small amused smile flitted across her mouth. "The way he jockeys that crazy sports buggy you *can't* help but notice him." The smile dissolved and her brown eyes clouded gravely. "Mr. Cameron, has this anything to do with the murder?"

It was the first time she'd mentioned it.

"You've heard about it then?"

"I should think everyone has. Poor Mr. Whitman. It must be terrible for him. And his fiancée . . ." She winced, shoulders shuddering. "It's dreadful."

"You acquainted with Harlan Whitman, Connie?"

"Yes, he's Dad's lawyer. I've seen him umpteen times. Why?"

"Nothing." I was about to ask if Whitman had ever featured in the pictures she'd seen, but I remembered Hal saying he had never met Christine Danhurst's husband.

"You haven't answered my question," she reminded me. "Do you think that man I saw has anything to do with—with what happened?"

"Uh-huh. But nobody else does. The sheriff thinks I was dreaming."

"But we both saw him. I'll go with you and tell him so."

"No you won't," I told her gently. "You don't want to get involved. At least, not unless it's absolutely necessary. I've a hunch the person you saw might have some connection with the way Bridget Cole died, but exactly how and why is something I can't begin to explain. I can't offer the sheriff anything concrete, and until then I don't really blame him for being skeptical."

"Then you're working on the case also?"

"I'm trying."

"For Mr. Whitman?"

"Yes, for Hal Whitman."

"I wish you luck." She smiled, shoved forward a small hand. "And—and if I can help, please call me. I'll gladly tell them what I saw."

I took her hand and then walked with her to the newsstand where she selected the papers she'd come to purchase. Another few minutes were spent at the door before saying goodbye.

As things turned out we never had any need to call Connie March as a witness for anything, and watching her small, trim figure moving away down the sidewalk was the last I saw of her.

I went back to the counter and ate. One of the more useful pieces of information extracted from the girl was Sheriff Mulder's home address. This she'd given me while we stood at the entrance to the lunchroom.

The blue ranch wagon was parked in the drive. In the garage, the door of which was open, stood a white Lincoln convertible of very recent vintage. Next to the garage an ugly Great Dane lay watching ominously as I approached the gate. The house was newish, not large, but smart and modernly attractive in a neighborhood filled with similar houses, each of them boasting modest luxury. The dog rose slowly to its feet when I unlatched the gate, a low growl rumbling out of its thick throat. I held the gate and stood still.

Still growling, the dog advanced. Around its throat was a thick silver-studded collar from which led a heavy chain, the other end secured to a steel pin cemented into the ground near the garage. I gauged the distance, hoped the dog couldn't reach the gate, and opened it to step onto a black slate walk leading to the patio and front door. The growling stopped, only to turn into angry barking when the dog leaped forward. The chain brought him to a choking stop. He strained at it and continued to direct the barking at me. I hesitated, not certain how strong the chain was, or precisely what the animal had been trained to do should it break.

Then the front door opened and an attractive woman came out onto the patio, scolding the dog to quietness. Happily he obeyed her, lamped me suspiciously, then dropped down onto the grass, watching balefully while I went to the woman.

Her hair was long and black, inclined to deep waves. Her skin a soft olive, her mouth round and full, its color natural. She stood tall and every inch of her shaped to near-perfection. Proud, sharp breasts thrust against the fabric of a low-cut blouse and the outline of long legs was visible under a light flared skirt when she stood, feet apart, in an oddly masculine manner, waiting for me to speak.

I said: "I'd like to see the sheriff."

"He's asleep," she snapped, but not angrily. "He has work all night. He is asleep now."

Up until then I'd only guessed at her ancestry.

"He *was* asleep," another voice boomed. " 'Til that damned dog started barking." Following the sound of his voice, Mulder came through the door. "Oh," he snorted, surprised to see who it was that had aroused the animal. "It's you. What's the matter? Changed your mind? Decided to tell me where he is?"

He was still in the clothes I'd seen him in at the hotel, and he still had not shaved. But instead of boots there were now a pair of scuffed slippers covering his feet.

"No," I said, "but something happened that I think you should know about."

He turned to the girl. "Okay, Paula, inside. We'll talk out here." She smiled at him, went silently back into the house and the door closed. "We can sit out here where it's cooler." Motioning to the plastic patio furniture he slumped down into one of the queerly shaped chairs.

"You have a nice home, Sheriff," I said, climbing the two steps that brought me up onto the green tiled patio.

"It passes and it pleases," he grunted. "But you didn't come here to wake me up and discuss real estate, did you now? What gives?"

I sat down opposite him and told about the shell and about being attacked. He listened with interest, moving only to get a cigar from his pocket and put a flame to it.

"Pity," he growled when the report had been exhausted. "You lost the shell and you didn't see who it was that jumped you."

"I didn't lose it, it was taken from my pocket."

"Same difference. We still got nothing to go on." Cigar smoke drifted into my face. I moved my head and Mulder asked: "What made you go out there in the first place? Didn't you notice the road was blocked off?"

"I was curious. As it turns out the trip may have been worthwhile. Whoever hit me must have wanted that shell pretty badly."

I waited for him to say more about me having driven beyond the road barriers, but he didn't.

"Think so?" he asked instead. "Why?"

"Because it perhaps explains how a man happened to be bleeding."

The thin cigar came out of his mouth and another cloud of blue smoke crashed into my face. "I've been waiting for that. You on that kick again?"

"I've never been off it."

"Geeze, Cameron, we checked out every damned hospital, every doctor in the vicinity. There's been no sign of anyone with that kind of wound. If, as you seem to be trying to suggest, someone got hit with a bullet, we'd know it by now. You want to see the file, you can. It'll show the checks we made after getting your report about the bleeding character you allege having seen."

"He was seen," I said. " And in case you're doubting the other business, you might like to feel the lump at the back of my head."

Mulder unwound himself from the chair, shouted for the girl Paula. When she appeared he told her to bring two beers.

"Not for me, thank you, Mrs. Mulder," I said rising.

"She's not my wife," the sheriff corrected. "I'm not married. Paula looks after the house for me, is all."

Paula's lips pulled down at the corners. His words had stung, but she said nothing, retreating into the privacy of the house instead.

"I'm sorry," I apologized to the closing door. To Mulder I said: "I'd like to stay for the drink, but better not." For a few seconds I watched the smoke dribbling through his pursed lips. "I don't suppose you'll do anything about what I've told you?"

"That's where you're wrong." He grinned wolfishly. "I'll get a man to go out there and have another look around—though I don't hold much hope of finding anything." He examined the ash at the end of the cigar, then knocked it off into the air with his little finger. "Since we found the girl's body I've had a man staked out there watching the car, just in case the boy who did it got brave or worried enough to go back and make sure his tracks were properly covered. I called it off this ayem. And that, in case you've wondered, is why the car's still out there."

"I was. I was also wondering about something else. The Danhursts' doctor."

"McGill? What about him?"

"I don't know. A short while ago, when I visited him, he'd only just woken up, and from his appearance and smell I don't think I'm wrong in saying he'd been on the sauce last night."

"That so? Maybe he's got himself a new hobby," Mulder mused. "Didn't think he did that kind of drinking."

"Ever seen that place of his?"

"Once or twice maybe. Why?"

"It has all the looks of a down-at-the-heels business. And McGill acted nervous as hell when I told him how I'd been hurt. He dropped things, things he had trouble finding in the first place."

"You trying to tell me something? What is it, Cameron? Think there's something fishy about his setup?"

"Take a visit and judge for yourself. I'd be surprised if McGill has a dozen patients. All I'm suggesting is that in his own surroundings he doesn't look like the kind of practitioner who would be on the Danhursts' payroll."

"The way I hear it he doesn't need a dozen patients," Mulder supplied. "He came here with money and always he's acted more like a semi-retired quack than one out trying to establish a big practice."

I walked to the patio steps. "That may be it then."

"Heard from Whitman?" he asked.

"No." I considered telling him about the two I'd encountered at the motel in Fresno, but decided I should see Whitman first before doing anything like that.

Paula came out of the house carrying a tray and a tall glass of beer that made me feel sorry I'd turned down the invitation. Mulder took it from her and drank deeply.

"You want to tell me anything else?" he asked stuffing the cigar back into his mouth just as soon as the glass left it.

"Uh-uh."

"Don't like me much, do you, Cameron?"

"It isn't a case of liking," I said. "You're a little too tough for my blood, that's all. But I don't have to like you, do I?"

"Damned right you don't." He plucked the brown weed from between his lips, attacked the beer again, then said: "As for being tough—that's something I got to be. It's how I come to have this job. I was born with nothing, and for a long time had to live with nothing. I worked like a dog in the fields so I could pay my way through night school. But I was still nothing to the people of this county. Then along came the war. I was shipped off to the Philippines and there I learned fast that it was important to be tough. That way you got to stay alive. I came out of that brawl with a whole stinking bunch of medals and damned little else. But I found out something important. It was the tough ones who survived and bought themselves a piece of the world. When I came back I was suddenly somebody for a little while. The local boy with a chest full of bronze and silver who'd made good. I even got my picture in the papers."

He paused, sneering, as if the memory of his home-coming was something distasteful. "It bought me nothing—except a job as a cop. I worked hard at it and I was good at it. But I was getting no place fast. You see, I'd forgotten about the toughness. I quit the force and came here to take a job as deputy. And here I was different. After a time I got the chance to be top dog. I'm somebody now, Cameron. I'm sheriff of this whole damned county, and I'm serving my third term in office. This town is clean and I'm the one who made it clean and keeps it clean, and the people here like it that way. They don't mind that I'm a little hard. So you see, if a little toughness is what you don't like, then it's just too goddamned bad for you."

It was a long speech and he probably realized it, because in one long swallow he got rid of what remained of the beer.

A long speech that was probably meant more to impress than explain. Trouble was, it left me even more wary of the man.

"You may have a point," I agreed, looking at the house and the cars. It was a lot more than I'd ever owned. "It seems to have got you what you want." I waved a hand and started for the gate.

The dog growled when I passed it, but I didn't stop. My talk with Connie March was giving me other things to think about, and something Mulder had casually mentioned had given birth to an idea.

I went back to the hotel to work on the telephone directory.

EIGHT

THE WOMAN who opened the door to peer inquiringly up at me was another fairly tall one and, from what could be seen, also nicely assembled. Under yellow satin lounging pajamas a figure swept in and out at all the right places, enough of it swelling against silky cloth to prove that no help had come from foundation specialists.

She was about thirty with large sultry eyes and a mouth, naturally red, that pouted prettily. Hair the color of golden wheat was tied away from her face by a narrow strip of yellow ribbon. From delicately formed ears dangled long crystal adornments, but on her feet she wore nothing but pale pink nail varnish. I had the odd impression of a wealthy girl playing the role of a Chinese peasant.

"Miss Gallagher?"

Leaning against the open door she eyed me critically before answering.

"I'm Mona Gallagher. You were wanting something?"

Her voice was deep and throaty, the kind that belonged to a female who could fill yellow satin pajamas the way she did.

"Someone," I said. "Hal Whitman."

The satin strained as she pulled herself up straight. "Why look here?"

"No special reason. He mentioned you, that's all. It seemed like an idea worth following up." I waited a moment for some sort of response, and when getting none, asked: "Is he here?"

"Hal gave you my address?" Her tone accused me of a lie.

"Not your address, Miss Gallagher. Not even your name. He told me you were a friend of Bridget Cole's, that you operated a hobby shop in town. The address of the shop is listed in the directory. It was the only one of its kind. A few questions here and there got me the name of its owner. The directory provided the rest. Is Hal here?" I asked again.

"No he isn't. And I think you've some nerve suggesting he might be." Still deep, still under control, but now a small amount of indignation tinged her words.

"Well, it was an idea. If he was here I thought it better I see him before the sheriff finds out and sends someone to pull him in." I made as if to leave. "Sorry if I troubled you."

"Wait," she said. And when I stopped: "Who are you?"

I told her who and what. "I'm supposed to be working for Hal."

"This business about the sheriff—you trying to be funny or something?"

"Miss Gallagher," I answered patiently. "I've an aching head and it's been a rather trying morning. The last thing I feel like is being funny."

Large eyes inspected me again. This time with a great deal more care. Apparently satisfied I was not someone who could create big black headlines, she opened the door wide.

"Perhaps you had better come in."

I went in. Through a short hall into a living room that could have been a page clipped from *Good Housekeeping*. Every item complimented the other, and each in what seemed its proper place. The furniture could have been bought and arranged only that very morning.

Mona Gallagher closed the door and walked over to a long white leather couch. She didn't sit down or invite me to do so.

"Where is he?" I asked.

Biting her lower lip and avoiding my eyes, with a toss of her head she motioned to a closed door.

"He's sleeping. And before you wake him you'd better understand something. This isn't what it might seem. He came here yesterday afternoon, full of hooch and loaded with tears. I was someone he knew, someone whose shoulder he wanted to use." The yellow satin slid provocatively over jutting breasts when she shrugged. "Look, he needed someone to listen to his troubles and I happened to be that someone. That's all there is to it. No more, no less."

"He's been here ever since then?"

"Except for a couple of hours this morning. This morning he developed a grand idea about going to Brid's apartment in case there was anything there that might clue him in on who had killed her. I told him he was crazy, that it was the sheriff's job to do that. But—"

She left the rest of it to my imagination. I considered it and didn't like it much.

"He found nothing, I take it?"

"Found? He didn't even get inside. There was a deputy's car parked outside the building." Her hands made a movement that meant nothing more than possible confusion or frustration. "He came back here and started on the bottle again until I finally managed to talk him into getting some more sleep."

"It took a couple of hours to do that?"

"I don't know what he did. He didn't offer me the details and I didn't ask for any. All I know is what I was told." Folding her arms she affected a pose that challenged me to doubt her. "So what's with the sheriff wanting him? What's he supposed to have done?"

"What he's done, I don't know. But Mulder fancies him for the killer."

One arm dropped to her side, the other went to her mouth and smothered a tiny gasp. Her head shook in vigorous disbelief.

"That's impossible! Not Hal! He—he couldn't."

"That's about how I feel," I admitted. "But hiding out here doesn't make the picture any prettier. Mulder has an idea he's deliberately avoiding him, that perhaps he's even taken the long ride out of town. If Hal's got any sense he'll go and see the sheriff and tell him where he's been." I paused to wonder about a small private thought. "Would you mind? Having them know he was with you, I mean?"

"Of course I'd mind!" she snapped back. "What girl wants that kind of news gossiped around a town like this?" For a fistful of seconds we stood and listened to the silence. "Oh hell," she cried suddenly. "Why should I mind? Their sharp little tongues can't hurt me. And besides, who could stand still while they try to blame him for something he didn't do?"

"You like him, don't you?"

A slow flush crept over her face, but instead of denying it, she said: "I like him."

"Before we go in there," I said, thumbing the bedroom door, "do you mind if I ask a question or two more?"

"As long as they're not too personal. You've already had your quota of those."

"Hal told me you saw Miss Cole driving out to the Danhurst place the night she was killed."

"I saw her. Or to be more precise, I saw her car going out that way. I had no reason to think there was anyone else driving it."

It took care of the next question I had. Mona Gallagher would not have noticed if the girl was with anyone.

"According to certain people I've talked to, Miss Cole was acting somewhat strange these past weeks. Did you notice anything like that?"

"Yes . . . I noticed. But when I asked she brushed it aside, saying she was just tired. I accepted her word, but I had ideas of my own."

"Which were?"

"Brid had a problem. A big problem, Mr. Cameron. And something was frightening her."

"But she never told you why?"

"Oh, I pried, but whatever it was she kept it to herself." Turning her head from me she glanced at the bedroom door. "I thought I heard something in there."

"You did," I said. "Just one more question then we'll go get him. Did you ever see her with other men—those you might know?"

Her blonde head wagged from side to side. "Not the one Hal was told about. "But—" Cutting it short to check the door again, she said: "Look—I've never told anyone about this, and the only reason I'm telling it to you is because if he's in trouble I don't care who I involve."

I waited, listening to the faint shuffling sounds from the bedroom.

"There was one guy who tried to make time with her and never did. Gerry Danhurst. She told me how he used to phone her and how twice he tried visiting her at her apartment. She made me promise not to tell Hal."

The noise in the bedroom was more pronounced now. It ended the discussion when the knob rattled and Whitman jerked the door open.

He didn't look so good. His clothes were a mess and he was still bleary-eyed and still a little drunk. He spotted me and put on the brakes.

"Paul? What're you doing here?"

"Trying to find you. And it looks as if I just got lucky."

Dragging his feet across the carpet he looked at me, at Mona Gallagher, and embarrassed all three of us. With care he lowered himself down onto the whiteness of the couch.

"Don't get ideas, buddy. Mona's a good friend. A damned good friend."

"I know. She told me." To the girl, I said: "Can you fix some black coffee?"

With a quick nod she left us and vanished through a swing door that revealed a kitchenette on the other side just before it swung shut.

"You've got to get cleaned up, Hal. The sheriff wants to see you and it won't look so good if he has to pick you up here." I went on to sketch in the rest.

By the time I finished he was sitting bolt upright, head moving in slow but emphatic rejection of what he'd been told.

"He's crazy, the stupid son of a—! Geeze, Paul, you don't think—? Hey, not you! *You* don't think it was me?"

The following instant he was on his feet.

"No," I said. "I don't."

"Then stop looking at me like that. You're supposed to be working for me, aren't you? So stop looking like you think Mulder's stupid notion might be a good one. It isn't! For God's sake, you're supposed to be my friend, aren't you?"

"Why do you think I've been trying to find you?"

"That's better, buddy. Much better. That look on your face had me worried."

"Mona told me you tried to get into Bridget's apartment this morning. She said you were away two hours. Want to tell me what took so long?"

"Hey now," he drawled slowly and sat down. "Hey, you—you're starting to think just like Mulder."

"Two hours is a long time to go to her apartment, find you can't get in and then drive back here. And, incidentally, where is your car?"

"Parked under shelter at the back of the building. You can't see it from here. And yes, it took me two hours to do what you heard." His tone had become dry and brittle. "Two hours to do that and then try to get into my own place. And you know why I couldn't get in? There was somebody watching there as well! I parked and waited, but that boy of the sheriff's wasn't moving. *That*, my alleged friend, took two hours." He scowled up at me. "What do *you* think I was doing?"

"Nothing," I said. "But if you've any sense you'll sober up and go and see Mulder. If she has to, Mona will tell him you've been here with her."

"Don't tell me what I must do!" he shouted angrily, making a futile attempt to lift himself from the couch. "I know the law. I know what I can and can't do!"

"I went to see McGill," I told him gently, mainly to switch the subject and shut him up for a while. "There's someone who might just know something we could use. Would you know if Bridget was ever one of his patients?"

"Him? That miserable quack's got only one patient he cares about. The Queen of Retreat—the Matriarch of Misery Manor. Mrs. Christine Danhurst! Dear Dr. McGill doesn't need other patients. He's got enough loot to quit playing around with that black bag and stethoscope. And I should know. I'm his lawyer." A bitter laugh rattled around the room. It ended as abruptly as it had started. "Say now . . ." he said thoughtfully. "I wonder why he should worry about her so? She's too fat to—" He laughed some more, a crazy drunken laugh that was totally alien to the person I knew. "Or maybe these little guys like their women big and fat, huh? How about that, friend?"

The kitchenette door swung open and Mona Gallagher emerged balancing a tray in her hands. Here face was a little flush. I guessed she'd the last of what Whitman had just said.

"Get some coffee inside of you," I said, my impatience with his attitude starting to show. "It'll sober you up. Then we'll go and report to Mulder."

With a leap he was up again.

"I'll see Mulder all right! I'll see him and I'll set him straight once and for all. But I don't need any help to do it. I'll go there under my own steam. And when I'm good and ready."

"Hal!" Mona cautioned, looking for a place to deposit the tray.

"What's eating at your liver?" I asked him.

"You! You act like they've made you an honorary deputy or something. Why're you so anxious to turn me over? What's in it for you?"

"I'm trying to help you," I answered, trying hard not to feel offended. "That's what you hired me for, isn't it?"

"Yeah, and what've you done for me? What've you found out?" he demanded. "All you do is sing your song about going to the sheriff because it's for my own damned good."

"Not afraid, are you?" Personal anger was slipping free and I couldn't prevent it . . . didn't especially want to.

"What are you trying to say?" The words traveled slowly, but they were sharp and vicious. And suddenly his fist was swinging.

I moved back and the intended blow missed by a foot and more. It robbed him of his balance and he toppled backward onto the couch.

"Get out of here!" he yelled. "Get out before I get up again. Otherwise I swear you'll never walk out of here in one piece!"

"Hal!" Mona cried, getting rid of the tray and its contents. "Have you gone mad?"

He ignored her and turned back to me. "Get out. You've just been fired!"

I walked to the door.

"When you're feeling better, see Mulder. Don't and you'll be helping him knot the noose."

"Beat it!" he shouted. Then for effect, added: *"Friend!"*

I opened the door. Mona came quickly after me.

"Mr. Cameron, wait. Hal's still drunk. Don't take any notice of him," she pleaded. "He doesn't know what he's doing. When he's sober it will be different, you'll see."

"I went through part of a war with that hardhead," I told her. "I know him well enough to think different. He's got it into his skull that I'm no longer to be trusted, and when he wakes up from this drunk he'll hang onto that idea. Anyway, he isn't that drunk."

"Will—will you tell the sheriff where he is?"

"No, Mona, I won't. But try and persuade him to report in. It's in his own interests. You understand that, don't you?"

"I'll try," she promised, then turned sharply when Whitman called her name.

A hollow and empty feeling accompanied me back to the car.

Pleasant feelings were at a premium back in the hotel room. Adding to my problems was a head that was aching again. I went into the bathroom, ran a glass of water and swallowed two of the tablets McGill had prescribed. I didn't enjoy what had happened with Whitman and me, but I didn't entirely blame him for behaving as he had. He'd been drinking, and only recently his girl had been killed. Mulder had been riding him from the beginning, and perhaps I could have handled him better than I had. Under similar circumstances I would probably have acted much the same.

The phone jangled and interrupted my unhappy reverie.

The receiver was barely at my ear before a voice asked: "Mr. Cameron? It's Mona Gallagher." A sharp intake of breath, and then: "He's gone. But not to the sheriff!"

I sat down on the bed. "Where then?"

Hurriedly her voice babbled into my ear.

"What does he hope to achieve by going there?" I asked when she stopped talking

"I don't know, but I'm worried stiff. He was in a foul mood when he left and I'm scared he might . . ."

"I'll try and get to him before he does anything stupid," I promised. "Was he still crocked when he left?"

"A little, but—"

"Sit tight," I said. "I'll go over to McGill's place now." Then I thought of something and asked: "How did you know where to find me?"

"I asked Hal about you after you left. He told me where you were staying but made me promise not to contact you. I promised, but I couldn't help myself."

"You did right," I assured her. "I'll buzz you back later."

I hung up, grabbed my coat from the bed and went downstairs, moving as fast as I could. Under my ribs my heart thumped heavily, and in my head the voice was back, calling me every kind of idiot.

His car was parked against the curb in front of the squat lilac-colored house. I braked behind it, swung out onto the sidewalk and walked quickly up to the front door. Bayo Street was very quiet that afternoon. From behind the walls of the house there echoed not a sound. A tomb by comparison would have been noisy.

The door was slightly ajar when I reached it, so I ignored the bell and went right in. I stood in the hall and listened. Movement sounded off to my right. A faint, short, shifting sound that had no meaning. Quietly I moved in its direction. Another door stood open and the little I could see of the room beyond showed rows of books and old but shiny brown leather chairs. I hesitated before pushing the door further open, my skin suddenly chilled and clammy.

Hal Whitman spun around as I entered, his mouth open, searching for elusive words. In his hand he gripped a small black gun that was pointed up at my head. He stepped back involuntarily, his own head making quick, negative signs. I ignored him and brought my gaze over to the desk.

A small figure slumped over a once green blotter, its face resting in a pool of sickly red. The thin white hair stretched over the pink scalp told the rest. Whitman watched apprehensively, his face drawn and devoid of color, the close-cropped blond hair like an absurd wig on the head of an old man.

"Not me," he announced nervously, at last dredging up the words. "He—he was like that when I got here. I never—"

"Give me the gun," I interrupted. "Then we can talk."

His eyes blinked, their focus shifted to the gun he held, and I took the opportunity to get nearer. As soon as I moved he jerked upright. I stopped, but by then I was within reaching distance.

"No!" he shouted defiantly. "Paul—I didn't—He was dead when I arrived, for God's sake! The gun was on the floor. I—I picked it up because—because . . ."

"Because?"

"Nothing."

"Why did you come here, Hal? What the hell were you thinking?"

"I was going to make him tell me what he knew." He flicked a quick, jerking glance to where McGill was sprawled. "You—you said he might know something useful. I—I thought . . ."

"I remember," I admitted. "I was dumb."

"I thought maybe—maybe I could get him to tell me what he knew. The door was open when I got here and he—he was like that. This"—he indicated the gun with a shake of his right fist—"was on the floor. I—I picked it up. And then . . ."

"And then I arrived?"

"Yes," he muttered. "Yes . . . you arrived."

"What the hell made you pick up the gun? You're a lawyer; you ought to know better than that. Why didn't you call Mulder, or me?"

"Because it's my gun. You hear that? It's my gun, that's why I picked it up. Look!" Opening his fist he pointed to a small 'HW' metal monogram sticker fixed to the butt. The gun was a .22 Colt Junior automatic, the monogram black and gold and obvious against the blue finish.

There was nothing intelligent I could offer.

Uncertain of what might be going through my mind, he continued: "I forgot about it. I gave it to Bridget weeks ago. It—it used to worry me, her driving alone at night. I told her to take the gun. She didn't want to—told me I was worrying needlessly. But I insisted and she took it. I—I'd almost forgotten about giving it to her."

"Until only now?"

"It was on the floor. I couldn't help but recognize it."

I stuck out my hand. "Better give it to me. This is going to take some working out."

He stepped away. "No!"

I made a grab for it, but he was either sobered now or just naturally faster than I was. With a lithe jerk the gun was pulled out of my reach. He swore and pushed me aside with his free hand, and a little too late I saw the short barrel of the weapon swinging at my head.

The blow was not heavy, but I'd been hit before, not long ago, and the hard contact released all the pain the tablets had so far been able to subdue. I went down on one knee . . . heard him going out of the room. Everything around me became hazy and red, the desk teetered and the walls seemed to be sloping and swaying crazily. By the time I reached the study door I heard a car's engine kick over, and when I made it outside, Whitman's convertible was hurtling down Bayo Street. I leaned against the wall, knowing that any effort to give chase would only make him run faster. And in his present state of mind . . .

I shucked off the thoughts, not wanting to think of further unpleasantness, and reached for a cigarette.

I drew smoke down deep into my lungs. It made me feel slightly better. Until a familiar blue ranch wagon turned the corner and slid up slowly behind my car.

Doors opened and a uniformed deputy followed Mulder up to the house. Neither showed any surprise at seeing me there. On the first step Mulder stopped, removed the slender cigar from his mouth.

"Didn't think to find you here, Cameron."

His clothes were fresh and his face had been shaved.

I said: "Hadn't expected to be here. Somebody call you?"

"Nope. After what you had to say about McGill I figured I'd come and talk a bit." He looked at me inquiringly, put the cigar back between his lips and spoke around it. "Any reason I should have been called?"

"McGill's been shot. He's dead."

He grunted once only before pushing me aside. The deputy flashed a dirty look that was perhaps meant to disable me, then followed his chief into the house. I took a few more drags at the cigarette before throwing it away and returning to where McGill had died.

With a slim ballpoint pen inserted into the barrel of the little automatic, Mulder held it to his nose and sniffed.

"This here when you found him?"

I nodded, surprised to see the gun, unable to make sense of his question.

"Anything else you care to tell me? Like who else was here maybe?"

"Where did you find that?" I pointed to the gun.

"Here by the door where it was ditched." He chewed at the cigar. "Dumb thing to leave behind, wouldn't you say? Especially when it's got initials like this on it."

"Dumb," I agreed. "Or perhaps the one who dropped it was in a panic. Or perhaps it was left here for a purpose." I moved my head to give McGill some attention. The deputy was fidgeting around the body. Even though I didn't want to believe he had triggered the gun, I felt scared for Whitman. There were other things that worried me, but most of all, and more immediately, what he might do now that he knew his gun had been used to kill.

Mulder broke into my thoughts. "Recognize the initials?"

"It belongs to Whitman," I said.

"Figured as much. A check of the serial number will make doubly sure." Carrying the gun over to a wall table he deposited it there with a great deal of care, removed the pen and clipped it back into his pocket. "Where'd he go?"

"I don't know."

"So he was here?" he accused, spinning quickly around, ripping the brown weed from his mouth.

There was no point in trying to lie now. They would have Whitman picked up sooner or later and eventually all the facts would stand revealed. Covering for a homicide suspect can carry a heavy rap—especially if the suspect is ever proven guilty. Although I couldn't bring myself to believe Whitman's guilt, the possibility could no longer be ignored. Now more than ever.

I said: "If he killed McGill do you think he'd leave the gun behind?"

"What I asked you is, was Whitman here?"

"I've already as much as told you he was. And although I don't believe he had any part of this, I think for his own sake it will be better if he's picked up. He's panicky and he's been drinking. That's a bad combination."

"McGill hasn't been dead long," declared Mulder. "You can see that for yourself. Look at the blood. So if Whitman was here he's got one hell of a lot of explaining to do. If he's clean, why'd he run? That the way an innocent man would act?"

"His girl's been murdered, you've been riding him hard, and now he's started doubting whether in fact I'm his friend or just someone working with you." I stopped to run a hand tenderly over my throbbing head. "Right now he must feel like a man without a friend: a man with the whole damned world ganging up on him. With all that crowding his mind he isn't likely to act rationally."

"He'll get every chance to defend himself. Once we get him, that is. Anderson!" he called to the deputy. "Get onto headquarters. I want an APB put out on Whitman. They've got his description and the number of his car. Tell them I want action and I want it nice and fast. Get it to all stations. I want Whitman by tonight. And I mean tonight."

The deputy reached for the telephone on the desk near McGill's outstretched hand. Mulder bellowed at him:

"Not that one, damnit! Use the car radio."

As if the phone was electrified the deputy jerked away from it, muttered: "Sorry, Chief," and scurried out of the room.

Alone with me Mulder grunted irritably. "You pick the best you can and even then half of them haven't enough brains to put their pants on right way round." Realizing he was knocking his own department, he changed the subject. "Better tell me in detail what happened here."

It didn't take long. When I wound it up, he said: "Glad to see you're co-operating, Cameron. I know how you must feel, Whitman being an old army buddy and all. But," he shrugged broad shoulders and in a fatherly fashion that did not become him, put a hand on my shoulder, "people change, do funny things, and it's hard for us, their friends, to accept what they do. Take that gun for instance. It's a .22, or didn't you notice? This morning you told me a funny little story about a .22 shell, remember?"

"I also told you about a man bleeding," I reminded him. "We haven't explained that one, nor have we explained what that shell was doing out on the road. We haven't even established that it came from the same gun."

"We haven't," he agreed amicably, removing his hand from my shoulder to take a square transparent envelope from his pocket. "This look familiar?"

I took it. Inside was a spent .22 cartridge case. "From Whitman's gun?"

"Uh-uh. Found it over there by the desk."

I gave him back the packet and its contents.

"Well?"

"The one I picked up was also a Remington," I said.

"Uh-huh." He studied the contents of the plastic envelope. "Got a man on the road now, looking for anything he can find. If he's lucky enough to pick up another shell we'll be able to match them. As for how the shell came to be on the road, I don't know. Maybe he fired a few shots to make sure she wouldn't try to run. Could be he was drunk and trying to scare her." He put away the envelope. "That being so, he'd have good reason for not wanting the shell found, wouldn't you say?"

"It still doesn't explain away the party I saw bleeding," I said.

"No, it doesn't. But until we find more evidence of such a character, you'll still need to convince me about him." A heavy pull at the cigar, a cloud of acrid smoke exhaled over my shoulder, and then he asked: "You're sure the guy you saw wasn't Whitman?"

At the moment I wasn't sure about anything. I'd seen the man. I hadn't seen the blood. For that I had only Connie March's word.

"Anyway," he went on, deciding I wasn't going to comment, "Whitman will be able to fill us in on the things we don't know, once we get him. And that shouldn't take too long. Maybe he'll even tell us where he got to on Friday night. Could be you'll even learn who it was that hit you out there."

"Do you want me to hang around?" I asked.

"Nah, you can trot along. We'll need a statement from you, but tomorrow will be time enough for that."

The sun was starting to slide out of the sky when I parked at the hotel, collected my key, went up to my room and conveyed the bad news to Mona Gallagher. There were tears in her voice when she hung up, and she wasn't ashamed that I could hear.

After swallowing a beer that had been sent up to the room, I stretched out on the bed and thought all kinds of weird and troublesome thoughts while waiting to hear if Hal Whitman had been apprehended.

Since Rudge, the *Reposado Record* reporter, had talked to me a vague idea had been floating around inside my head. It had been smothered so far because it was the kind that seemed too far out to be worth consideration. But now with my client on the run, the law closing in rapidly and his chances of crawling out from under looking dismally grim, I decided to play it out. Perhaps only because I was trying to salve my own conscience. From the start I'd made up my mind that I would take nothing from Whitman to do as he had asked. At the time I saw the job as a way of paying back a little of what l owed him. The debt hadn't been reduced one iota yet.

I picked up the phone, got through to the newspaper office and was lucky enough to find Rudge in. Before I could ask a question he rushed in with a list of his own.

"Just got back from McGill's place," he informed me. "Mulder's not saying much. How about you?"

I let him ask, and answered each question truthfully. He didn't get much from me either, but it satisfied him enough to listen to the queries I had.

"That paper I gave you," he said, "means nothing now. It was a good idea that fizzled out cold. The Leonard kid died under circumstances much the same as those of Bridget Cole. My idea was to do a comparison speculation story to keep the interest in the case going. But the coroner's report that the Cole dame was strangled washed out that one. As for seeing the parents, you can. That's if you fancy a trip up to Boston. That, I seem to recall, is where the mother is living these days. Tom Leonard died some years ago and his wife packed up and went to stay with relatives."

I told him thanks, hung up, and sucked on another bitter cigarette.

In Reposado the time was five-twenty. In New York it would be somewhere after nine. I got a number from the telephone operator and after several attempts spoke to a man there who had made headlines of his own in a profession we both shared. He didn't know me, but he knew of organizations with which we were both associated, and on the basis of that agreed to do a small job of work.

"I'll wire you whatever I dig up," he promised. "Shouldn't take more than a few hours. Probably get it off to you sometime in the morning."

At seven-thirty I went downstairs for dinner. After that I dropped in at the sheriff's office. The place was buzzing, but Whitman was still on the loose. I stayed around until they let me know I was getting in their way, went back to the hotel and lay on the bed, waiting, trying to make sense of things that made no sense at all.

Without knowing it I drifted off into sleep and slept through the night.

While I slept, Reposado had visitors. And that night two men died.

NINE

THE NEWS was communicated to me the following morning when I came downstairs and slid my room key across the counter.

"Seen the paper?" asked the desk clerk.

Somewhat absently, I said I had not. I was still wondering why the character on desk duty at the sheriff's office had been so grouchy. Soon after awakening I'd tried to contact Mulder. But an impatient telephone voice let me know he was out and not expected back for at least another hour or more. Whitman had still not been brought in, the voice advised reticently, adding that they were loaded with work and if I didn't want to leave a message or talk with one of the other officers, would I mind very much if he got back to some of that work.

The clerk was still talking. "Looks like the whole darned town's flipped. Yesterday Doc McGill stops a bullet in the head, and now—last night two guys shoot each other over at the museum!" Ducking under the counter, he brought out a newspaper and unfolded it before me. "Here, take a look."

I picked up the tabloid. It was a morning edition of the *Record,* and people had worked fast to rearrange the front page so that in three inch black headlines it screamed:

TWO DIE IN DARING MUSEUM ROBBERY

Kronstead Collection Stolen

As I read, coldness like the caress of a spiritual hand seeped through me. The story contained only raw facts, padded out to fill the columns. During the night two men, thus far unidentified, had entered the museum by forcing the lock of a back door in the building, overpowered the guard, opened the safe in the curator's office, and lifted the entire Kronstead collection which, according to the story, was estimated to be worth in excess a hundred thousand dollars. But the caper had not been without snags. The guard had recovered, fired at and killed one of the men, and then had himself been shot dead. The assumption that two, perhaps even three people had participated in the crime was based on the fact that the collection was not found in the possession of the dead burglar, or anywhere in the museum.

Sheriff's men were reported to have been on the scene within minutes of being notified about the sound of gunfire. The man who'd reported the disturbance was named, so was the dead guard and the county sheriff, the latter promising personal supervision of the investigation and an early arrest.

McGill's death had been dropped to the lower half of the page, his headlines reduced in size. It carried pictures, which the first story didn't. But it had nothing new for me.

After paging quickly through the rest of it, I folded the paper and gave it back to the boy.

With a mild expression of horror contorting his features, he said: "Heck of a thing, ain't it? I mean in the town's whole history nothing like this's ever happened. Now suddenly there's three killings in one day."

"Count what happened to Bridget Cole," I told him, "and you've got four in three days."

"Hey, yeah! Yeah! So much's been going on I forgot about that one. Say, you think . . .?"

Before he could draw me into a discussion on the subject, I made a getaway.

Skipping breakfast, I tooled my car along to the newspaper office. I wanted information, and it seemed unlikely that I'd be getting any from the sheriff's office.

Rudge was at his desk when I got there.

From a battered Underwood he looked up, waved absently to a chair. "Park your butt. Be with you in a minute."

While I sat waiting he continued the furious hammering of the typewriter keys. From the looks of him, he'd been up a greater part of the night. Red rimmed his eyes and, though seated, in the wilted white shirt he appeared to be even lankier than I remembered. A razor hadn't been near his face in it least twenty-four hours, and judging from the number of crushed plastic cups in the wastebasket, he'd been using only coffee as fuel during the night.

At last the hammering stopped and the sheet was ripped from the machine and laid on top of a small pile of similar pages. He turned his chair to face me.

"Reckon you've heard what happened?"

"I read your story."

"You here for information? Or, that it should happen to me this morning, you brought along something I can use?"

"Depends. Your paper said the man killed hadn't been identified. How about it?"

"That was last night." Rubbing his eyes he tried to stem a yawn. And failed. "Know anything about the newspaper business?"

"Enough to keep silent in the company of an expert."

"All right. So you know something about how it's put out. Yesterday we had everything set to roll. McGill's murder was page one news. Then, and I repeat *then,* just before we put her to bed—wham! We've got two more killings and a hundred thousand dollar collection lifted right from under our noses. I've been up all damn night trying to rake together enough information to make the morning edition. You know what it takes to hack out a story under those conditions? You got any idea of the work that's involved in reshuffling the front page?"

"Hold it," I interrupted. "I'm not here to gripe about poor news reporting."

Reaching for the packet of cigarettes on the edge of his desk, he shook one loose, lit it, and grinned. "Ah, what the hell. Don't mind me. I'm tired, and that story *was* lousy. Only last night I could get precious little out of Mulder. Had to use what I could get."

"How'd they open the safe?"

"These guys were experts, Cameron. No explosives, no mess. There were two locks on the safe, both of the key type, and they opened each without much trouble. Some tools, the kind a locksmith might use, were found in the office." Flicking ash onto the floor, he went on: "They came through the back door, and that offered no problem at all. A kid with a pocket knife could have done it."

"No alarm systems?"

"Seems no one ever figured any need for one. Not in a place like this."

"How about identification? Any been established yet?"

"Yeah, it's been made. Why Mulder couldn't give it to me last night, I don't know. The guy had papers in his pocket." He grinned, but it was small and sardonic. "Personally, I think our sheriff's becoming a little rattled, what with all these killings suddenly landing smack on his doorstep. He's always boasted of how clean this town's been of even minor crime since he took office. And now? Now he's got four bodies in the morgue and he's still chasing Whitman." He sucked hard on the cigarette, took it from his mouth, looked at it, screwed up his long face and forced smoke through his nostrils.

"Do I have to wait for the next edition to learn who he was?" I asked quietly.

"Why? Think you might know him?"

"I might."

"Mathews was his name. Kent Mathews."

He toyed with the cigarette packet and waited for my reaction.

The name drew a blank with me and he sensed it. "Don't know him?"

"It was a wild idea to start with," I murmured, and got up from the chair.

"This help?" Shifting papers on the desk he found a glossy photograph and held it up for my inspection. It was a poor head and shoulders portrait of a man, and it might have been a hurried enlargement from a license photograph.

I looked at it and experienced the same tremor of excitement I had first felt when reading the museum story.

"I met him once briefly," I said. "On Saturday night. He was using the name Carl Myburgh."

A soft whistle came from Rudge. "Interesting. There more?"

"Uh-huh. But you're going to have to do me a favor."

"Thought I'd already done you one?" He waved the photograph at me then tossed it back onto the desk.

"If I tell you, you're going to have to give me your word not to use any of it just yet. Break into print what I've got and it may take a lot longer to get back the collection, or to get our hooks into the guy who assisted Myburgh, or Mathews, or whatever his real name was."

"It was Mathews," Rudge put in. Then, after but a moment's consideration: "You're asking a hell of lot of me, Cameron."

"I know. But it may be worth it in the end."

"Think you can find him, that it?"

"I don't know. I'd like to try, and for more reasons than one."

"One being the insurance?" He leaned forward, squashed the cigarette butt into an over-loaded ashtray.

"If I can recover the coins, they'll pay," I admitted.

"The other reason then?"

"Bridget Cole. She worked at the museum."

He waved at the chair. "Sit down. I think we can talk business."

I sat down again and told him about my visit with the Sheltons in Fresno, about Bridget Cole's alleged relationship with Mathews, how they'd dealt with me at the Silver Horn Motel. "They knew her," I said. "And it was them who lifted the collection and killed the guard. There's a strong connection somewhere."

Rudge nodded. "And if there is, it could mean clearing Whitman, that it? That's if we're operating on the same wave-length."

"Do we have a deal?"

"We have," he said, expression thoughtful.

I got back onto my feet.

"Want to tell me where you think the other half of the team is?" he asked.

"At this stage I'd rather not."

"Suit yourself." Slowly, almost reluctantly, he drew his rangy frame out of the chair. "When do you think you'll get back?"

I didn't bother to ask how he'd guessed I was about to take a trip.

"With luck, tonight."

"Then I wish you lots of it. In the meantime I'll sit on the story."

"Just one thing more. Exactly how many coins are there in this collection?"

"Not many. The lot could be carried in a small bag." Attacking the contents of the desktop again, he came up with a typed sheet.

"What are they made of?" I queried. "Gold!"

"Some. Most are in what is known as proof condition, and that's apparently one of the things that make them valuable." He tapped the sheet with his fingers. "Listen to this, it's a list of the coins. One 1822 Half Eagle, valued at sixteen thousand, five hundred; an 1880 Four-dollar gold piece—value: six thousand, five hundred. An 1870 San Francisco minted Silver dollar—five thousand; an 1883 Double Eagle—three thousand. Want me to go on?"

"No, I get the picture. Got an extra copy of that?"

"Take this one." He passed over the list.

I took it and quickly scanned the close type. "When was it first known that the collection was to be exhibited here?"

"A few weeks back, as I recollect—when first the arrangements were confirmed."

"Your paper give it any coverage?"

"Some; not much. A couple of short columns."

Folding the list I tucked it away in my pocket.

"You know," Rudge mused, "when I first saw that list I started wondering just how many times I might have handed over five thousand for a purchase worth a quarter."

"And if certain pennies are worth a hundred bucks, think how much the use of a public convenience might have cost you."

"And there've been times," he chuckled, "when I wouldn't have minded a bit."

"Know who insured the stuff?"

"Sure. West Coast Mutual Fidelity. If you're planning on seeing them, they've an office right here in town."

From the newspaper offices I made my way to those of the organization that provided insurance cover for the Kronstead collection.

A man with a nameplate on his desk that said he was Kevin L. Dewey, District Manager, put up a protesting argument, but with a little persistence I persuaded him to communicate with his L.A. office before making any final decision. It was a routine I'd been through before, and would probably have to go through a few more times if I stayed in the racket.

I'd previously handled recovery work for West Coast, and they knew me in L.A. After the call had been made, Dewey was even less happy. Although they refused to pay the usual percentage should I succeed in locating the coins, Dewey reluctantly agreed to the addition of a fee of one hundred per day, with a minimum of five hundred in the event of the job taking less than five days. He agreed only because he had every confidence that the local authorities would have the collection returned in less than that time. I asked for a letter confirming the agreement, and that sent his temperature a few degrees higher.

Fifteen minutes later, with the signed letter pocketed, I thanked him and left to pick up a publicity brochure and have my car gassed up. What Dewey had not known was, that regardless of any decision he might have made, I would still have gone ahead with what I intended. Only this way, if I was lucky, I stood to show a profit of some kind for my stay in Reposado.

The sun was warm when I drove out of town, winding my way toward the Sierras, but the air started to cool pleasantly as the climb began and the miles diminished. Ahead, Mount Whitney thrust its majestic dome up at the heavens, as though stiffly proud in the knowledge that it towered above anything in the country, and that Alaska did not exist. It made me feel small and transient and very alone.

A National Park Service Ranger collected the entrance fee and directed me to the lodge. At the coffee shop nestling in the shadows of a grove of giant sequoias, I parked and went in to take care of a breakfast I'd so far delayed, but which my stomach had not forgotten.

Filled and feeling better, I took the publicity folder from my pocket and checked it once more. It was identical to the one I'd seen in the suite Mathews and partner had been using at the Silver Horn. On that one two places had been ringed in pencil, and unless my memory had committed a betrayal, I was now at the nearest of the two. I settled my bill and went back to the car where I fixed the holstered .38 to my belt and slipped a pair of handcuffs into a hip pocket. Then I got the car moving toward the rustic and canvas-topped cabins.

Not many appeared to be occupied, judging from the number of cars on view. Otherwise their occupants had taken their vehicles with them wherever they'd gone. Those that remained were mostly from other states. I checked all I could see before returning to the long black Olds.

It was the only one that carried Nevada's plates.

On the way to the front door of the cabin, I remembered the dead museum guard and loosened the gun on my hip. Without creating very much noise, I laid knuckles upon the wood.

The knock fell either upon deaf ears or emptiness. I tried again.

When still nothing happened I reached down for the handle, turning it slowly. It was unlocked and the door made only the smallest creak as it moved inward. I pushed it further, trying to ignore the crawly sensation between my shoulder blades.

The room had all the untidiness of recent occupation—used ashtrays, a bottle and glass on a low table, the mustiness of stale cigarette smoke, and over near a rumpled couch, a pair of shoes. For a long moment I stood absorbing everything, while on my back the hairy spider crawled higher. I let go of the handle and took a cautious step forward. The door made another tiny creak and the room returned to silence. Very slowly I started to turn, then forgetting about the gun clipped to my belt, gave the door a vicious kick that sent it slamming back against the wall.

From behind came a sharp sound of surprise before it came swinging back at me. I reached across my body for the .38, but before my fingers could close over the butt, the one who had been concealed behind the cabin door leapt out into view, his thin brown hair ruffled in spite of the glistening oil, his eyes wide and round and wild. The fingers of his right hand were clenched tightly around a gun I had seen once before in his possession.

"Shut the door!" he grated.

"Sure, Joey."

I took a hold on the door and closed it quietly.

"Now get over there," he directed. "And keep those paws up where I can see what they're doin'."

Between us there was about three feet of stale air. The pointing gun probed the space like a malefic reminder, but the hand holding it trembled while sweat glistened on the face of its owner. I raised my hands but didn't move.

"I said to get over there!" The hiss was the sound of a startled snake. "Don't give me trouble!"

"I've already given it to you, Joey. Try popping that thing off around here and you'll be dead a great deal sooner than you expect to be."

"Shut up!"

"Nervous?" The smile I tried was no more than the stretching of lips. "You're sweating like a pig. The dead guard bothering you that much? Or is it what's to follow?"

"I said to clam up," he screeched, lifting the gun in a swift movement that was designed to lay the barrel across my teeth.

As his arm went up I stuck out my raised left and blocked the blow, dropping my right to swing a fist at his protruding belly. Joey did two things simultaneously. He went high up on his toes and the gun flew from his grip as though suddenly red-hot. It fell with a thump on the bare boards at his stockinged feet and a sickening sound whooshed out of his open mouth. Groaning still, he grabbed for his middle, turned his back on me and lowered himself to the floor where he curled up into a small bundle to make sounds like an injured cat.

I stooped to retrieve the fallen gun, conscious of the dampness on the back of my shirt.

"Get up."

Rocking rhythmically against the floor, he held onto his belly and went on making the animal noises.

"Oh, Geeze," he cried, "you bust it. You bust it!"

Sticking the gun in my pocket I got a grip under his arms and dragged him over to the couch. His face was wet with sweat, screwed up in agony, the flesh gray when I propped him into a sitting position.

"What's wrong?"

"My gut," he moaned. "I think I got an ulcer, and I think you bust it. Oh, Geeze, I feel like I'm gonna toss a tiger!"

And with that, unconcerned about anything I might do to stop him, he got up and staggered wobbly to the bathroom.

I went with him, waiting until he was through turning his inside out. I felt a little sick myself when we returned to the room and he flopped back onto the couch, searching his pockets until finding the plastic box and the tablets it contained. With three of them down his throat he seemed to become a little calmer.

From my pocket I took the handcuffs and clamped them around his wrists. He made no protest.

"Okay, Joey. Where are they?"

"Cameron, I'm a sick man. I don't know what you want with me, but I ain't fightin' you. I'm sick, can't you see? I need a doctor, for crissakes!" The manacled hands tenderly massaged the bulge under his soiled shirt.

"The coins, Joey. Get them and we'll start back for town where you can get all the medical attention you want." I paused to smile thinly. "It's an odd thing, the way they care for a prisoner until they're ready to dish out the cyanide pills."

He said nothing, avoiding my face.

"A guard was killed at the Reposado Museum last night, Joey. Your pal died there also. It's asking a lot for us to believe that Myburgh, or as we now know him, Mathews, shot the guard as he was dying. Or that he shot the guard first and as the guard lay down managed to trigger off one last fatal shot."

"He did!" he whispered hoarsely, sweaty face grayer than cold ashes. "That's what happened. That's exactly what happened. You can't pin that on me. I never killed him . . ." Realizing his mouth had run off a little too fast, he clamped it sullenly shut and stared down at his imprisoned hands.

"Now that we've established that fact, let's get to my question. Where are the coins?"

"In there." He inclined his head towards the bedroom. "There's a leather bag stuck in bottom of my case."

As I started to move, he called: "Cameron, I had nothing to do with that shootin', I swear it. Kent clubbed the guard and we both thought he was out for the count. But just as we're cuttin' outa there he comes round and goes for his gun. Hell, Kent hit him so hard we never even worried to take away the old coot's rod."

"Keep going, Joey. You've got an interested listener."

"I had the stuff in my hand," he continued. "I wasn't even thinkin' about no guard, just about cuttin' outa there, like fast. Then the next thing, Kent is swearin' and jerkin' at his gun. There's one helluva boom and he goes slammin' backwards. I turn and there's that guard up on his elbow, his rod pointin' at Kent. I freeze solid 'cause sure as hell it's me he's gonna hit next. Then suddenly, next to me there's another shot and instead of me bein' dead the old guy's wearin' a big hole. I turn where Kent is standin', but he's halfway to bein' dead himself. He just swears some more, throws away his rod and goes down on his face. That's how it happened. I swear it on my mother's name, that's what happened. I never fired one stinkin' shot!"

"But you grabbed the coins and ran for here," I supplied. "Why this place?"

"It was Kent's idea, bein' outa the way like it is. We didn't figure on no guard comin' to like that. This dump was booked a week back already. We was plannin' on spendin' a few days laying low before cuttin' back to Vegas." He shrugged, winced and dug fingers into his swollen middle. "I was in a sweat. I wanted to drive straight back home, but I figured like how maybe the cops got the roads blocked or somethin' . . . Anyway, I came up here. Only now it don't look like it was such a hot idea." His eyes shifted to the bottle and glass. "I think I need a drink."

"If it's an ulcer you've got, that won't help."

"I need a drink, I tell you! "

"Then help yourself. You can manage."

I waited until he'd sloshed a liberal quantity into the glass, downed it and returned to the couch. Once seated he picked up where he had left off without any need for prompting.

"They can hit me for the robbery," he moaned. "But I'm not gonna die for a killin' I had no hand in. I wasn't even an accomplice—I didn't know there was gonna be a shootin', did I? How could I? It just went sour and . . . and . . ."

I didn't try to help, or to argue the point. "Why the coins? What did you hope to gain by lifting them? You can't sell those things without raising a lot of questions. Or didn't that thought occur to you?"

"I don't know." There was a note of sadness in his voice and his head wagged wearily. "Kent, he had this bright idea when he read about the collection bein' brought up here. He knew some guy, he said, who'd pay us a good price for the stuff. I thought he was crazy and I told him he was nuts, but he made it look as easy as pickin' your nose. I went along with him. It looked easy and if it'd come off we'd've picked up a nice piece of change."

"Who was Mathews planning to sell them to?"

Joey's damp face tilted up and a look of stupidity clouded his unhandsome features. "He never told me," he answered softly. "I never even worried to ask him. He was bossin' the show so I left it all to him. Like always."

"And you've been sitting here with a collection worth well over a hundred grand, planning to do exactly what?"

"Listen—please—I don't feel so good. My guts is killin' me."

"You'll live long enough to answer my question."

"Okay, okay. I was plannin' on cuttin' outa here tomorrow. My guts was actin' up otherwise I'd've got out today. I had me an idea I could maybe unload the stuff somewhere up north. Bein' worth all that loot there hadda be somebody willin' to cough up a fair price for it."

"Uh-huh. And where does the Cole girl come in?" I moved up against a low wall cabinet and leaned an elbow on its top. "Was she in this with you?"

"She was what started the whole damn thing," he complained sourly. "If it wasn't for her none of this would've happened. Kent and me used to work for a guy called Mel Formento over in Vegas. He—"

"The one who runs a dive called the Casino Crescendo?" I remembered what Marge Shelton had told me during my visit to Fresno.

"The same," Joey answered quickly. "Mel had a big thing goin' for that twist, but she wasn't havin' none of him. It used to be a joke among the boys how Mel couldn't make first base with her. Only one night . . . one night Mel tries to play it cute. He invites her up to his room, like it's supposed to be business, y'know? Anyway, once she's there she finds he's got a table all rigged for dinner—candles, champagne—the works. But this doll latches on real quick about what Mel's schemin', and she tries walkin' out on him. I guess Mel made to stop her and there was a little rumble. The next thing we hear is the dame chargin' outa the room, her dress all torn, and Mel is yellin' like he's been killed. We go up to see what's wrong and there he is with blood all over his puss. Turns out the dame picks up a fork from the table and sticks it into his face as deep as she can get it. But while all this is goin' on nobody thinks to get hold of the dame in case there's gonna be trouble, and when somebody does start thinkin' in that direction, she's already packed and gone. The same night she grabs a bus outa town, and that's the last any of us hear about her."

Perhaps it was the pain in his gut, or the thought of impending death that had him talking faster and more readily than I'd hoped. And he wasn't through.

"All that was a couple years back and now everybody's kinda forgotten what happened. We know Mel would like to fix the dame good for the way she loused up his kisser, but he never mentions it—makes like it's ancient history. Kent and me, we nearly forget about it also, until we stop in Reposado one day and see her." His hands went up to his face and tried to do something about the sweat. "That's how it all started. Kent tells me to hang around, that he's gonna talk to her. When he gets back he's grinnin' like he's just taken the craps table for its last buck, or somethin'. I ask him what gives, and he says to sit tight, that he's plannin' to take the dame back to Vegas with us. Only it's gotta be done quiet, with no fuss and noise. I'm not so dumb I can't figure what's goin' on in his head. Kent was a real hot pants himself, and I figure what he's really thinkin' is how to cut himself personally in on a piece of what the broad's got.

"But I don't say nothin', it's his business and his funeral if Mel ever gets wind of it. We sit around town a couple days until he picks up a paper and reads about the coins. He shows it to me, tells me the dame works at the museum where the coins are gonna be displayed in a few weeks time. To me it don't mean a thing, but the next day we're movin' out, up to Fresno where we live at different hotels—until you come bargin' into the last place. Up there Kent lays out the deal for me."

Wincing when something happened inside his stomach, he looked up, frightened. But seeing I was still waiting to hear the rest of his speech and nothing about the state of his health, he picked up the story again.

"He claims he knows someone who'll come across with at least twenty-five grand for that junk. Maybe more. Like I been tellin' you, in the beginin' I don't want no part of it. It's right outa our line. But Kent soaps me up and the next thing I'm in."

"Either the girl helped you or she was taken back to Formento? That the play?"

"Yeah, that's how it was gonna be." Raising his arms he brushed the sleeve of his shirt clumsily across his face. It came away damp. "Kent had her scared right outa her pants. So every Friday when she comes up to those friends of hers, she visits us also, and brings him things. Other times he drives down to Reposado and meets the dame there. First thing she gets for us is the dope about the floor layout and how many guards they're gonna use at night, and what kinda locks they got on the back doors. That kinda stuff. Then she gets us impressions of *the* keys for the safe. Kent gets a set made then gives them back to her so she can test them in the safe. He shows her how to put on some purple stuff so that any parts what don't fit will get scratched. When she brings them back he files away the scratched parts and she takes 'em away to test again. All the time she's squawkin' about what he's makin' her do. But he shuts her up quick, tellin' her to remember what Mel will do if we take her back, or even if we phone and tell him where she is. So all right, she does what he wants and we get ourselves a set of keys that are supposed to fit. On Sunday night, the same day the stuff's brought to the museum, we pull off the job."

The sad look moved back onto his pained face. "It shouldn'ta gone sour like it did. Not with all that plannin'. But I guess I knew somethin' lousy was gonna happen. I got that feelin' just as soon's I heard how the dame got herself killed."

"Yet even knowing she was dead you went through with it?"

"I didn't want to. But Kent reckoned we'd already put in too much to pull out now."

"What about the tools left in the curator's office, Joey? Was that window dressing?"

"Yeah, that was another part of Kent's idea. The dame wasn't supposed to run away like she tried. After we opened the safe we was gonna leave some tools behind to make it look like the box was cracked by guys who knew what they was doin'. That way nobody would start askin' questions, like where'd the guys who lifted the stuff get keys? Kent didn't want the dame involved. If she got hooked she'd've led the cops straight back to us."

"Then why did she decide to run?"

"She got scared." Changing his position, but still holding his belly, he said: "Cameron, my guts is goin' mad."

"You sure?" I asked, ignoring the last piece of information. "You sure that wasn't another part of Kent's plan? Let her start running so that he could kill her—so that she could never shoot her mouth off to the police? Where was Mathews on Friday night?"

Joey's eyes grew wildly frightened again, and for a moment he forgot about his discomfort. "No . . . Kent wouldn't've killed her! That wasn't in the plans! She was scared, I tell you. She was runnin' away before anythin' happened. Kent didn't kill her. I know why she was runnin'."

"Then tell me, because I sort of like my first idea—the two of you stopping her on that old road so you could beat her to death and shut her up permanently."

"No!" His head shook furiously. "No, we didn't have no part in that, I tell you! She was just scared. She was runnin' 'cause she'd pulled a double-cross on us, that's why! She told us the keys fitted, but they didn't. They didn't fit, you hear me? That's why we took so damn long—that's why the guard had time to wake up and shoot Kent! Those damned keys never fitted. She knew it and she was runnin'. She lied to us—left us to look stupid."

"If they didn't fit, how did you get the locks open?"

"That's what took the time," he answered, his tone pleading to be believed. "We had to work on the things right there in the office. It took time to file until they did fit. The night she got herself killed she was supposed to bring us the last dope about the guards and stuff. That's why Kent was so anxious to get hold of her. That's why he phoned her friends when she didn't show."

I straightened up, wondering how much truth was in all he had told me. It placed parts into position, but didn't account for others. I left him stretching for the bottle and went into the bedroom to find his suitcase.

A chamois leather bag was stuffed at the bottom of the case under an untidy pile of dirty clothes. Inside it a small pile of coins, each sealed in a separate transparent case. I took them back to where the perspiring Joey waited, placed them on the table and counted them, checking the number against the quantity shown on the list Rudge had provided. It would have taken too long to check each identification, even if I knew how.

With the coins back in the bag, I stood up.

"Get your shoes on. We don't want to keep the people waiting."

TEN

MIXED REACTIONS greeted our arrival at the sheriff's office. Mulder was happy to have the coins returned: glad to have someone who could be legitimately charged as an accomplice in the robbery. But not overjoyed by the fact that someone outside his department had made the arrest and recovery. Especially since the job had been accomplished through facts unknown to him.

I asked for and was given a receipt for both coins and man. It was something I would need if I hoped to collect payment from the insurers.

After Joey Ortell, or as his identification revealed, Joseph Inskip, had been taken away to a cell and a doctor summoned to attend to him, Mulder led the way to his office and had me go over the entire story a second time.

I gave him everything I knew, including my meeting with the two men in the Fresno motel and Joey's version of Bridget Cole's involvement in the robbery.

"Don't get the idea I don't appreciate what you've done," he said when I wound it up. "I do. It's saved me a lot of work. What I'd like to know, though, is why wasn't I told about Mathews and that punk before now?"

"Would you have believed me? I seem to recall experiencing difficulty having you believe other things I reported."

"I guess I asked for that, didn't I?"

He stood up and I did likewise.

"What Joey told me," I said, "could explain why the girl went to Christine Danhurst for the five hundred, even if it doesn't explain what eventually happened to it. It's a reasonable bet that she planned to run at the last minute, that's why she didn't have time to draw money from her banking account. Or perhaps she didn't want to arouse anyone's curiosity by making a withdrawal of that size. Joey's story also gives Mathews a reason for wanting the girl dead."

"That's true," he conceded, moving around the desk to the office door. "But it doesn't explain why McGill was killed. You forgetting it was Whitman's gun we found there? The bullet that killed McGill was fired from it."

I shook my head. "He told me he gave it to the girl for protection during those night drives. If Mathews killed her it's possible he took the gun after she was dead."

"There's that possibility. But first we'd have to prove he was in town on Sunday the time McGill was shot. That jerk in there"—he jabbed a thumb in the general direction of the cell block—"he claims they drove in here after midnight, only minutes before hitting the museum, and I don't think we'll have an easy time getting him to change his statement. In any case, we've got Whitman now and it'll be interesting finding out which one of them is lying."

The information he provided so casually left me with little to say.

"We got him a few hours ago," Mulder explained. "Highway Patrol found him at a filling station getting the car's tank topped up."

"Has he said anything?"

"If you mean has he confessed? No." He opened the door to show me out. "But something happened this morning while we were still looking for him. A woman calling herself Mona Gallagher came to see me."

He waited to see if the name meant anything to me. When I failed to react, he continued.

"She gave us a story about how Whitman had been with her all of Saturday and the best part of Sunday. Also, she says, he came to her place after leaving that party Friday night. He was down in the dumps and stayed there with her until pretty late." Smiling, he reached into his shirt pocket. "According to her, that is."

"You don't believe it?"

"I'm not sure." He put the cigar taken from his pocket in his mouth and searched for a match. "If what she says is true, it could mean she and Whitman were a little bit more than just casual friends, wouldn't you say? And if they were that, it could maybe point to the real reason why the girl was killed."

"You know the reason?"

Before answering he fiddled with the cigar and got it burning. "Nope, not yet. But when there are two dames and only one guy, the motive usually turns out to be a pretty uncomplicated one."

"Which means you don't think much of the idea that Mathews might have been the one who murdered the girl?"

"Do you?"

"I'm still thinking about it."

"Listen—I'd like nothing better than to prove it was Mathews. Believe that. It would make everything that much tidier. Only I don't see why he would want to kill the doctor."

"Can I see Whitman?"

"Sure, I don't mind. But I've a hunch he won't want to see you. He thinks it's you who sicced us onto him."

He bellowed for one of the uniformed men and told him to take me to Hal Whitman.

The detention block was located behind the square brick building. It housed six ceils, each arranged in such a way that the prisoners could not communicate with each other, explained the deputy as he led the way. I had no opportunity of seeing how many of the cells were occupied, for Whitman was seated on the narrow bunk of the first we arrived at.

"Someone to see you," the deputy told him loudly.

Whitman moved his head, saw me standing at the bars, then swung his face back to the bare wall he'd been staring at previously.

"Hal?"

"Get the hell out of here!" he snarled. "There's nothing I want to discuss with you!"

"Hal, you're being stupid. I'm still trying to help you. If nothing else, try believing that."

The strange laugh I'd heard from him before echoed in the confines of the small cell. "That supposed to be funny?" He laughed some more, and then turned it off sharply. "Get out of here, Paul! I don't need you. I was a damn fool to think I ever did."

A hand touched my arm. "Better leave him," the deputy advised. "He don't seem to feel much like talking."

With a last look at Whitman's back I turned and followed the uniform out of the building. From there I returned to the hotel. There was no other place go.

At the desk the clerk handed across the room key and an envelope. As I was about to walk away he suddenly remembered something else.

"Oh—Mr. Cameron. There was a young lady in see you a couple of times."

"She leave any message?"

"No, not even a name. Came in three times, but I told her I had no idea when you'd be back." He grinned widely when another thought jogged his memory. "She was a real good-looker."

I walked away from the desk and ripped open the envelope to read the telegraphic message it contained.

"REGRET NO RECORD OF INFORMATION REQUESTED STOP SURE YOU HAVE NAMES CORRECT STOP ADVISE IF FURTHER ACTION REQUIRED STOP CONDOR"

Folding the message, I put it back in its envelope and shoved it into a side pocket. A feeling of depression entwined its arms unlovingly around me and suddenly I was tired and feeling defeated. Instead of going up to my room I headed for the bar.

There were few people in the place, and those that were there appeared to be in moods similar to mine. They paid attention only to their drinks and ignored my entrance. The barman sidled over to where I sat down, listened when I ordered, and then without comment delivered a cold beer.

I was near the bottom of the glass, half-listening to the radio that played too loudly from the shelf on the other side of the bar, wrapped up in thoughts of Hal Whitman, when I saw her. She was seated at the far end of the counter, staring into the mirror behind the bottles, her face pale, her forehead lined with tiny furrows that made her look slightly older and a little sadder than I remembered. I picked up my glass and went over to her.

At the sound of my voice she whirled around, stifling a soft frightened gasp.

"I was told an attractive young lady had been looking for me. Was that you, Sandra?"

A small smile fought for a place on her face but quickly lost the battle. She reached for her glass, took a very short sip and set it down again.

"You—you surprised me, Mr. Cameron. I didn't think you'd be back today."

I signaled for the barman and inspected the clothes she wore. A white skirt, a blouse as dark as her hair and a pair of flat saddle shoes.

"Can I get you another drink?"

"No, please don't. I—I'm not used to it. I only came in here because . . ."

"You were waiting for me?"

Nodding mutely, she averted her face.

The barman arrived and took my order. I said nothing until he put down another beer and dropped my change onto the wood.

"What's wrong, Sandra?" I asked gently, lifting my drink.

"Wrong?" Her face visible again. "What—what do you mean?"

"It's written all over you. Most of all in your eyes. That sort of look doesn't belong there." I swallowed some of the beer before going on, watching the indecision that flickered in the deep blue under the long lashes. "You've heard about Hal Whitman. Is that it?"

Again the silent nod. But this time she went on looking at me. "What—what will happen to him now?"

I shrugged. "The way the sheriff talks it sounds as if he's fully satisfied with what he's got."

"They could prove him guilty, couldn't they?"

"They could."

Sparkling white teeth nibbled at her lower lip while she struggled with the next question. "Could he be sent to the . . . gas chamber? I mean even if he didn't do it and . . ."

"You mean even if he's innocent of the charge but found guilty in spite of it?" I toyed with the glass and pretended to think. "Yes, he could be executed if sufficient circumstantial evidence exists. From where he sits the picture isn't an attractive one."

"Mr. Cameron?" Her hand touched mine in an urgent plea. "Isn't there anything you can do to help him? He didn't kill her. You don't believe that, do you?"

"No, Sandra, I don't. Do you?"

By returning to her hardly touched drink she managed to delay the answer.

Using the pause to light a cigarette, I swung myself around on the stool and concentrated on her reflection in the mirror. It looked dream-like staring back at me from there. Like something seen in the desires of a forlorn drunk.

"You know Hal Whitman didn't kill anyone, don't you, Sandra?"

"No," she returned quickly. "I—I just don't believe he could do such a thing. I—I don't want to believe it."

"Sandra," I began in a voice that sounded foreign to my own ears, "the night I drove into Reposado I saw a man with blood on his clothes. There was someone with me who also saw him, so it wasn't something I've imagined. Everything I've discovered so far seems to point to one thing. The man I saw had been shot. The weapon I believe was a gun that was in the possession of Bridget Cole the night she was killed. The trouble is that so far we've not been able to find any person who was wounded like that."

Next to me the girl breathed heavily, but still she did not attempt to in-terrupt or get up and leave. She listened and I knew I was at last digging in the right place at the right time. That she had to be the one I was using did not make me feel any better.

"If there was such a man, and that man was wounded by a bullet or bullets, it means that somewhere someone has been giving him shelter and protection."

Her movements were very slow, but the way she downed what was left in her glass, it might have been something no stronger than spring water.

I said: "He's at your house, isn't he, Sandra?"

The glass slipped through her fingers, bounced on the counter and did not break. I caught it before it toppled to the floor.

"No," she cried softly. "No, it wasn't him." Her voice was a faint whisper of pain. "Clevedon's dead. It wasn't him!" Her head shook in emphatic denial of the accusation I had made, blue-black hair swirling as if caressed by a breeze she alone could feel.

Under other circumstances there may have been satisfaction in hearing the unintentional admission. But the expression of pain on her face, the round open mouth and the lip that quivered with frightened realization, brought only a feeling of guilt. I took the telegram from my pocket and read it to her.

"This is the result of an inquiry I requested," I told her. "Your brother Clevedon was supposed to have died as a child in New York. I asked for a check to be made for the record of death. This is the reply."

She went on staring, open-mouthed, like someone who'd just been backhanded

"I had to do it, Sandra," I said, finding myself unconsciously offering an apology. "It was the last place I had left to look."

Tears welled up in the darkness of her eyes, spilled over the edges and tumbled down her cheeks. I stood up killed the cigarette and steered her out to my car.

She came willingly, like a child being led.

The gate to Retreat was wide open when we arrived there. The girl looked at it and almost to herself whispered: "I . . . forgot to close it . . ." Then turning to me she cried: "The Buick! It's still in town!"

"We can get it later," I said, assuming she meant the car she had used to get into town. And as we passed through the gateway: "I want to see your brother, Sandra."

"Everyone will see him soon," she remarked dejectedly. "And then everyone will know." The tears, which had stopped only shortly before arriving at the great house, started to run again.

During the drive she had allowed the words to bubble out. They'd been words stored up for too long a time. Not much of it made sense, and I doubt that she quite understood it all herself. She couldn't even fully appreciate her reason for trying to find me, except that she knew Whitman had not been guilty of any killing and that she was seeking some way to help him. Perhaps without realizing it she had wanted the truth known. And that part I could understand. At least to some extent. Both she and her brother Gerry had been living under a shadow of fear and doubt most of their lives. Both harbored fears that in their bodies lurked the same qualities that had made Clevedon Danhurst what he was. I had time to think back on the brief meetings with Sandra and Gerry, during which both had expressed opinions of their own mental health.

Only one other car stood in the drive when we pulled up quietly at the entrance to the house. The white Triumph. I opened the door and slid off the seat, going around to help Sandra. As I did so I glanced up at the tiny balconies above us, in time to see something dark move out of sight.

To Sandra, I said: "Let's go to your brother before we talk to anyone."

Nodding silently she led the way up the stone steps and into the house. There was nobody to greet us, only a stillness that belonged behind the walls of a cathedral. Motioning for me to follow, she started up the broad arched hallway. We passed the room in which I had met her mother. The door there was slightly ajar and through the gap I could see the fat woman slumped in the big rocking chair. It was dim inside the room, and she appeared not to see us passing. At the end of the hall Sandra quietly opened the door, on the other side of which a few cement steps descended to another level of the house.

The steps ended on a square of scrubbed concrete, and in one wall was set another door, heavier than any of the others I'd seen in the house. A large slide bolt kept it securely closed. With fingers that trembled, the girl pulled back the bolt and creaked the door open.

A putrescent stench, warm and mixed with the strong odors of medications, wafted out at us. Sandra pushed the heavy door open wide until

I could see the bed and the man in it. The covers were drawn up to his neck and his eyes were closed. The beard stubbled face was a thing of gray wax, the hands stretched stiffly at his side in a pose I had seen many times before. It was not one with which the girl was familiar.

"He's sleeping," she whispered to me.

"Sandra . . ." As gently as I could I put an arm around her. "He's dead. You know that?"

Her face lifted and the dark eyes grew puzzled. "Yes . . . Yes, he's dead. I—I forgot. I mean I . . ." Her head moved slowly from one side to the other, trying it seemed, to get her thinking organized again. "I—I forgot. But—but that's why I tried to find you, isn't it . . .? There . . . there wasn't any doctor to call, you see. He died. He died and it was all over. All . . ." Emotion flushed through her face as she squeezed her eyes tightly shut. "He's dead!" she cried loudly. "He's dead!" And as she burst into racking sobs her entire body suddenly slumped and collapsed against mine.

I caught her, got an arm around her back and another under her legs. She weighed hardly anything at all. With her in my arms I took one last long look at the dead face. Connie March's reason for thinking of Nathaniel Danhurst when seeing him on Friday night was there in that face. The resemblance to the painting that hung on the wall of the Danhurst living room was striking.

I turned away from the body and the sickening odors and carried the girl out of the room. But as I reached the steps the door above them was flung open and Gerry Danhurst stood framed in the aperture. A small bore automatic pointed down at where I stopped.

"You slimy son of a bitch!" he hissed loudly. "Couldn't keep your nose out of our business, could you? You had to keep interfering!"

"Your sister's fainted," I said. "Let's take care of her before continuing the fight."

He stood aside to let me pass, then followed carefully behind while I made my way to the room where his mother waited.

She was cradling a phone when we entered and it was the first time I had seen her standing. She looked even larger. But under the fat something had died. Christine Danhurst had become aged and sick. She resumed her place in the rocker and glared at me.

"I knew you were trouble from the start, Mr. Cameron." She squinted at me, puzzled . . . or seemingly so. "Why have you done this to us? Was it the money Whitman is paying you?" Her voice had also changed, grown tired. The hardness was still there, but gone was the bite it had previously possessed.

Sandra stirred when I put her down into one of the chairs near the dark piano. Gerry Danhurst stood where he could keep the gun pointed at me.

I said: "Most everybody works for money, Mrs. Danhurst."

"And how much were you expecting to receive from me?"

"For what?"

When she didn't answer I turned to Gerry. "Get your sister a drink. She's going to need it."

He hesitated, then deciding he could still use the gun if I were to try anything, moved towards a cabinet and poured out a shot of brandy. At no time had he tried to find out if I was armed. I wasn't.

"How much to go away and forget everything that has happened here?" his mother asked when I was again facing her.

I waited until Sandra's eyes were open. Gerry spoke softly to her and after that she sat perfectly motionless, her eyes vacant things of blue that watched us.

"You're forgetting that a man may die for something he didn't do," I said to the fat woman. "Doesn't that bother you?"

"There is no proof that he didn't do it!" she returned, trying to stoke up some of the fire that was dying within her.

"Your son killed the girl, Mrs. Danhurst. All of us here know that. Somehow he got onto that road, found the girl having trouble with her car, and attacked her. Before she died she shot him. He was seen bleeding the night of the murder. Since then you've been hiding him out here, and unless I'm badly mistaken, your late friend, McGill, has been doctoring his wounds."

"Did my daughter tell you this?"

"Sandra told me very little," I answered. "It was an idea I got after talking to one of your ex-servants, a boy named Raul Ybarra. He told me a story about seeing Gerry drunk in the yard one night, and how Gerry had suddenly recovered fast enough to beat him up and throw him off the premises. What he told me didn't make a great deal of sense. Not until I started thinking about the person I had seen the night Bridget Cole was killed. That person was bleeding, yet none of the hospitals or doctors around here had treated anyone with such an injury. It meant that someone had to be hiding and caring for him. It also suggested that the wounded man was someone none of us knew about. When Ybarra told me about seeing Gerry drunk I wondered if he hadn't been confused, if it hadn't been someone else he'd seen." I took a breath and watched her face. "It wasn't Gerry, was it? It was your oldest son, the one everyone believed to be dead. Ybarra only assumed it was Gerry, because Gerry was the only male he knew to be living here."

From the son came a soft curse that accompanied Raul Ybarra's name.

"After that," I went on, "I had someone in New York check the records for your son's death. There wasn't one."

Again there was nothing but silence from any of them.

"Why the secrecy, Mrs. Danhurst? I've already gathered that Clevedon was some sort of mental deficient, but I don't and can't understand the reason for locking him away like an animal. Why wasn't he sent to an institution before he could hurt anyone?"

"My husband would never permit it! " she said harshly. "Nathan was a proud man. He—he was ashamed that his first son should be— unbalanced."

"The fear of shame made you do this?" It was difficult to believe; yet others before had done similar and worse.

"You wouldn't understand. How could you?" Her gaze slid away from me to her children. "Nathan was an important man. I too had a reputation to consider. There would have been the type of publicity neither of us could afford . . ."

Though both Gerry and Sandra had to be hearing everything, neither offered a word. "There were also my children, Mr. Cameron. What sort of lives do you think they would have had if it was known their brother was in an asylum? Do you think any man would have wanted to marry Sandra? Do you think that any woman would dare risk having Gerry's children? Do you?"

"Lots of people have relatives in institutions," I said. "It hasn't affected the lives of those that are left. Because one kid is mentally handicapped it doesn't follow that the others are also."

"Would you have risked it?"

My answer would have sounded too self-righteous, so I asked instead: "What happened on Friday night?"

She returned to silence, looking down into her lap at the fat fingers that picked at her skirt like bloated pink worms.

"He didn't mean to kill her," she said as softly as her gravelly voice could manage. "It wasn't his intention to kill her. I know it couldn't have been. She must have frightened him, otherwise he would never have done anything like that."

"Some years ago there was another killing here," I said. "In 1950 a child named Marlene Leonard was murdered in much the same fashion as was Bridget Cole. They never found her killer, but at the time the sheriff seemed convinced it was the work of out-of-town hooligans. Do you feel like telling me about that?"

Gerry Danhurst had been staring intently at his mother. Now he slowly turned to glance down at Sandra. It occurred to me that the murder of the Leonard child was something new to both of them.

Christine Danhurst never looked up. She went on studying the fidgeting fingers in silent fascination. Seconds crawled by before her voice rasped again.

"He's dead. It's all over now. All the years of worrying and fretting are over."

She didn't see my nod. "It was Clevedon then also, wasn't it?"

"Certain things fascinated and intrigued him," she murmured hoarsely. "Especially long hair of a certain color. He loved anything soft and fair . . . When I was young he loved so to—" She let it drop and raised her heavy head. "It was an accident. He didn't mean to harm the child. He was no more than a child himself then." Her stare moved past me, focusing on something she alone could see. Something that was a long time ago. "That night he slipped out of the exercise yard and we didn't know about it until too late. When—when we found him he was still with the child. He—he was fondling her long hair."

"What did you do, Mrs. Danhurst? Take him home and pretend none of it had happened?"

"It was an accident," she insisted earnestly. "The child must have somehow angered and frightened him. Otherwise he would never have harmed her. He never once tried to hurt any of us. It was only when he was scared. He—he couldn't control himself then."

"Don't you think that that was the time something should have been done? There are institutions that could have treated and perhaps helped him."

Color returned to her round face and rose high in flabby cheeks. "Stop talking about those places! I told you why we couldn't do that!"

"Yes. The shame. So, tell me about Bridget Cole."

Her bulk slumped deeper into the upholstered chair and she set it rocking. Neither of us were enjoying what was happening and at the back of my mind I wondered about her willingness to tell me these things. Then I remembered her son and the gun he was holding. In some way they didn't expect me to make any use of the things I was being allowed to hear.

As if controlled by an independent life, fingers still moved nervously in her lap. She glanced briefly at them before starting again to talk.

"I don't know everything . . . Only the little they told me. Cleve couldn't remember very well. At times he could not even remember his own mother." A heavy sigh shook her massive body. "It—it was hard for him to tell me these things. He never spoke much, you see. He—he couldn't. Sometimes he'd sit for days staring into space, and then—then sometimes he would talk to me and he was very quiet . . . very passive."

Regardless of what was to happen to me afterwards, I realized the woman had a reason for telling all this. She needed to have her actions understood. Possibly not so much by Cameron the intruder, but by the boy and girl who listened. It seemed important.

In some way she succeeded in reaching into my mind and plucked at the question I had there.

"He was not really violent," she said defensively, as if the question had been asked of her. "We only kept him locked up because—because sometimes he had those spasms of rage. But that was only when he'd been annoyed. No one can blame him for that." Her eyes closed but she went on talking. "For years he made no attempt to run away from here. I suppose we grew lax watching over him. Then . . . on Friday night Gerry was careless, and I have no doubt why." The eyes flicked open, almost glaring at her son. "It was because that girl was here. He was interested in her and wanted to share her company." Again her eyes closed, this time only for a moment or two, as if to dismiss the thought. "Instead of staying with Cleve the usual hour in the yard, he left him alone. The wall is high, but there are a few places one can climb over. It was only some time after the girl had left that we discovered he was missing.

"Somehow he must have made his way up to the old road and stumbled upon her when her car gave trouble. I do not know what really happened. You see, he couldn't tell me very much about it. But of this I am sure—he only wanted to get near her—to touch her. She must have become frightened, panicked and shot him. He wouldn't have hurt her, not unless something like that happened."

While she continued to speak I began to see a partially complete picture of the events that Friday night. In it was the girl alone out on a dark road, wondering what to do about the flat tire of her car. If suddenly Clevedon Danhurst were to appear on the scene it would have been more than enough to frighten her. Especially knowing the two from Vegas might be on her tail. If she had a gun and the Danhurst boy refused to go away, or was unable to understand her and the meaning of the gun . . .

"Gerry found him wandering about in the brush. He—he was badly hurt." She stopped to take a breath that shuddered through her body. "Myron McGill took the bullets out, but—but he needed a lot more attention. Then"—a long despairing sigh hissed across her lips—"then Myron was murdered."

"How long was McGill treating your son?" I asked.

"For a long time."

"Ever since you and your husband were married?"

"Yes."

"And he didn't mind helping to keep your son's existence a secret?"

"Myron would have done anything I asked of him," she said, and this time the color in her face was not from anger.

I disliked having to ask the next question in front of the children, but it was necessary and there was no way to immediately avoid it.

"McGill was in love with you, was that it?"

"There was nothing between us!" she retorted in defense of their relationship. "We were good friends, and no more. Myron was aware of my marriage and my devotion to my husband and children. He never tried to be anything more than just a good friend, even after Nathan died."

McGill had loved her. In his own way he had made himself a willing slave to this woman whom the years had changed from a youthful beauty to a mass of misshapen flesh. Further questioning would have perhaps extracted such a confession, but it wasn't necessary and I didn't really have to hear it. It was there in her face.

"The other woman in the house," I said. "Luisa. Did she know what was going on here?"

"Luisa was with me long before I met my husband. She is as much a part of this family as are any of us."

"One thing bothers me, Mrs. Danhurst. If your first son was mental, didn't it trouble you about having more children? Especially since the possibility of either Gerry or Sandra getting married and having children seemed to concern you so much. By the time Gerry was born you would have been aware of the state of Clevedon's mental health."

Christine Danhurst shifted uncomfortably in the large rocking chair, as if trying to shrink into its upholstery. She made no effort to answer the question, but for the first time fear brightened her eyes.

"Was Myron McGill that good a friend?" I asked coldly.

"Cameron!" Gerry blurted. "Don't you—"

"Shut up." I told him. "This, I think, is something you and your sister should hear."

Outside a car door slammed and interrupted the proceedings. None of us had heard the car arrive, and with the gate still open there had been no warning from the bell.

Leather soles slapped quickly against stone and then the front door was thrust open. Footsteps trod down the hall to where we were gathered.

The half-closed door was pushed open and Sheriff Walter Mulder walked into the room.

"What the hell's been happening here, Cameron?" he demanded.

"For a change," I said, "people have been talking the truth."

From me he turned to the others.

"Maybe I should hear some of it, huh?"

"You should." And leaving out most of the unnecessary details I filled him in. While I spoke nobody interrupted. But they were no longer watching me. Mulder's arrival had shifted the spotlight.

When I finished he stepped over to where Gerry Danhurst still held his gun on me, took the weapon out of the boy's hand without any trouble, and said:

"Seems like you've managed to get your client off the hook, doesn't it?"

"Seems."

He chuckled. "Imagine it. All the time it's been a loony that's had us bamboozled. You figured out how he killed McGill?"

"He didn't. McGill was killed because he was afraid. He didn't mind covering up for the Danhursts and taking care of the boy, but when it came to murder he couldn't handle it. Perhaps I should say when it came to the second murder."

I waited a few seconds for someone to say something, but none did. "McGill," I said, "was killed with Whitman's gun, and the gun was left behind after the killing so that it would lead us to Whitman. The person who had that gun would either have to have taken it from the dead girl or from Cleve Danhurst. Either way it would appear that person was up there on the road shortly after the girl was attacked."

"Makes sense," Mulder agreed. "There more to it?"

"A little. To start with, I don't think Cleve killed the girl. I think he beat the hell out of her after she shot him. Then he ran away, wounded.

The coroner found indications that a man's boots had been used on her body, remember? That way he wouldn't have spilled blood on her, not if he only kicked her when she was already down. Someone who was out looking for him found the girl and realized what had happened. Let us assume that whoever found her also realized that if she lived she would be able to identify her attacker and blast the lid off the secret the Danhursts had kept guarded all these years.

"The protection of that secret must have been very important to the one who found her. He must have decided it would be better if the girl was to die so that she could never talk. So she was strangled. Then to cover up existing traces of what had happened, the car was rolled further back down the hill into the bush. Afterwards the girl's body was dragged there as well. I found a shell up on the road, but it was several yards from where the car was found. I'm pretty certain that's where the murder really took place, not where the body was eventually found. And the reason for that could only have been to steer your men away from where the attack actually took place, just in case there was still something there— something like a spent .22 shell the killer couldn't find in the dark."

Mulder inclined his head to where Gerry Danhurst stood. The boy backed away to the wall. His mouth opened to protest against the silent charge, but his vocal cords had frozen.

"Whoever took the gun knew enough about such things to make sure it belonged to Whitman," I told them slowly, "not merely to assume ownership because of the initials that were on the butt. That person had to be in a position to check the serial number without arousing curiosity. At the same time that he picked up the gun he also picked up five hundred dollars from the dead girl's purse."

The grin on Mulder's face was wide when he turned to me. It was a grin of cold self-assurance. "Reckon you're pretty damned smart, don't you?"

Ignoring the remark, I said: "After I visited McGill he became scared. He didn't know what I intended doing or how much I knew. He was afraid that unwittingly he had positioned himself where he could be charged as an accomplice in murder. He knew about the girl, and as far as he was concerned the Danhurst boy had killed her. He turned to you for advice, and you in turn, fearing McGill might talk of the wrong things, decided to silence him. You had Whitman's gun and at the time Whitman's position in the business was somewhat precarious. Everything was shaped up nicely so that you could put a knot into each of the loose ends." I shut up, then asked: "Need I go on?"

Still smiling, he shook his head, and the gun taken from Gerry Danhurst was pointing at me. "The question now is what to do with you, Cameron. I've got too much at stake to let you run around blabbing about any of his"

"You've known about the boy for a long time, haven't you?"

Nothing, except the grin.

"How long? Since the Leonard child was killed?"

"Clever," he muttered, moving backward to the door. "Real cute; real clever."

"And instead of doing what you should have you used your knowledge to lever money out of the Danhursts and to promote yourself in this town. Is that how you're able to afford a house like you've got, a flashy car and a mistress? Is that why Christine Danhurst phoned you just now and why you're able to enter this house without knocking? Like McGill, did she expect you to provide protection?"

He was close to the door now, but near to where I was standing. The grin was gone from his face, but he made no attempt to respond to my questions.

While waiting I looked down at his boots. They were shining, not dusty like they'd been the Friday night when I had first met him in his office. The dust from the old road had messed up my own shoes when I had gone out there. It could have been the same dust that had dirtied his boots—after he'd taken care that Bridget Cole would never talk to anyone again.

"On Friday night, after I reported to you about the man I had seen, you made a phone call. Was it to here—to let them know where Cleve had been spotted and where they should look for him?"

"Shut your mouth," he snapped. "You talk too damned much. I should've killed you when I had the chance."

"That was something else I'd nearly forgotten, Sheriff. You left my hotel room shortly before me on Sunday. You had the best opportunity of all to wait and see where I was going, and to follow. When I found that shell you sapped me down to get it because it might in some way have led us to the man who'd been wounded. You didn't want that."

"You're wasting what little breath you've got left, hot-shot. So why don't you shut up and save it?"

"In front of all these witnesses?"

"Mulder . . ." Christine Danhurst ventured.

Either he hadn't heard or didn't want to. He said:

"There won't be witnesses. You've fouled up everything, and now there's only one way left to finish it." He stepped backward, closer to the door so that he could watch all of us. "When I'm finished it'll look like Christine here shot you, then realizing what she'd done, killed the kids and blew her brains out. When we find what's locked up downstairs everyone will understand what happened. There won't be questions."

Sandra sat still mutely in her chair, but her head moved fractionally from one side to the other. Her brother saw this and went to her side.

"You wouldn't dare kill us," he said. "You'd never stand a hope of getting away with it if you tried."

"Oh, crap!" Mulder retorted. "You want to get it first just keep talking like that. I'd figured on letting your little sister here be the one—just in case she starts screaming. I hate screaming women. They unnerve me. But keep yapping and I'll do you the favor of putting you first in line."

Three drawn and frightened faces stared back at him. From the painting on the wall Nathaniel Danhurst looked down upon the scene and his old eyes seemed to possess the knowledge that the end was in sight and that it had been inevitable, that all along he had known it would be like this and had been a long time waiting for it.

The gun in the big man's hand leveled itself at Sandra, the finger whitening around the trigger. The girl cringed back in the chair, hands folded in supplication at her breast. I tensed myself to jump; to do the last possible thing there was left to do. But as I was about to move I saw something in the doorway, the black shadow I'd seen up on the balcony.

Mulder must have sensed something for he suddenly heeled about.

I threw myself down onto the floor and out of the path of the shattering death that thundered through the room like the slamming of a door in hell.

Stray lead slammed into the wall behind where I had been standing and several voices screamed in unison. Mulder's was the loudest, but the shortest. His huge body was flung backward across the floor, landing in a heap near where I had dropped. The small gun was still gripped loosely in his hand, but no shot had been fired.

Slowly I got to my feet. The screaming had stopped, but Sandra was sobbing, loudly, wildly, into her brother's chest. Entering the room came the one thing, the one person Mulder had overlooked; the dark figure of Luisa, the shotgun still in her hands.

"You weren't a moment too soon," I said gratefully. "Or were you standing there all this time?"

"Do not be too grateful, Mr. Cameron," she answered, the shotgun pointed at my middle. "When I saw you arrive with Sandra I sensed trouble. I have been listening to you since. If he"—she motioned with the gun barrel to Mulder's body—"had not arrived, I think I would already have shot you."

"And now, Luisa?"

"That will depend," she said.

"Put down the gun, Luisa," Christine Danhurst instructed. "There will be no more killing." She gave her attention briefly to where Mulder lay before speaking to me. "And you? What will you do now?"

I waited until Gerry had helped his sister out of the room and away from the sight of Mulder's broken body before answering.

"There is only one thing I can do. The authorities will have to be called."

"And everything will be in the papers?" She lifted her plump hands and then let them fall heavily back into her lap. "I suppose it's inevitable now, isn't it?"

"It has to be, Mrs. Danhurst. But at least Gerry and Sandra will now have a better chance. The courts will decide what happens to you, but somehow I can't imagine them being too harsh."

"It matters little," she said. "My years have been numbered for a long time. It is of little importance how what's left is spent. Not anymore."

"Then spare the kids what you can," I urged. "They helped you only because you had them believing they could never live normal lives, that they were like your son. Now tell them the truth."

"What is the truth?" she asked, her voice distant and softer than it had ever been.

"Clevedon looked very much like your husband," I said. "Gerry and Sandra don't. They don't even resemble each other. Surely that thought has occurred to them before now?"

The old woman bowed her head. She said, and there was in her voice a sound that was perhaps the closest she could get to a sob: "Gerry has already questioned that—many times. But they are my children. Whether or not they are my own flesh and blood, they *are* my children."

"And there's nothing wrong with either of them, is there, Mrs. Danhurst?"

"I was afraid to lose them, that's why I told them those things about themselves. Can you understand that? I was wicked and selfish, but I—I was so afraid to be left alone. I couldn't bear the thought of living alone with Cleve, not knowing what would become of him when I died, yet not wanting him locked away." She sighed heavily and raised her head, eyes shifting to focus on the painting of her late husband. "My husband wanted more children, but when Cleve's condition was discovered Dr. McGill warned against it. He helped to arrange private adoptions, keeping it a secret so that no one would ever know. Before we got Gerry I went to New York and spent several months there so that the people here would think I had gone away to have my child. With Sandra it was the same. Nobody ever questioned it. Nathan didn't want it known that he'd been compelled to adopt children. He was a proud man. Such a very proud man . . ."

From the wall the painted image smiled down at her without pity.

I turned away and went to look at Mulder. The badge on his broad chest looked like a miniature starfish in a crimson sea, his face torn and hideous in death.

At the door I paused in front of Luisa who still clung to the shotgun.

"You'd best call the sheriff's office," I advised her. "I'll be waiting outside."

Gerry Danhurst was in the hall when I reached it. He stopped when seeing me.

I asked: "How is Sandra?"

"She'll be all right," he muttered. "But I'm going to call a doctor. She's had a hell of a shock."

I nodded and started to turn away.

"Cameron?"

The question was smeared across his face.

"I think your mother has something to tell you," I said.

"It's true then?"

"Does it make a lot of difference, Gerry?"

"No, I guess not. She's the only mother we've ever known." Self-consciously he rubbed at his jaw, and in that moment the toughness seemed to leave his body and he was just a boy unsure of what next to do. "You still think I'm pretty dumb not to have thought about it before. But I did. Often. Only the conclusions I arrived at weren't nice. I tried not to think too much about it."

"She's waiting for you," I told him.

Outside I hung a cigarette on my lip and lit it. The day was fading into grayness. I looked toward the trees near the big gate and remembered my meeting with Sandra there. Now I knew what had been troubling her that night. It was all part of life's pattern, I had told her. At the time the words had been easy. Easy to say and easy to believe. Now I could only hope that if there was such a pattern, in it there would be a time of happiness for her and her brother.

I was still there, wondering about my own part in the pattern, when the first of the cars arrived.

THE END

THE

SHARP EDGE

ONE

FEET SLITHERED stealthily up to the other side of the door in the rat hole which still posed as an hotel off Third Street in downtown Los Angeles. Through the flaking painted wood a cautious voice asked:

"Who's it?"

"Santa, with ten thousand," I answered, feeling again the neat, tightly wrapped package in my inside pocket. In a side pocket another package bulged uncomfortably, pulling my coat out of shape.

"Got a name?"

I told him what it was.

Another pause, while down the hall the rattling elevator stopped to disgorge a plump and puffy female with a mop of straw hair. Unsteadily she made her way to one of the rooms, checked the number, then fumbled a key in the lock, cursing not softly when it failed to fit the first try. Downstairs someone pressed a button and the elevator creaked and rattled again.

Behind the door at which I waited the voice spoke.

"Who sent you here?"

Straw Hair got the key to cooperate at last and stomped off out of sight.

"Look," I said impatiently, "do you open up or do I go back and tell her you were too scared to show your face?"

He answered with something I couldn't hear before snicking back the lock. The door swung in on a room lit by a single light that tinted everything in it a dull, unpleasant yellow. Even the sallow skin of the man who stood aside waiting for me to enter.

Under a narrow window was an old iron bed, its black paint chipped and scratched. An ashtray loaded with mementos of a wait, a dying bottle and a smeared glass perched on a table next to the bed. A cheap plywood wardrobe, a battered dresser and a kitchen chair shared the rest of the space with a cracked hand-basin and a speckled mirror. Covering the warped floor, a square of scuffed linoleum that contrasted hideously with the blue curtains stirring gently at the open window. Across the street a green and yellow neon blinked out a message concerning the benefits of a certain backache cure. The name was very familiar. Not a room in which to grow rich quickly. But that's the way the man who closed the door and came over to sit on the bed had planned it.

He wore only a shirt and the pants of a gold-fleck suit. Sharp pointed black shoes covered small feet, fastened by cross-straps with decorative silver buckles. Strung over the post at the foot of the bed was the suit coat and a dark red tie. Back in his teens he might have been good-looking, but since then things had been encountered which had etched sour lines into a face that hadn't seen much of the sun in recent years. Dark hair beginning to thin out slightly was heavily lubricated, while down the right side of his face, near the ear, ran a thin white scar that had been the work of something sharp. A droopy mouth was the only fault in an overall presentation of hardness.

He held out a hand that had lost its steadiness. "Okay, leave us not waste time. Give."

"Not so fast. There's a lot of money involved. Got something to prove you're Baxter?"

"What the hell . . .? I'm Baxter. What's there to prove?"

"You may know it. I don't. So let's see something that tells me you're not kidding."

"How about I see the money?" He got up from the bed, fingering the damp collar of his shirt. "How do I know you're not trying to pull something?"

"You don't," I answered. "But my instructions were to hand over the loot to a Dan Baxter, not to just anyone who might be occupying this room."

Sitting down again, his hands appeared to have grown even shakier. "Then we're both wasting time. I'm not carrying identification with me. You got my word, is all. Take it or leave it."

"Supposing I do? What guarantee have I got you'll keep your part of the bargain?"

A hollow laugh gurgled out of his throat. "You got none. But like I told her, I'm not aiming to string this thing out. Once I get the cash I'm cutting out and she won't be hearing from me again."

"And if you don't get it?"

"Then I sing to the papers," he returned quietly as curiosity mixed with uncertainty in his eyes. "They'll eat it up. 'Specially now she's becoming a big name."

I nodded. "Care to tell me the tune?"

Again the laugh. "Balls to you, friend. That's strictly between me and her."

"And ten thousand dollars."

"Yeah, right." He gave me a thin, frozen grin. "Ten thousand. And that's what I'm still waiting to see."

I shrugged and felt inside my coat. "All right. We'll play along with you. But get something straight. There isn't going to be any more. This is the first and the last payment. Trouble her again and you'll find yourself holding the wrong end of a very dirty stick." I flipped the package onto the bed. "Count it. I'd hate to be accused of trying to short change someone like you."

Eagerly he ripped away the paper protecting the one hundred century notes. While he busied himself with that I sneaked open the two drawers in the dresser. Both were empty. He was counting the money and didn't bother to look up when I stepped over to the flimsy wardrobe, turned the tarnished key and opened the door. Except for an expensive leather suitcase, that too was empty. I took out the suitcase.

"Hey! What the hell you think you're doing?" He was up from the bed, the wad of money open like a hefty fan in his left hand.

"Just move in?"

"What's it to you?" he snapped back.

I dropped the case on the bed.

"And obviously not planning to stay very long, were you, Mr. Baxter?"

"You nuts or something?" There was more he wanted to say, but as a certain disturbing thought began to penetrate, he switched the theme. "What's your game, Mac?"

From the side pocket of my coat I pulled loose the other item and handed it to him. After a moment's hesitation he took it gingerly, his narrowed gaze glued to my face.

"That's something else for you. A sort of bonus for all the trouble my client's been put to."

While he gaped at the oblong box I bent down and unsnapped the locks of the suitcase. He made a tired attempt to stop me, but with both hands occupied he didn't stand much of a chance. I elbowed him back onto the bed and it seemed to cancel out any similar notions he might have had.

"I get it," he announced, a faint smile trying hard for a place on his face. "You think the stuff I got on the dame is in there maybe. Well you're wrong, Mac." He tapped the side of his skull with the black velvet-covered box. "It's all up here, and that's where it stays now I been paid. That's the deal, ain't it?"

When the clothes inside the suitcase were sufficiently disarrayed, I straightened up, lifted his coat from the bed post and went to sit on the hard chair near the door.

The bed springs received a little further exercise as once again he tried to get to his feet. I reached across to my left hip and brought the .38 Colt Agent out to where he could view it.

It stopped him.

"You haven't looked at your present," I reminded softly.

His glance flitted from the gun to the black box to the coat held across my knees. "There—there's nothing in there."

"Open the box. Or aren't you interested?"

A reluctant hand laid aside the money as he prepared to open the box. I watched carefully. For a full thirty seconds he gaped at the contents. It was worth gaping at. Lips moved soundlessly when at last he let the lid snap closed and placed the box carefully next to the money. A pale tongue sneaked out and rubbed itself against the corner of his mouth.

"What—what's it all about?"

"The necklace? It's part of some jewelry lifted from a home in Beverly Hills last night. Or haven't you heard? Some people named Rigby had a visitor while they were out. A burglary, Mr. Baxter."

"So what? What's it got to do with me?"

"I received a tip," I answered, "that you could tell us something more about it. That's one of the reasons I'm here."

"You crazy?" he almost yelled. "I never seen that thing before now—before you gave it to me!

"We'll see. Last night the Beverly Hills cops picked up a few fingerprints at the Rigby house. I'm willing to bet they'll match those on the clasp of that jewelry case. How about you?"

He made a grab for the case, but I moved the gun and he left it alone. "A frame! A dirty, stinking frame!" he screamed. But doubt strained the force of the accusation.

"Someone will be joining us shortly," I informed him. "Try telling him that. In the meantime, let's find out who you really are."

"You know my name; I told it to you," he protested feebly while I felt in the pockets of his coat and found his wallet.

"Sure." I looked toward the window. "But I can also read. Like that sign outside, for instance."

Very slowly his head turned in the direction of the open window.

Colored neon continued to blink out its message: *Aching Backs Receive Instant Relief With Baxter's Balm.*

"Perhaps you should have drawn the curtains before I arrived." Letting the coat fall to the floor, I opened the wallet with my left hand.

Inside were two old letters, a few dollars, a small collection of cards and a driver's license issued to one Frank Antonio Cugino at Taywood, California, in 1943. I slid it back and let the wallet drop onto the coat.

Sweat beaded the sallow face as he sat trying to grasp the situation.

"What's it you want?"

"Nothing, Frankie. It's out of my hands now. From here on the law will have to decide what happens."

"This her idea?" he demanded sullenly. "She dream up this caper? Or was it your personal brainwave?"

"Knock it off, Cugino. You talk like you've been done an injury. Yet you're the lad who had ideas of blackmail and burglary. Anyone would think we were trying to hang something on you."

Cugino nodded, picked up the money, examined it briefly, then put it down again. "There's something you haven't figured, smart guy. You and the cops try to plant a thing like this on me and I'll yell my head off about what I got on that chick. Let's see how smug you'll look then. A thing like this could cripple her career. I mean cripple, but good. She'd be dead in the business."

I shook my head. "The police have agreed to cooperate with us. Whatever you've got to sing about will go no further than the police records. If that far. Unlike you, they're not concerned in trying to smear people. Besides, just exactly what do you think you know that's so important?"

Ignoring the question, he said: "You forgotten the papers? Certain rags go big for something like this."

"They'll be taken care of," I told him. "The studios carry a lot of weight."

Before he could come up with something else there was a loud knock at the door. Cugino jumped no more than a foot.

I got up from the chair.

"It's open."

A big man with a hard red face and a protruding middle came into the room and shut the door loudly. His hat was tipped to the side of his head and in the corner of his mouth dangled a thick cigarette that moved continuously as his jaw made slow chewing movements. He looked every inch what he was supposed to be.

"Meet Sergeant Runyon," I told Cugino who was lamping the huge man with added uneasiness. "The sergeant's interested in some missing jewelry."

"This the punk?" Runyon asked.

"That's him. Frank Cugino. And that's something I found in the room. Seems we got here just in time. He was all packed to leave."

"You touched that stuff, Cameron?" His deep voice was all business.

"Uh-huh, but you'll find at least one of his prints still on it."

Cugino's face was damp and glistening. "You dirty bastards!" he spat. "You lousy, stinking—"

Runyon let the cigarette fall from his mouth, put a number ten shoe on it and took the two long steps that brought him up to the smaller man. His hand lashed out and sent Cugino down hard onto the bed.

"Want to repeat that?" he inquired mildly.

Cugino didn't.

Runyon produced a handkerchief, wrapped it carefully around the velvet box and wedged it into his pocket.

"We found the other stuff," he told us gruffly. "This jerk must've dropped it in the dark and got too scared to go back and look for it. This's the only item still unaccounted for." To Cugino, he said: "On your feet, punk. You and me are taking a little ride."

The man on the bed sized him up, decided against resistance, and slowly raised himself.

"Just a minute, Sergeant." I touched his arm. "We had a deal, remember?"

"Sure." He paused to shape up a contented grin. "But this cat's for us now. We'll keep the lid on this thing he's supposed to have on your client. Let him open his yap just one teeny little bit and he'll wish his head was made of rubber. We know how to handle his kind, and we know how to take care of the press. There'll be no publicity. You have my word on it."

"All the same," I insisted, "I'd prefer not to take chances. You've got back the necklace and I'm fairly certain that's all Rigby will want. Whether or not Cugino is put away won't bother him very much."

"You suggesting I turn him loose?" Runyon asked with pronounced astonishment. "This guy's a cheap little crook, he's—"

"Perhaps he'll deal with you," I said. "Perhaps he'll prefer to save the state some expenditure and himself a lot of inconvenience."

Runyon screwed up his large face and pondered the suggestion. It didn't take him long enough, I thought.

"Okay, Cameron. I still owe you a favor or two. What's it you got in mind?"

"In return for his immediate release get him to promise to clear out of California and forget he ever heard of my client."

"A promise? Him?" He chuckled deeply. "You got to be kidding, kid. A punk like this doesn't know the meaning of a promise. Soon's he was out of our way he'd try it all over again."

"Then you'd know how to handle it, wouldn't you? You've got his prints, and without too much effort I think you could dig up a little more on him. Say something that would net him twenty years or so in the shade."

"Yeah," Runyon muttered. "Yeah, I could maybe do that. And something tells me it won't be hard to do either." He turned sharply back to Cugino, "Where've I heard your name before, punk?"

The sallow face grew startled. He shook his head vigorously. "You got nothing on me."

"Says you," Runyon charged. "Well? You heard the man. What's it to be? Ride with me, or let us take a chance on you losing your memory?"

Cugino shrugged his shoulders. "I got a choice?"

"A helluva lot better one than you deserve. So make up your mind. I'm not enjoying this crummy room so much I want to spend the night sharing it with you."

"I'll blow." The voice was very soft.

"Right out!" the big man growled, the sound only a fraction softer than thunder. "You got twenty minutes to blow this fleabag and start for the state line. And,"—he grabbed a fistful of Cugino's shirt—"pull a stunt like you tried down here and I'll nail you no matter where you happen to be. And when I do you can be damned sure there won't be anyone around to remind me of favors I owe."

"I said I'm going," Cugino complained. "What else you want? A signed contract?"

"Don't give me ideas, punk. I might just make use of them." He shoved the sweating Cugino in the direction of the open suitcase. "Start packing. Twenty minutes don't allow time for leisure."

While Cugino hastily bundled his clothes back into the suitcase I stepped around Runyon's big frame and retrieved the money from the bed. Peeling loose one of the bills I pushed it into Cugino's hand.

"Here's train fare. Use it all."

"You're too soft," Runyon admonished sourly.

"Yeah," I grunted. "I'll leave you to see him off."

"Sure. Run along. Sonny Boy here ain't going to try any double-cross. Are you, punk?"

Frankie Cugino went on packing.

Runyon spun him around.

"I asked you a question!"

"I won't try anything. I'll cut like I said." His face was a mask of glistening sweat now and I had a funny feeling that the pressure Runyon was exerting was not the sole cause of it. There was the smell of fear about him.

I walked to the door, took another look back, and exited.

Out on the street I sat in my car, lit a cigarette and waited. From there I had an unobstructed view of the hotel entrance.

Ten minutes later Runyon appeared, his hand on Cugino's shoulder to help him on his way. A few words were exchanged as they stood on the sidewalk. Cugino pointed down the street. Runyon nodded, gave his companion a shove that sent him stumbling, placed another cigarette in his mouth and came over to where I was parked. Cugino kept going, not once looking back. The leather suitcase slapped against his leg as he went.

The door on the curb side opened and Runyon put his bulk down on the seat next to me.

"In case you're interested, he's got a car parked further down the line."

"I am," I said. "Let's find out where he's going."

I turned the key in the ignition, got the engine ticking over and waited until a car pulled out onto the street.

"That's it."

"Check," I answered, tramping enough gas into the engine to get us moving.

"I do okay?" Runyon asked.

"You nearly had me believing it," I said. "Anytime you get tired of loafing you could try out for TV."

He chuckled softly. "Hell, I had enough practice, didn't I?"

Observing all the traffic rules, Cugino tooled his brown Chevy toward the boulevard and stayed with it until hitting Venice. We remained a safe distance behind, neither saying very much.

At Barry the Chevy made a left turn, slowed down and rolled up into a slot near a small apartment block—a drab piece of pink stucco with only a few lights behind the windows to lend it any appearance of brightness.

"Want me to follow?" Runyon asked when I switched off the car's lights and swung in against the curb.

I nodded and he got out, ambling down the street at a deceivingly casual pace.

A soft breeze that tinged the air with the scent of the sea had turned the night cool. Recorded music echoed from a distant window. There was nothing else to see or hear.

Runyon returned in less than five minutes.

"Number eight. Mailbox says it belongs to someone named Rose Lang. Do we wait?"

"No need for you to hang around," I answered. "You've done your part. Me too for that matter."

"But you're going to wait and see what happens, huh?"

"I don't have a wife at home, Vic."

"This wasn't your idea, was it?" The way he said it, it wasn't a question;

'No."

"And you don't think much of it either, huh?"

"I don't have to. It's the way he insisted I play it," I said by way of an explanation. "Anyway, he's paying the tab and I've done exactly as instructed."

"You think Cugino bought that line we handed him?"

I made a shrug he probably missed. "I hope so, Vic."

"Me," Runyon said quietly, "I think it stinks. I was a cop too long to believe in promises made by Cugino's kind. He'll try again. You can make book on that. Hell, he knows that once he's out of town, never mind the state, we'd have one sweet time finding him again. He could go away and start the trouble all over. Then what?"

I didn't comment.

Minutes later he again spoke: "Think I'll ship off. Unless there's something else you want me for?" He took the jewel case from his pocket, freed it from the handkerchief and placed it next to my thigh.

I told him there wasn't and thanked him for his help. He got out of the car, touched his hat and started off up the street in search of a cab. I watched his impressive figure fade away in the dim reflection of the rearview mirror. An ex-cop who took it quiet and easy these days. A big humorous man who knew how to be tough and who was less than putty in the hands of the woman who'd been his wife for nearly thirty years. But though happily retired, Runyon was the kind of ex-cop who could never resist the sort of job I had offered him that morning.

Sit alone in a dark car on a quiet street at that time of the night and you can entertain a strange line in thoughts. Like of Vic Runyon, for instance, and his wife and the home they shared out on Cortlia Way, of the difference between it and the place where Ross Rigby lived—the man who had hired me. The big-time agent who had insisted upon all the fancy stage work in spite of my protests. And thinking of them inevitably brought me back to Allison Page . . .

Exactly what Frankie Cugino had on her I never knew. Rigby had declined to provide that information and Allison Page I had not even met. But I knew of her and about her. Her voice was as familiar to my ears as my own. And perhaps that was why I had agreed to working in the dark, why I had taken on the kind of assignment that would normally have received a flat rejection.

The thoughts were at the point of becoming depressing when Cugino appeared on the narrow sidewalk. He carried another suitcase and was concerned only with getting to his car. If he knew I or anyone else was watching, it didn't appear to bother him.

I stuck on his tail along the Pacific Coast Highway until we crossed the city limits, and only then did I notice that his car was wearing New York registration plates. He kept traveling, making no stops. A few miles beyond Topanga Beach I gave it up, turned around and started back.

It looked as if he was keeping his part of the deal. The first part, anyway.

TWO

IT was long after eleven when I passed Linden and Roxbury and the other drives where many of the big name stars have set up house. But Ross Rigby had insisted that I report personally as soon as the job had been completed, and a personal report he was about to get.

At Beverly Drive I departed from the Santa Monica Boulevard and continued up to the six-point intersection at the Will Rogers Park. No less than two police cruisers slowed down as they passed, their occupants giving my two-year-old heap the practiced once over. It was natural enough. If there's another place as well policed as Beverly Hills, nobody has ever told me about it. They didn't stop me, but on the rest of the way to the big house that overlooked part of Benedict Canyon I found myself being less generous with the gas.

A broad black-topped drive swept in behind huge olive trees that screened nearly all of the house. Lights glowed from behind several draped windows and out on the drive waited a silver Stingray that didn't shrink away when the Plymouth pulled in at its gleaming rear.

Rigby answered the door personally. Between large white teeth he held a long black cigarette holder and a freshly lit filter-tip. Perhaps someone had been telling him too much about lung cancer. Relief showed in his face upon seeing who had prodded the bell.

"Ah!" he piped, taking the holder from his mouth. "Cameron. I was beginning to get concerned." A carefully manicured hand waved me inside. "Come in. We'll use the study."

The study could have accommodated the better part of my apartment, and that which it missed wouldn't have been very important. Thick tufted carpet capable of hiding a Pekinese between cleanings covered the floor from wall to pine-paneled wall. Shelves of beautifully bound books and a small collection of tasteful watercolors were on prominent display. Hogging a lot of carpet near a glass sliding door which faced out onto an illuminated swimming pool was a carved oak desk that probably cost twice as much as the down payment on the Corvette parked outside. A leather couch and a few club chairs had been strategically placed around a broad natural stone fireplace, spoiled only by the electric heater nestling in the hearth.

Rigby stepped behind the desk after inviting me to sit down, slid back a panel of the wall and asked: "Can I offer you a shot of something before we get started?"

I studied the array of bottles with appreciation.

"Whisky wouldn't hurt."

"Bourbon, Scotch or Irish?"

I said it didn't matter. I wasn't that much of a drinker.

Between the time of pouring the drinks and bringing them around to where I sat in front of the desk he had disposed of the cigarette and the onyx holder. On the street the high-class flesh peddler could easily be mistaken for a prosperous doctor, or even a college professor. His hair was heavily streaked with gray and over his eyes were plain rimless spectacles. It wasn't until you got around to noticing the darkness of his skin, which was probably the result of exposure to a sun lamp, the broad band of gold with the big green stone entwined around the little finger of his right hand, the cut of his clothes, and caught the ready smile that your first impression would undergo a quick revision. It might well have been his deceptive appearance that had brought him the success and luxury by which he was surrounded.

I took my drink, sipped at it and waited for him to get parked. The stuff in the glass was a high jump from the brands I could usually afford.

"Well? How'd it go? He buy it?"

"Exactly as you predicted," I replied, removing the package of money from my pocket to slide it across the desk. "You'll find a bill missing. I gave it to him to buy distance."

Picking up the money, Rigby glanced at it briefly before shoving it carelessly aside as if it were no more than the colored confetti they used when filming. For a moment I wondered about its true value. He tasted his drink, set down the glass, leaned back in the upholstered chair and started chuckling.

"Didn't I tell you?" he asked, putting the brakes on the laughter. "Didn't I say you were too pessimistic?"

"You did, and I'm afraid I still am. When you outlined what you wanted done it sounded too fancy—too phony to work. It seemed even phonier when we pulled it."

"Ah, but Baxter's gone, hasn't he?"

"He's gone."

"Which means *he* believed it." He reached for the glass and disposed of a little more of the iced bourbon. "Baxter accepted the play because he didn't know it was phony. You, on the other hand, were uneasy because you realized that in a pinch we could never make our threats stick. That's if he insisted upon forcing the issue. My boy," he went on, "it's probably an occupational hazard of people in show business, but blackmail is something that has touched several of my clients too many times. I've had to devise a way of dealing with these people. The act you set up for Baxter has been worked not only tonight, but a number of times before. I say worked because so far we've always come out on top. I've no reason to believe this time will be any different." Some more of the drink found its way down his throat before he smiled with satisfaction. "Come on, drink up and don't look so damned glum. Drink up and tell me exactly what happened."

"There is one consolation," I said. "I don't think he was a pro. The way he handled the thing was too clumsy. Also, he was scared. Why, I can't explain. But I don't think it was simply us jumping him that brought on the sweat."

Rigby went on smiling. "Tell me what happened. From the beginning."

"To start with, his name isn't Baxter. It's Frank Antonio Cugino." If the name meant anything to him he didn't let it show. I carried on, leaving out nothing, and by the time I arrived at the part where Cugino was still traveling after having left the city, my drink was finished. I put the empty glass on the edge of the desk then felt in my pocket and produced the jewel case. "Mrs. Rigby will want this back." I placed it next to the glass.

Light dancing in his eyes, Rigby sat watching silently from behind the rimless spectacles. "By damn!" he said softly. "I wish I could have been there. I'd have given a bundle to see his face."

"Then you're satisfied?"

"Perfectly." He got up and walked around the desk. I stood and he had to reach up to clap a hand on my shoulder. "Naturally I had every confidence it would go off smoothly, but it needed the right man to put it across. I'm satisfied, my boy, and to prove it"—his hand left my shoulder and dipped into his coat pocket—"and to prove how sure I was of success, I took the liberty of preparing this in advance. I think it'll take care of your fee and any expenses you've incurred. Take a look, and if it isn't enough, say so."

I opened the unsealed envelope. Inside was his personal check for five hundred dollars.

"It looks a little excessive."

"Don't be funny. When a man saves you ten thousand dollars and maybe a lot of unwanted publicity, a sum like that is piddling." His smile was that of a much-pleased child. "Put it away."

I did.

"One other thing," he said, retaining the smile. "If ever again I need a man in your line you can be sure I'll be calling your number. And that goes for anyone else to whom I can recommend you."

I said thanks, putting out a hand which he seized and pumped vigorously.

"Ah, but don't trot off right away," he said. "There's someone else who's insisted on saying thanks."

Behind me I sensed the presence of a third party, and turned around. The door to the study had been left open and her footsteps had made no sound on the thick carpet.

Though tiny, no more than five foot and a bit, she was formed to absolute perfection, looking ten times better than the miniature version I'd seen many times on TV. A petite blue-eyed honey blonde whose hair curled softly around her face to accentuate the gentle tan. Sparkling white teeth showed between lips parted in a smile that was all warmth and friendliness.

"Mr. Cameron?" The long tapering fingers of her small hand reached up and got lost in my paw.

". . . Miss Page . . .?"

There had been blondes before. Bigger and better stacked and loaded with all the sex and know-how that's supposed to make a man's juices run faster. She was none of these and my pulse rate didn't even budge. Yet my voice sounded like an old man's dying croak.

At last she took back her hand. "As Ross said, I did want to thank you personally. And I do—most sincerely. Thank you." The last was a throaty whisper.

For me there was nothing to say.

"Please don't be angry that I eavesdropped," Allison Page continued softly. "It's just that I didn't share Ross's confidence. I was afraid of the worst."

"You weren't the only one lacking confidence," I replied, noticing the small frown that had crept onto her forehead. "Anyway, it's over now."

"All over, Mr. Cameron?"

Before I could answer, Rigby said: "Of course it's all over, darling. Didn't I promise you everything would be all right? You can go home now and forget the entire thing ever happened."

I looked at my watch. "It's time I also rolled."

"Won't you stay for one more drink?" the little blonde asked, and in the invitation there was all the sincerity of an earnest desire. But most likely I had just wanted it to sound that way.

When finally I answered it seemed like I had taken too long to decide. "I'd like to, very much. But there are still one or two things I have to do tonight."

"Then perhaps in the very near future." And again she let me have her tiny hand.

"Sure." And I wondered what the odds were against that ever happening.

At the door Rigby and Allison Page again extended thanks, then watched while I descended the steps to my car.

Behind the wheel I again reassured myself that declining her invitation had been the bright thing to do. Allison Page fitted in too well with my ideas of the ideal woman, and the circle which had accepted her was still not for people like me. A woman joined Allison and Rigby as I drove away. Until then I hadn't thought about the whereabouts of his wife.

Arriving at my apartment I hung up my coat, unclipped the gun from my belt and loosened my tie before going into the kitchen to prepare something to eat. While the coffee percolated I went back to the living room, sorted through a pile of discs and placed two on the record player. Her clear soprano carried through to the kitchen. It was a familiar voice in those surroundings.

I poured a cup of coffee and paused to listen as the opening chords of *The Italian Street Song* rang through the apartment. The number ended. I looked up from the steaming coffee cup and in doing so caught my reflection in the glass door of a wall cabinet.

It sneered back and my own voice growled: "Grow up, why don't you?"

2

Sunday morning was spent locating a witness to an auto accident, while a large part of that night was consumed in tracking down a partner of an Oregon organization who had taken an extended leave of absence from his office. I found him holed up in an apartment with a kid not much older than twenty and enough booze to pickle them both for eternity. I left him there sleeping off the long drunk and phoned his partner to fly down and make the collection. Monday started off with all the promise of being one of those days when not even the telephone would be exercised. The morning mail brought only one letter of any significance; from a woman in Glendale who wanted an appointment to discuss the possibility of gathering evidence to take into a divorce court. I put it aside for later and began typing up a report that was owing to one of the out-of-state agencies for whom I occasionally worked.

Only a few minutes after signing the report and sliding it into an envelope for mailing, the telephone jangled.

No secretary made the connection. The call came direct from Rigby's desk.

"Cameron, something's happened. I have to see you right away."

"Want me to come over?"

"No, stay put. I'll be there in under twenty minutes." I couldn't see his face but I'd have laid odds on it being minus the usual smile.

"I'll be here," I promised, and hung up to wait.

The buzzer fixed to the door of the reception room squawked exactly eighteen minutes later. I got up from behind the desk.

Rigby wasn't smiling when I opened the door. He was worried and looked more like a college professor than ever. I ushered him in, waited until he was seated and then lowered myself into the new swivel chair which was the start of a refurnishing plan.

"He got to her again," he said, inspecting the office quickly and wasting no time with preliminaries. "Last night he phoned her and right afterwards she left to meet him."

"With money?"

He nodded. "I don't know, but I'm reasonably sure she took it with her. It was hers, the stuff you used the other night. I returned it to her before she left my place."

"She tell you about Cugino's call?"

"Not a word. And I wouldn't have found out about it either had I not gone to her house this ayem. And the only reason I did that," he explained, "was because she had an appointment at my office for nine. When she didn't put in an appearance I phoned her home. The maid told me she'd left at about eight-thirty last night, taking an overnight bag with her."

"Then it was the maid who told you about the contact?"

"She didn't know it was Cugino, of course," Rigby said with a swift wag of his head. "All she knew was that someone phoned Allison last night and that whatever was discussed had a most upsetting effect on the girl. After the call she piled a few essentials into an overnight case and told Terry—that's her maid—she might not be back until early this morning."

"What makes you so sure this has anything to do with Cugino?"

"What else would make her break an important appointment with me and take off without a word to anyone?" he asked, his tone insinuating that I wasn't too bright this morning. "Allison's not like that. She has a great deal of consideration for other people. Sometimes too much, I think. Unless she had a damned good reason for breaking the appointment she wouldn't have stood me up. Not without first phoning to explain. It isn't her style. Besides, the appointment this morning was almighty important to her."

"Still—"

"And there was this," he said, ignoring what I had started to say. From between the folds of a gold-edged wallet he removed a small pink square of paper and pushed it across the desk.

The paper measured about four inches square and was totally devoid of writing.

Rigby elucidated: "That's the top sheet of a telephone note pad I found in her room. The impression of whatever she jotted down on the preceding sheet is on that piece."

I nodded, already trying to read it. The handwriting was a neat light script that hadn't made much indentation.

"Looks like Vadear Point or something," I suggested.

"That's what I took it to be," the bespectacled agent agreed. "There's more, but I can't decipher it."

"That's two of us then."

"Do you know where that place is—Vadear Point?"

"Up along the coast in San Luis Obispo County, I think."

"It is," he confirmed. "I checked it on the map before coming here."

"And?"

"Can you go up there? Right away?" There was an eagerness and an out of place urgency in his words. "God knows what this bastard Cugino is playing at, but the kid may be barging into trouble."

I pushed myself up out of the chair.

"I can leave in a half hour. You coming with me?"

"No," he answered, also rising. "I can't. I've got to be at the studio within the hour. That's why it was so necessary I see Allison this morning. We're negotiating a contract for her first picture. With the success she's had on records and television, and now that they're making better musicals again, well. . . ." Breaking off the rest he fell silent, before muttering: "I was an idiot, wasn't I?"

"About Cugino?"

"Yes, about Cugino. I should have listened to you instead of being so damned cocksure of my plan."

"It worked before, you said. You thought it had a good chance of doing so again." I picked up the pink square and slid it into my pocket. "What exactly do you want me to do now, Mr. Rigby?"

"First find Allison. Make sure she's done nothing that can make for future trouble. If she hasn't already contacted Cugino, make sure she doesn't."

"And then?"

He hesitated before answering, as if deciding precisely what action he wanted. "Get her back here. Cugino I'll leave to you. Do anything you consider necessary, just as long as it doesn't invite publicity. I've stressed that point before, so I don't need to go into details again. Allison, at this stage of her career, can't stand up against that kind of thing."

"There's only one way to handle him. You know that, don't you?"

"Just as long as it doesn't mean publicity, I don't care what you do. From here on you've got *carte blanche.*"

"I asked you this before," I said slowly, "and you declined to answer. I'm asking you again now, and this time I wish you'd try trusting me. What is it Cugino's holding over her?"

Elegantly tailored shoulders shrugged then slumped wearily. "I declined simply because I didn't know. I still don't, and so I still can't enlighten you. It isn't that I don't feel free to trust you, Cameron, or that I don't want to break a client's confidence. It's just that I've no real knowledge of what it's all about. Allison wouldn't even tell me."

"But you've formed some ideas."

"Only the very vaguest. A possible indiscretion in her past. I don't know. That's the usual thing in a case like this. Allison could have done something that Cugino knows about, or . . ."

"Or he could be an acquaintance from her past?" I offered.

Rigby's answer was a reluctant one. "There is that possibility, of course, and I've not overlooked it. The man, however, is a complete stranger to me. I'd never heard mention of him before."

He drew back his sleeve and checked his watch.

I took the hint and asked for details of the car she would be driving.

3

After packing a few things into a grip, arranging with my answering service to take care of incoming calls, and filling the car with gas, I started off on U.S.101 to Vadear Point.

It took nearly three hours to reach the place. Where the sign pointed west I swung off the highway and followed a partially paved road down toward the rocky coast holding the Pacific at bay. At my right the Coastal Range loomed large and smug, while inside the car the heat was starting to become slightly oppressive. A few cars passed, some traveling fast enough to send little pebbles rocketing into the air to bounce off the Plymouth's side. Another sign cropped up further ahead, announcing to all weary travelers that only a half mile further waited the Crescent Palm, a dozen modern units and TV at reasonable rates.

Something gelled at sight of the sign and I pulled to the side of the road, took the piece of pink paper Rigby had given me, and again inspected the faint impressions. Vadear Point was still distinct enough, and that was about where I was. The rest of the wording could well have been Crescent Palm. It could also have been a hundred other things. Resting in my pocket the shallow indentations hadn't grown any clearer.

I drove on.

A rainbow of pastel colors appeared suddenly at the right of the road, and up front were even a few tall and healthy palms poking up between ornamental shrubs sporting bright red blooms. It wasn't necessary to read the sign to know what the place was, but I found myself looking around, trying to establish the motive for the "crescent" part of the name. There wasn't anything noticeable, but what I did see looked brighter and a lot better than many of the places that had rented me a bed in recent years. Even though the amount of cars parked on the concrete apron suggested business was not all it might be. I drove in through the single entrance cut into a low white wall, moving slowly so that I could check out the cars. The one I wanted had been docked crookedly in the last bay, the off-side wheels straddling the black painted dividing line.

I parked next to the silver Stingray, checked the registration number Rigby had given me, and then stepped out onto the warm concrete. As if admiring the owner's choice of transport I moved around the badly parked car. The number on the plates tallied with the one in my pocket. I walked toward the building nestling in the middle of clustered geraniums, on the wall of which a small sign said: OFFICE.

It was empty, but from behind a closed door leading to somewhere beyond came the sound of a voice raised in anger. Not that it was any of my business, or that I was remotely interested, but I waited and listened. The door was too thick to hear much, so I struck the bell on the desk. It made a louder noise than expected of something its size, and faded into

silence the voice behind the door. A moment later the door opened and a
squat man with closely cropped black hair, thick black eyebrows that
knitted across the bridge of his nose, and heavily muscled shoulders,
strode slowly into the office. He looked surprised to find a customer.
Then remembering his face still boasted a scowl, quickly exchanged it
for a smile that showed lots of teeth.

"Howdy. Didn't hear you drive in. Accommodation?"

"If there's a vacancy."

"Just you?" he asked. And after I'd confirmed that fact: "Easy right
now. Later may not be so easy. That's when the place starts to fill up."
From a box behind the counter he selected a printed card and gave it to
me together with a ballpoint pen. "Fill that in and I'll get your things.
Unit's ten bucks a day and you can watch TV all you want. No charge."

I completed the card and returned it to him along with two five dollar
bills. "That's for tonight. I'm not sure how long I'll be staying."

"Just let me know when you're ready," he said, taking the money then
the card. "But try to make it early, will you? Sometimes we get a rush on
sudden like, and 'less I have to, I don't want to turn nobody away."

I promised I would and was about to ask about the silver car when I
noticed a woman standing in the doorway. Upon seeing me she came all
the way into the office, offering a small nod of greeting, but no expression. She went directly behind the counter and started fussing with a
bunch of papers that lay there. Her hair was tinted a shade of auburn and
she still sported a fairly good figure in spite of breasts and hips that the
years had made heavy. Her face was handsome, somewhere in the last
part of its thirties, and one which in a not so long ago youth would have
been pretty. The man glanced sideways at her but said nothing. The tension between them was a thing that reached out and touched.

"Let's go," he suggested, taking a key from a drawer hidden from
view.

A white T-shirt stretched tightly across his back and blue beach-
comber jeans were like a second skin around thick legs and waist. He
looked like an ex-light-heavyweight, but there was a roll to his walk that
seemed to suggest some of his life had been spent at sea.

I said: "Disagreement with the wife?"

He looked up. "You heard us, huh?"

"Not what was said. Besides, it wasn't any of my business. Forget I
asked."

The muscular shoulders shifted restlessly. "Nah, it was nothing. We
often get a little hot around the collar. This time it was about the bill for
the paint. Notice all the unit's got new colors?"

"I noticed," I admitted.

"Figured if we're going to have to buck the competition in town we
better brighten the place up. We got a good place here and I got lots of
plans for it," he told me proudly.

"Sounds like it's a recent acquisition."

"You mean like we just bought it?" he questioned. "Nah, we got it for a year now. That's nearly as long as me and Ann have been married." He laughed at some private thought. "Guess that's why we fight, huh? Newly-weds?"

They didn't look newly married but I was prepared to take his word for it. There were other things I was more interested in. "They say the first years are the hardest," I said as we stopped at my car. "But it's only something I heard. I've never tried it yet."

When the trunk was unlocked he reached in for my bag. "You oughta try it. It's a good life. 'Specially when you got something to work for. Like me, I got this place. I'm going to make it something, you watch and see. One day this'll be the biggest and best motel along this part of the coast. I got plans."

He was about to move away and continue talking after I slammed the lid shut. Then he saw what I was looking at.

"Nice, huh?"

I nodded. "Very."

"A beauty." He laughed quickly. "But a wreck compared to what's driving it."

"Blonde?"

"Nah." He shook his head and frowned at the way the car had been parked. "Brunette. But who can tell about a dame's hair these days, huh?"

The grip shifted from one hand to the other. It wasn't that heavy, but I accepted the hint.

Inside the unit it smelled of fresh paint, but whoever had wielded the brush had not gone crazy with color. Perhaps the wife had some say about the interiors.

"My name's Newton," the dark man announced, depositing the bag on a stand near the door. "Mike Newton. You want anything just lift the phone. There's no restaurant yet, but it's coming. I fixed up a cool little bar in the meantime, and if you do get hungry during the day it's only a couple minutes drive into town. Mornings ain't no problem. I'll bring coffee and if you want something light the wife can fix it. No problem."

When I was alone at last I got rid of my coat and shook a smoke loose from the pack. With the curtains drawn slightly apart it was possible to watch the row of parked cars. I sat down upon the bed and considered ways of making contact with the owner of the Corvette without having to ask Newton any more questions. Short of knocking on the other eleven doors, the only solution appeared to be to sit and watch and hope she would decide to use her car soon.

The wait ended before it had hardly begun. A girl appeared carrying a small blue overnight bag. She wore a pale lemon dress and a matching peasant scarf that concealed most of her hair. I stubbed out the cigarette in a cheap ashtray and got up fast, reaching for my coat. Enough of her hair showed to prove Newton correct. She was a brunette. But Allison Page was a too familiar memory for me to be taken in by a black wig.

By the time I got the door open she was in the car, tucked in behind the wheel. I broke into a run, wanting to shout after her, yet hesitant about using her name. Before I was halfway to the parking lot there was a roar from the engine as the car reversed jerkily, pausing only while she straightened the wheels to thrust the flat nose at the single exit. There was still a slim chance of stopping her, but whatever plans I had were promptly rearranged by the sudden appearance of another car converging too fast upon the motel.

The two vehicles arrived at the entrance within short seconds of each other. The Corvette swung hard to the right in a frantic effort to avoid the other car, cleared its fenders by less than half an inch, got a grip on the road and then shot off in a screeching streak of silver. The other driver wasn't that good. When at last he brought his wagon to a stop it was angled across the entrance with the motor stalled. A door burst open and the driver leapt out, yelling loud uncomplimentary things about crazy females and an equally insane law that permitted them licenses to drive. The twin exhausts of the Stingray replied with a loud raspberry.

I stood where I stopped, listening to the verbal rockets being fired at the departing car, now only a gleaming speck in the distance. It was too late to consider following it.

Allison Page would be well on her way to L.A. or any other place south before the entrance was cleared and I was able to get my own car out on the road. The trip looked like a washout.

The driver of the stalled ranch wagon, a tall freckle-faced number with a blank spot in the centre of his pale hair, turned around, saw me and quickly forgot about the near collision.

"Hey!" he shouted. "Hey!"

I went to him.

"Got a phone I can use? Emergency!" His sunburned face was sweated and he looked both scared and excited.

"In there," I said, directing a thumb at the office. "Trouble?"

Suspicion slithered quickly into his eyes as he licked his lips uncertainly. But we both knew he was too agitated to keep whatever was bothering him a secret.

"Plenty! But not mine. I have to call the police." He swallowed hard and added loudly: "Back there—there on the beach—a dead guy!" The Adam's apple wobbled when he took another deep swallow. "Geeze, what a lousy mess!"

The red face contorted itself sickly before he pivoted abruptly and stalked off to the office.

THREE

A HALF mile south of the Crescent Palm the ranch wagon turned off into an opening on the sea side of the road. I had offered to follow Genders to the scene of his discovery; to wait there with him until some law arrived. He had welcomed the suggestion. Mike Newton had wanted to join us, deciding afterwards that he had better stay in case his presence was required at the motel. There was no reason why I should have felt uneasy about the short trip, but by the time the car ahead left the road to swing into the narrow clearing, I was wound up tight with expectancy.

I trailed the balding redhead's car down a much used strip into a space shrouded by sturdy, windblown bushes, barely wide enough for a car to turn in. The silence was like partial deafness when we stopped and got out onto the sand, with only the occasional screech of a gull, the lazy murmuring of the Pacific and the noise of a distant vehicle as a reminder that other life existed. Far down on tile beach a man in a wide straw hat and rolled up trousers dug into the damp sand with a fork. Under the afternoon sun his brown back glistened as smooth as seal skin.

"Up there," Genders indicated, pointing between dunes on which green bush clustered thickly together. "Better tie down your stomach before you go in. It's not pretty, that I can tell you now."

I said nothing, starting after him to the place his finger had indicated.

At a small sheltered section in the clearing he paused. The ground was littered with rusted cans and a few sand-logged bottles. An old faded blue sneaker that would never see use again lay near a broken circle of smoke blackened stones that were the remains of somebody's campfire. A stench that didn't belong lingered heavy in the air.

"Over there," Genders said. "You can look if you want. Once was enough for me."

Something flat posed upon the sand near a bush that had been partly burned. From where we stood it looked like an old and dirty length of driftwood. Sand flies hovered above it, others already settled in to exploration. I went in for a closer look.

Man or woman, it was difficult to tell at first. Someone had dragged the body onto the sand, doused it in gasoline, or something else that would burn as well, before dropping a lighted match. The flesh was no more than badly charred meat, the clothing long since consumed by the flames.

Judging from the persistent and nauseating stink, the act hadn't been committed very long ago. Waiting until my stomach reseated itself I took a better look. The arms and legs were stretched out in line with the body.

Everything had been touched by the flames. Even the shoes were now just black blobs against the pale ground. I got down onto my haunches and looked at what was left of the shoes. The one on the left foot still retained a fancy buckle, now dulled and tarnished.

Genders held out a cigarette to me when I got back to where he waited, lighting it with a hand that had developed palsy.

"Geeze," he exclaimed hoarsely. "How can you do it? I mean look at it so long? I had one look and when I realized what it was I nearly hurled my breakfast."

"How did you manage to find it?" I asked instead of answering the question.

"I wasn't looking for anything like it, that's for goddamned sure," he said in an attempt at humor. "I was driving up to Monterey when nature started calling. This clearing appeared and I figured it was as good a place as any. So I drove in—to take a leak. Hell, I was all through before I even noticed the stink! Then I looked around and saw that—that there."

"We'd better get back to the road," I said. "The police should be arriving soon and it'll look better if we're there waiting for them."

Without a word he followed me back to the cars. Down on the beach the clam digger had stopped work. The straw hat shadowed his face, but it was a good bet that he had stopped to watch us.

We drove the cars out of the clearing and parked at the side of the road, completing the maneuver in time to hear the fast approaching wail of a siren edge in on the silence.

An under-sheriff who introduced himself as Phillips arrived with two deputies. They examined the scene Genders showed them, made notes of our names and addresses, and after satisfying themselves we were no more than tourists with nothing helpful to add to the information already provided, allowed us to leave.

Genders was happy to get away. I would have liked to have stayed a little longer, but to Under-sheriff Phillips I was merely a curious citizen, and for the time being it was preferable to keep it that way.

Instead of returning to the motel I traveled the rest of the way into town. Vadear Point was only a small place consisting of a few shops, most of them aimed at the tourists, two or three hotels and one long street. Finding the post office was easy, and from a vacant booth there I put a call through to Los Angeles.

A seductive voice told me Ross Rigby was out and not expected back for at least another hour. Could he return my call?

I told her he could, that it was urgent, and left her with my name and that of the motel. He could find the number in the directory.

Newton's wife was pottering around in between masses of geraniums planted near the office when I arrived back at the motel. I walked up behind her and for a few seconds she continued working, unaware that I stood watching. She wore a simple plaid blouse above a light tan skirt, and the legs that showed from under were still good and firm. She was a lot of woman and even the tinted hair and the rather heavy hips and breasts still retained a strong physical attraction. I moved my feet against the concrete.

"Oh!" she exclaimed, turning and rising in one easy movement. "You startled me. It—it's Mr. Cameron, isn't it?"

"Sorry. I didn't mean to creep up on you."

She smiled back. "That's all right. Whenever I get a chance to tend the garden, and that isn't often, my mind simply drifts a million miles away. I didn't even notice you drive in."

There were few lines in her face, but under tired gray eyes a harsh darkness. She stood taller than her husband and she was something he would want to hold onto. Like his motel. Ten years from now she wasn't going to look very much different.

I said: "You've a very attractive place here, Mrs. Newton."

"Thank you. I'm glad you like it." She moved her head to make a quick survey of their little domain. Some of the tiredness left her eyes and in its place was reflected a little of the pride I had detected in her husband's voice. "Mike has big plans for it. Some rather grand, I'm afraid. But then, he maintains, that's the only way to plan."

"Mike—your husband tells me you've only had it about a year," I said, trying to lead into the questions I really wanted to ask.

"That's true. You should have seen it before we took over. I thought then the money had been wasted." Her face came all the way back to me. "Was there something I could help you with? That's why you wanted to speak to me, isn't it?"

"Two things," I said. "Mike told me you've got a bar on the premises. After seeing what was up the road I could do with a drink."

Mrs. Newton's attractive face became serious. "What was it? Was it really a—a dead man?"

I nodded. "The sheriff's men are there now. I don't know what happened, and it wasn't something to stand and watch on a day like this."

"Yes," she said unemotionally. "I hate things like that myself. I don't even like thinking about them. Well. . . ." She shrugged away a shiver that ran through her body. "The bar is at the back of the units. Don't expect too much, though. It isn't quite complete."

"As long as I can buy a drink of something cold I wouldn't care if it was served in a tumbled-down henhouse. The other thing I wanted to know was . . . Well, to be honest, I'm not sure how to frame this question. You see, I was supposed to meet someone here last night. Only something happened and I couldn't make it. Now I'm afraid he may have left without waiting for me. If he has, I might as well move on."

The deep gray eyes were fixed firmly on me. "Your friend have a name?"

"That's the difficult part. You see he's in a business where often it's necessary to travel incognito. If I had made it here last night there wouldn't be any problem. Now, because I'm late, I'm not sure what name he would have used. Probably Baxter, it's one he's used before. But I can't be sure."

A little more interest moved into the woman's face. Along with a touch of suspicion. "This all sounds rather mysterious, doesn't it?"

I laughed, but it sounded flat and artificial. "Not really. If you want privacy these days it's one of the few things left to do."

Removing the white gardening gloves from her hands, she said: "Let's go into the office. Offhand I don't recall registering any Baxters. But the cards should tell us."

Behind the counter she shuffled carefully through a small pack of white cards which she'd removed from a green file box. Arriving at the last one, she replaced them in their container. "Sorry, no Baxter."

"When you were going through those registrations you didn't happen to notice the name Cugino?" I asked quietly.

"Cugino?" Her hands shut the box and froze stiffly over it.

"Was that the name he used?"

"No." Her head shook. "It's just that . . . the name came as a surprise."

"It's his real one," I informed her slowly. "Was he here?"

"I don't know," she answered. "If he was he didn't use either of those names." Lifting the green box she returned it to the shelf behind the counter. With her back to me she stood looking at the wall. "What do you really want, Mr. Cameron?"

"Nothing. I'm looking for someone. Nothing more."

She came around, gray eyes darker by shades. "Why?"

"I told you why. We had an appointment."

"Yet you didn't think it necessary to enquire about him when you arrived. Nor did the lateness of your arrival appear to matter just now when you offered to go along with that—that man in the ranch wagon." Mingled with the accusation there was now both disbelief and scorn.

"True. But the immediate got the best of my curiosity. It's things like that which make me late for appointments."

She didn't swallow it, but neither did she wish to turn the subject into a debate.

"This man. What did he look like?" The flat emotionless quality which spoiled her voice had returned.

Briefly I described Cugino.

"If anyone like that registered here I never recognized him," she said stiffly. "Yesterday I told your friends the same thing." She paused, watching for my reaction. "Didn't you believe them?"

"Friends? Which ones would they be?"

"Two men came here," she explained patiently. "Late yesterday. They were also asking questions about a person called Frank Cugino. I told them nobody of that name had booked in, but they didn't believe me. One became rude and insisted on going through the registration cards himself."

"Can you describe them—these men?"

"Need I? They were associates of yours, weren't they?" A hand brushed unnecessarily at her tinted hair.

"No. If anyone else was to meet Cugino, it's news to me."

"They didn't act as if they had come to meet him, Mr. Cameron. They were *looking* for him. If they weren't friends of yours then I apologize for what I said. As for what they looked like, I hardly remember. I was far too upset to take all that notice. One was tall and gaudily dressed. He spoke with a slight lisp. That's about all I can tell you. Needless to say, they never introduced themselves."

"I'll wait around," I said. "He might still show."

There was little chance of that, but I needed an excuse now to delay my departure. At least until Ross Rigby got around to phoning.

"You're paid up in advance," she said coolly. "For tonight, anyway."

"Mrs. Newton, those two men are people I don't know. And I don't think I want to know them either. If they upset you, I'm sorry. What they wanted with Cugino is anybody's guess. But it has nothing to do with me."

'Nor me," she returned, the coolness turned to frost. "Nor is it any of my business. On the other hand, I don't want any trouble around here. Please try and remember that." The papers she'd been working with when I arrived that morning were still on the counter. They got her attention again and I found myself dismissed.

Mike Newton was in the small bar he had built. It hadn't been completed yet, but what he was trying to achieve was fairly obvious by the results so far. Hardboard cut-outs of palm trees and crescent-shaped moons had been painted black and secured to three walls. Behind them soft lights and appropriate colors were supposed to create the effect of a tropical island sundown. Although only partially finished the effect was pleasing.

One other customer sat at the bar, drinking quietly by himself at the far end. Newton saw me come in and raised a hand in silent greeting.

"A cold beer," I said in answer to his "What'll it be?"

He opened a bottle of Budweiser and set it on the bar top with a freshly polished glass.

"That business the guy in the wagon was fretting about—you see it?"

"Uh-huh."

"Motor smash?"

"I doubt it. Someone managed to get himself killed, that's all I know. It wasn't pretty. He'd been set alight."

Newton responded with a remark that contained an infamous four letter word and which got attention from the other customer. "Probably some drunk. Could even be it was a woman that fixed him. That beach and them rocks are favorite places for guys too cheap to take their fluff to a motel. Not," he threw in quickly, "that we cater for that sorta trade here. Annie wouldn't stand for it. Me neither. It gives the place a bum name, and that's something we don't want. I got ideas for this place. Going to make it a motel for families—you know? Like a place where they can stay longer than just one lousy night, or in some crummy hotel. That's the kinda business I'm aiming for. It's steady."

"You think what happened might have any effect on trade?" I asked for want of nothing better to say.

"Hell, I hope not. It's none of my concern what happens off these premises, and I don't even want to know about it." He paused to look at me. A worried frown made deep creases in his forehead, bringing the heavy black brows into a straight line. "You think it might steer customers away?"

I shook my head. "I doubt it. If anything, it'll probably bring them in."

It brought a laugh. The kind that needed crutches.

I briefed him on my talk with his wife, bringing the subject around to the two men she had told me about. He listened attentively, nodding whenever I mentioned something his wife had disclosed.

"They were the kind of jokers we don't see around here too often, thank God. Back in San Francisco I saw enough of them—too many. They're trouble, and don't try telling me different. We told them nobody like that had checked in, but they got tough—acted like we were lying. The big guy, the one that talked funny, he got awkward and went behind the counter to look through the cards himself. I wanted to toss them out and call Phillips—he's in charge of the sheriff's sub-station up in town— but I figured why make a scene? They weren't planning on sticking around once they knew the guy they're looking for wasn't here."

"Get a good look at them?"

"Not much more than my wife did. One was pretty ordinary. The other one, long and dressed fancy. He's the one with the queer way of talking. Like a fairy."

"Mike?" It was his wife's voice. We both looked over to where she stood at the door.

"Yeah?"

"There's someone to see you at the office."

"S'cuse me," Newton said, moving out from behind the bar. "Won't be long. You want a refill, help yourself."

The other customer left soon after Newton. I dawdled over the beer, then lit a cigarette and wished Rigby would phone so that I'd know what to do. It was over two and a half hours since I'd seen Allison Page drive away in an obvious hurry. It seemed like only minutes.

I was down to the bottom of my glass when Newton returned.

"Phillips," he said, explaining the reason for being called away. "From the sheriff's office. Guess you already know him, huh? I mean you would've met him back there."

Back there I assumed to mean the place where the charred body had been found. I nodded.

"Remember that snazzy little bus we were looking at when you got here this morning? That Corvette Stingray—the silver one?"

"What about it?"

"I wondered why in hell she would take off in such a tearing hurry. Didn't even stop to hand her key in. Just left it stuck in the door." Without being asked he produced another bottle of beer and uncapped it. "She was out this morning, just before you got here, and it seems one of the places she was at was there where that dead guy's been found."

I put down the empty glass I'd been fiddling with and poured from the new bottle.

"A guy who was digging for clams along the beach saw her. He didn't know about the body, of course. That part he found out later after seeing you and the other character show up, and afterwards when the sheriff's men started crawling over the place. When he saw the sheriff's car pull in there he quit digging and came over to find out what was going on. He told Phillips about the silver car, and now he's been here trying to find out if we'd rented her a place."

In my mouth the beer had gone sour. "Your cards should give him that information."

"Yeah," he agreed. "Only I don't know that it's going to do them much good. You see, I got an idea she didn't use her own name, and the number she wrote down for her car was phony also."

Using another name was something I would have expected her to do, considering she'd gone to the trouble of donning a black wig. But the number of her car was something she might have forgotten about.

"What makes you say that?" I asked.

"Don't know. Call it a hunch if you want. But this morning when I was looking at that bus I seem to remember seeing a lot of sevens in the number. The one she filled in on the card didn't even have one seven in it."

The beer began to resume a little of its original taste. But only a little.

"You think she could've killed that guy?" He had both elbows on the counter now, leaning forward, anxious for an opinion.

"Well," he said when I shook my head, "they do weird things with their hair so who's to say what they're likely to do with a man."

He thought that was pretty good. I wished I could have laughed with him.

FOUR

THE beer had made me drowsy while waiting for Rigby to phone. I turned on the television, then propped the pillows up higher and went on warding off the nagging call of sleep. Each time I relaxed dark things crawled into my thoughts and it was becoming more difficult to free myself of them. No matter how I tried to redirect my concentration to the glowing screen, the dark images remained—mental scenes of a dead man, a blonde girl and a can of gasoline. As I swung my legs over the side of the bed to switch off the set, the telephone jangled loudly.

With all sleepiness instantly gone I grabbed for the receiver and spoke briefly with an unidentifiable voice before waiting for Rigby to come onto the line.

"Cameron? That you?"

"It's me. I've been trying to reach you."

"I know, but I was out until now. I've only just received your message." I could hear him take a deep breath. "Have you contacted her?"

"Hold it," I warned. "This is an extension phone I'm using."

There was an abrupt silence as we tuned in on the hollow purr that echoed through the wire.

"You think someone might be listening in?"

"It occurred to me, but I don't think it's happening."

"You've found her then?" he asked, trying to subdue the eagerness in his voice.

"No. I missed making contact by seconds. I arrived shortly before she left in what seemed like a great big hurry. This minute she's on her way home—if not already there."

"Cameron—has something happened?" Gone was the eagerness, in its place sudden, sharp concern.

"I'll get to that when I see you. Right now I need your help for something." Without waiting for agreement, I continued: "I want you to get over to her place, and if she's there, stay with her until I arrive. If she hasn't arrived yet, wait. Can you do that?"

"Of course, but—"

"I'm leaving as soon as I hang up. I'll meet you there," I said, sidestepping the started protest. "Better give me her address."

Rigby read it out to me, and when he was through, asked: "What happened? You make this all sound so—so . . ."

"A man died. She was seen leaving the place where it happened."

"Oh, no," he groaned, and I could see the professor-like face lose its usual good humor and fold up in anguish as clear as if he were in the same room.

"I'm leaving now. Get to her and stay with her."

"Wait," he shouted, anxious to squeeze in one more question before I rang off. "This man . . . Was it—him?"

"I think so, but there's no way of being positive yet."

"Oh, my god," he groaned again. "Cameron, you don't think . . . ? No, that's impossible! She wouldn't . . ."

"I'm hanging up," I said, and did.

Newton's wife asked no questions when I returned the key and told her I was checking out. I had a feeling she'd been expecting it ever since I'd spoken to her about Cugino. Yet, for some reason I found it necessary to offer a lame explanation. She listened politely while those brooding gray eyes called me the poorest kind of liar.

2

It was already dark when I arrived back in L.A. and parked in front of her house. As I got out of the car the tiredness returned and I felt strangely reluctant to proceed any further. The house was neither as large nor as distinctive as any of its closest neighbors, but with lights burning behind all the wide windows it glowed warm and bright. The sort of place it would be pleasant to own, or even rent. But to do that you'd need to be in a position to easily afford other things—such as the latest in Cadillacs parked in the short drive. I couldn't.

"Mistuh Cameron?" an outsize black female enquired upon opening the front door.

She waved a fat brown hand, beckoning me to enter as soon as I confirmed who I was.

"Mistuh Rigby's in the livin' room. Been waitin' for yo' some time now." In her starched uniform and white cap she resembled a walking commercial for someone's cake mix.

"I had a long way to come," I said, and followed her broad rolling hips into a living room that had been furnished and decorated by somebody who knew what he or she was doing. Nothing in it was flashy or there only because it was costly and would be an item to show off to visitors. A talented and sober mind had been responsible for what was in that room. Including, perhaps, the man who lounged wearily in a rocker near a window commanding a view of the Santa Monica Mountains.

Rigby looked older, his face more lined that I remembered. In his hand he clutched a large glass. Drinking from it before rising, he said in a flat voice:

"She's gone, and God knows where to."

I looked at him, then at the uniformed maid who had preceded me into the room.

"Tell him, Terry," the agent instructed.

"It's okay?"

"Of course," he answered, irritated by the question. "Mr. Cameron knows everything that's happened. Tell him."

"Well," she started off self-consciously, plump hands fidgeting with each other in front of melon-like breasts, "Miss Allison she come home not so long ago, and she was all nervous—she'd been cryin' too. I asked her wha-for she was so upset, but she jest said never to mind, jest to help her pack her bags." Her round-eyed gaze roved from me to Rigby to make sure we were listening.

"Go on," I prompted.

"Well, I helped her pack her things. But land sakes, that chile never even cared about what she took. Some of her real pretty dresses she jest ignored, left 'em behind like she didn't care. She was in a real hurry about things, never even worried about changin' what she was wearin'. Well then, after she was all packed an' everythin', she come in heah an' used that there recordin' machine. She tol' me that when Mistuh Rigby come around I got to make him listen to what she put on it. When Mistuh Rigby come I done jest like Miss Allison asked and tol' him about the machine. He played back what she recorded. Ain't that so, Mistuh Rigby?"

He confirmed it with a curt nod.

I said: "And she left right after recording what's on that tape?"

"Yessuh."

"Did she say where she was going?"

"Nosuh, she didn't. She just hugged me there by the door an' promised me she was gonna be okay. Then she went off to that li'l car of hers an' drove away to the Lord knows where." She paused. The hands became still as she opened her mouth to add something more. But Rigby spoke before she could find the words.

"What happened down there?"

"Just a minute," I said. "Were you going to say something, Terry?"

"Nosuh. I was jest gonna ask if Miss Allison's in some kind of trouble, thasall."

"Why?"

"Why?" she echoed. "'Cause I been workin' for Miss Allison a long time now, that's why. That chile is like my own, an' if she's in trouble I want to . . ."

"Yes, Terry?"

"Oh, nothin'. I was gonna say I want to help her. But what can ol' Terry do? She ain't got neither the brains or the money to help people what's in real trouble." From out of her wide apron pocket came a foot-square handkerchief. It went to her nose as she sniffed noisily.

"You can pray," Rigby put in without sarcasm. The gentle manner of his voice surprised me even more than what he had said. "Allison's in a little trouble, it would seem, but we're here to try and help her if we can.

In the meantime it's important that no-one else knows about it. Do you understand, Terry?"

"Natch'ly, Mistuh Rigby," her voice answered hoarsely from behind the handkerchief putting in overtime at her nose. "I jest knew there was somethin' gonna go wrong. Ever since that phone rang on Sunday night I jest knew somethin' was gonna happen."

"How about some coffee," he suggested. "I'm sure Mr. Cameron could use some after his drive. So could I for that matter. Or"—he looked my way—"maybe you'd prefer a drink?"

"Thanks. Coffee sounds fine."

Terry's head bobbed when I gave my answer, then she turned quickly, as though anxious to get away and do her sniffling in private.

"Want me to tell you what happened, or do I get to hear the tape first?" I asked.

"Better listen to the tape, not that it helps us. She's given no indication of where she's gone."

Over at the wide wall cabinet that housed, in addition to a TV set and record player, a tape recorder, Rigby pressed a button that started the spools revolving.

Allison Page's voice was hushed and hurried as her words were fed through the big dual speakers:

". . . By the time you hear this, Ross, I shall be well on my way out of Los Angeles. Where I'm going does not really matter, but I am sorry that what I have to do—what I must do—is going to put you to a great deal of inconvenience. I'm sorry, Ross, believe me I am. But it's better that I do this now before we get ourselves involved with any contract. Running out on you like this must seem terribly ungrateful, and there are no words I know of to really apologize for my actions, or even to assure you how deeply grateful I am for all the faith you placed in me—all the work you've done to help me. I don't have a great deal of time to say what I have to, but I must try and explain my reasons for—for running away like this . . . On Sunday night I received a call from that man, the one who said his name was Baxter. He accused me of having pulled a—a double-cross, and explained how he'd been compelled to fall for it. This time, he said, things were different, that he didn't care if the police arrested him. He said things to the effect that he couldn't be any worse off than he was now. I didn't know what he meant, but he sounded desperate, Ross. I think even frightened. Again he demanded money. This time he insisted that I deliver it personally, and that if I failed to do so he would tell all the newspapers about—" There was a small choking sound followed by a lengthy pause before her voice returned. ". . . I was instructed to go to a motel at Vadear Point, a place called the Crescent Palm. There I was to wait until he contacted me. Baxter, which was the name he was using again, told me how he'd know if I brought anyone else along, or if we attempted to stage another trick. When he rang off I was scared. I wanted to call you, to get your advice. But I was afraid,

Ross. Not only for myself, but for others very dear to me. So I did as he instructed. I still had the money we used on Saturday night . . . I drove to the motel and booked in under another name. I even went to the trouble of wearing a dark wig I'd used in one of the shows. Most of the night I sat in my room and waited for him. But he didn't come or even phone. This morning I didn't know what to do—except that I had to get out of that room. All the while I kept remembering our appointment at the studio . . . I—I took a short drive just to get some fresh air, but it turned out to be a dreadful mistake. There was a place off the road with a beautiful view of the ocean. It—it looked so peaceful that I drove in and got out of my car. I even took off the wig, thinking I was entirely alone. Then— then on the beach a man appeared. I think he was clamming . . . He saw me and waved. Automatically I waved back, and then I moved out of sight, walking further into the clearing and out of his view. There—there was an old picnic spot or something where I stopped. I stood there for quite a long time, thinking about Baxter and what I ought to do . . . I didn't want to return to the motel, but at the same time I was afraid to come home without first seeing him . . . Then—then I saw that—that . . . Oh, Ross, it was awful! I've never seen anything so awful before. That poor person had been burned . . . I—I don't know what I did after seeing it. All I know is that he or she was dead and . . . Ross, I feel ill when I think about it even now. The next thing I remember was racing back to the motel . . . My mind was in a turmoil, but suddenly I realized what would happen if I stayed at the motel. I had been seen on the beach near where—where that body lay. When the police were notified of what was there that man on the beach would have been able to give them my description—he'd seen my car and he'd seen me without the wig. I knew I had to get away from there before anything like that happened— regardless of Baxter. But—but even as I was leaving the motel a man tried to stop me. He looked familiar, but I was in too much of a panic to take a better look. Ross, I have no idea of what will happen now. Baxter will probably give the papers what he has, and if he does . . . Well, I don't think Lynx would want me after that. Nor, for that matter, anyone else. I ran from that terrible scene, Ross, because if the police were to question me everything would come out—my reason for being there, for using an assumed name—everything about Baxter and. . . . This is probably not the best way, the way I am going about it, but right at this moment it seems like the only way. If I simply fade out of the picture perhaps the police will not bother looking for me, perhaps even Baxter will give up his ideas . . . But I suppose that is too much to hope for. Everything seems to have become so hopeless. Ross, please believe one thing. It isn't merely what the publicity would do to me, it's—it's the awful hurt it will subject others to—others who are very precious to me. They're worth more than the kind of career I had hoped for, and which, with the help you have given me, was beginning to look like a reality . . . Perhaps I'm a coward. I suppose I am. Everything has suddenly turned so dark and confusing. One way or another everything Baxter knows will be made public . . ."

There was more, but not much, and most of it consisted of apologies to Rigby and a few requests to dispose of the house and to give Terry whatever she wanted of its contents. Then the tape rolled on in silence.

Rigby switched off the machine.

I said: "No hint of where she's gone. Or do you have any ideas?"

"None." He flopped down into a nearby chair, removed the rimless glasses and massaged the space between his eyes. On his finger the ring glinted like an evil green eye. "None whatever." Looking up at me, it was a while before he said: "I guess you'd better tell me what happened down there."

I sat down and told him everything, of Allison's hasty departure; of the finding of the body; of my talk with the motel owner's wife and the information she'd provided, including that which Mike Newton had told me about the unknown clam digger telling Under-sheriff Phillips about the blonde he'd seen on the beach.

"When I phoned you at the motel," he said when I was through spreading it out for him, "you said you had reason to think the dead man was this—this Cugino. Are you sure?"

"Reasonably."

"Isn't it possible it's someone else, someone completely unrelated to this business with Allison?"

"It could be," I admitted, "and until the police are able to make a positive identification no one can be absolutely sure who he is. The body was burned beyond recognition, but what was left of his shoes still contained fancy silver buckles. I saw the same kind on Cugino's shoes Saturday night."

"That isn't much to base identification on, is it?"

"No, but if it is Baxter, or rather Cugino, it explains his failure to contact Allison last night."

"Cameron," he said thickly, "you don't honestly believe she could have done a thing like that, do you?"

"I don't want to."

"You're not answering my question."

I got out of the chair which was beginning to remind me that I was tired. "Let's look at it from the point of view of the police. Their working hypothesis would probably be something like this: Last night Allison met Cugino to pay him off, but instead she got rid of him. This morning she returned to the scene to make sure what she'd done had been done right, that she'd left nothing behind that might later incriminate her."

"But she couldn't have!" he protested, returning the glasses to his eyes. "She's only a little thing. How could she ever overpower a grown man like him? He'd have to have been unconscious first."

"Cugino didn't die by fire," I said. "When a man dies like that his body generally contracts into a certain position—a sort of fighting stance with the legs drawn up and the arms poised above the face. Cugino—and let's call him that for the sake of reference—was stretched out stiff when I saw him. I'll give odds on the autopsy revealing he was dead long before being set alight. Burning the body afterwards was probably only an attempt at preventing identification."

"And you honest-to-God think *she* could have done *that?*"

I shook my head.

"Why?" he wanted to know.

"Mainly because I don't want to. But there are other things that provide cause for doubt. I told you about some of them. There were those two men looking for Cugino. I'm certain he knew who they were and that he was trying to avoid them. When I spoke to him on Saturday night he was jumpy, and as I told you then, I didn't think it was the stunt we pulled that brought out the sweat."

"Then you think they could have done it—those men?" He'd been offered a slim straw and was clutching at it with both hands.

"Could be. Proving it would be another thing. But that's a matter for the authorities."

The graying head nodded thoughtfully as he got up and began to pace about the room.

"That kid had a career ahead of her, Cameron. Lynx Studios will sign her up. After I found she was missing from here yesterday I even arranged a delay in the signing of the contract. But Friday's the deadline. If they don't get her they'll sign with someone else so that production can get started." He stopped moving to explain further. "Now that the studios have discovered there's again big money to be made in good musicals they're all jumping on the wagon, and they're looking for new talent—real talent. Most of the old-timers who made their names and fortunes in those kind of pictures are either dead or retired. So new faces have to be found. Faces with voices. In this town that isn't as tough a chore as it might sound. Hollywood's lousy with singers and would-be actresses. The studios could take their pick from the best of them. But Allison has everything to offer. A face and a figure and a voice that is unique. Dammit, when she sings she sounds like a female! And don't think the people who count don't know it. There's a contract ready for her to star in *The Song You Hear*. All it requires is her signature and . . ." His sigh was like a dying breath. "But now!"

"Yeah," I agreed glumly. "If whatever she's afraid of is as bad as she's made it sound, Lynx and the others will have a rapid change of heart. But what about her?"

"What do you mean?"

"Do you just drop her now? Leave her running?"

Blood rushed into his face, deepening the already dark tan. "You think I want to?" he asked sharply as Terry returned carrying a tray. "You think I like what's happened?" While the maid set down the tray, doing her best to pretend she had missed his outburst, he simmered down.

"Supposing she was here to sign up with Lynx, and supposing that after signing the thing she's been hiding is made public, thanks to something Cugino might have fixed. Can you imagine the stink it would create? She'd be dead before she ever got started." Shrugging helplessly he let his arms drop loosely at his sides in an expression of total defeat. "Friday's the deadline and she won't be here. So Lynx signs up someone else not half as good."

When I made no comment, he muttered: "What are you thinking about?"

"Do you know what it's like to be really frightened?"

"All right." He sighed again. "What do you suggest I do?"

"As a start you could try finding her. And somebody could check into Cugino's activities, find out who he was and how he came to have such a hold over her. That way perhaps you'll also learn who killed him. Blackmailers sometimes have more than one victim on their books."

"But after Friday—"

"That's still a way off, Mr. Rigby. Anyway, I was thinking about her, not the contract."

It took him only seconds to decide.

"You're prepared to do this?"

"I wasn't suggesting myself," I answered. "My business consists of only me. That's not enough for an operation of this size. For that you want a big agency with a large staff."

His head shook determinedly. "No. What's happened is to remain confidential—between us. I don't want anyone else brought in."

"Mr. Rigby," I said patiently, "if I worked twenty-four hours a day I couldn't hope to produce the results a staffed agency could. Anyway, not in twice the time it would take them to cover the angles."

"You brought up the subject. It was your suggestion. And if you're worrying about money, don't. I'll personally guarantee to meet any bill you present."

"It's not the money that's—"

"—You just don't want to, that it?" he snapped before I could finish.

"You're baiting me, Rigby."

The maid was watching him with eyes like brightly polished saucers.

"Supposing I am?" he returned.

It became my turn to shrug. "Okay. I'm hired," I said, and wondered why I'd started to argue when all along I had wanted to do the things suggested.

Rigby returned to his chair and flopped down heavily into it. "Drink your coffee and we'll talk about it."

We drank and talked, but he was unable to dredge up a single idea of where Allison Page might have gone. A quick search was made of the house for letters or anything else that might provide a lead, but it was wasted effort. Terry let us know, once informed of what we were looking for, that her mistress stored what correspondence she kept in a small wall safe in the master bedroom. And to open that without knowing the combination would have called for a far more talented hand than any of us there possessed.

What I did learn during our quick tour of the house was that Rigby had not been Allison's agent for very long, and consequently knew very little about her personal background. She'd been singing since around the age of fifteen, or so she had told him. Later she had won herself a contract with a small recording outfit. Very little money had been derived from the venture. Gradually she had progressed to a better known label, but it happened at a time when the beat groups were becoming popular, when long-haired males and noisy guitars were starting a new trend in the music business. A trend that put good singers, like so many of the big name bands who had been famous for years, into premature retirement. Allison had been one of the few who had refused to quit. She'd stayed in there fighting for survival as a straight singer. And during that time her marriage had cracked up. Less than eight months ago Rigby had caught her act at a benefit performance, realized her potential, and signed her up. In those months he had helped her increase her number of television performances, finally swinging a deal where she had her own show for six months. The movies had beckoned and at last her star appeared to be ascending.

I listened with genuine interest, especially about the broken marriage, for part of the small record buying public which had still been prepared to lay out the green for singers like Allison Page had included Cameron. The fact that she had been married before arrived as news which brought a feeling of disappointment.

Not bothering to explain why, Rigby lingered behind when I decided to leave, and it was Terry who appeared and walked me to the door.

"Mistuh Cameron," she said, holding the door open, "you're really gonna find Miss Allison, ain't you?"

"I'm going to make a good try, Terry."

"An' I'll be prayin' for you," she promised solemnly.

I patted her thick arm softly, then went out into the night.

3

Down in Venice there was a chill in the air and a reminder of the dark unseen Pacific. I found a parking place near the pink apartment block, locked up the car and went into the building.

Mailbox number eight had a card tacked to it, on which someone had printed in crude block letters: ROSE LANG.

I climbed the concrete steps to the second floor balcony and found number eight at the far end. It was the last apartment in the eight-unit structure. Gloomy darkness blackened the closed windows, but I put a thumb on the bell and held it there for longer than is customary while a soft breeze laid a chill across the back of my neck.

Inside there was not the slightest indication of life, but responding to the same impulse which had made me jab the bell in the first place, I glued my finger back on the button and listened to it ring. From within I heard nothing, not until a woman's hard voice demanded cautiously:

"What's it?"

I gave the bell a rest when reminded of another night, when Frank Cugino had asked a similar question. I told the voice my name.

"What d'you want?"

"I've got a message for Frank."

A short silence preceded her answer. "You're lying. What d'you want?"

"I told you."

"And I told you you're lying."

"Please yourself, Miss Lang. But think of Frankie's reaction when I tell him you wouldn't open the door."

"Frank never sent you," she spat back.

"Okay. I was bluffing. But my business concerns both you and Cugino, and it's important. So how about opening up?"

"Get lost—leave me alone." But her voice had undergone a change, sounding softer, and unless I was imagining things, frightened.

"What's wrong, Rose?"

"Nothing's wrong. Just go away, willya? I got nothing to say to you or anybody. Frankie don't tell me his business."

From my pocket I took a business card and pushed it under the door.

"That's my card. If you change your mind, give me a ring. Only tomorrow may be a little late." Late for what I didn't and couldn't say. But it was the kind of threat that sometimes brought reactions.

More soft noises rustled through the closed door. If it hadn't been dark in there I'd have thought she'd picked up the card and was reading it. I waited, but so did she, making no attempt to touch the lock.

"I'm going," I told her, moving my feet so that the shuffling sound could be heard. "Remember, I did try to talk to you."

"Wait. Hold it a minute."

A light went on inside the apartment, but the curtains were thick and I couldn't see so much as a shadow. While I was waiting the light went out again and the door lock scraped back. An inch at a time the door began to open.

"C'mon in," the hard voice invited carefully.

I went inside and the door slammed shut immediately I was clear of its swing. The room was dark and stuffy and I had only a vague idea of where she stood.

"Don't move from where you are. I got a gun pointed at you, and s'help me I'll use it you lift one lousy finger."

Her position shifted and a switch clicked sharply a second before hard white light flooded through the room. It took a little time for my eyes to adjust to the new light. When at last they did I turned slowly around.

"I told you—stand where you are!" The words came fast and nervous.

She was barefoot, her toenails wearing chipped pink varnish. Light brown hair that looked as if it hadn't been brushed in days tumbled untidily down to the shoulders of a red satin robe that gaped widely at her throat. Her hand trembled as she kept the small revolver trained on my chest. She was scared, and if her face held any clue to the cause of that fear, I didn't blame her for acting as she was.

Her lower lip was swollen and split, and not long ago the hard knuckles of a swinging fist had painted her left eye a cruel blue.

FIVE

"YOU can put the gun away," I said. "I'm not here to make trouble."

"It stays until I hear what you want," she snapped back, trying to sound defiant.

"You're Cugino's girl?"

Instead of answering she drew herself up stiffly. The red robe pulled further apart. Underneath was flesh as pale as paper, and very little else.

"I saw him come here on Saturday night. Later he left carrying a suit-case," I told her.

"So Frankie's someone I know. You haven't started telling me what you want yet."

"Can we sit down? I'm not carrying a gun, and if it makes you feel better you can hold onto yours."

Rose Lang took her time considering the request, deciding at last that she held the upper hand as long as she clung to the revolver. She waved it at the furniture.

"Find yourself a place."

The room was a mess. Furniture had been pushed about sloppily, as if a drunk had been stumbling around in the dark. Ashtrays spilled over with filter-tipped butts, while the pages of shattered newspapers littered the couch and skimpy carpet. I pushed some of the papers off the couch and made room to sit. The girl came and stood by a chair as soon as I was settled.

"You who it says on here?" Quickly she checked the card again before letting it drop to the chair.

"Uh-huh."

"Got anything else that says so?"

"In my pocket. Want to see?"

Waving the revolver absently. "What the hell's it matter? What you want is what I'm waiting to hear."

"Frankie's in trouble," I said, "and from the look of your face it would seem you've experienced a little yourself. What happened?"

"I walked into a door," she cracked. "What's it to you?"

I shrugged. "Were you in on the blackmail deal with Cugino?"

Her face tried to blank out expression, almost succeeding except for the quick flicker of her one undamaged eye.

"Believe it or not, Rose, I'm here to offer you a break—a chance to square yourself before the action really gets rough."

She tried to laugh but the effort hurt her swollen lip. "Nobody ever gave me anything but headaches, buster, so don't hand me that crap. You don't even know me, but you're going to give me a break. Tell me something really funny."

"I know all about Frankie's attempt to blackmail a certain party in town," I went on. "I know what happened on Saturday night, why he cleared out and where he went. And I've seen him since."

"So you're the bastard!" she hissed scornfully.

"Is that how you picked up the mouse and the broken lip?" I asked her.

"Can the cute talk, Cameron. I'm not in the mood. You said you saw Frankie. Where is he?"

"Right now, with the sheriff's men up at Vadear Point. And very soon they're going to connect him to you. I don't know your opinion of the police, Rose, but I think you're intelligent enough to realize they'll get to you sooner or later."

Her bruised and puffy face started to fall apart as the last remnant of confidence slipped away.

"I had nothing to do with Frankie's business. They can't rap me for anything he done. All I did was give him a place to stay till he got sorted out. There a law or something against doing that?"

"The police are only part of the problem, Rose. From where I sit, the very least of your worries."

Around the small gun's trigger her finger whitened when her arm lifted.

"Meaning you? Like you can hand me trouble? Not while I got this, brother. While I'm holding this nobody's giving me any more trouble."

"I was thinking of two other people, not myself."

"You're talking a foreign language," she said slowly. "Like Dutch. Me, I don't understand a word."

I got up. The newspapers rustled harshly when I moved and the girl took an involuntary step back.

"I came offering you a break," I said. "But it seems I'm wasting my time."

"These other people," she said, motioning with the gun for me to stand still. "What about them? You said they're looking for Frank?"

"I didn't, but they were. I was hoping you could tell me something about them. One was a big guy. A flashy dresser with a slight impediment of the speech. He lisped."

"Strode." The whisper was harsh and not intended for my ears.

"You know him?"

"I might." Her good eye fixed its focus intently upon my face. "You said the cops got Frank. That mean those two—the ones you mentioned, they never found him?"

"That's why I'm here, Rose." I wasn't sure how I was going to tell her about Cugino. The hand holding the revolver was unsteady and at that range she'd have difficulty missing—even if the shot was only the reflex action of shock.

"What're you holding back?" her hard voice demanded. And something in my face must have provided a hint. "Something—something's happened to him?"

"He's dead, Rose. He was killed."

Her entire body stiffened. I took advantage of it to reach out and grab the gun. It came willingly, as if her hand was anxious to be rid of it.

"You lie . . ." she accused woodenly. "He can't be. . . He . . ." Turning her back on me she clung with both hands to the back of the chair, her head bowed low. I waited for the sound of crying, but it never came.

So far Frank Cugino hadn't added up to much in my book, but watching the girl, the cheap red robe strained across stooped shoulders, it was apparent that Rose Lang used a different system to measure a man. I said: "I'm sorry."

"The poor, crazy little bastard," she mumbled. "I warned him. He said he'd clear out. He said he'd . . ."

I put a hand on her shoulder. "Rose."

"Don't worry about me," she said, dislodging my hand when she turned. "I'm a big girl. I don't cry anymore." She sat down in the chair and pulled the robe tightly closed around her throat. A tremor flitted through her body and she shivered. "Besides, it was me who told them where to find him. They came here looking for him and I fingered him." Carefully she caressed her left eye and lip. "I didn't want to tell them, but they gave me this. There were other things they were going to do—so I told them. That makes me kind of responsible for what happened, don't it?"

"If you warned him, it makes a difference."

"Some difference," she scoffed. "After they roughed me up I got through to him at the motel and told him what happened. He said he was getting out right away. But I guess he must've waited too long." Her face tilted upward and the question was silently repeated. "You said you'd seen him. What'd they do to him?"

"It wasn't nice, Rose. You don't want the details."

"I asked you what they did."

I sighed, and only because I thought it might anger her enough to tell me more about the two men, told her how Frank Cugino had looked when found. Manipulating emotions in order to gather possible information. One of the less honorable aspects of an already much maligned profession.

She listened quietly, without any comment or outward display of emotion.

"Those men, the ones who beat you up. Do you know who they are, Rose?"

Tiredly her head wagged from side to side. "The big one's name is Strode, that's all I know. I heard the other one call him that. He was the one who talked like a queer, the one called Strode." Scarlet shone where the split in her lip had opened again. Her finger touched the blood and she studied the tip without concern before fetching a handkerchief from the pocket of the robe. There were other spots of dull brown on the small crumpled square.

"Do you know why they wanted Frankie?"

Her head shook behind the handkerchief. "Yesterday, when they came banging their way in here was the first time I laid eyes on either of them." Satisfied that the bleeding had been temporarily stemmed, she said: "They killed him, huh?"

"It seems a possibility. Did Frankie ever mention them to you?"

"No; not by name. But he told me there was certain people after him, and that they wanted him dead. He'd been running ever since he was sprung back in New York. For over a month he'd been holing up in one place and another before coming down here."

"He was in prison?" I queried, recalling how pale his flesh had looked that night in the hotel room.

She nodded wearily. "For the last five years. I knew him before he went inside. He was a big spender back then," she added somewhat nostalgically.

"Five years is a long time. What did he do?"

"You tell me. All I know is he was tied up with some big shot mob. Frankie wasn't one to tell anyone his business. We used to knock around together for a time, but he hardly ever told me anything about what he did. Then he found some new piece and all of a sudden I got forgotten. I was a dancer back on the Stem and guys weren't on any ration list, so I didn't waste time grieving over what happened."

"Were you still in New York when he was arrested?"

"Uh-uh. I cut out from there. Some bum promised me he had strong connections that could get me into pictures, and I fell for it." She chuckled mirthlessly. "Imagine that, huh? One of the oldest and corniest lines and I went and took it. Oh, he had connections in pictures all right, the kind where you do gymnastics and other things in the raw. When I found out I gave him the gate." Shoulders lifted and slowly fell. "Oh, well, give him his due. He treated me right even after I told him I wasn't interested in his proposition."

"And now?"

"Now nothing. Here I am, a hoofer in a town that's already got a few hundred too many. Broke and bruised and—and if I still knew how to cry I'd do a little of it right now."

"How did you manage to tie up with Cugino again? He know you were living here?"

"No. He was just as surprised as me when we run into each other again. I was sitting in a bar when he came in and bought a drink. For nearly fifteen minutes he sat there right next to me before I recognized him. Frankie was thinner and paler than I remembered him, but seeing him there like that I forgot about where he'd been all the time."

"And he talked you into letting him move in here?"

"Something like that," she confirmed. "We kicked it around a bit and I got the idea he was scared of something. Personally, I had no yen to include myself in on any of his problems, but he let me know that he'd taken care of me back east, and how I owed him a favor or two." Red-clad shoulders performed another shrug of dismissal. "Tell the truth, I felt sorry for the little bastard. He had a few bucks and a car, but he was peanuts to the guy I used to know. So I said okay, move in. It was only going to be for a short time, so what the hell."

"You said he was running," I reminded her. "He told you that?"

"Yeah. But that's all. Frankie wasn't the kind that went in for details. He said only that there were some guys out to make sure he got dead. Why, he didn't know."

"He didn't know who and he didn't know why?" The disbelief must have been strong in my tone.

"I never said that. I said he didn't know what they wanted to hit him for—or so he told me." She hesitated before continuing quietly. "I think he knew who they were. I think he knew why they wanted him, too, only he didn't talk about it."

"And you think it was the two men who came here? Strode and his companion?"

"Who else? They said they'd tailed him to this dump and they wanted to know where he was. First they took the place to pieces like they was looking for something. They wouldn't tell me what it was supposed to be; just that it was a package Frankie's supposed to have had. They seemed to think I knew what the hell they were talking about."

"Did you?"

Her answer was a mute one-eyed glare.

"Rose," I said patiently, "if those two were responsible for Frankie's death, do you know where that leaves you? You're the one who told them where he was staying. That makes you a witness of sorts. If you want help, don't start holding back anything now."

"I'm telling you everything," she insisted adamantly. "I didn't know about any package. I still don't. If Frankie had anything like that I never saw it. And he sure as hell didn't mention it to me."

"What made him go to the motel?" I asked.

"Which motel?"

"The Crescent Palm."

"How should I know? He was running and it seemed like a good enough place to hold over for a while."

"He wasn't registered there under his own name. How did you know what name he'd be using when you tried to warn him about Strode?"

"Simple. He told me what name he'd be using. Fred Carter."

"And the motel's name?"

"How else would I know where to reach him?" She pulled the robe tighter together and shifted her position irritably. "While he was here he was always playing around with maps and things. Like he was planning on what to do and where to go in case there was sudden trouble. When he had to leave on Saturday night he picked that place at Vadear Point because it wasn't so far away, I guess."

Or so that he would be able to take another crack at Allison Page.

"Tell me about the blackmail," I said. "Do you know who Cugino was working on?"

"No."

"The truth, Rose."

"Look," she flared hotly, "you don't want to believe me, knock off the questions and take yourself the hell out of here!"

"But you knew he was blackmailing, or trying to blackmail somebody, didn't you?" I said, ignoring the outburst.

Her reply was slow in coming and sullen when it arrived: "I had an idea about what he was doing, but I didn't know who he was working on. All he told me was that he had a way of picking up a lot of quick change—enough to take us both far from here. Europe was what he talked about. Frankie was all hepped up about it. He said he wanted to take me along with him, and that from there on all our troubles were going to be over. We were going to live like royalty, he said, and we wouldn't ever have to scratch for a buck again."

"You believed him?"

"I listened to him. And I admit it sounded good. But I'm a girl who listened to a fairy story before, remember?"

"I remember."

She said: "Your card has your business on it. You working for her?"

"For who?"

"Her. I don't know who—the dame. The one Frankie was trying to blackmail. If that's what he was doing," she nailed on quickly.

"She's my client," I said, and smiled. "You're sure you don't know her name, Rose?"

"Didn't I already tell you I don't? Frankie said it was a dame, that's all. The rest he kept strictly to himself."

"These promises he made you . . . Were they made when he met you in the bar?"

Her head negatived. "No. I think the idea of making some quick money was something he dreamed up when he was loafing around here." She touched her lip gingerly, making sure it hadn't started to bleed again. "I got the big speech when I came home from work one night. Frankie was real hot about it, like a kid who's found a hole in their neighbor's bathroom window. He told me he'd been using my phone to make some long distance calls. He even parted with a few bucks to take care of the bill when it arrived."

"Know who he was calling?" I asked casually.

"How many times I got to tell you Frankie played things close to his vest? I wasn't even a junior partner in the enterprise!" Even the swollen blue eye tried to open and match the other's roundness when her face reddened in quick anger.

The smile I gave her could have been interpreted any way she wished. She received it the way I had hoped, calmed down and said:

"Who he called, I don't know, except it was someone up in Tayward, or Taywood, or something. And the only reason I know that is because there was a collect call for him here one night. I took it, and the operator told me where it was coming from. Okay?"

It was difficult to know how much of what she had given me was the truth, or whether the information provided was simply that which she had decided was safe enough for me to have. Rose Lang had encountered the school of hard knocks as part of her basic education, and lying for someone like her would require no special talent. By her own admission, a dancer. And probably a dancer with some acting ability. Yet the way she told her story had been in a manner of total dejection and defeat, as if speaking to me could no longer alter matters or their ultimate outcome.

Frankie Cugino's driver's license had been issued at Taywood, California, but I never told her that. Perhaps she already knew and had snatched at the name to pad out the story of the long distance call.

I said: "What was going to happen to all of his plans, those to take you away with him?"

"What do you mean?"

"He skipped out, didn't he?"

"Sure. But he was forced to. You oughta know. It was you who leaned on him."

"And that was to be goodbye to the boyfriend and the promised Utopia?" I suggested.

"He promised to send for me. He said nothing had changed. Things had just been delayed and that I had to wait here till he contacted me again."

"Which you've been doing," I said to fill the gap.

"There was something else I could do?"

"You could have gone with him."

"Oh, no. Not again, brother. Until I saw the color of the loot he was bragging about getting I wasn't moving my butt nowhere. There's a saying about being bitten once or something."

"What do you do now?" I asked her.

"You mean with Frankie being dead?" She stood up, let her shoulders perform another slow rise and fall before plowing her balled-up fists into the dressing robe's pockets. "What's there to do but go on working and waiting till something better comes along."

"I was thinking about Strode and his friend. It might be smart for you to leave this apartment. There anywhere else you could go?"

"New York's my home, but getting there will be something else again." Her open eye peered at me with new interest. "You really think those two could come back?"

"Why take chances?" I took out my billfold and opened it. Inside were a hundred and sixty-three dollars. I removed all but two fives and three singles and held them out to her.

She took them before asking: "What's this for?"

"Call it a contribution to your transportation. And if I can make a further suggestion, I'd advise leaving first thing in the morning. Hanging around could prove dangerous."

"Thanks," she murmured after counting the thin sheaf of bills. "I've still got a few bucks of my own, and with this there's no reason to sit around waiting for trouble, is there?"

"None at all."

"Why are you doing this for me?" she asked cautiously, and the suspicion in her voice seemed to throw a shaft of light into her eye that made it shine. It looked solitary and evil.

"I saw what happened to Frankie," I answered. "You've still got a lot of living to do. Besides, if the police get to you before Strode does, and if they chose not to believe that you knew nothing of Cugino's affairs . . . Well, you're still pretty young to go inside."

"And you're Big Hearted Ben who's going to save me from all that, huh?"

"I've lost more than that on horses," I said.

She grinned, but the eye still looked like glass. A globule of blood squeezed out of her lip. "This money—I suppose it'll be part of your expenses, no?"

"I could book it to that. Why do you ask?"

"Just thinking." She turned so that her face was averted. "This dame you're working for must really be loaded."

"If you're trying to say something, Rose, why not trot it out so we can both understand."

I waited for what I had expected to come much earlier.

Her face returned, the swollen lip twisted in a painful attempt at a smile.

"Maybe it wasn't those two bums that knocked off Frankie. Could be it was this dame, this rich bitch he was going to work on who did it. You thought about that?"

I said nothing.

"How about that? Couldn't be you're trying to buy me off, could it? Get me out of the way?"

"Get dressed," I said, "and we'll go and have a talk with the law. You can tell them all you've told me. After that you can make up your own mind about things. I've offered you what I can but I can't force you to accept it."

"Forget it," she broke in. "I was only kidding. I know what the score is, Cameron, and whether it sounds like it or not, I'm grateful for the dough. After tomorrow you won't be seeing me again. Not unless you happen to be up in Manhattan sometime."

I went to the door and turned back the lock.

"So long, Rose. Take care."

"The best," she said.

Outside her apartment I waited until the lock snapped into position and her bare feet padded away from the door. Like a foreboding star the memory of her bright eye followed me all the way to the steps. I wondered about the investment I had made.

In the dim light of the stair well a man leaned against the wall. He looked sleepy as he came erect and took something out of the shabby green suit which pulled tightly around a belly gone to fat. He smiled when I stopped, allowing the light to flash on the square of gold in his open mouth, and brought his hand into view so that the double-action .38 wouldn't be mistaken for an artificial extension of his arm.

"You been a long time, pal," he said. "Let's go."

"Anywhere in particular?" I asked, looking for a way around him.

"To see a man that wants to talk to you. C'mon, let's get moving."

I said, without moving: "Tell him to make an appointment."

"I'm making one for him. Now—with this." The gun was thrust forward. "It good enough for you?"

"It's good enough."

When we reached the sidewalk he slipped the gun back into his pocket and steered me across the street to where a long black Imperial waited. The back door swung open as we neared it.

"Inside," the one behind instructed, and a hand placed on my back helped my progress.

Another one was waiting on the back seat. Like the man in green who opened the driver's door and wedged himself behind the wheel, this one also held a gun. He pointed it at my face. The gun was less conventional than the weapon his partner affected: a .22 automatic target pistol with a long fluted barrel.

Even seated he looked tall. In the centre of his long face a large lump of flesh posed as a nose. Above it the slanted eyebrows were pale and bushy. He wore a dark straw hat with a band like a drunken rainbow, a sports coat with noisy gray checks, and black and white moccasins.

"Thit nithe and thtill," he advised, "and there won't be any trouble."

SIX

LIKE an impatient dark fury the big car weaved its way out of Venice, hurrying in the direction of Santa Monica. Little was said as we moved along, but I was given the impression by what I managed to draw out of them that they'd been watching Rose Lang's apartment, waiting for someone like myself to put in an appearance. I had a feeling also that the sloppy one had been leaning his ear against her keyhole.

Eerie blue light lit up twin windows of a florist shop, lending a funereal atmosphere to the display behind the glass. There the Imperial slowed down and turned into an alley at the side of the building, halting in front of a low concrete ramp.

The one in the green suit got out of the car and opened the back door. The gun had returned to his hand. "Out," said the one at my side.

I hesitated, but only briefly, before sliding off the seat and into the alley.

"Watch him, Bo," the voice from behind warned. "I have a feeling thith one could be cute."

Bo snorted contemptuously, waving the Smith and Wesson. "Quit worrying. I got a cure for that kind of ailment."

We mounted the ramp, and while Bo kept watch over me, his partner unlocked a wicket gate in the steel roll-up door and held it open for us to pass through. The smell of the graveyard dominated the dark interior.

Before the gate was slammed shut a light went on inside. The room in which we stood looked as if it were part of the florist set-up. Crates and cartons stacked closely together consumed much of the floor space. Long wooden tables were positioned against one wall, their scarred tops damp. On the floor once-green stems had been squashed into the cement, along with flower petals blackened by rot. Across the room was another door.

The one I'd heard called Leo said: "Keep him here. I'll go and tell The Earl."

Bo made another gold patch grin when the door closed behind his partner. "You heard the man."

The next five minutes were spent watching the green man, the gun he held, and glancing around at the things in the depressing room. Then Leo came back.

"Take him up," he said.

I was taken through the door into a short lobby and up a straight flight of stairs to a narrow landing, and from there into a murky smoke-filled room where a very little man sat munching a torpedo-shaped cigar. Poker chips and playing cards were strewn upon the round table at which he sat.

From the stench of smoke, the state of the ashtrays, the positions of the cards and the three unoccupied chairs, it looked as if the other players might only recently have retired to another part of the building.

"Close the door, Strode," the little man instructed from around the fat cigar, and quietly Leo obeyed.

"He'th unarmed, Erle," Strode told him, coming back to stand behind me. "Hith name'th Cameron. A private thtar." From the side pocket of his jazzy coat he took out my identification folder which had been removed during the ride to Santa Monica. He pushed it across the table to the man in the chair.

Bo moved noiselessly to the other side of the table and leaned against the wall. From there he and the .38 continued their vigil.

"Siddown, why don't you?" the little man said.

Strode's hand fastened on my shoulder and pressed me down onto one of the chairs standing way back from the table. As I sat down and watched my property undergo inspection I began remembering certain things. Had Strode not mentioned his name I would not have recognized him, even if his pictures—usually in the company of female companions—had frequented several newspapers in the last year. Now as I looked at him much of what I had read started to return. Erle Donetti—racketeer, alleged gang boss, self-professed businessman, self-proclaimed lover. Hoodlum.

Up until a year ago he had been an almost unknown quantity. Then his brother had died and suddenly the younger Donetti was making news. More than once he'd received mention in connection with gang killings, but so far no one had been able to make much more than a parking ticket stick. For a long time certain government agencies, including the Bureau of Narcotics, had maintained a close interest in the activities of his brother. Now those same agencies watched and waited for the younger Donetti to make that one slip that would put him in a similar place to the one in which his brother had died. Erle Donetti. Or as he enjoyed being called—The Earl.

I said: "Apparently you've never heard about the Little Lindbergh law."

He tossed aside the leather case. "You howlin' that you've been kidnapped?"

"Technically, that's what it is, isn't it?"

"Want to lodge a complaint?" Donetti asked, sliding back his chair and rising to his full five feet-odd height.

I checked the smile on Bo's wide florid face, the gun in his fist. Both looked equally as deadly.

"I want to know why I've been brought here."

Donetti took a few aimless steps, clasped his hands behind his back and frowned down at me. In his mouth the cigar was like an obscene extrusion. The dark suit adorning his slim frame was of an expensive Italian cut, the trousers narrow, the coat pockets slanted sharply. In his buttonhole he wore a large white blossom. A precisely folded handkerchief peeped out of his breast pocket and matched the gleaming forty dollar silk shirt. His shoes were pointed, highly polished, and on his head the smooth shiny black growth looked as if it had been cultivated from the same material as the footwear. Behind a florist's counter Donetti would have seemed a natural.

"Strode and Fletcher, my boys here, say you've been visiting with the Lang woman." Rocking back on his heels, head canted slightly, he took another drag on the cigar before going on. "What'd you want with her?"

"A private discussion. Why?"

Something hard chopped down on my shoulder from behind and my left arm went numb. Strode said:

"Don't be cute, hard boy. Jutht anther the quethtion."

"I was looking for someone," I said, massaging my arm. "She was a lead."

Donetti took the cigar from his mouth, studied the ash thoughtfully before flicking it to the floor. "This person you're looking for. He got a name?"

"Cugino. Know him?"

"Never mind about me. What'd you want with him?"

"Something private."

Angrily the cigar was wedged back into his swarthy face. He pulled hard on it, jerked it free again, and blew smoke hard at me. "There's something you wanna understand, my friend. When I ask a question I get an answer, not lip. Now, nicely I ask you just once more. What is it you wanted with Cugino?"

"Your zip's down," I muttered.

Involuntarily Donetti's gaze and one hand flashed down to his pants. Before I could see his reaction the chair in which I sat lurched backward and toppled to the floor. I went with it—the back of my head slamming hard against the bare wood. Above me I saw the pouting lips on Strode's long pink face twist ugly. The toe of his shoe crashed into my ribs, then took a jab at my skull. Somewhere far away I thought I heard Bo Fletcher chuckle.

I must have slipped under for a few seconds because the next thing I remembered was having Strode prop me back in the chair. My head ached and my vision was hazy. Strode held on to my tie so that my head wouldn't sag. Behind him Erle Donetti smiled.

"You wanna be taught some manners, it can be arranged. You wanna be co-operative, we'll treat you nice. Please yourself how it's going to be." He filled his lungs with more blue smoke, letting it dribble out through thin, flared nostrils before again asking: "What was your business with him?"

My answer was slow in coming, so Strode pulled hard on my tie as a reminder that people were waiting.

"He was blackmailing a client," I choked, my head beginning to clear.

"The name of this client?" Donetti snapped. "Quick!"

I reached up and jerked the tie from Strode's hand. "That's my business. You want to play rough, go right ahead. In the end it will still be only my business."

The back of Leo's hand slashed twice across my face, snapping my head sharply back. My eyes felt scalded. "Want me to work him over for you, Erle?" Bo Fletcher offered from where he lounged against the wall. "I'll have him singing like a thrush inside of five minutes."

The Earl nodded and resumed his place at the table. Fletcher came at me, stowing away the .38.

"This's going to hurt, pally," he grinned happily. "But anytime you want it to stop, you know what you got to do. Savvy?" He bent down slowly and I braced my neck for the impact of his fist. But it wasn't my head he wanted. His right shoulder made a sudden drop and air gushed out of my mouth when his fist dug itself deep below my belt. Before there was time to gasp, it happened again. Very quickly things began to grow painfully dim.

I heard voices, felt hands on my face, slapping, jerking, and I wanted to be sick. Somewhere in between there was a lull in the proceedings and I heard Bo's voice. Snatches of what I heard were things I'd said to Rose Lang and what she'd told me in return. Then they were working again, and afterwards there was the groaning sound of my own voice. It was all vague and unreal and I had no idea of what or how much I told them. At last Donetti's voice broke through and the hands released me. I fell from the chair and lay on the floor, gasping, squinting at the light that filtered through my eyelids, wondering how long it took to die.

Someone was pouring fire down my throat and I was back in the chair. I gagged on the liquid and spat it out.

"Swallow it!" It was Fletcher's voice.

I swallowed slowly. It burned all the way down, but it brought back some life to my body. There was no pain, just numbness. Even the desire to throw up had vanished. I shoved the hand and glass back shakily and felt my face. There was no blood and all my teeth were intact. I felt in my pocket for cigarettes and took a long time to get one going. Nobody tried to help.

"Satisfied?" I mumbled.

"You're not tough, Cameron," Donetti replied from where he sat back behind the table. "But you're a stubborn son-of-a-bitch. Either that or you're leveling. You changed your mind about telling me who's paying you."

I blew smoke into my lap. For the first time in years it tasted good. I wondered if it was so because there wouldn't be another.

"Bo could go back to work on you. You'd like that? Or maybe this time I'll let Leo take over. He's got a little more talent. There's tricks Leo knows that Bo never even heard about. You wanna see them?"

When I didn't answer, he grunted: "Okay. So okay, it isn't that important. How about the package Cugino's got stashed away? You know about that? You already told us some of it."

I sucked deeply on the cigarette before trying to speak. "If I told you anything like that it was only what I picked up from the girl. She told me your two animals were after something Cugino was supposed to have. But she didn't know anything about it. Neither do I." The cigarette slipped out of my fingers. I left it smoldering on the floor. "Why not ask Cugino? He ought to have all the answers."

"Because the bastard's dead, that's why!"

My head lifted.

"It was on the news," he explained. "They found a body up along the coast where Cugino's been hiding out. It came over the news a few hours ago."

"I saw the body," I informed him tiredly. "It was burned beyond recognition."

"It still is," Donetti said guardedly. "The cops up there are still trying to put a name to it."

"But you know it's Cugino," I said, looking at Strode. "You said Leo knows all kinds of tricks. That one of them?"

Short, stubby fingers laced themselves together as Donetti leaned back in his chair. "I sent Leo and Bo up there to find him, but I didn't give no order to have him liquidated. He had it coming, only not yet." He paused. "You know who I am?"

I nodded.

The smile was the kind of proud smirk I had seen on faces of others who had clawed their way out of sewers to establish reputations that had elevated them to the top of the rackets. "Ever hear of my brother? Gino Donetti?"

I shook my head in a silent lie that brought a look of disappointment to his smooth face.

"So all right. It was a long time ago, and besides Gino operated in New York. He was a big man up there," he added with what sounded like a small note of sourness. "Cugino worked for him, but he was a no-account rat. He made a mistake and the cops picked him up. Cugino was the worst kinda fink that lived. When the cops put the arm on him he blew the whistle on my brother—got him sent up for a long stretch. Gino got sick and he never got out again." Lids lowered themselves halfway over the listless eyes. "I was with Gino when he died. You know what it's like to be with your brother when he's gotta die with a lot of stinking fuzz watching? No"—he shook his head—"you wouldn't. But I did, and because I did I got good reason for wanting Cugino dead."

Any comments I had, I kept to myself.

"You wanna know how I know it's him that's dead?"

"It should be interesting," I answered, feeling the numbness give way to pain crawling into my stomach.

"They found a car. It was pushed over a cliff into the sea. A brown Chevy. It also came over the news. You know what kinda car Cugino was using?"

"A brown Chevy."

"Yeah. And that's how I know the bastard's dead. I can put two and two together."

Which meant exactly nothing. If he had ordered the kill he certainly wouldn't admit it to me—or to anyone else. Not on his own accord. I said:

"You were acting anxious about a package."

"Yeah, the package." He produced another cigar, methodically stripping away the cellophane. "It belonged to Gino. Frankie had it when the cops put the arm on him. He kept quiet about it and when he was sprung he picked it up from wherever he had it stashed. But it belongs to me. Cugino figured nobody else knew about it, but he forgot me, Gino Donetti's brother—The Earl. Me, I don't forget. Gino told me about the merchandise and I was waiting for Frankie when they turned him loose."

I waited for the rest while he flicked a gold lighter and nosed the cigar into the flame. "Trouble is, Frankie was too slippery, or else the boys were asleep. He got away from us. That was over three months ago. We been chasing him across the country since then." A cloud of smoke disintegrated in my face. "I want that stuff back."

"What has any of this got to do with me?"

"Just this. You got any ambitions about going after it yourself—you figuring on getting your hands on that stuff, forget it. You had a taste of what we can dish out. There'll be more. Maybe of a permanent nature."

Like with Frankie Cugino?

"What's supposed to be in the package?" I asked, although I already had a reasonably good idea. If it was important to Erle Donetti, it would be only one of three things, and the first could be struck out because it didn't make sense of past events.

"What'th it to you?" Strode queried quietly.

I directed my reply to his boss: "Supposing I find it? What happened here hurt, but it isn't going to stop me from completing the job I've started. Cugino figures in that and it's just remotely possible I'll stumble across that package before you do."

For the next few seconds the cigar held his complete attention. At last he spoke:

"Supposing you do? You thinking about making a deal with me?"

"What sort of deal?"

"Like maybe trying to sell it back to me? If so—*don't.* That stuff is mine. Nobody else owns it. But"—he poked the smoking cigar back between his lips and reached under his coat for a bulging wallet—"I'll do this much. Take this." Several bills of large denominations were plucked from the wallet and spread out on the table. "You find that package, or you find out where it is, you let me know. Either way—you return it to The Earl, or tell him where it is, and I treble what's there."

I shook my head. It hurt and things seemed to move inside.

"Whatsa matter? Not enough?"

"Not for what you want."

"How much then?" he asked guardedly.

"It's no deal, Donetti. I'm not looking for what Cugino's supposed to have had. But if I do find it, it goes to the cops. Besides, I wouldn't even know what to look for."

"Cameron," he breathed wearily, "you're either a damn fool or an idiot. I don't know which. Maybe you're a bit of both. That's a lotta money there. You don't need money?"

"I need money," I said, "but not that much. Let Leo and Bo go sniffing for it. I'm not for that kind of hire."

"You know what the stuff is?"

"I could make a guess."

"My money's dirty, that it?"

"You said it, not me."

He stood up and walked around the table, hands behind his back again. From the other side of the wall I thought I could hear someone laugh. After that there was only the sound of the little man with the majestic air pacing about thoughtfully.

"You know we could get rid of you without no trouble?" he said, stopping before me.

"I've thought about it. But you won't."

"No? What makes you so damn sure?"

"Because you can't be certain I don't know what Cugino did with the package. Only you're wrong. I don't."

For the first time he chuckled. "Know something? I don't get you. You coulda kept your face shut, let us go on thinking anything we wanted to think. Maybe even sucker me into a phony deal that would give you time to get outa my reach. But no, you go ahead and make things easy for me to dispose of you. Whatsa matter? You some kinda nut?"

"Maybe Leo loosened something in my skull when I fell."

"Supposing I let you go? What you going to do? Run to the cops and bleat about what happened here tonight?"

"Would it help? Your money could buy lawyers who'd make me sound like an imbecile in a court room."

"Quite so," he agreed. "Then again you make trouble for me, we'll just have to make trouble for you. And trouble's something I don't especially want. What I want is what's in that package. All right"—he made a silencing gesture with his hands—"you won't work for me, I can't force you. You force people you ask for a double-ex and more trouble. So I take a chance. I let you go and no hard feelings." From the table he scooped up the three bills and gave them to Strode. "Give it to him."

Leo took the money and tucked it into my pocket.

"That's for what happened. Call it compensation for the going over the boys gave you. I ain't going to apologize. You were uncooperative. You asked for a lotta what you got."

Strode's voice pitched high with disbelief: "Erle, you—you going to turn him loothe?"

"What you want I should do?" Donetti asked sarcastically. He turned back to me. "Get up. The boys are gonna take you home."

I stood up, wanting to take the money from my pocket and return it to him. But that would have been inviting more of what I'd received, and more of that I could do without. Under the weight of my body my legs were like old pipe cleaners and my stomach hurt so bad that I had to bend slightly to relieve the pain.

"I'm letting you go, feller," Donetti said slowly, his voice an icy chill that cut sharply across the room. "I'm taking a chance on you going outa here and minding your own business. You rat to the cops, you make trouble for me or you try and latch on to that stuff yourself—you're like dead. Get it? No matter where you go, you're dead. Read me?"

I leaned across the table and retrieved the case that contained the photostat of my license and other identification. It was in my hand when Strode spun me roughly around.

"You were athked a quethtion!"

So far I'd been pushed, kicked and knocked about. I'd been stuck on the receiving end of everything they had wanted to dish out. Including Donetti's generous gesture to turn me loose under the shadow of a death threat. Perhaps because I'd been in no position to do anything effective until then, a childish impulse urged me to strike back in some way. Without thinking, I said:

"You've got an awful lot of mouth for a mutt who can't even pronounce his own name."

There were stupider things I could have done, but that was enough to draw the wrong kind of reaction from Strode.

He exhaled a slow curse and shot his left deep into my middle, following with a quick right that was there to greet me when I doubled up. Donetti said something. But I didn't hear and was beyond giving a damn.

2

It was either the cold air caressing the side of my face or the overpowering stench of whisky that finally lifted the darkness and snapped my eyes open. That, or the sound of labored breathing and the vague awareness that a hand was carefully pawing through my clothes. I listened to the breathing and tried not to move as the unseen fingers felt their way to my hip pocket. Somehow I had returned to my car, propped over the steering wheel, looking and smelling like a drunk who shouldn't have belted back the last one.

The hand had discovered my billfold and was gently tugging it loose from my pocket. At the side of my head the breathing was heavier, and over the whisky fumes there was more than a mild suggestion of halitosis. When I was sure I could move again without making a fool of myself, I pushed away from the wheel, twisted and drove my left elbow upward to where I imagined the face would be, hoping it belonged to Leo Strode. The sound of impact was sharp; the surprised cry of pain loud. I reached out clumsily for the dark shape that hulked over me, but he was too quick. With the attempt to roll me abandoned, and with both hands now free, he lashed out desperately. A fist barely missed my head but jabbed itself into my shoulder with sufficient force to rock me back onto the seat. Then there was nothing except my own heavy panting and the diminishing echo of shoe leather slapping itself against asphalt.

I pulled myself up and squinted through the windshield. A small figure that could have been man or boy, or anything else with bad breath, was hurriedly spreading distance between it and the car. As I watched it turned swiftly onto the sidewalk and gave itself to the protection of the shadows.

It had been a bad night for both of us.

In my pocket I found cigarettes, now badly crumpled, and hung one on my lip, pulling the car door shut as I fished around for a light. My shirt front was damp and explained the reason for the booze stink. I got the cigarette going and looked up at Rose Lang's apartment block. Apparently all its occupants were in bed, for not a light burned in the building. I thought about going up to check on her, but discarded the idea. Instead I twisted the key which had been considerately returned to the ignition switch. Very slowly I let in the clutch and crawled out of the neighborhood.

In the security of my own apartment I began peeling off the soiled clothes, examining the work Bo Fletcher had executed. It looked as lousy as it felt. Then I started thinking of Rose Lang again. I sat down on the bed and hunted up her number.

On the eleventh ring a sleepy voice answered.

"What the hell do you want now?" she demanded after learning who had interrupted her sleep.

"Just wanted to make sure you were all right," I said, and apologized for waking her. "Better leave early in the morning, Rose. Those guys are still around."

She said something I missed hearing before slamming the receiver down on me.

I dropped the phone back into its cradle, looked at the bed, and was unconscious again before I reached the pillows.

SEVEN

SUNLIGHT pressing down on my face and chest like a broad open hand dragged me back from the sleep of the dead. Overnight ten years had been added to my thirty-four: from my neck to my hips there was a stiffness that ached when I breathed, and in my mouth the taste of a hairy foot. I had a rough idea of what The Lip's opponents felt like the morning after the fight. Except that they had a share of the purse to compensate for the bruises and bumps. Outside the traffic murmured steadily back and forth. Busy people going about their daily business. Healthy people. The time was twenty minutes before nine and it was Tuesday, and three days before Friday. And Friday was D-Day for Allison Page—the deadline declared by Lynx. Three lousy days. California, I reflected wearily, was a large piece of real estate, offering over 158,000 square miles in which to hide or get lost, and I had a Chinaman's chance of finding her before the end of the week. The bed felt luxuriously comfortable, clinging to my back with a tenderness that was more enticing than the arms of any woman.

The battle from the bed to the shower was a long one.

Cold water pounded down on my head and dispelled some of the fogginess that had clogged up between the ears. I turned the water up harder until the spray was torturous, and bit back a yell. Around my stomach the skin had turned a greenish blue and my left ribs were swollen. But by the time I shut off the water I was again feeling like something to which the human race had grudgingly granted acceptance.

Before completing the job of shaving and dressing I put on one of her recordings, and after the disc had played itself out knocked together a light breakfast and swallowed cups of black coffee.

Erle Donetti worked his way into my thoughts. I started thinking about the package he was so anxious to recover. Last night I had formed a crude idea of what it might contain. This morning I was more certain. Money was out, for Frankie Cugino had been in want of that commodity, trying blackmail to satisfy his needs. That left records which, if allowed to fall into the wrong hands, could prove disastrous to The Earl's activities. Or else the stuff in the package was dope, a supply entrusted to Cugino before his arrest in New York. The last I liked best. At six hundred dollars an ounce, it wouldn't take a great deal to make a small package very valuable to the wrong kind of people. I thought sourly about the way I'd been soaked in booze and dumped back in my car. If I'd been unlucky enough to have been woken up by the law, a tough time would have been had explaining the situation—even if the alky test proved negative. And if any eager badge had bothered to check out Donetti, all he'd have found was a group of card players ready to swear that the entire crew, including Fletcher and Strode, had been intact all evening.

The coffee began to get bitter.

On the way to the office I bought a copy of *The Times,* dropping it on my desk before picking up the phone to call Rigby's office. Once again I talked with the seductive voice, and once again heard that Rigby was out, not expected back until after lunch. I broke the connection and fingered through the book for Allison Page's number. It wasn't in the listings. I hung up the receiver and returned to *The Times.*

Vietnam, racial trouble in San Francisco and a sex slaying in Ventura took care of the lead pages that morning. The story I looked for was locked away inside, but it carried a picture of Under-sheriff Phillips and one of his assistants, together with a shape on the ground that could have been anything but which was identified as the burned body. Except for a footnote to the story there was nothing I didn't already know. Details of the blonde seen near the spot where the body had been found were given prominence, as was the description of her silver car. The footnote told of another car, a brown Chevrolet, which had been salvaged from the sea. According to Under-sheriff Phillips the car had been run off the edge of a low cliff but had hit a submerged rock during its descent. Otherwise it might still have been underwater, undiscovered. The registration plates and other identification had been removed and the sheriff's men were now in the process of running down the engine number. Found in the padding of the driver's door had been a hole that had led to further investigation. A .22 slug had been retrieved from behind the panel—one which matched three other slugs the coroner had removed from the body of the burned man.

I read the story a second time. Neither Genders nor I were named. I closed the paper, put it in a bottom drawer and lit a cigarette. It made me a little dizzy, the way the first in the morning always does. I looked at the phone, felt my bruised middle, and spent ten minutes pondering the validity of an anonymous call to Vadear Point. There was a certain .22 automatic target pistol I knew of that would, I was sure, provide the law with some interesting information. I picked up the phone, but contacted my answering service instead. The girl had no messages.

I told her I planned to be out most of the day, that if Rigby should call she was to either take a message or find out where I could reach him.

The various directories in my bookshelf couldn't tell me what I needed to know, so I locked up the inner office, drove down to the City Library, and checked through theirs. It was a routine long shot that paid off. The name and address I sought was in the first directory checked.

Back in the car I flipped a mental coin. It came down heads, so I made for the Hollywood Freeway and from there headed south-east, picking up the San Bernardino Freeway to cross over into the nation's largest county.

At San Bernardino I stopped for something cold before continuing north-east on the wide paved highway of Route 66. Groves of oranges and lemons gleamed cleanly under a hot midday sun, while a half hour distant was Taywood, the city that had waited a long time for something like a boom to happen.

Back in the eighteen hundreds when a handful of Mormons purchased enough land from some Spanish ranchero to begin what was now the City of San Bernardino, another religious group led by a man named Taywood secured a stretch of land further north. There they set about establishing a city that would make the Mormons' attempt look like the floundering feat of amateurs. But Taywood had put his dreams on a pair of deuces, his opposition, it appeared, on a royal flush. And while San Bernardino had flourished rapidly, the growth Of Taywood had been agonizingly slow. San Berdoo had never needed to concern itself over the competition. If the way I had heard the story was true, a certain non-Mormon would probably be lying face down in what was left of his coffin by now.

2

Built almost entirely around a wide open square in which stood an impressive church, its steeple spiraling desperately towards the heavens as if hoping to snag at least a passing cloud, the city sprawled at the foothills of the mountains. I slowed down where the sign warned of a speed limit and spent several minutes getting directions to the Hillside district.

The neighborhood had gone to seed, but at one time it would have been a good middle-class address. Only a few of the houses there were making any sort of attempt to retain something of what had originally induced their owners to buy. Trees grew tall and untidily along the sidewalk, cypress hedges high. But only here and there was the monotony broken by the color of flowers. The house I wanted had neither flowers nor hedge. In places bare wood showed where the paint of years past had flaked away. A piece of cardboard with faded blue print still visible from the outside kept the weather from entering a broken window. The house was at the lower end of the street where its neighbors could perhaps pretend it didn't exist.

I pulled in against the opposite sidewalk and got out. My middle remained stiff and sore, but the discomfort was something I could live with without too much strain.

At the door I pressed the plastic bell button, and when nothing happened inside the house tapped loudly against the glass panel. A dusty old Chrysler in need of a wash was parked in front of a garage that no longer had a door. A gray cat sat on its roof and watched me with narrowed suspicious eyes. I was about to knock again when the dull curtain screening the glass panel in the door jerked aside and a shadowy face peered out from the gloom. The curtain dropped back into place and the door opened.

"Yeah? What do you want?" He was old and dirty, with wisps of hair sprouting stiffly from a huge, balding head. Around his chin the stubble was days old. His face was lumpy and pale, like a bowl of cold porridge.

"Mr. Cugino?"

"That's me. What do you want?"

"A little discussion that I'd prefer conducting inside."

Watery blue eyes blinked twice before he said loudly: "Not until I heard what you're after. If you're selling, you're wasting your time with me."

I took out my identification and let him see the license stat. "My business concerns a Frank Antonio Cugino."

"Cop?" He was squinting at the license, but I didn't think he could read much of what was on it.

"I'm a private investigator, Mr. Cugino."

"Hah, one of those!" he snorted, throwing back his head. "What's Frankie done?"

"Do you want the street to hear?"

His head turned from me to inspect the house next door.

"Okay. Come in. That bitch over there's got her nose to the window again, I bet. If she could get herself a man now and again maybe she'd keep her gawdamn beak where it belongs. Maybe if she wasn't so damn miserable I'd oblige her myself."

Before he could change his mind I went in. He shut the door and the passage turned dim.

"This way if you want to talk," he said, shuffling past me.

We went into a room that was filled with a mixture of dark, ancient furniture; dusty and neglected. A yellowed print and framed photographs of a woman and a group of people hung from a black picture rail above wallpaper that still showed off some of its original design. The smell in the room was strong enough to walk on.

The old man creaked slowly down into a chair, motioning me to another. As I lowered myself into the depths of a nearby wing-back something dark and furry leapt from the corner of the seat and ran meowing to the door.

"You said you wanted to talk. So talk. Tell me what you've got to do with my boy. He ain't in trouble, is he?"

The once-white shirt he wore looked like something that doubled as pajamas. The blue slacks were creased and stained with grease spots. On his feet were felt slippers without socks. A bare toe peeped from a hole in the left one. I studied him for a few seconds before nodding silently.

"Got a cigarette?" he asked, leaning forward.

"Frankie's in trouble," I said, reaching for the Camels and shaking one loose. He stretched across and plucked it from the deck.

"What I figured. You expect me to be surprised?" The voice was smooth for a man of his age, apparently having discarded emotion a long time ago. "Frankie's been in all kinds of scrapes ever since he was born. I don't get surprised anymore when I hear about it." He looked at the cigarette, poked it into a hole between the whiskers and rubbed his chin. "Got a match?"

I had it ready and put a flame to the smoke. He sucked on it hungrily.

"When did you last see your son, Mr. Cugino?"

From behind a stream of feathered smoke he shrugged. "Eight years ago. Maybe more. I never kept check."

"But he kept in touch with you, didn't he?"

"Like hell! Frankie was no letter writer. Once or twice he sent me a note, and now and again a few dollars. You call that keeping in touch? And me with just a measly pension and nearly all my savings used up. You'd think a man's only boy would want to look after his old man, wouldn't you?" I was wrong about the emotion. He still knew how to talk in tones of self-pity.

"Mr. Cugino," I said slowly, "we have reason to believe your son phoned you more than once from Los Angeles during the last few weeks. What I'm here for is to find out what he wanted."

Another long drag on the smoke while eyes like small wet marbles rolled cautiously, as if trying to find something more about me than I was letting show.

"Frankie phone me? You must be crazy. That's the last thing he'd waste his money doing. You got your information from the wrong people, mister. Which reminds me. You never said what your name was."

I gave it to him. "Look, Mr. Cugino, I don't know how you felt about your son, or how he felt about you. But for your own sake I'd suggest the truth. Frankie phoned you, didn't he?"

The cigarette received one last drag before it was dropped to the floor where a slippered foot squashed it to a shredded smear.

"Don't go calling me a liar, sonny. I ain't the type that stands for that sort of lip. Not from nobody, cops included. And you're no real cop. You don't like it when I tell you the truth; get your ass the hell out of my house."

"Who else would he phone here?"

"Why don't you ask him?"

"If it were possible, I would."

The cat returned to the room and sprang onto the old man's lap. He let it get comfortable, a gnarled hand stroking its black coat. The only sound in the room was the cat's purr.

"Go on," he said. "Tell it. What's happened to him that he can't answer your questions?"

"Your son's dead," I told him.

The withering hand tightened over the cat. It squealed and clawed at his thigh. He knocked it off his lap and swore loudly. Then he got up and came over to my chair, glaring down at where I sat.

"What kind of game you playing, mister?"

"It's no game," I answered carefully. "A man was shot to death and then burned so that he couldn't be identified. This happened along the coast at Vadear Point. A car, the same kind Frankie drove, was fished out of the Pacific. The police found a bullet hole in it and all the obvious identification removed. The bullet they took out of the car matched those taken from the body."

The whiskered jaw moved soundlessly, masticating the information before digesting it piece by piece. He looked at the hole in his slipper, then brought his head up to face me.

"Just because they found a car like Frankie's is no call to think it belonged to my boy. You said the body was burnt so they couldn't identify it."

"I saw the body, Mr. Cugino. I also saw Frankie the night before. If it wasn't him, the corpse had borrowed his shoes."

"That still don't necessarily mean it was him."

I kept quiet.

Cugino exhaled loudly, rubbed hard at a bearded cheek and turned away. He shuffled to his chair, stopping to look at one of the pictures on the wall.

"He's gone, Millie," he muttered quietly. "Just like you always prophesied he'd go. Frankie's gone to hell."

I stood up. Cugino turned around.

"Who did it?"

"That's one of the things I'm trying to establish. One of the reasons I was hoping you could help me. Did you know what sort of business your son was engaged in?"

The lumpy face negatived. "But whatever it was I knew it wasn't no good. I got a letter from him in New York one time when he was in prison. But he never went into details."

"He worked for a man named Donetti," I said. "A racketeer who, among other things, dealt in narcotics. While in his employ Frankie was arrested. He turned states witness and drew a shorter term than Donetti. Donetti died in prison, and since his release Frankie has been running from Donetti's brother. It seems Erle Donetti blames your son for his brother's death."

The watery blue eyes slitted as his forehead creased up in a fleshy frown.

"Your son ratted on Donetti," I explained. "The way Erle Donetti sees things, his brother would still be alive had he not been forced to live behind bars."

"And this feller—this Erle Donetti—he the one that killed Frankie?"

"I believe so. Or at least he had one of his men take care of the actual killing. But Donetti wanted something your son was supposed to have had. He still hasn't got it, and he's still looking."

"For what?" he queried.

"A package."

"Of dope?"

I said nothing.

"Well?"

"Do you have it, Mr. Cugino?"

"You got rocks in the head? I told you I never saw Frankie for more than eight years!"

"Then what made you ask if the package contained dope?"

"Mister," he said slow and ominously, "don't try to knot up my words or s'help me I'll toss you through that gawdamned window and don't think I can't! You said Frankie was mixed up with people who sold that damned stuff, didn't you? What else you want me to think was in that parcel they want back—this Donetti?" The gray face became dark while hands trembled at his sides. I didn't think he'd be able to carry out his threat, but at the same time I had no desire to tangle with him. He looked like the kind who had never learned that men in their twilight years are supposed to scorn the rough life.

Placatingly I said: "Forget it. I'm not interested in that stuff."

The hands stopped moving and he blew out his breath. "It was dope then, huh?"

"I could be wrong, but I don't think so. Apparently the package was in Frankie's keeping at the time the law put the arm on him. Neither he nor Gino Donetti noised it about during their respective trials, but when he knew he was dying Donetti told his brother all about it. That's one of the reasons Erle Donetti was after your boy."

"You got another cigarette?"

I gave him another and lit it.

"Who told you all this stuff about Frank?" he asked, after a few deep drags had been taken from the cigarette.

"Donetti," I said.

"That's who you're working for?"

"No. My association with him is purely incidental. The job I'm doing seems to have cut across his activities, that's all."

"Then how come you're so interested in the package? What's the idea of insinuating I might have it? You think Frankie'd leave anything like that with me—even if he did come to see me, which he never."

"It was just a question that came up," I said. "If what Donetti is looking for is dope, it should be turned over to the authorities."

A small gleam entered his eyes. "Must be worth a bit of money to make it so important to a feller like this Donetti, huh?"

"Quite a bit. But Donetti has outlets for that kind of merchandise. To anyone not in the rackets it would be worthless—and dangerous."

"What do you mean? How dangerous?" The glint still lingering in his rheumy eyes.

"I thought I told you. Donetti's still looking for it. Whoever's sitting on that stuff might as well be parked on a keg of gunpowder."

"Well," he shrugged, removing all that was left of the cigarette from his mouth, "I sure as hell ain't got it." He looked at the short butt in disgust before dropping it to the floor. He used cigarettes the way most people use water. "These days these things seem to burn out faster than ever."

I took the deck of Camels from my pocket and held them out to him. "Keep them."

"Well, thanks. But don't go thinking I was throwing hints or anything like that." The packet was transferred smoothly from my hand to his shirt pocket. "It's just that these days I got to ration myself. Got to watch what measly pension I get."

"Why did Frankie phone you?"

It was a weak try which he didn't buy.

Looking pained, he said: "You forgotten already? I told you he never once called me."

"All right. Then I'll have to accept that. Also that you don't know anyone else he might have called."

"That's right. There ain't nobody I know who he'd be calling. Frankie never had many friends in this town." He scratched himself under the arm and waited for me to contribute something. When I didn't, he inspected his thick, dirty fingernails and murmured: "This call you're so concerned about. It connected with that parcel of dope?"

"I don't know."

"Ain't got much to go on, huh?"

"There seldom is in the beginning."

"Yeah, guess so." He gave the nails on his other hand a fast check, then lifted his gaze back to me. "You said you weren't working for this Donetti. Who's hired you then?"

"I'm not at liberty to say. Except that they're important people. That's why I was hoping you could help. It might save us both a lot of trouble."

"Because your client's important?"

"Because your son was trying blackmail and ended up dead and made a mess of quite a few things," I said. "Because if I don't succeed in doing what I've been hired to do the matter could fall into the hands of the police, and then into those of the news hounds."

"Slow down," he said, raising a hand to stop me. "You left me behind some time ago. What've the police got to do with this?"

"They're investigating Frankie's death. Pretty soon they'll learn about the call he made and the one he received the same way I did. Only they'll have ways of tracing the calls."

"Yeah," he nodded. "Yeah." He thought about it. "How'd you find out about them?"

I told him of the collect call Rose Lang had received.

Scratching his beard thoughtfully he went back to his chair and sank into it.

"Supposing they find out? There ain't no law in calling up anyone anywhere, is there?"

"Not unless it can be established that the call was part of your son's blackmail scheme." I watched him sitting thoughtfully silent for a few more seconds and then took out my billfold and removed two fives. I went over and put them on the arm of his chair.

He picked up the two bills. "What's this for?"

"I'm still trying to save you some trouble, Mr. Cugino. But at the same time I'm prepared to pay for any information I receive."

Studying the ten dollars speculatively, he considered what I'd said, and then asked: "Don't suppose you could jack it up a little, could you?"

I added another five to what he held.

"That's real kind of you, mister. Don't like asking for more, but times are hard and a body's got to live."

"Tell me about the call."

"Guess you knew it all along, eh? You knew Frankie phoned me?" Without waiting for an answer he went on: "He called me, but sure as I'm sitting here I never knew what he wanted the information for. That's gospel, I promise you. He never mentioned nothing about blackmail, otherwise I would've told him to go straight to hell. I'm poor and I'm old and money don't come easy, but I don't aim to get hooked in anything crooked just to make an extra buck or two. Frankie asked me to get him a list of names, that's all. He promised to send me five hundred bucks if I did him that favor."

"A list of what names?" I prompted when he fell silent.

"Just names of all the people mentioned when old Eugene Green got himself killed." A few more seconds of silence while again scratching under his arm. "I been thinking. Now that Frankie's been killed, I won't be getting paid for my trouble, will I? Hell," he said sourly, "I figured it was too good to be true. That's the kind of miserable luck I always had."

"This list of names—what was it all about?"

Shoulders rose and fell as a limp hand gestured helplessly. "Damned if I know. All I did was jog down to the library and look up some old copies of the *Taywood Times*. I just wrote down all the names I could find and phoned them through to Frankie at the number he gave. That's all he wanted, and don't ask me why because I already told you I got no idea."

"Any thoughts about why he should be interested in this man Green?"

"None, mister. That part sort of puzzled me, I admit. Old Eugene was chopped to death in his garage nearly twenty years ago by that McCord kid. Way back in forty-six it was. It was a cut and dried case and just about forgotten by folks around here. But when Sam Ettman was Deputy Sheriff of these parts he checked up on everybody he figured might've done Green in. He even pulled in Frankie for questioning, but he let him go right afterwards. It was the McCord boy that done it and there was no proof to make anyone think otherwise."

"Do you still have that list of names?"

He shook his head. "Nope. Threw it away right after I was finished passing everything on. But I guess you can get it same as I had to. The library's still got the papers. They'll let you see them if you ask."

"You said Frankie was often in scrapes around here," I reminded him. "Any of them involve Green?"

"Not that I ever heard of. Sam Ettman pulled in my boy just on account of some nosy bitch like I got next door told him she'd seen Green hollering at Frankie and chasing him off his premises one time. But that was just on account of Green didn't want Frankie seeing his daughter. Figured she was too good for him, Green did. There was nothing more to it. Frankie was in scrapes, sure. But they were the harmless kind boys get into. Never was nothing really serious, though his ma used to fret a lot about him, always saying how he'd end up no good. Guess she was right after all. Look how he up and left me."

"How long," I asked, "has it been since he left here?"

"A few months after that Green business. But," he added quickly, "it had nothing to do with that. Frankie and me had a pretty rough argument about him not wanting to hold down a steady job and bring something into the house. His ma'd been dead three years already and it was hard for me alone to keep a rein on the boy. We had this fight and the next day he up and told me to go to hell, that he was getting out for good. He came back visiting 'bout eight years later. All duded up and driving a big snazzy auto. But he didn't stay long. Gave me some money and that's the last time I ever seen him."

"About this man Green," I said. "Why was he killed?"

"All I know is what I read," he replied with a show of reluctance. "Seems this McCord kid was caught lifting stuff out of Green's garage, and when he was caught he upped with an axe and hacked old Green's head in. They found stuff near the body that led them to McCord, but it was too late to do anything to him by then."

He waited for me to query the last bit. I obliged.

"It's like this," he explained. "When the kid left he must've been in one hell of a panic. He was driving a delivery truck and tried to gun it just a little too fast in getting away from what he'd done. The thing turned over and killed him." He stood up, tucking back some of the soiled white shirt which had crept out around his belly. "Anyway, you can get the whole story down at the library if you're interested."

All he had related made very little sense when combined with what little I already knew. So far there was nothing to indicate anything Cugino could have used to scare Allison Page into paying the kind of money he had demanded.

I said: "Are you sure you've told me everything?"

"Everything I know. That's what Frankie wanted me to do and that's all I did."

"Was there any name or names he showed particular interest in?"

"If there was he never said so."

"How about the name Page?"

"Never heard of it. Who's he?"

"No one special," I lied, and moved to the door.

Cugino stopped me by grasping my arm.

"I been thinking about that package you mentioned. You think Donetti will come here looking for it?"

"I hope not, Mr. Cugino. They're rough people to entertain."

"Well," he shrugged, "if they did they'd be wasting their time. I ain't never seen it and I don't know nothing about it."

He came with me to the front door, and during the short walk succeeded in thinking up another question or two.

"You happen to know who'll bury Frankie?"

"No. But I suppose you could claim the body once the police have established identification and the coroner is through with it."

"Hell," he said worriedly, "I ain't got the kind of money to finance a funeral. You think maybe the police will take care of that part?"

"You could ask them."

"Don't suppose," he said slowly, "you'd know if Frankie was carrying any insurance?"

I looked down at the old and dirty figure that waited for a reply.

"Oh, boy," I said, shaking my head.

He didn't throw one at me. But it wasn't until I was getting into my car that the door slammed loudly, like a rifle report on the quiet street. In the house next door a curtain moved at the window.

EIGHT

THREE women were performing different duties behind the wooden staff enclosure when I entered the library building. I drew the youngest, a plump bespectacled bathroom blonde with a face masked by layers of make-up that didn't quite hide all the small brown freckles. Her arms were spattered with them, too, but there it didn't seem to matter. Eyes fluttered behind the thick spectacles while she smiled and listened to what I wanted.

"Certainly," she answered chirpily. "We have copies of every edition, dating back from the very first up until the last. The paper changed its name a few years ago, you know? One of the bigger concerns bought it and then . . ."

But I was no longer listening to her chirp. A tall severely dressed girl had come away from a cardex cabinet that had been getting all her attention when I'd come in and was now standing behind Freckles. The latter saw where my gaze had strayed. Slowly she turned around, pink eyebrows arching high above the spectacle frames.

"It's all right, May," the other girl said. "I'll take care of the gentleman."

"That's quite all right," Freckles returned, sounding a bit peeved by the intrusion but trying hard not to let it show. "All he wants is—"

"I am aware of what is wanted," said the other girl with a calmness that carried a chill. "I'll take care of it. A lot of books have been brought back. You can look after that."

Freckles didn't move and for a few awkward seconds it looked like she was going to present an argument. But apparently there was a question of seniority involved, for with a haughty lift of her yellow head she turned and stalked stiffly off to the other side of the enclosure.

I smiled at the tall brunette.

She said: "If you'll come this way, please."

The smile was put back into mothballs while I waited until she came through the low swing door so that I could follow.

She had a good face that required little assistance from cosmetics, but which would have looked even better had she accepted a little of what Max Factor and the mob were selling. Dark hair drawn away from her face and tied tightly behind her head; trim, shapely legs that disappeared beneath a tight black skirt, and above that a tailored blouse with thin vertical stripes, made her look older than she probably was. Which was very likely only a few years past thirty. She made me think of a history teacher

I knew way back when who had the male half of the class speculating wildly about her personal history.

The hike ended in a basement room that was windowless and stuffy. High shelves with glass doors ran the full height of all the walls, and behind these, large bound volumes with names and dates printed on the spines in white ink. A long dark table and six uncomfortable chairs filled what was left of the room. The girl stopped at one of the shelves and for the first time I saw that she was carrying a small ring of keys. I looked at the rest of her hands and found only one other ring. A small, plain affair that didn't appear to have any significance.

"Was there any particular month you wanted?"

"There is," I said, "but I don't know which. I'll just have to wade through the lot."

Still without smiling or showing any other sign of interest, she said: "That could take a very long time. A year's supply of newspapers makes up a great many pages. Even a small paper like the *Taywood Times.*" She looked up at the shelves and transferred the keys to her left hand. "If I knew what you were looking for I could perhaps help."

"Back in forty-six there was a man murdered here," I said. "A guy named Eugene Green."

Her reply was a little slow in coming. Something moved in her face, but for only a fleeting second before it was gone. "It's those editions you want?"

I said they were.

She turned her back on me and unlocked the glass door in front of which she had been standing. "That was during April."

I went and helped her free one of the large bound volumes from the shelf and carried it to the table.

"May I ask of your interest in that particular case?" she inquired softly after the glass door had been locked.

"I'm a writer," I said, resurrecting the smile. It still had no purchasing power but I left it on my face to lend support to a lie that had been convenient on other occasions. "Every now and then I knock out a feature for one of the true crime magazines."

Her nod was barely perceptible. "Well, everything you need to know ought to be in there." She turned and left, high heels tapping sharply against the cold floor tiles.

I sat down and began turning pages.

The story ran to five editions before starting to fizzle out. After that it became only smaller items relegated to the inner pages. I went through everything twice, and some stories once more, and when I was through it was late. I studied the photographs but they meant little or nothing to me. There was a photograph of the murdered Eugene Green, taken before his skull had been opened with an axe; one of his seventeen-year-old daughter; another of the housekeeper—the two who had discovered the body in the garage. There was also a picture of Green's killer; a handsome youth named Clark McCord. And in a later edition, pictures taken at his funeral which showed his parents and younger sister.

When the story had first broken into headlines the paper had used all kinds of pictures—of the house, the garage, the murder weapon, pictures of the investigating team which included a deputy named Samuel Ettman, and even one of the wrecked delivery truck in which Green's killer had died. I wrote down names, addresses and dates into a notebook and then closed the big folder and sat back to try some thinking which didn't work out very well. Eugene Green had cast a long shadow—after his death. Twenty years long.

The soft jangle of keys and the tapping of heels descending stairs snapped me out of it. I stood up.

"Did you find what you were looking for?" she asked, stopping just inside the room.

"Thanks. Give you a hand with this?" I lifted the volume of newsprint.

We went through the routine of getting it back on the shelf and for the first time I was close enough to smell a perfume that appeared to be no more than lavender water.

After locking the shelf door and finding I'd made no move to leave, she asked: "Was there something else, Mr.—?

"Cameron," I filled in. "Did you know Eugene Green?"

"Of course not. What sort of question is that?"

"Sorry. I thought you might have had a personal interest in the case."

Her face went like marble. "What do you mean?"

"Not sure. Just that out there you seemed anxious to give me your personal attention. The way you remembered the date of the murder. The way you went straight to the correct shelf. There was no having to look around." I felt in my pocket. "Perhaps I'm a little too curious. Maybe you anticipated my request?"

"I never knew Eugene Green, Mr. Cameron. I was much younger at the time of his death. As for the rest, the explanation is simple. Though I'm sure I don't see that I have to explain anything. However, if you're that curious I'll tell you this. Only this morning there was a woman in here asking for the same papers. When you arrived but hours later with the same request I was a little more than surprised. Very few people look at those old editions." Her eyes made a swift downward shift. "If you're looking for a cigarette I'm obliged to remind you that smoking in the building is prohibited."

"No cigarettes," I said, remembering where mine had gone. I let her see my empty hand. "What did she look like, this woman?"

"I fail to see why a description of her should be necessary. After all . . ."

"It's not. But if one of my competitors is after the same story I'd like to know who I'm up against."

Curiosity would persuade her to tell me, we both knew that. Yet she stalled her reply, as if having to decide whether it was a contravention of any of the library's rules.

"She was a fairly ordinary-looking woman," she said at last. "Perhaps a little hard looking, with light brown hair and reasonably good clothes. She wore dark glasses which she never once removed. Not even down here. She wasn't from Taywood, and she too claimed to be a freelance writer. I might add she didn't look very much like one. Nor did she speak like one."

"Do they look and speak special?"

"I'm rather busy, Mr. Cameron," she replied testily, drawing a line under the discussion. "If there is nothing further you require, I'd like to get back to my work."

"Sure," I said. "Thanks for the help."

At the start of the steps she paused. "Do you think the case will make a story?"

I shrugged. "Don't know. It has a few coincidences, but not much more. I doubt whether the readers would go for it."

She nodded, starting up the steps quickly, leaving me to follow on my own time.

At the top she said nothing, not even goodbye. But my friend Freckles was watching, so I waved to her. She didn't wave back. Maybe they had laws about that, or maybe she had decided I was fickle. At the front door I stopped to look back. Straight into the eyes of the tall librarian.

Outside I searched for a phone and found one two blocks from the library. In the local directory I discovered a Samuel C. Ettman still listed. I dialed his number and gave him the same story I'd used on Freckles and her colleague, asking if I could call on him. He said to come on out.

2

Ettman's wife was a short, round, cheerful little woman who greeted me as if I were a close friend. She took me into what she called "his den", a big airy room at the back of the house that had shelves of books, an old desk, an Indian rug on the floor, photographs of a man in uniform on one pale blue wall, three official-looking framed documents that could have been citations, a gun rack, a bunch of fishing rods, stacks of magazines, a big leather chair and a tall man seated in it playing with a box of fishing lures. A king-size pipe dangled out of the side of his mouth. There was no tobacco in it. His face was ridged and toughened by years of exposure to the sun. The lank hair on his head snow-white, hanging in a cow-lick against his forehead like a hank of freshly spun silk. His clothes were cowpuncher boots, working denims and a red check shirt. A Stetson perched at the crown of his head and two silver Colts strapped to his hips would have completed a perfect picture of a TV peace officer—had they been there. They weren't.

He didn't get up when I entered. Acknowledging his wife's introduction with a curt nod, he said: "There isn't another chair. 'Less you want to fetch one, you'll have to use the desk."

"The desk will be fine," I said, hitching myself up onto a corner.

"I'll get some lemonade," his wife said, smiling. "Mr. Cameron looks hot, and if you two boys are going to talk you'll need some refreshment." She was the kind of woman who would always regard men as boys no matter what their age.

Waiting until she had departed, Ettman picked up a handful of the lures, glared at them briefly, then dumped the lot back into the tin and shut the lid. "Darned woman. Can't leave my stuff alone. Always fussing around, tidying things. Now my stuff's in a mess." He put the tin down carefully upon a shelf close to his chair.

He didn't want me to comment, so I didn't.

"You married?" he asked, taking the pipe from his mouth to scowl at the empty bowl.

"Not yet."

"You ought to be. It's the only life. When you retire and end up around my age you'll realize why. So they mess around with a feller's stuff, so what? There's other things that count, boy, things that matter a whole lot more. You should get married. How old are you?"

I told him.

"I was married at twenty. Don't regret a day of it. You're wasting good time, boy." He stood up, stretched and silently took stock of what sat on the desk. "So you figure on doing a story on the Green case? Why?"

"I might not," I said. "It all depends on how much I get from you. What was in the papers at the library didn't offer enough for a feature— unless I play up the part about the accident. That was pretty coincidental."

"And probably a darned good thing for the boy's family," he grunted, going back to the chair. "A trial's hell on the family."

I nodded solemnly, and before I could open my mouth to speak Mrs. Ettman brought in a tray with a frosted jug and two tall glasses. She poured from the jug, handed us each a glass, then left without contributing a word.

Ettman said: "What exactly do you want from me?"

"You were Deputy Sheriff in Taywood before a city police force was established. According to the papers you headed the investigation with hardly any outside help. What I'd like is to hear the story from you, in your own words. As well as any personal opinions you might have."

In one long pull he drained the glass and set it down on the shelf. "If you read the papers you know it all. My office got a call that there'd been a motor accident on Alpine Street, that somebody'd got himself killed. We checked it out and found it was a delivery truck belonging to Striker's Hardware. The driver was a young sixteen-year-old kid named

Clark McCord. Seemed he took that corner on Alpine too fast and didn't quite make it. There's a sharp one at the end of the road," he explained, "that points downhill and needs to be taken real slow. The kid didn't, not according to the skid marks we found on the road. So the truck over-turned and he was tossed out and killed. Got his neck broken. Died instantly. This what you want to hear?"

"Uh-huh." I tasted the lemonade. It was home-made and good. It tasted like nothing I'd swallowed in more than twenty years. But it didn't vanish as fast as Ettman's had done.

Ettman put the pipe back in his mouth and sucked on it thoughtfully before continuing. "We tied that one up and were hardly through when there was another call. This time from the Green's place up on the same street. We went and took a look and found Eugene Green sitting in his garage with his head split in two and looking like a lousy amateur butcher had been using him for practice. Somebody'd taken an axe to him. We found it lying outside the garage on the grass. He'd been dead a couple of hours by then."

"It was his daughter and housekeeper that called you?" I queried. "The paper didn't elaborate on the details."

"It was Clarice Sutton, the housekeeper," Ettman supplied. "Seems she'd been out shopping and was on her way home when she met Felic-ity-Anne, that's Green's daughter, in the same bus coming home. The girl'd gone to the library after school to do some research on a homework project or something and got home later than usual. Otherwise, thank the good Lord," he said, lowering his voice, "she might've been the one to stumble on him. It ain't nice to find your old man all chopped up that way."

I thought it might look better if I made a few notes, and got out the notebook and pen. Ettman watched.

"When they got to the house Green's car was parked in the drive. Fe-licity was the first to notice it 'cause Green should normally have still been at his office that time of day. But it appears he'd been nursing an ulcer for years, and that afternoon it was giving him particular hell. That's why he quit the office early. Anyway, they went into the house and after they couldn't find the old man they started looking around. It took them some time to consider the garage, and when they did and went there, all hell broke loose. The daughter fainted dead away and the housekeeper just started screaming and ran out on the street yelling that there'd been murder."

"I haven't seen the house," I said. "Just a newspaper photograph. The picture of the garage was separate. From what I saw the two buildings are not joined. Is that correct?"

"They weren't," he confirmed, sucking contentedly on the pipe. "The garage is behind the house where it couldn't be seen from the street. The drive goes right around the house in a kind of circle arrangement."

"Were the papers right about your first clue being a packet of nails?"

"They were. If it wasn't for that we might've had quite a search on our hands. Afterwards we tried looking for another motive that would fit the killing, but there wasn't none we could find. Anyway, there was this packet of two-inch nails lying there in the grass, and finding it reminded us of the capsized truck from Striker's Hardware. We contacted Striker and learned that the McCord kid had been out making deliveries—a part-time job he held down after school. Well, as it turned out one of those deliveries he was making was for Eugene Green. Another look was taken at the stuff that was in the truck at the time of the accident. Amongst the junk we found was a carton marked for Green, complete with an un-signed delivery slip. One item was missing. The two-inch nails. That was the first lead, just like you read. After that it was only a matter of testing for fingerprints, and we were lucky to pick up two on the axe. They matched McCord's all right. And if that wasn't enough, there was blood on the boy's trousers when he was picked up dead. Thing was, Cameron, he hadn't been bleeding. The blood was tested and compared with Green's. Same type. Cut and dried. And a lousy one all round. I hated it."

"That why you rounded up all those other people for questioning?"

"It was routine," he mumbled. "Just routine. I had hopes, even though I knew it was hopeless."

"Hopes, Mr. Ettman?"

"Sure," he growled, and jerked the pipe out of his mouth. "Hopes. I knew the McCord kid slightly, same as I did his folks. He was a good kid. His folks were honest, God-fearing people, and it was a hell of a thing to have to happen to them. Myself, I didn't want to believe it at first. But there it was. Cut and dried. There was no question about what happened there that afternoon." He inspected the pipe again, scowling even deeper than before. "Darned doctor's limited me to only five smokes a day, so I got me the biggest pipe I could buy. But it just ain't no good. Too long I been a heavy smoker to start sucking air most of the day." He dropped the pipe into his shirt pocket. "Cut and dried, I said. No two ways about it. It was temptation and nothing else that was the cause of it. Could've happened to any other one, I guess. Too bad it happened to Clark McCord. But there it was. You get a boy making a delivery to a house, only the housekeeper ain't been told about it and she takes off for town to do her shopping. When the boy gets there no-one's at home. So he looks around a little. He goes into the garage and maybe there's a couple of things there he can use. But while he's at it Green pulls up on the drive. The boy doesn't hear him. Then suddenly Green is there in the garage, maybe catching him in the act of looting. The boy panics and tries to run. Maybe Green grabs him. The kid is scared and the next thing there's that axe in his hand and he's defending himself—he thinks. Only he's not; he's doing murder. Next thing he knows Green is dead. So he picks up the carton of stuff that was ordered after throwing away the axe, and hightails it out of there. But he drops something in his hurry—a lousy packet of nails which later we find.

"Temptation," he grumbled. "That's the cause of too many crimes. Temptation. I ain't saying it's always so. I'm just saying it accounts for a lot of it. We put things in the way of youngsters, we stock up store windows with a lot of junk that tempts all kinds of people who never thought about swiping a nickel before, and we let the girls wear skimpy clothes that can attract all kinds of sex crackpots."

"Was there ever any trouble between the boy and Green?"

"Never," he answered promptly.

"Do the McCords still live here in Taywood?"

"Nope, not anymore. Moved a few weeks after they buried their boy. Guess you can understand their reason for not wanting to stick around here after that."

"Do you know where they went to, Mr. Ettman?"

He shook his white head silently. I didn't believe him, but I didn't push it.

"I'm told that when you pulled in these other people for questioning a youngster named Cugino was included in the group."

"Yeah?" Suddenly there was suspicion in his voice. "And who told you that?"

"A friend of Cugino's," I said easily. "He was the one who suggested I look into the case."

"You know Cugino?"

I shook my head. "He's no friend of mine, if that's what you're asking."

"He was a bum," Ettman said, his tone still suspicious. "He'd been chasing Green's daughter that's why we took him in. A couple of times he'd been around to their place and seen her. But he was nearly twenty, older than she was, and her old man booted him out. Trouble was, Frankie was the kind of bum that never learned. He went back sneaking around the girl and Green caught him. There was a minor ruckus. Green belted hell out of him and he never even tried to fight back. Just crawled away like the bum he was. Where's he now?"

"Last I heard, in real trouble," I said. "I don't know the exact details." It wasn't exactly untrue.

"Figures. He never was any good. Never had the kind of stuff that amounts to anything." The pipe, though cold and empty, found itself back in his hands and then in his mouth. "He was clean. We let him go inside of an hour."

"Did McCord know Green's daughter?"

"Nope. They went to different schools and stayed at opposite ends of the town. Besides, she was a year older than him, and girls of seventeen don't date younger boys or even get real friendly. Least they didn't when I was a kid. Nope, they never knew each other."

"What sort of girl was she, Mr. Ettman?"

"If you're trying to find out was she ever in trouble, forget it. She wasn't—not ever. And get it out of your head that the kid was loose. She wasn't, not that I know about. And I never heard anything that made me want to revise my opinion either. She was just a kid that had the misfortune to come home and find her old man butchered. When it must've happened she was in the library, and there were witnesses. Think I never troubled myself to find out where she and the housekeeper were?"

"I wasn't trying to imply a thing," I said, sliding off the desk. "I'm sure the investigation was conducted expertly, and from what I've read and heard everything appears to have been pretty straightforward." I put the notebook and pen away. "I'm grateful for your time."

Slowly he pulled himself out of the chair, biting hard on the oversize pipe. Erect, he towered over me. Thin and wiry with a lot of hard years behind him and still a lot of cop left over.

"Going to do that story?"

"I'll have to give it some more thought," I said. "I'd liked to have talked with Green's daughter, but I don't suppose she's still living here, is she?"

Ettman wagged his head. "You suppose right. Got married the last I heard of her. Can't recall the feller's name, though I met him once. Green's wife died when the kid was still a toddler, so after her old man died Felicity went to stay with the Hammonds. Dave Hammond was a darned good friend of Eugene's. But she's not there no more. Moved away from here just a couple of years after she was married. Least, that's what I heard from my wife."

I checked the time on my wrist. It was moving on fast.

"Now that I've opened up to you," Ettman said a little too casually, "care to tell me what's your real interest in all this?"

"A story," I answered.

"My butt," he retorted. "I spent too many years in the law business not to smell a cop a mile off. Besides, I remember seeing your name in print when that stink broke up in Reposado [1]. And if you were a writer, why'd you go to the library instead of the newspaper offices to check the details of that story? Their morgue would've had a hell of a lot more for you than just the stuff they put into print."

"And have some reporter ask the wrong kind of questions?"

"What're you trying to do, feller?" There was no hardness in his voice, no threat, no nothing. No more than a question.

"I'm sorry," I said. "I'm not free to tell you that. I'm a cop, yes. The private variety, which, I hope, explains why I can't discuss my interest in the case."

"Cugino!" he sneered through bared teeth.

"I don't want to lie to you Mr. Ettman."

"So?"

"So how about we lay off the questions? I'm not trying to reopen the case if that's what's bothering you."

---

[1] From SHADOWS DON'T BLEED

"Cugino," he snorted. "Okay. Play it your way. In the days when I still had a badge I'd have got the truth out of you, but they don't pay me for that kind of thing no more. Now I got only my own business to tend, and I'm happy to do just that. But if you think reopening that old case worries me, you're chewing on a rotten apple. Trained men checked the evidence and qualified men reached the final decision."

"Look," I said quietly, wanting to leave as someone in whose wake he wouldn't spit, "I'm convinced of the facts. I'm neither working for nor trying to help Frank Cugino. All I'm trying to do is save something pretty important. That's all there is to it."

"Okay, Cameron. No more questions. The Green case is dead. Twenty years dead, and I'm not a cop anymore. Go ahead, do what you want. I can't stop you."

"Thanks," I said, offering him my hand. "Right now it looks like I'm going to fall flat on my face, but this thing has become important to me."

Ettman didn't shake hands immediately. He looked down at my projected paw for several seconds before slowly crushing it in a grip which, twenty years ago, could have broken bones. When he gave it back, he said:

"Don't fret about it. You've got the kind of face that will take a fall."

On the way out of the house, warm cooking odors reminded me of another meal I'd missed.

From Ettman's house I drove into town and found a place that looked reasonably clean and which had a number of vacant tables. Over a well-done steak I tried adding up the things I'd learned.

At a nearby table four young men only recently escaped from their teens were discussing the merits of the current *Green Hornet* television series. One, it appeared, had differing views on the subject and was not loath in expressing them. I listened with a detached sort of interest as the subject moved to comics and magazines which, worthless a few years ago, were today fetching fantastic prices. Something like the Green case which had been dead, buried and forgotten. Now, suddenly, to certain parties it was of immense interest and there could be only one reason why.

I drank the last of my coffee and went out.

3

Most of the stores were already closed and the streets were beginning to empty. It wasn't dark yet, but the sun had sneaked out of sight and within the hour street lights would be burning. It had been a long time since I felt so alone. I smoked a cigarette and when it was dead took the Plymouth down to the hotel on the next block. In the car's trunk was still the grip containing the change of clothes I'd taken to Vadear Point. I carried it into the hotel where a desk clerk with impeccable manners, a frozen smile and a built-in desire to please let me sign the register while he rang for a bellhop.

It was one of those things that happen once in a rare while. But then in a town the size of Taywood there were not many hotels and the odds against something like it happening would be reduced. Out of habit I had scanned the entries which topped mine in the register. Three lines above where I had signed appeared the scratchy signature of an *R. Lang.*

I noted the room number, checked over the pigeon holes behind the desk and found her key missing. Then I turned to where the bellhop was nursing my grip and followed him to the elevator.

In the room I took off my coat, loosened my tie, sat down on the bed and picked up the phone. I told the hotel operator who I wanted, then hung up, stripped off my shirt and went into the bathroom.

The phone rang while I was drying my face.

"Cameron?" Ross Rigby said as soon as I identified myself. "I returned your call but the girl on your answering service said you might not be back at all today. What the blazes are you doing up there? Don't tell me that's where she went?"

"No," I said. "I'm still no nearer to finding her. This was just a lead that needed following. I'm not certain, but I've a fair idea of what he was holding over her now."

"Who? Cugino?"

"Uh-huh. But let's not discuss it now. I'll fill you in later. Anything at your end?"

"Everything," he groaned across the distance. "I've just arrived home and I feel terrible. It's been that sort of day. I went to see Lynx about an extension to the deadline, but they weren't even remotely interested. Their schedule is set and they refuse to alter it. And to make matters worse, I had a visit from the police."

I kept quiet, listening to his anxious breathing. Or perhaps it was my own I was hearing.

"It's all in the evening papers," he went on. "No names yet, thank goodness. Just a short piece about the L.A. police working in conjunction with the Vadear Point sheriff's office and being anxious to contact a certain blonde female celebrity."

"How did they get into the act?" I asked.

"Someone provided an anonymous tip," he explained. "Oh, the police were very decent about it all, assuring me that it was simply a lead they had to follow, and that it was strictly routine. But when they started asking questions I was in no position to answer they began showing signs of suspicion. Apparently they'd already been up to Allison's house, and when they discovered she wasn't there came to my office and waited for me. They know all about the kind of car she owns and that she fits the description of the girl detailed in the morning press. They don't like the fact that she's not available for questioning."

"What did you tell them?"

"What? Just a minute." The wire became muffled, as if a hand had been placed over the mouthpiece at his end. I waited, not caring for the news he had conveyed.

"Still there?" he queried, coming back on the line.

"Uh-huh."

"Sorry about that. Visitors just pitched up. I was expecting some from the gentleman of the Fourth Estate, but apparently the police haven't released anything about Allison yet. However, I'm going to have to make the rest of this brief."

"You were going to tell me what you told the police."

"Yes. Yes, of course." Another pause. "I'm afraid my story wasn't very convincing. But I tried. I couldn't tell them outright lies or refuse to answer their questions; you appreciate that, don't you?"

"What did you tell them?" It came out harder than intended.

"Only that I had no idea where she had gone. Probably on a short motor tour, but that I couldn't say where. I told them her TV series had been completed and she wasn't due to report for work for another six weeks, that she'd mentioned plans of a short vacation."

"What about the maid?"

"Terry told them nothing. Before I left there last night I briefed her on what to say in case a thing like this occurred. She told them her mistress was away on holiday. She hadn't told her where she was going because she wanted to rest without interruptions. Before I left I took the precaution of removing that tape from the machine."

I could appreciate the police being suspicious of a story like that, but I didn't tell him so.

"Anything else?"

"No. Only that they've identified the body as that of Cugino's. They told me how—something about tracing the car and dental impressions, and something about a tattoo on an unburned portion of his skin. I'm vague about the details."

"This tip the police received. Any ideas?"

"You mean who could have phoned it in? I don't know, Cameron. A girl in Allison's position is bound to have rivals. Professional jealousy could have prompted any one of them to do it. One of them could have read her description in the paper, realized that it suited Allison and that she drove a silver Stingray and . . ."

"And tipped the cops," I finished for him.

"Doesn't look very hopeful, does it?"

"It doesn't."

"This other business, this lead you've followed. I don't suppose it helps either?"

"Not the way we want. But it provides a few possible answers."

"You don't sound very happy about it. Does what you've uncovered make—make—things look any worse?"

"Just more complicated," I answered. "I'll follow through with what I have and contact you again. Meanwhile there's something I meant to ask you."

I asked and after a short but obvious hesitation, he answered.

After I'd hung up I sat staring at my reflection in the dresser mirror for a long time without really seeing anything. After a while the room seemed to shrink around me. The small sounds that had emanated from the passage and the adjoining room had vanished; the breeze entering the open window at my back now suddenly cold. I began to dress without any enthusiasm.

Downstairs the bar was noisy but not quite full. Pink tinted interior lighting heightened the facial complexions of those seated at the long bar and at the tables placed close to the wall. With the exception of five male drinkers huddled in a corner, the rest were matched couples. Except one. I made my way to a vacant bar stool and was almost there before I saw her. She was wearing the dark glasses the librarian had described. I bought a drink and went over.

A smile creased her very red mouth when I sat down. "Following me?"

"Should I be?"

The glass she held went to her lips, but before drinking, she said: "I saw you check in. I wondered."

"I thought you'd be on your way back east, Rose."

"Had a change of heart," she said, smiling back with what seemed like reconstructed confidence. "You're not going to beef about the dough you put up, are you?"

I tossed off half the Scotch. "It was a gift. No beef."

"So? What brings you here, if not me?" The shades completely hid her eyes but the lipstick wasn't thick enough to camouflage the split lip.

"Reading old newspapers, Rose. Same as you."

"Found out about that, did you? Well, there's no harm in it, is there?"

"Not unless you were thinking of picking up where your friend Cugino left off."

She wagged her head and killed her drink. A waiter materialized as if he'd been waiting for that moment. I told him to bring us each another and he went away.

"Well?"

"Uh-uh," she said. "Frankie was crazy to get himself mixed up in that sort of deal—and I had nothing to do with it. What he had he kept to himself, like I already told you. Blackmail buys you grief, Cameron, and me; I had enough of that to last forever." Unconsciously her fingers slid behind the black lens over her left eye, softly massaging.

"Then what are you doing here?"

She shrugged. "Same as you, I guess. Finding out what it was Frankie was trying to sell."

"And?"

"I found."

"And now?"

"Now I make myself some easy money. Legitimately."

The drinks arrived. While I paid for them she sat eyeing me across the table. When the waiter faded, I said: "Trying to be funny?"

"Not with you, sweetheart." Another too red smile. "Don't believe me?"

"All right, Rose. You're going to tell me, so stow the suspense routine."

"The magazines, Cameron, the magazines and papers. After you left my dump last night I got around to thinking why the hell it should be me that has to run out with nothing to show for my troubles. She's big time so she's got money to hire guys like you to keep her lousy past under wraps, and me, I'm nobody so I got to blow quietly with nothing but bruises. Nuts to that. This time I figured it'd be worth some more trouble to make some real money. Not a fortune, honey, but more than little ol' Rose's seen in a long time. Anyway, enough to give me a good start someplace else. And best of all it's strictly legit. Nobody can give me trouble over it."

"I get it," I said. "Blackmail's too dirty and dangerous, but you're quite prepared to sell what you know to any of the rags who'll print that kind of muck."

"Call it what you like," she returned calmly. "I'm taking care of my end and the hell with the rest. There's nothing crooked about it."

"And all the time you've been insisting that you had no idea of what Cugino was doing?"

"So I had to lie a little." She sipped at her drink. The smile was still there when the glass came away from her mouth. "But not about everything. I wasn't in on Frankie's scheme, but I could add two and two together so it comes out four. Like when he phoned her that night the first time and I was supposed to be in the kitchen where I couldn't hear. That part I didn't tell you. Thing was I did hear. Sure, it was just names and dates that meant damn little to me, but just in case Frankie tried to ditch me before coming across with what he promised, I wrote them down. This morning I came up here and dug up the rest of the details." She sat back, turning the smile into a challenging grin.

I didn't know how long she'd been at the bar, but judging from the looseness of her tongue quite a few drinks had been knocked over before I'd joined her.

"What makes you think you know anything?" I sneered. "Nothing in those old papers mentions her or anything she's supposed to have done."

Rose Lang laughed loudly. A hard, coarse sound that had heads turning in our direction. But she never noticed. She drank some more, putting the glass down heavily.

"Who're you kidding? I can read as well as the next guy and it was all there to read if you knew what to look for. Her kid brother was a lousy killer, that's what! "

"Keep yelling," I warned, "and you'll have everyone aware of the details before you have a chance of offering them to a buyer."

"Screw them," she grinned, but lowered her voice. "Anyway, I already have. What d'you think I'm celebrating for? I phoned a magazine back in L.A. and they've promised to put up a nice fat little bundle for baby if the story's all I said it'd be. A nice fat little bundle that'll be legit right through to the last buck. And it'll be all I promised them. In this morning's paper there was a piece about the cops trying to learn more about a certain blonde seen there where Frankie got himself roasted. The time they get to her everyone'll be interested and the magazine that's got the full story of why she went there in the first place will sell a million copies."

"It looks as if things have fallen into your lap very nicely," I said. "You'll forgive me if I don't offer congratulations. Her brother—and he wasn't her kid brother—killed a man here twenty years ago. We both know that. We also know that he got himself killed a short while later and that at the time all this happened she was probably no more than seven. What happened she couldn't prevent or help. So what makes you think she should be made to pay for any of it now?"

"Nobody's got to pay for anything," Rose flared. "That was Frankie's idea. What I'm doing is selling facts to the press. There's nothing crooked or personal about it. The public's got a right to know that that sweet-faced little so-and-so with the screeching voice had the kind of brother who went around splitting people's heads open. There ain't nothing personal. I'm just taking advantage of a good opportunity, that's all."

"He killed one man," I corrected. "And for all we know, under provocation."

"Screw the two-bit words," she snapped. "He killed a guy and she killed Frankie."

"You believe that?"

"Why not? She had good reason."

"Tell me one thing, Rose. How did Frankie know who she was?"

"You mean about the Page chick being McCord's sister?"

I nodded.

"Take a look." She shuffled things around in her purse and came up with a page ripped from a magazine. "Frankie used to live here. He recognized her real name, I guess."

I took the sheet from her and read. It was a one-page biography of the singer torn from a movie or TV fan publication. In it the author had included very little I hadn't already heard from Ross Rigby. But only a half hour ago, when I'd spoken to him on the phone, had he told me her real name. The writer of the biography had known it also. Judith McCord.

"Funny thing," Rose mused, refolding the page I returned to her, "that was the first time her real name's been in a magazine. That I know about, anyway. And I should know. I read enough of them. How Frankie came across it was sheer fate."

"That's what started it off?"

"Nothing else. I guess he came across it when he was holed up at my place. Then he got someone up here to check the old newspapers so he could get all the dope. Frankie used to live here, you know that?"

"So you said."

"I found the piece torn out of the book and then went out and picked up another one just to find out what was in it that'd got him so interested. Call it curiosity, if you want, but it paid off."

I toyed with my glass and then swallowed what was left in it. We sat looking at each other in silence. The noise in the bar seemed louder; the lighting darker.

"Hell," the girl said at last, "she's just a client. She can afford to pay and retire for a few years on the loot she's already made."

"Yeah," I grunted. "Did you ever meet her, Rose?"

"Now where the hell would I get to meet her kind? Say," she drawled with sudden amusement. "Don't tell me you're hung up on her?"

Ignoring the question, I asked: "Was it you who tipped off the L.A. police about her?"

Whatever amusement had been in her face died abruptly. Her mouth clamped shut in a crooked red line.

"Like that, huh?"

"You're talking foreign," she said softly.

"Frankie phoned her at her home," I said. "How did he know her number? It isn't listed."

"There're people who sell numbers like that. You ought to know, being in the racket you are." She paused, reached for her glass, only to discover it empty. This time the waiter didn't appear. "What's this jazz about tipping the cops?"

"Somebody did. I thought it might have been you."

"Well it wasn't."

"No difference. It's been done and the police are trying to contact her. Know what will happen if they do, Rose?"

She didn't answer.

"Everything will surface," I said. "All the details of Cugino's blackmail attempt, what he had on her, the facts about Green's death—the works. Your story will be second-hand the time it's published. That's if they still decide to run it."

She kicked back her chair and stood up. "That's what you think! They'll print it, and the hell with both you and her. You're not conning me into changing my mind. Tomorrow I'm giving them the whole story and it'll be printed. Besides, it comes out weekly, so it doesn't matter if the cops do get her before it's printed. Remind me to send you a copy," she spat, turning on her heel and stalking off.

Her exit caused heads to again turn. Several pairs of amused eyes followed her wiggling rear from the room before slowly swiveling back to where I sat.

I got up and went to the bar.

NINE

THEY were paging someone over the hotel's public address system, but to my ears it was just another sound adding itself to the clamor inside the bar. Working my way down through a new drink, I was well on the way to feeling the effect of the others when the barman bellowed:

"Anyone here named Cameron?"

"Me."

"They've been yelling for you to take a call." He sounded very put out. "Didn't you hear?"

"Uh-huh. But I prefer the sound of your voice. Where do I take it?"

He told me, and in the lobby I closed myself in the booth and got through to the switchboard. They made the connection and a female voice I couldn't recognize said:

"Mr. Cameron? This is Diane Riley."

"That's nice." I waited. "And who's Diane Riley?"

Her voice hesitated before answering: "We met at the library today. I showed you the newspaper files."

"Oh? What'd I do—tear a page?"

"Are you all right?" she queried after a further short bout of silence. "You—sound strange."

"I'm fine," I assured her. "Been having a little one-sided chat with John Barleycorn and feeling just great. Was there something you wanted, Miss Riley?"

From the booth I could see the reception desk and the people at it. A man moving away with his back to me looked familiar, but he didn't stay in view long enough to be recognized.

Diane Riley was talking again: "At the library you said you were going to do a story on the Green murder case."

"And you appeared not to believe me."

"I'm afraid I still don't. But just the same, I believe I'd like to talk to you about it."

"Where?"

"Anywhere you choose. I'm at home now. If—if you prefer you could come here. Otherwise I'll meet you wherever you wish."

"You're making it sound important."

"It is. Will you come?"

"I guess so. What's the address?"

"Eighteen Cerro Street," she supplied after some hesitation. "It's not far from your hotel."

"Talking of which, Miss Riley, how did you know where I was staying?"

"If you were staying at all," she said seriously, "it had to be at one of the hotels. There aren't many and it didn't require much effort to make the necessary inquiries."

"I'll see you at your place shortly," I promised, and rang off.

In the hotel lobby I looked around for the man I thought looked familiar. But he was no longer there, nor in the bar or loitering outside the hotel. I gave it up, but it bothered me a little. He had looked a little like one of Donetti's stooges: Bo Fletcher.

With detailed directions and a crude pencil drawn map received from the desk clerk I had no trouble finding Cerro Street and the small house with lights burning behind the widest front windows and over the porticoed entrance. A pleasant, quiet street, the only noticeable sounds the hushed whisper of palm fronds and the chirp of a cricket that had established residence in the front yard.

Diane Riley had the door open before I had a chance to look for the bell.

"I heard your car," she said. "Please come in."

The living room, if over furnished, was cozy. In order to make room for two oiled-wood rockers that looked like recent acquisitions, an old upright piano had been pushed into a corner near a shelved alcove presently being used to store a few books and a few dozen tiny glass animals. On the mantel stood a pair of silver vases and another glass menagerie.

"My mother," she said nervously when I picked up a miniature green giraffe.

"She collects these things?"

"It—it looks like it, doesn't it?"

I selected one of the chintz covered chairs and sat down. "You live here with your parents?"

"My mother. Father died when I was nineteen."

She was out of her working clothes now. In their place skin-tight Capri pants of a shimmering silver fabric and a loose fitting midnight blue shirt. Her hair was down on her shoulders, but there was still only the barest hint of make-up on her face.

"Can . . . I get you a drink?" she offered.

"Thanks, no. I've had my quota for tonight." For a week, I corrected silently, my head feeling like something molded from cheap polystyrene.

She nodded without comment and found a seat on the couch which was only a few feet from my chair. Anyone seeing her then would have agreed she was perhaps the sister of the librarian, but hardly the same person. Along with her working clothes she'd shed the haughty attitude. With fingers laced together in her silver lap she assumed the subdued pose of a nervous little girl, sitting there waiting for me to say something.

So I said the obvious: "Well, I'm here."

"Yes. And—now I don't know quite how to start."

"The beginning's not too bad a place. You might try there."

Her dark head bobbed. "Will you first answer one question?"

"If I can."

"What is your real business, Mr. Cameron? What do you really want here in Taywood? You're no writer; I know that."

"That's two questions," I said. "Look, I'll make a deal. You tell me why I was asked to come over and maybe—I said maybe—I'll tell you why I'm interested in what happened to Eugene Green."

"Very well." White teeth worried her full lower lip while her hands tightened together. "I don't want the case publicized again. I don't want all the dreadful details of that—that affair brandished before everyone's eyes all over again."

"It's important to you that they aren't?"

"Yes."

"Why?"

"Why?" she repeated, surprised by the question. "Isn't it obvious? When Green died his death involved a lot of innocent people. Many were hurt by the publicity—people who will be hurt again if the case is publicized."

"And you were one of them?"

"Yes, I was one."

"That was twenty years ago. You couldn't have been much more than a kid then."

She lowered her eyes, said nothing. And then the nickel dropped.

"You knew him. You and the McCord boy . . ."

"We—we were only kids, but I was his girl. We—we were going steady." Her chin came up defiantly. "That sounds terribly juvenile to you, I suppose."

"Get the chip off your shoulder," I told her. "I wasn't born yesterday. I know how it is with kids."

"With Clark it was different," she went on earnestly. "As soon as we were old enough we were going to be married. We had our entire future mapped out, even to the kind of home we would build, where we would live, and the kind of careers we would pursue."

"Were you ever married, Diane?"

The full shapeliness of her body tensed. "What has that to do with—with the rest of all this?"

Without trying for a reply I took out the new packet of cigarettes and looked around for an ashtray. There wasn't one at hand but she saw what I was looking for and got up from the couch.

"No," she said, going to the mantel. "I never married." I waited until she returned and placed a large square hunk of clay on the arm of my chair before asking:

"Your mother home? You said you lived here with her."

"No—fortunately." Resuming her seat she tucked her long legs in under her and leaned against the couch's floral armrest. "She's spending a few days with her brother in Arizona."

"Fortunately?" I put a light to the Camel hanging on my lip.

"Yes, Mr. Cameron, fortunately. Mother would hate to know you're interested in—in what happened to Clark. She wouldn't enjoy knowing that old ashes might be raked over again. If—if she was home I'd never have suggested you come here."

I chewed on the cigarette. She was a lot of woman, beautifully put together. Every inch of her screamed sex, and yet there was something wrong with the overall presentation, something I couldn't find.

"Is that why you never married. Because of him?" And when it looked like she wasn't going to answer: "Your mother?"

Her head moved so that she would not have to look at me. "I—I prefer not to talk about it."

I stubbed out the cigarette and pushed myself up out of the chair. "Please yourself. Just remember it was you who suggested the talk. I thought you'd give me at least one good reason why the case should be left where it is. Looks like I was wrong."

"There—there were other people as well," she said quickly. "I was thinking of them. Clark's parents. Do you—do you have any idea how much they suffered when it happened?"

"No," I admitted. "I haven't. But I'm beginning to get some about you. You're a big girl, Diane. You're pretty and you're not built like a clothes rack. You've got everything it takes to make a healthy guy pant."

"Please—don't."

"Don't what? Tell you things you already know? Care to tell me why you go to work looking like the leader of the temperance league; why you stand a yard away from the lipstick when you're using it? What are you trying to hide from, Diane? Men?"

"You're drunk! You've—you've no right to say such things."

"Right, on both counts. Only I'm not so drunk I can't see." I drew a deep breath and went on looking down at her. There was a damp glitter in her eyes but I couldn't be sure of the cause. "Okay. It's none of my business, but it's time you realized memories alone are poor company. You can't live with ghosts for ever." I took four slow steps to the door.

"You're going?"

I stopped. "Any point in staying?"

"You—don't know what it was like," she said so softly it only just reached me.

"Then why don't you tell me?"

Very slowly she rose to her feet. Her movements smooth, unpracticed and unconscious. But they would never need to be any different.

"Please sit down. I—I'll get something to drink. Will brandy be all right? It's all we have in the house."

I started to say no, thought better of it and nodded an okay.

By the time she returned from the kitchen I was back in the deep chair. I took my drink from her and waited until she was once again seated before trying it. The first sip told me I was making a mistake.

"You were wrong," she said. "People can live with no more than memories. I know. I've been doing it long enough."

"You loved him that much? Even after what he'd done?"

"Nobody will ever make me believe that," she returned with a firm shake of her head that made her black hair swirl as if caught by a sudden angry gust of wind. "They never knew him as I did. None of them did. There was no violence in him. He was gentle. He wouldn't hurt anyone or anything."

"The police appear to have thought different," I said. "Or was there something you never told them?"

"No, there was nothing I knew that would have helped. Besides, who would have listened to me then? I was only a young girl who loved him. Even my own mother was ready to believe everything they said about him. She . . ."

Not wanting to press her I took some more of the brandy.

"I guess that's what really started it. After mother discovered what Clark had been involved in she wouldn't permit me to go out with any of the other boys—even if I had wanted to, and I didn't—not for a long time. Even Clark's old friends were not allowed to visit the house." The dampness in her eyes was growing as her thoughts ventured back across the years. A tear crept out of an eye and streaked swiftly down her cheek. She didn't disturb it. "I used to come home from school and spend the afternoons in my room—every day, every week. Oh, at school the boys tried to date me, but I turned them down. Even the casual invitation to a Coke at the malt shop was something I learned to avoid. I was lonely and there were times I welcomed their company, but after a while I think I started believing some of the things mother said. There were times when I would lose hold of my belief that Clark was innocent of the crime he'd been accused of. After it happened I wouldn't listen to a word anyone said about him or the things the papers printed. Mother would show me the stories, but they meant nothing. Sometimes, though, I would think it was perhaps true, that he had killed Mr. Green. But . . . but that the man had invited the attack by doing or threatening something fearful. Sometimes—sometimes I would get terribly confused and I would stay in my room all afternoon crying, wishing I could also die."

There were things I could have said then. Things the Taywood paper had printed and the same things ex-deputy Sam Ettman had confirmed. Things that involved fingerprints, blood stains, proof of presence, time and opportunity.

"The whole horrible affair upset mother terribly," she continued. "I think at first she was ashamed. Shocked that her only daughter had been going about with a killer. Dad was more tolerant and sympathetic, but he was never a force in the house. By the time I graduated and started working I had gained a quiet reputation as the girl to be left alone. Behind my back things were said that would make the other girls giggle and think up names like Ice Berg, The Untouchable . . . and some much worse. You said no-one can live with memories. Believe me that also occurred to me. I realized one day what I was turning into and what sort of life lay before me. So when a certain boy asked me out I accepted. It was the worst thing I ever did. When mother discovered what I'd done she fainted and had to be put to bed. She was there for three entire days. And for just as long I listened to what I had done to her. Do you know what I had done, Mr. Cameron?"

"Paul," I said. "No, what had you done?"

"I was jeopardizing her life and our happiness by exposing myself and her to the possibility of the same kind of shocking publicity. How did I know that the boy I was dating wasn't of the same breed as Clark McCord?"

"You swallowed that?" I muttered.

Her head wagged negatively. "It was ridiculous, I knew that. But it didn't make the situation any the less embarrassing. So I cancelled the date. And it wasn't until over a year later that anyone ever invited me out again. This time I didn't tell her about it. Instead I fabricated a story about having to work late and met my date in town. It was a simple, harmless evening: a movie, a hamburger and coffee after the show, and then straight home. It—it was one of the most enjoyable evenings I'd had since—since Clark died." A heavy sigh punctuated the silence when she stopped to sip from her glass. "Only one thing ruined it. Mother was waiting for me when I returned. She had phoned the library after I'd left and discovered I wasn't there. There was another scene, much worse than any before. She locked herself in the bathroom and tried to slash her wrists. Thank God Dad had been dead a few years by then and there were no men in the house. Otherwise she might have found a razor blade sharp enough to do what she had threatened. Oh, she found a blade, but it was an old one, probably the only one in the place. Somehow the cuts, when I got to her, were little more than harmless scratches. I pleaded and cried for her to let me in, but it wasn't until I tried to phone the police that she relented and opened the door." Breasts swelled against the dark fabric as she shrugged off a tremor that rippled through her body. "After that I resigned myself to the company of memories." She stopped and let the silence stretch, as though inviting comment. Getting none, she asked: "Now do you know why I'm afraid of publicity?"

"Uh-huh," I said, and finished the rest of the brandy. "You're scared she'll throw another wing-ding and try another suicide."

"I don't know what she'll do," she answered quietly. "All I know is that I don't want anything like that to happen again. I . . ."

"Nuts," I grunted. "She's been trying to scare you. Because one youngster was involved in and accused of a homicide is no sane reason to have your daughter avoid all men in case she happens to meet up with another with similar instincts."

"I know that," she agreed meekly. "So does she—I think. But in fairness I should admit that the publicity *was* very hard on her. Dad, too, for that matter. For weeks afterwards people who had been her close neighbors started ignoring her. Every time she went out they would point and whisper and say: 'There goes Theresa Riley. She's the one who allowed her kid to run around with a killer. Even had him in her home.' Dad experienced the same kind of thing where he worked, only there the men treated it as a big joke and kidded him about it. It used to hurt him, I know, even though he never ever discussed it with me. But he would talk things over with mother and often I would hear them and . . . and . . . They had no more friends when eventually we left the neighborhood to move here. Dad lost a lot of money on the sale of the house, and what made it worse was that they loved the place. Much more than this one."

"You were old enough to move out and live on your own," I said. "Ever consider that?"

"Often. Once I went as far as suggesting it. There was another scene. That, I think, is when I started wondering what it was mother really feared most. The possibility of being associated in the publicity of another murder, or just being left alone. Dad's death changed her. Even that she blamed on the publicity—the strain it had put on him. Before he died things were bad enough, but it was only afterwards that she started doing these things, threatening to take her life and . . ."

"She wouldn't," I assured her with a confidence that had a lot to do with the grape juice. I was feeling very relaxed.

"And if she did?" the girl questioned. "What then?"

"You mean how'd you feel? Forget it. Most people who threaten suicide the way your mother's been doing seldom ever kill themselves."

"I've heard that. But mother could be the exception."

"So what are you going to do?" I finished the drink and put the glass aside. "Continue living the way you've been doing? Going to chart a course straight for the old maids' home?"

"It will work out in time. I know it will. It must. In the meantime my mother is old and I feel obligated to take care of her. You see—in spite of what you've said and what I might believe I know she would do something dreadful rather than face the kind of publicity which would result if the case was brought into the open again. She's never forgotten the first time. On the contrary. Instead of putting it out of her mind she's constantly reminded us both of it—enlarging upon the facts, making it much worse than it really was. It—it's become a sickness with her."

"And in the meantime you're prepared to sit around and wait until she kicks off?"

"Please—don't talk like that. What I'm doing in the meantime, or rather what I've been trying to do, is show you why I want things left the way they've been." She smiled crookedly, and when next she spoke there was a very audible quaver in her voice. "But I don't think I've succeeded, have I?"

"Feeling sorry you talked to me?"

". . . No. No, strangely enough I'm not. You're the first person I've ever discussed it with. It—it's made me think. Perhaps I should have talked to someone long before this." Looking into her glass, at the last drops that clung to the bottom, she said very quietly: "When I asked you to come here I was scared. I was afraid of what might happen had mother decided to return home early for some reason. But I'm not anymore. You're the first man who's been here since Dad died, and . . . strangely, I'm no longer worried." She put down the glass. "Perhaps it's just the brandy and no dinner. Perhaps I'll wake up in the morning and it will be the same as before."

"It doesn't have to be."

"No, it doesn't." another long and inviting pause. "What will you do now?"

"What I started. And that, in spite of what you've been thinking, is to try and prevent the Green case hitting the headlines. You guessed right," I said getting up. The room tilted and I had to blink my eyes before it settled back into position. "I'm no writer. I'm a private cop."

"Then . . . Then why—?"

"Why I let you tell me those things about yourself? I was interested. It's not often that an attractive woman takes the trouble to find out where I'm staying so she can invite me to her home. I'm glad I came, and if it's any consolation, what you told me goes no further than this room."

"Can—I believe that? It's true—you're really a detective?"

I said: "Sam Ettman can tell you if you don't believe me. And there's this." I took out the I.D. case, opened it to the proper place and gave it to her.

She examined it carefully. "Then if it's true about not wanting the case reopened you must be working for someone! Somebody hired you to—to . . . ?"

"Don't ask me the details," I said, "because I can't and won't tell you. Just believe that I'm as anxious as you to ensure the case remains only a memory."

Her head bobbed in silence. Then: "That woman. The one who came to the library before you . . . Is she the one who . . .?"

"No questions, remember?"

"But—"

"But I'm going to ask you a few more. Did you know someone named Frank Cugino?"

For an answer she shook her head.

"How about Green's daughter?"

"Felicity? Of course. We attended the same school."

"What happened to her? After her father was killed she went to live with people named Hammond, then she's supposed to have married and moved away."

"That's right. She married a fellow named Daryl Merrit. He was a telephone technician or something. Their pictures were in the social pages of the *Taywood Times,* that's how I know about it. Then, of course, there was the usual talk at work. They moved to San Francisco after her husband received a promotion."

"What sort of girl was she, Diane?"

"No different to any other, I suppose. Why?"

"It was just a question. Ever hear her name linked with that of the Cugino I mentioned?"

"No—never. But I didn't know her that well and—and after her father was killed we purposely avoided each other."

"The people she went to live with. Are they still in town?"

"Yes, the Hammonds still live here. I don't know their address, but I suppose they would be in the phone book. Are you going to see them?"

"I don't think so."

"Paul," she said softly before I could ask anything more, "why are you asking these questions?"

"I don't know." And it was the truth. "But ever since I started on this thing I've had a funny feeling that someone's left out something. Still, it's not important to what I'm trying to do. The questions come from habit."

She sat looking at me, making no attempt to speak, her brow creased with shallow furrows. "For just a little while," she said at last, her voice hushed, "I thought you were going to say there was a reason for doubt . . ."

"I wish it were possible, Diane. For your sake, and maybe for your mother's and a few other people. But it's not. Ettman struck me as a responsible type of person. His investigation would have been pretty thorough."

She sat fingering the leather case I had handed her and said nothing. Disappointment flooded her eyes.

"Did you ever see the McCords after it happened?"

"I wanted to, but mother wouldn't allow me near them. Anyway, they didn't stay very long after Clark died. Years later I heard that they had moved to Imperial. Once when I was feeling very low I wanted to write to them. I went as far as searching for their address. Mother never knew what I was doing, of course. Then—then after I found out where they were living I—couldn't do it. I tried to write, but the words wouldn't come."

"Where were they staying?" I asked slowly.

"I don't know the exact address any longer. It was written in a notebook which I mistakenly threw away. But it was somewhere in El

Centro, I know that." She lifted herself from the couch and held out the identification folder. "You—you won't bother them, will you?"

"No, I won't bother them."

"Please don't, Paul. They were the ones who suffered the most. When it happened the shock was too much for Mrs. McCord. She had a heart attack and was never the same person after that." Still holding the case for me to take, she said, as though the thought had just occurred to her: "She—she may not even be alive now. And little Judith . . . I wonder what she's doing."

I took the folder from her. Or rather I started to. But something went wrong. I took her hand instead and the case dropped to the floor and neither of us moved to retrieve it. Her hand trembled in mine and I squeezed it to stillness.

". . . No," she breathed.

But by then I had her other hand, drawing her close. I was like a third person watching the scene move in a crazy kind of slow motion that had no connection with reality, and after that everything was lost in a jumble of murmurings and movement as her body brought itself hard against my own, her lips quivering unresistingly when I found them.

Something was happening and neither of us wanted to question it. Perhaps it was the loneliness to which she had been subjected for so long, or perhaps the one miserable glass of brandy, or even the constant thoughts of Allison Page which had been living with me since that Saturday. But it didn't matter at all what it was. There didn't have to be a reason. Her arms wound themselves around my neck and in between her soft cries her lips became demanding and alive. On her cheeks I felt moisture when my fumbling fingers explored her face, and afterwards there was quiet sobbing as she lay spent at my side in the all white bedroom that was hers.

I woke up about five. It was still dark, and aches that had been forgotten soon after arriving at the house, returned. Diane lay cuddled in a small ball next to me, as peaceful as a child. I put my hands behind my head and stared at the dark gray ceiling as thoughts of the things she'd revealed paraded through my mind. She'd been honest about the men in her life.

Other thoughts joined the march, and then quite suddenly I was thinking about Frankie Cugino and a package of heroin—if that was what it really was. *Cugino running . . . Cugino running . . . Donetti chasing . . . Cugino running . . .*

I got out of the bed as quietly as I could and collected my clothes from the floor. In the living room I dressed quickly and picked up the I.D. case from where it had been left lying open on the carpet. Then after carrying the two glasses and ashtray to the kitchen and washing and drying them, I tiptoed back to the door of the bedroom. She hadn't stirred. When she awoke it would be better if I wasn't around, and maybe after today things would be different. I hoped so. She had too much to offer, to much to let wither and waste.

Out in the garden the cricket chirped a bright good morning as I went to my car.

TEN

THE desk was unattended when I got back to the hotel. I touched the bell and glanced around the silent, empty lobby in which most of the lights had been doused. Suddenly, for a reason I could not then understand, a coldness fingered my spine, caressing my flesh as though something spectral had stepped up beside me. It was an unpleasant sensation and I shrugged it away to pound the bell once more. From the office behind the counter a chair scraped hard against wood and then a sleepy number wearing the uniform of the hotel poked his head around the door, knuckling sleep from his eyes as he inspected me across the distance.

"Something you wanted?"

"My key." I told him the room number.

With movements that would make a sloth look zippy, he dragged it out of its pigeon hole and dropped it on the counter. Tired eyes asked questions, but it seemed like too much effort would be required to transfer them to his mouth.

I rode up to the fifth floor and once in the room got rid of my clothes and went into the bathroom to scrape off the day-old beard. *Cugino running . . . Cugino dying . . . Donetti and his precious merchandise . . . Cugino running . . . .* The thoughts swirled around in my head like a drunken dervish while I tried to sort them into some kind of order that would show up the one thing that didn't fit.

Under the shower, instead of the water helping to clear my thinking, the thoughts became only more jumbled. I shoved them aside, turned off the water, and started toweling down. Erle Donetti and the stuff he was trying to locate were only incidental; neither had any direct connection with the work I was being paid to do. The only link was Frankie Cugino. *Cugino running . . . Donetti chasing . . .* Something about the setup was cockeyed. Unless . . . I started to laugh, but the sound was hollow and short-lived, for even if I was right it didn't help my end of things one bit. Already Rose Lang had arranged to sell what she knew, and once that story was in print there wouldn't be a studio who'd want to touch the blonde. Finding Allison was one thing. But after that?

And then, like a fist slamming low under the belt, it hit me.

Her key was in the rack!

I dressed quickly and went downstairs to hammer the desk bell.

"The woman in 407," I said when the night clerk showed his face. "When did she check out?"

"Who?"

More slowly, I repeated the question.

He inspected the pigeon holes and shrugged. "Search me. All the time they're coming and going. To me they're just people. I don't pay much attention."

"How about the register?"

With a grunting sigh he flipped open the book and ran a long nicotine stained finger down the entries. "Be out of line I ask how come you're interested?"

"She's a friend. We weren't supposed to be leaving until later today."

He glanced up from what he was doing and the little smile pulling at his lips said: "Like that, huh?" The finger went back to searching, and then it stopped. "Ten-forty," he muttered, closing the register with a muffled report.

"Who was on duty then?"

"Me—since last night." Tight lines began to wrinkle his narrow forehead.

"Didn't it strike you as a peculiar time to leave?"

"So what?" He shrugged again. "It was her business. She paid up and left. People do it all the time, y'know?"

"Not at that time of night they don't."

"So perhaps she got restless. Look, if she—"

"Was she alone when she left?"

"Mister, I told you. I don't pay attention."

"That's something you would have noticed, isn't it?"

"Look," he said, gesturing with his hands. "If she wanted to leave I couldn't stop her. We're not responsible for what the guests do or who they leave with. *If* they leave with anybody. And I'm not saying she was with anyone. All I'm saying is—"

"Who was with her?" I asked before he could finish the explanation.

"Now wait—I didn't say there was somebody else!"

"You didn't have to. Who was it?"

"I don't know, so knock it off, wilya?"

I took out my billfold, extracted a five and spread it out between us. "That help your memory?"

"Mister, when it comes to money I'm no different to the next joker. But that you can put away. It's not worth my job to take it. The hotel don't like to get itself mixed up with the troubles of people who rent rooms here." His hand reached out and started to push the bill away.

I wrapped my own around his wrist. He tried to pull back, fingers disappearing into a tight fist that clutched and crumpled the five spot. I said: "There's no trouble, amigo. But there just might be a whole lot of it if you don't tell me who she went with. Or perhaps you'd prefer I took it up with the management?"

"There was two of them," he said with a deliberate show of reluctance, and jerked his arm from my grip. "They stood away from the desk when she was squaring up her bill and I didn't take much notice of them. One of them was a pretty tall feller. The other guy just average-looking.

He was the one that carried her bag."

"What else?"

"Nothing else. Only . . ." Then deciding a little more to what he had already declared couldn't worsen matters, the hesitation ended. "Well, she acted sort of jumpy. I don't know how to explain exactly—maybe it was just my imagination. But twice she dropped her purse when she was trying to get her money out, and the second time it happened one of her friends came over and picked it up for her. The tall one. He said something to her, but I couldn't hear any of it." With another impotent gesture he wound it up: "Then they left."

I nodded my thanks and walked away from the desk. "Hey." he shouted. "Your money!"

But I was already leaning on the elevator button.

Through the window of my room I watched the sun pushing shadows off the roof tops as I tried to decide my next move. Today and tomorrow and then it would be Friday. Two days to go. I left the window and began gathering my few things together. What I had to do wasn't going to help Allison Page, not any way that I could see. Yet it had to be done.

At a gas station on the edge of town I had the Plymouth's tank topped up. That done, I turned the car around and pointed its nose back to Los Angeles.

2

At her apartment a neighbor let me know that the noise I was making with the bell was a waste of time. Rose was not at home.

From Venice I linked up with the heavy flow of late morning traffic, fighting it all the way over to Santa Monica. Suburban to Los Angeles, Santa Monica is a residential and beach resort town. It's also the place where the Annual Motion Picture Awards are presented. A lot has been written about that town, and not all of it the kind of stuff the chamber of commerce would want to record. The last time I had been there was when Fletcher and Strode had taken me to meet their boss. The memory of that Monday night made the almost forgotten bruises around my middle throb back to life.

During the ride there with The Earl's stooges I had noticed a few landmarks, but even after picking them up it took a good half hour to run down the florist shop.

I pulled up beyond the alley siding the building, and when I left the car the .38 was clipped to my hip.

The alley was completely deserted; the roller door above the loading ramp lowered, the pass door locked. A board fence brought the alley to a dead end and there was no other way into the building. I gave up looking and went around to the shop entrance.

The character leaning on the counter was a small, pale specimen that might well have been cultivated in a pot in the shade. His belly was carried like a basket ball under the sleeveless shirt hanging over his pants. Spread in front of him was an unopened newspaper from which he looked up when I entered and closed the door. I was on top of him before he said anything.

"Ain't got much today," he continued when I failed to answer his first question. "See for yourself. If there's something there you fancy . . ."

Even if I had been in the market there was nothing there I'd have offered a nickel for. Already three quarters on the way to being dead, the stuff on the low stands looked as if they'd been stolen from recently filled graves.

"Where's The Earl?"

"Who?" The protuberance in his throat jumped when he spoke.

"Donetti. And don't tell me you never heard of him."

"It's the wrong place you got, buster. This's a flower shop, or maybe to you it ain't obvious?" A limp hand waved at the withering plants. "Nobody named Donetti here."

I put my hand under my coat and brought the gun out front. Arms shot stiffly up into the air and he reared away. The wall at his back stopped him from going very far. Squirming against it, his head made curt, negative signs, his tongue flicking at his lips like a startled pink worm. I stepped behind the counter, took hold of his shoulder and yanked him in the direction of the door situated further to the rear of the shop.

"Let's take a look behind there." I nudged his spine with the Colt's short barrel. "Open it, and while you're at it, remember what this is in your back."

He did exactly as instructed, opening the door as though it might be wired to an explosive. Very slowly he pushed it in until we could see into the dimness of the short lobby. The stairs I had been taken up when first brought there were only a few yards away. I looked at them, then at the railed landing above, and in the small moment of time it took to do that the gun shifted its position and the runt developed a sudden case of bravery. Lunging sideways, he spun around, clawing for the Colt, his mouth wide, screaming:

"Whitey! Whitey—!"

I pulled the gun away from his grasping hands, brought it up in a fast swing that ended hard against the side of his head. He went down in a soft whimpering heap that didn't even twitch after it touched the uncovered floor.

Upstairs there was the sound of heavy footsteps. I stepped over the shape on the floor and ran for the stairs, flattening myself against them as a door was flung open above. Then followed absolute silence. With the gun leading the way I started crawling upward. Nearly at the top, I heard the feet move again—a moment before a shot blasted through the silence. Using the cover of the noise I went up the final three steps and peeped over the top.

He was standing there pressed against the wall so that he'd be out of range from any gun aimed from below, but in a position where he could look down on the open door to the shop and the little man lying there. In his hand was a black army-type automatic, but it was pointed down to the door at which his shot had been aimed.

In his huge fist the weapon looked quite small. He fanned it out slowly in front of him, eyes straining for whatever he thought he had seen downstairs.

He was tall and fat, with a crop of white hair sitting on his head like frosting on a pink cake. I waited until he moved closer to the balustrade rail before raising myself.

"Drop it, fat man!"

The hammy paw jerked, but the gun stayed put as the rest of him froze rigidly.

"Drop it!" I ordered again. "And don't turn around unless you want your head blown off!"

The hand that clutched the automatic began to lower, and for a few careless seconds I forgot that it wasn't some punk kid playing the heavy who stood there, but someone being paid to carry the gun and who was supposed to know how and when to use it. When it seemed he was about to back down he took a nimble unexpected backward step, turning dancer smooth on his heel while the big .45 bucked and belched thunder.

Without thinking about it I let my face hit the step, aware of the thing that hissed past like a frightened wasp, of another shot being triggered off . . . and it wasn't until he screamed that I realized the second shot had been from my own gun. The heavy automatic came unstuck from Whitey's fingers, bounced at his feet and slid across the boards. His right hand went to his shoulder as he performed a jerky pirouette that sent him reeling against the wooden rail. His weight hit it too fast and too hard, and in the position his arms were it was too late to do anything about the balance he'd lost. There was no sound when he went over and out of sight. A hundred years later, it seemed, the sound of his body smashing against the downstairs floor shook the building.

My hands had difficulty remaining still when the silence returned, thick and dull. Slowly I got up and went to the front door, inching it cautiously open to look into the room where Donetti had greeted me from the card table. The table was still there. So were the colored chips, the stale stink of cigar smoke and the butts on the floor. But that was all.

The door from which Whitey had made his entrance was still open. I sidled up to it and listened. Inside something metallic made a tired creak.

"Come on out!" I said sharply, pressing against the wall.

"I'm coming," a familiar voice replied. "I ain't armed, so don't get anxious." The thing I couldn't see creaked again before he shuffled to the door.

"You?" said Bo Fletcher weakly when he saw who was there. Then he turned and went back into the room. I went in after him.

ELEVEN

INSIDE the smudgy green-walled room there was a chair and a steel army cot on which a cheap gray blanket hid the mattress. A naked bulb hung from the ceiling like a suspended lump of candle wax upon which flies had been staging daylight orgies. High up in an outer wall a narrow window framed a small piece of sky and provided the only light. Fletcher flopped down on the cot, bringing another squeaking protest from its springs.

His shirt was torn and stained dark with sweat. Damp hair lay in untidy tendrils across his forehead while the rest of his wide, florid face was camouflaged with an assortment of ugly lumps and bruises. Blood had run from his swollen nose and he hadn't yet managed to clean it off his upper lip.

"Geeze, Cameron, if anyone ever told me there'd be a time I'd be glad to see you, I'd've told them they was on Pentothal." The gold tooth glinted like a bright cavity when he tried to grin. "What happened to that son-of-a-bitch Whitey?"

"He's out there. What happened to you?"

The tightening of his jaw dissolved the grin. "What's it look like? I been to a beautician?"

"Fletcher," I said, motioning with the gun, "a minute ago I had a hell of an experience and my insides are still jumping. Don't let me have to take it out on you."

"Donetti," he returned sullenly, allowing his shoulders to ride up and down in a surrendering shrug. "He didn't like a couple opinions I expressed so he let Leo and that fat bastard Whitey do what he couldn't handle personally." Squinting up, he touched the side of his battered face and called Donetti a purple name I hadn't heard since Korea.

"Where are they now?"

"You'd come maybe fifteen minutes sooner you'd of run into them all. They left Whitey and that little creep downstairs in case I got restless for other places."

"And the girl?"

The disfigured face went stupid. He looked away.

"Rose Lang," I said. "The girl you and Leo Strode took from the hotel in Taywood."

"You know things nobody's told me about," he muttered. "I never heard about any such dame."

"Ever hear about the law being only one phone call away?"

His head came around fast. "The cops can't touch me. There's nothing I've done that's cop business."

"You're obviously ignorant about a lot of things, Fletcher. Forgetting everything else that's happened in this place, I'm sure they'd be interested in the testimony of witnesses at the hotel. You and Strode were seen leaving with the girl. Or have you forgotten the night clerk who checked her out?"

"Okay. So that was another of Donetti's ass-about ideas." Sweaty shoulders slumped slowly forward. "After we dumped you the other night me and Leo staked out the dame's place in case she got ideas about taking off. We watched her pad the whole night until she grabbed a bus next morning for that jerkwater burg. Then we reported back to Donetti. He got all steamed up over it; made us go after her to find out what she was up to. So we followed and when she got there all she did was waste a lot of time in the goddamn library and soak up booze at the hotel. When Donetti was told about it he gave orders to bring her back here."

"For what purpose, Bo?"

"Donetti figured she knew where Cugino'd stashed the stuff. When we got her back here he let Strode apply his personal style of questioning." He stopped talking to look up again, trying to find out if what he was saying was being accepted. "For crysakes, I'm telling you the truth! I got no reason to lie about anything. Not now. As far as Donetti's concerned I'm through—kaput!"

"Get on with the rest of it. And while you're at it, remember who I am. The mug you and Strode left hurting."

"She talked," he said lamely. "Leo really went to work on her this time, and she talked. She told them everything they wanted to hear. And that," he added, fingering his swollen nose and the black bruises mottling the side of his face, "is about when I bought this."

"Where is she now?"

"They let her go about an hour or more before they left. She was no more use to them."

"Try again. I've just come from her apartment. She isn't there."

"So maybe she was too scared to go straight home. How the hell'm I supposed to know where she's got to?"

"Want one more try?" I asked quietly, moving the .38 in case he had forgotten it was still there. "And this time give it some thought."

"I'm telling you the truth, damnit! They let her go!" A shade louder and it would have been a scream.

"After she told them where Cugino hid the stuff?"

"Yeah, she told them," he said grudgingly. "She tried to hold out, but it didn't do her much good. Leo Strode's a first-class bastard when it comes to making people hurt. It didn't take long for him to turn her into a canary. After that they tossed her out."

"And now they've gone to pick up the stuff?"

"Yeah, I guess."

The room was warm and sour with the smell of human sweat and cigarette smoke. I felt a little sick standing there having to look at him; impatient at having to extract the information in pieces.

"Gone where?"

"To that motel where Cugino was staying. According to what the dame told them Cugino had the stuff with him when he blew town. Then when she tipped him we were coming after him he gave the guy that runs the joint a few bucks and had him lock the package up in his safe." Fletcher wiped his mouth tenderly against the back of his wrist, examining the damp smear before adding: "They've gone to get it. Donetti and Strode, and they took Pelser with them."

"Who the hell's Pelser?"

Fletcher's shoulders made the slightest of moves. "You'll meet him."

My insides turned cold at the thought of Donetti and his crew visiting the Crescent Palm. His impatience was making him reckless and if it wasn't stopped soon people were going to be hurt. I didn't want it to be the Newtons. I checked the time on my watch.

Fletcher went on without any prompting: "Cugino wasn't as dumb as we thought. He conned us sweetly. When we looked for him at the motel there was nobody by his name registered. Leo even went through the registration cards himself, and that dame there, that redhead, she couldn't remember anyone like him checking in. Unless he paid them some more to forget he was ever there," he ended thoughtfully.

"This stuff Donetti's after. What is it, Bo?"

"Hell, you were there when Donetti talked about it. You oughta know."

"I'm asking you."

"It's a package of H—about fifteen or more pounds of the pure stuff. Like it is it's supposed to be worth more than a hundred grand, and a hell of a lot more after it's been broken down for distribution. It's a supply Donetti's brother's supposed to have turned over to Cugino for delivery to one of their eastern outlets."

"And Cugino's supposed to have hidden it before his arrest and picked it up after his release?"

"Donetti told you so, didn't he?"

"He did. And it smells."

The face before me went as blank as a lump of red clay.

"If Cugino had that much unadulterated heroin," I said, "he could have sold it at half the market price and bought so much mileage Donetti would never have found him. He knew Donetti was after his blood and he was running scared. Yet he held on to the stuff and played the kind of games he did?"

Softly Fletcher chuckled. "You guessed it, chum. Me, I don't think there was anything Cugino ever had. Not a damn thing. I think Donetti's brother fed him a load of bullshit. Cugino was a nobody back east. A real nothing. So a guy in Donetti's position is going to turn over merchandise like that to a no-total like him? Crap! Gino Donetti was supposed to be a real hot shot. I mean like big, not like *The Earl* who just thinks he's big. Gino was a big man in his town. Well if he was, he wouldn't pull a dumb stunt like that. Trouble is, I had to shoot off my mouth to his brother and his brother didn't like it." Again fingers inspected the damage to his face. "Thing was, the way Strode was working on the girl made me sick. I don't go for that kind of stuff with the skirts. But I must've been nuts to mention what I was thinking to Donetti. The creep was probably thinking the same kind of things himself." Suddenly Fletcher became earnest. Leaning forward, anxious for me to understand what he was driving at, he went on:

"Look, when we had you here the other night you told Donetti how Cugino was trying to blackmail whoever it is you were working for, right? Well, I been thinking about it ever since, and it don't figure. What I mean is, if Cugino needed dough so bad he'd try picking up hush money it goes to show he never had nothing worth the trouble Donetti's been going to, don't it? So okay, maybe I should of mentioned it to Donetti before, or just shut up altogether. But when Strode was beating up on the girl I got so goddam sick of the whole thing I blurted out everything I was thinking. Donetti got mad as hell and told Whitey to shut me up. Then after the girl told them where Cugino was supposed to have left the stuff he let Strode push me around the room a little."

"Go on," I said when he paused to recapture his breath.

"That's it. After they let the dame go, him and Leo and Pelser took off in the car for the motel." He chuckled again. Dryly. "But Mr. Big Shot's in for a big disappointment, and I figure he already knows it. Hell, if he ain't figured out what his brother's done to him by now he must be the dumbest wop that ever swallowed spaghetti. When his brother was alive did he ever cut him in on a piece of his racket? Like hell! He let Erle scratch for himself, and the reason, the way I got it, is they was never real close like brothers. Once I heard they wasn't even brothers—real brothers, I mean." He had been talking fast, but now he slowed down, wiped the sweat from his neck and looked at me anxiously. "Okay, so how come all of a sudden when Gino is dying he sends for Erle and tells him about the big lump of H Cugino's got stuck away someplace?"

"You tell me, Bo."

" 'Cause when Donetti was put away the mob went to pieces. Somebody else picked up the bits and put it together again, but nobody wanted to know about Gino Donetti any more. So who's left to settle the score with Cugino? Who's going to take the time to make sure he gets paid off for singing to the fuzz? Nobody—except maybe Erle. And even he's not much concerned. He's too busy trying to make himself into a bigger number than his brother ever was. He's going to worry about a vendetta? Nuts! I guess Gino Donetti figured as much himself. That's why he sent for Erle when he was dying. He wants to go knowing Cugino's going to catch it in full for putting him where he is. But he knows Erle won't go to any real trouble over it. Not unless there's a buck involved. So he cons him with a story about Frankie Cugino having a packet of merchandise 'cause he knows *that's* something his brother will do something about. Savvy?"

I nodded, for as crazy as it sounded it made sense of events as I knew them.

"Donetti knows he's been conned," Fletcher said. "I could see it in his face when I told him. And that's why he's going along personally with the other two. You know why I've been left here with Whitey?" he asked suddenly. "You know why, Cameron? Cause they're not going to find any goddamn package. There never was one. I know it and Donetti knows it, and when they come back he'll do to me what he'd like to do to his dead brother and can't."

I looked at my watch. Donetti had a small start to Vadear Point, but it would still be some time before he got there. I still had a little time. Looking back at the waiting figure on the bed, I asked:

"What's this place used for?"

"It's Donetti's property. The runt downstairs sells flowers when he feels like it, but mostly Donetti rents out the store to some guys he knows. He's been using it for an office since we been in town on account of he didn't want the local fuzz to know who he's been seeing."

"He's been living here?"

"Nah, at an hotel. This is just for getting together."

"Who killed Cugino, Bo?"

"Huh?"

"What's the matter? The beating affect your memory?"

"I heard what you asked. It surprised me, that's all."

"Then how about an answer now that the surprise is over?"

Stroking his chin he tried to look thoughtful. His eyes peered questioningly at me. "If I told you I didn't know it wouldn't do much good, would it? Okay," he continued after I shook my head. "I can tell you what I *think*, that's all. What Donetti told you was the truth. We had no orders to hit Cugino—not until we got the stuff from him. But that night when we were up at the Point, after we drew a zero at the motel, me and Leo drove up into town and took a room at the hotel. We had a few drinks and then Leo decided he wanted to go out riding. I didn't—I was beat. So Leo went by himself and he was out late. Anyway, I was asleep when he got back. Next morning he was kind of quiet, but I didn't think anything of it 'cause he was like that sometimes. You know—withdrawn? Matter of fact I never thought anything about it till Donetti told us about Cugino's car being dumped in the sea and about that body being found burnt up there. I don't know for sure, but I'm pretty damn certain it was Leo's work. Could be that when he was out he ran across Cugino. Could be he worked him over a little too hard like . . . Later I read in the papers how it was a .22 that squibbed off Cugino before he

got the match. That's the same kind of gun Strode carries, or maybe you
never noticed?"

Tonguing his lower lip, Fletcher tried another grin. "Savvy what I'm
getting at? It's only a suspicion, but it makes sense. Leo'd never tell
Donetti if he killed Cugino—even if it wasn't intentional. I mean, not
when he killed him before Donetti had his hands on the stuff." The smile
stayed on his mouth as if glued to his lips. But a tenseness had entered
his body, making him lean still further forward. Then his eyes performed
a brief betrayal when flicking quickly to the door before again focusing
back on my face.

I stepped back hurriedly, forgetting about the chair that stood behind
me. Fletcher started a shout that was cut off sharply when a shot blasted
its way from the door, echoing loudly and deadly in the small confines of
the room. The chair caught me behind the knees, knocking me off balance. As I went down I caught only a glimpse of the pale specimen I had
left unconscious downstairs. His mouth hung open in wide, stupid
amazement while the gun drooped in his hand. From the floor I knocked
the chair out of the way, rolled against the wall and tried to get the .38 in
a position where it would be of some help. But by that time the doorway
was once again vacant.

Feet clattered on the boards of the landing outside as I scrambled out
of the room, hesitating only a moment to look down at where Fletcher lay
thrown back across the cot, his head angled awkwardly against the dirty
wall.

The little man was already crossing the downstairs floor to the entrance of the shop when I reached the landing. I shouted for him to stop,
throwing a shot at his legs when he didn't. It missed, but brought him to
a skidding halt.

"Throw down the gun," I shouted, and he did. "Now come back up
here. Slowly."

He hesitated, flung a glance at where Whitey lay folded up on the
floor, then looked up at where I waited with the Colt pointing down at
him. Raising his hands above his head he started for the stairs, mounting
them with extreme care, approaching with fear glistening brightly in
blinking eyes.

"Inside," I said, pushing him into the room where Fletcher was
stretched out on the cot, across his soiled shirt a wide patch of wet crimson spreading larger as it continued to pump slowly through the fingers
clutching at a hole in his chest.

The pale one stopped upon seeing the result of his work and I was
forced to give him another push. Fletcher opened his eyes, surprising us
by proving he was not yet dead. But it was only a matter of seconds and
at least two of us knew that. The third saw hope.

"Bo," he whispered hoarsely. "Bo, I didn't mean to . . ."

Fletcher peered weakly at the little man. "You—you stupid son of a—
a—" He gasped with the effort to talk and swiveled his eyes to me.

"Lied—Cameron. The—the girl. Downstairs. Make—the creep show . . . Make him show you." Air rattled from his throat, preceding a bubble of blood that broke at his lips and began the start of a thin trickle down to his chin. "Get—" He sighed deeply and never finished whatever it was he had wanted to say.

"Bo!" the little one cried pathetically. "Bo, I didn't mean—damnit, Bo . . . how was I to know . . . ?"

"You heard what he said." I took him by the shoulder and steered him out of the room. "Show me where the girl is."

All the fight had seeped out of him now. He made a tired shrug and led me downstairs to the storeroom. Near the steel roll-up door a long crate had been parked as if waiting to be collected. He pointed to it, saying nothing.

"Open it."

The lid of the crate was held down by a few thin ropes and it didn't take him long to get them untied. But once the ropes had been removed he straightened up and stepped quickly back.

"Get the lid off."

"No. Please."

I jabbed the gun into his back and repeated the order.

Slowly he stooped over, took hold of the lid, lifted and threw it quickly aside as if any prolonged contact with the wood might contaminate his hands.

She was inside the box, most of the clothing stripped from her body so that the bruises showed vividly on her arms and breasts. Her face was worse than Fletcher's; bloody and bruised, her mouth open, revealing the darkened red that clotted between broken teeth. I was glad her eyes were closed.

"I had nothing to do with it—it was Strode!" the runt pleaded, turning around. Sweat like bubbles stood out against the pallid flesh. Under his shirt the round belly heaved frantically.

"They—they were working her over and—and she just died on 'em. Honest to God, I had nothing to do with it. I swear it! I—I didn't even help when they put her in there—in the box."

"Why the box?" My voice sounded gravelly and foreign.

"They—they were gonna take her away in a truck. Dump her someplace. I dunno where. Honest I don't, mister. I had nothing to do with it. I work here, is all. The Earl, he made me stay with Whitey till they got back."

"Shut up," I said. "Shut up and get down on your ugly face. Be quick about it."

His head jerked obediently, the mouth chewing out soundless things as he got down on the floor and stretched out on his belly. I holstered the gun and used the ropes from the crate to tie his hands and feet together at the small of his back.

"Hey, please. . . . Mister, you're not gonna leave me here like this? Mister, please—not with her! For God's sake, not with her!"

But I was walking away from the sound of his pleas, fighting the surges below my belt, the ones that had started when Whitey had fired at me, which had subsided a little while with Fletcher, and which now, after having seen what was left of Rose Lang, returned with a vengeance. I was sick before I was halfway to the door of the shop.

To reach the shop I had to pass where Whitey had crumbled. He lay in exactly the same position he had fallen, but with a bullet in the shoulder and after having taken a twelve-foot fall, it was unlikely he'd be doing much moving again. At the door I stopped. I went back to the twisted figure. I felt for a pulse and found something that still beat with a small amount of vigor. The fat slob was still alive, saved perhaps by his bulk. I felt no disappointment. There's seldom any pleasure in the knowledge that you have killed. No matter who or what the man was.

Behind the counter I located a phone and from Information received the number of the sheriff's station at Vadear Point. But once I had the number I had a change of mind about calling Phillips and alerting him about Donetti. There was no sane reason for it; it was just a hope that was vague and possibly senseless. But that was all I could do for Allison Page now. Hope that there might still be a way out for her, a way to keep the Green killing in the past where it belonged. It was all that seemed to matter anymore. Her face, as I had seen it that night at Rigby's home, floated up before me as I hooked a finger in the telephone dial and spun out the number of the Santa Monica law.

So far I'd been able to avoid any direct involvement with the police, but that looked like being over from here on.

I told the voice who answered the call what had happened and where it had happened, and who was making the call. But when he started demanding that I stay there I put the receiver down on the counter and went away from the crackling sounds his voice made squeezing through the wire.

I went back to my car, wondering why the shooting had not attracted any interest from outside. But it was that sort of street. Or perhaps nobody had heard a thing. It happens.

Like a piercing voice that screamed for me to wait, the wail of the first siren arrived as I turned the car off the block, gunning the engine as fast as the legal limit would allow.

TWELVE

THE NO VACANCIES sign was burning when I arrived at the Crescent Palm, the multi-colored units already bathed in the gray shadows of late afternoon. Few cars were parked behind the low white wall fronting the road. One stood close to the entrance of the office; a sleek black Imperial almost as long as the building itself. I drove in past it, docking my car between two more conventional-looking heaps. During my first visit to the place it had been quiet. It was even more so now, as if all life had vacated the area. Then an infant cried shrilly, shattering the silence, following up with a series of loud, blubbering howls that were like something supernatural amidst the restful surroundings.

Inside the car I pulled off my coat, unclipped the holster from my belt and removed the .38. Holding the gun in my left hand I folded the coat over my arm so that the weapon was concealed.

Neither of the Newtons were in the office. In their stead, a thick-set, broad-shouldered number leaned against the shelves at the rear of the counter, a bent king-size cigarette dangling from his full lower lip. High on the bridge of his nose perched a pair of dark-lensed glasses that made his eyes invisible. But I didn't have to be warned that they watched with care as I entered. A white scar puckered the flesh on the upper part of his right cheek, lending his face a slightly lopsided appearance.

"We're full up," he advised calmly before I had a chance to ask any kind of question. "Didn't you see the sign?"

"I saw it. Then I figured it might have been switched on by mistake—judging from the number of cars parked outside."

"No mistake, friend. We're full, just like it says. No vacancies. You want a place for the night; better try the hotel in town."

The door at the end of the office through which the Newtons had appeared the first time I'd seen them was closed again. But this time no sound of any description penetrated its thickness.

"You the owner?"

"Uh-uh. Just watching things for him. He's occupied with something important." Manicured fingers removed the cigarette from his mouth, bent it fully in half, and dropped it to the floor. Levering himself away from the shelves that had been supporting his weight, he made a small movement and killed the smoke with his foot. "I was you, I'd try getting to the hotel early. There's a lot of tourists around this time of year. Be a shame the hotel's also full the time you get there."

"Your name Pelser?" I asked.

His face revealed nothing new as he slowly straightened up and allowed the trim fingers of his right hand to crawl casually toward the narrow lapels of his unbuttoned coat. "Who'd you say?"

I pushed my hand out from under the coat straddling my arm and put the Colt on display. "Leave it where it is."

"Cute." He dropped the hand, smiled. "Not novel, but cute. Going to tell me what it's all about?"

"Where are Donetti and Strode?"

"This a stick-up, pal? You don't look like no heist—"

"Strode," I repeated. "Where is he?"

"You got me. Never heard of no Strode. A friend?"

"Stay dumb," I said. "In the meantime get the gun out from under your arm and slide it across the counter. Fletcher's dead and Whitey's in a bad way."

"Oh . . .?"

"I thought you should know. Just in case you think there's a chance when getting the rod unloaded."

His hand inched back inside the coat. "You killed them?"

"As easy," I lied, "as I'd kill you if it became necessary."

The gun, an automatic that could have been the twin of the one Whitey had carried, came out carefully from the underarm rig he was wearing and was pushed across to me. I picked it up and shoved it down as far as it would go into my hip pocket.

"Now let's hear where Strode and Donetti are."

"Balls to you," he breathed softly. "You got the iron. You get nothing else."

"Put your hands on top of your head and keep them there," I said, waiting until he obeyed before crossing over to the closed door. For several long seconds I listened, hearing nothing. And then a man's voice spoke. I strained to decipher the sounds, but it wasn't any good. The voice stopped talking.

"Over here," I instructed softly, motioning for Pelser to join me.

His feet made heavy, unnecessary sounds as they walked him out from behind the counter.

"Open the door and go in. And be very careful about any other move you may be considering."

He turned on another of his empty smiles, shrugged and took hold of the handle. He said something in a voice that was too low to project its message, turned the handle and pushed the door in.

"I told you to thtay out there, didn't I?"

At the sound of the lisping voice Pelser stopped. I gave him a shove that sent him stumbling into the room and went in behind him.

"Put up the gun, Strode!"

Strode jerked forward, but recovered quickly, chuckling idiotically as he relaxed back against the couch. Curtailing the cackle, he said: "Better check the thituation, Cameron. One more move from you and the red-headed lady will be very dead!"

The room was a small lounge, presumably part of the Newtons' private quarters. Ann Newton sat on a low couch within touching distance of the tall blond Strode. Wearing another of his jazzy sports coats, Strode sat with his straw hat tilted to the crown of his head, the very pink pouting lips stretched into a thin smile that made the lump of flesh he used as a nose bulge even larger. Crossed legs supported his right forearm so that the long-barreled .22 nestling in his fist was in a steady position as it pointed at Ann Newton.

She tried to say something, but Strode silenced her with only two words and a hard jab from the gun. I looked at her, at the blouse torn open to reveal her brassiere and the bulging flesh above, at the auburn hair which had fallen loose and now caressed the side of her frightened face. I still couldn't see her husband.

"I don't know how you found out where we were, Cameron, or how it conthernth you, but you weren't very bright about it, were you?" The long face went on smiling confidently. "Now turn your gun over to my colleague before I get impatient and thoo—give it to the lady right now!'

"Who is he?" Pelser wanted to know.

"A private dick," said Strode. "A crummy private dick."

Strode's information brought a quick frown to Ann Newton's forehead as I continued to look at her. Her tear stained eyes came my way once more, then the gaze dropped to her lap and a hand rose to her breasts, tugging the blouse closed.

"A private dick?" Pelser echoed. "What the hell's he got to do with this?"

"Never mind about that," Strode admonished. "Get the gun from him. He won't try anything. Not now."

"He says Fletcher's dead," Pelser told him. "Claims Whitey's also in a bad way—that he's responsible."

"Did he now? Then we have another thing to take up with Mithter Cameron, don't we?"

Pelser still made no move to take my gun. Not that it made any difference to the situation. There was nothing I could do without endangering Ann Newton's life.

"Still looking for the package Cugino's supposed to have run off with, Strode?"

He didn't answer, so I went on:

"You've been going to an awful lot of trouble for nothing. Or didn't Fletcher tell you there never was anything? Donetti's brother suckered him."

"You talked to Fletcher, did you?"

"Before he died, yes. But there are other things to substantiate what he had to say. Want to hear them?" I asked. "Want to hear how Donetti's been using you punks as errand boys when there never was anything Cugino had in the first place?"

"No!" Strode shouted, a flash of anger darkening his face. "Get his gun, damnit!

Still uncertain of the score, Pelser took a deep breath, adjusted the dark glasses on his nose and reached for the gun with tentative fingers. I let him have it. Within the past few seconds I had discovered where Mike Newton was sitting—or standing.

With the Colt now his, Pelser released his breath and faced Strode.

"This's fouled things up, Leo. How we going to hang around now? Maybe this guy isn't alone."

Strode uncrossed his legs and stood up. "Then we'll have to leave. We'll take them along."

"I said he may not be alone," repeated Pelser.

"Which ith why we're taking them with uth. If Cameron hath anyone waiting out-thide they won't try anything. Not if we have him for cover and . . ."

"What's the matter?" Pelser asked uneasily.

"Nothing."

"You worried about The Earl—what he's going to say if we go back empty handed? The dame said the stuff was here in their safe."

"Well it wathn't!" Strode fired back. "Or were you blind?" Turning sharply he confronted the seated redhead. "But maybe we can find out the real truth before we go. Unfortunately, my dear," he said, addressing Ann Newton in a strangely hushed tone, "Cameron arrived at a very inconvenient time. Now I have no option but to hurry thingth up. And you're going to tell me where you've put that package our friend Cugino left with you. You're going to tell me and you're going to tell me quickly. If you don't that pretty red head ith going to be very ugly tomorrow morning. If," he added nastily, "you don't forthe me to kill you!"

Newton's wife cowered back against the couch, her head shaking from side to side in frantic denial. "I—we told you. Why don't you believe us? Why don't you leave us alone? Nothing was left here. Nothing! We never even saw this man you're talking about."

"Don't lie, damn you!" Strode hissed, raising the .22 menacingly.

"You're wasting your time," I chipped in. "Donetti's been chasing a bum steer."

"Shut your bloody face!" Pelser ordered.

"It's the truth!" Ann Newton cried. "Whoever told you that man was here is lying! Not us!"

All the while Strode and Pelser had been talking and deciding what was to be done next, a hand had been fiddling at my hip pocket. Now as it went away I tensed myself. As the blast of the .45 resounded through the room I flung myself at Pelser, landing on top of him when we hit the floor. A woman's voice screamed in terror and there were other noises as Pelser rolled me off him and fought to retain his hold on the gun. I butted him in the face with my head, knocking the glasses from his nose, but he only grunted and held on more tightly than ever. My fingers were locked around his right wrist, trying to shake the .38 from his grasp, but as he twisted and pulled I began to feel my grip loosen. Then when it seemed like Pelser was going to jerk free I saw something suddenly lash out through the air and connect with the side of his head. He went over sideways and before I could get at him again his head received another vicious kick. It was all he could take.

I got up and collected my gun from where he had let it fall. "Thanks," I said to Mike Newton.

He looked at the automatic in his hand, scowling deeply so that his dark brows knitted tightly together. Bunching up his muscular shoulders he hurled the gun across the room. Then without a word went to where his wife sat pressed into the corner of the couch, took her hand and pulled her up from it. With his arm supporting her waist he led her out of the room, neither of them once looking at where Strode lay with part of his head in splinters. Near his outstretched hand the colorful straw hat was perched on its crown, the narrow brim splattered with a slime that could have been part of its owner's brains.

I had Strode's target pistol and was picking up Pelser's gun from where Newton had thrown it when I heard the shuddering sobs of his wife echo from the office. I went out to where they waited.

Newton locked the door and went back to his wife. It took less time than I imagined it would for him to console her and shut off the tears. By then people were outside the office, some knocking on the closed door, demanding to know what was happening. Newton went outside and spoke to them. That left me alone with his wife.

"Thank God you came," she said. "I—I'm sure he would have killed us."

"That was true about not seeing Cugino?" I asked. "He left nothing with you?"

"I've never seen the man, Mr. Cameron."

I nodded. "Think you can get on the phone and call the sheriff's office?"

"Yes—I'm all right now." She reached for the phone. Newton returned as I was feeling in my pocket for a cigarette.

"What're you doing, Annie?"

"Getting some law down here," I answered for her, offering him the deck of cigarettes.

He took one and let me light it for him. Pulling deeply on the weed he held the smoke down in his lungs for a long time before letting it dribble through his nostrils. "I had to do it. You saw that, didn't you? I had to shoot him otherwise he'd have hurt Ann."

"The man you killed left a dead woman back in Santa Monica," I informed him. "And probably others before her. He won't be missed."

"You know what those crazy bums wanted? You know what they reckoned we had here?"

"I know," I said.

"They were nuts!" Newton shook his head, bewildered. "Who'd ever leave stuff like that with us?" Pulling again on the smoke, he said: "It was that blond feller's idea for me to sit there in the chair by the door. It was his idea, you know that? That way he could watch me and I could see what he was doing to Ann. We had twenty minutes left, he said, before he was going to give it to her. He was going to kill my wife if we didn't tell him where that stuff was. Geeze, Cameron, if I had it I'd've given it to him like a shot. Nothing's worth getting Annie hurt. But they were crazy, both of them. Where'd they get the idea we had anything like that?"

"From the woman he killed," I said. "I guess she was willing to tell him anything just to get away from them." I drew smoke down into my lungs and thought about how Rose Lang had looked spread out in the bottom of that crate.

Behind the counter Ann Newton put down the phone and reached for a handkerchief tucked in the sleeve of her blouse. While she repaired the damage the tears had done to her eyes, I said to her husband:

"That man everyone has been talking about . . . Frankie Cugino. He was here, wasn't he?"

Newton cocked his head to one side and scratched the short bristles of his dark hair. "Seems like he was. Anyway, that's what everybody's been claiming. Even you asked Annie about him when you first came here." He stopped the scratching and put the hand into a pocket of his tight jeans. "If he was, we sure as hell didn't recognize him, and he never used his real name, that's certain."

"He wouldn't have."

Newton permitted himself a grin. "I can't help thinking about that guy making me sit there behind the door. Even when you came in and I was hidden by the door he couldn't have no way of guessing it was going to be his big mistake."

I said nothing. I was looking at his wife again, watching the way she was swaying behind the counter.

"Hell," Newton said, "when you came in there and I saw that big old .45 poking out of your pocket—right there where I could get at it—"

"Mike . . . !"

We both went to her, but before we reached the end of the counter she had slipped away behind it.

"Annie!" Newton yelled.

I pushed him aside and lifted her head and shoulders from the floor. "Take it easy. She's just fainted."

2

Leading the way up to Vadear Point's largest hotel and to the room we wanted, Under-sheriff Phillips placed a heavy knock upon the door, loosening the gun at his hip while we waited.

Erle Donetti opened the door, one of the fat cigars he favored clamped between his teeth, listless brown eyes widening at sight of the star pinned to Phillips's shirt.

"Yeah?" Peering past Phillips to where I stood he took the cigar from his mouth. Recognition flickered and died quickly in his smooth face. "There something you wanted?"

"Your name Donetti? Erle Donetti?"

Donetti gave a mute nod.

Phillips marched him back into the room. "You got two men working for you, one named Strode, the other Pelser?"

"What if I have? What's your beef?" Donetti asked quietly, turning his side to us as he dropped ash in the receptacle standing on the night table.

"They your men is what I asked. Just answer the question."

"All right. So they work for me. Look, you going—"

"Get your coat on," Phillips ordered. "You're coming with us."

"What the hell for? What'd I do? I been sitting here relaxing till you come hammering down my door. What'm I supposed to've done? Those punks got themselves in some kinda jam that's their lookout. I'm not responsible for what they do in their own time, am I?" Stubbing out the cigar with exaggerated care he avoided facing either of us. "You never said what they're supposed to've done."

"I'll feed you the whole picture down at the station. Now get dressed unless you want me to take you as you are." To emphasize his seriousness, the gun appeared in the under-sheriff's hand.

"You arresting me?" Disbelief made Donetti's words a course whisper.

"Now how'd you manage to guess?"

"What for? What've I done?"

"Hell, don't you know another tune? How does murder suit you, Mr. Donetti?" Phillips moved his tall, wiry frame closer to where The Earl stood against the bed. Donetti shrank away until the bed prevented further retreat. "You know, I read about you several times, Donetti. I always had you pegged as some kind of a big shot. A hotshot hood. But you know what? Right now you look like just another lump of crap in a fancy suit. This the way you always operate? Sit on your fanny sucking those stinking weeds while your hired punks go out roughing up women for you? That the limit to your style?"

Donetti colored up but said nothing until he was quite sure Phillips had finished.

"You out of your skull, copper? Who's murdered who? Look, those boys got themselves in some kinda trouble that's their hard luck. You can't hold me for it. I let them go for the night. Where they went's got nothing to do with me." He stopped talking to loosen his collar and tug it away from his throat. "They—they killed someone?"

"Not here," I answered for Phillips, "but back in Santa Monica, at that dump of yours. A girl called Rose Lang. Remember her? Cugino's girl friend? There are also some questions waiting for you about the way Frankie Cugino died."

"I should never have let you walk outa there that night, you son-of-a-bitch!" he hissed venomously. "This's your doing, isn't it?"

"Why not go quietly with the man, Erle? I've got a feeling he'd enjoy dragging you out by the heels, and he's big enough to do it. Besides, you're all washed up. Pelser's been singing in high C for the last half hour. He's filled in most of what we wanted to know."

"And your other boy's dead. Seems he lost part of his head in a tussle of sorts," Phillips said, smiling at his own weak joke.

"And all for nothing, Erle," I said. "Cugino never had a thing that would have been worth a nickel to you—except his life. Your brother presented you with a fairy story about that consignment of divinity juice. There never was one. You should have listened to what Bo Fletcher tried to tell you."

"You're lying!" he cried indignantly, grabbing the front of my coat in both hands. "You lie! Gino wouldn'ta done that to me. He was my brother! He wouldn'ta played me for a patsy. You're a stinking liar, you—" As small as he was, his hands shook me violently, and as I reached down to knock them away I saw Phillips holster his gun and move toward us.

A big brown hand clamped down on Donetti's narrow shoulder and spun him around. Another hand, one balled into a hard fist swung up from Phillips's thigh and threw itself at Donetti's jaw. A gasping grunt came from Donetti's throat as he went flying across the bed, twisting over onto his belly and then lying extremely still.

"Soft," Phillips grinned, massaging his knuckles. As he reached across the bed to pull the little man to his feet, he said: "Always wanted to hang a good one on someone like him. It's made me feel a whole hell of a lot better now that I have."

3

At the sheriff's station I was ushered into a room where a burly deputy stood watch over Pelser, the latter nursing manacled wrists in his lap. Phillips brought in Donetti and thrust him down into one of the hard chairs that were the only furniture in the room.

"Stick around here, will you, Cameron?" Phillips said. "We're getting statements from the Newtons and after that we'll want yours. In the meantime I'd better get in touch with Santa Monica."

I lit a cigarette and prepared for the long wait. Donetti spoke once to Pelser, but his stooge bowed his head and played deaf. When Donetti got mad and started to yell the big cop told him what would happen if he didn't pipe down. Very meekly he shut up.

It was long after midnight before I got away from there. I recited everything I knew to Phillips, holding back at first about Allison Page's part in the affair. Until he said:

"There was a blonde girl out here the day Cugino's body was found. And as I recall, you were also there when we arrived at the place it happened. As it turns out I've been in touch with the L.A.P.D. and I also happen to know of a certain rather well-known blonde singer who drives a silver Stingray and who's vanished under circumstances that sound highly unusual. If she's your client, and I'm betting she is, I suggest you admit it and tell me everything—from the beginning."

"Does she have to be involved?"

"I don't know yet. If her part is all innocence like you're going to tell me it is, I'll see what I can do to help. I can't promise more than that. The papers have ways of finding out things for themselves."

"She never killed him, Phillips. Strode was the one."

"He admit it to you?"

"Not him. Fletcher. His ex-partner."

"And Fletcher's dead?"

I nodded.

"Pity."

"You've got Strode's gun. Also the bullets taken from Cugino's body and the car you dragged from the sea."

"Yeah, we got them and we'll check them, don't you worry about that. Now let's get back to the girl. What's her name? Allison Page? What was her connection with Cugino?"

I didn't answer.

"Give, Cameron. We can keep you here all night if we have to, but we don't want that, do we?"

"He was trying to blackmail her," I said. "But don't ask me what it was he was trying to sell, otherwise we'll be forced to sit here the rest of the night—and tomorrow."

But he didn't press the issue. He listened to all I had to relate, had the statement repeated to a stenographer and then let me sign the various typed copies.

"Your story tallies with the Newtons'," he advised. "About what happened at the motel, that is. So I guess you can go." And as I stood up: "I'll do everything I can to help the girl, Cameron. I don't like seeing people smeared unnecessarily. But don't bank on miracles."

"Sure. Thanks."

"One other thing. Back in Santa Monica there are some people anxious to talk with you when you get back. There your popularity rating isn't all it might be, is it?"

I left him and drove back to the motel. The Newtons were still awake, having only recently been driven home by a deputy. We avoided discussing anything that had happened, and Mike Newton gave me a key to one of the units without concerning himself over a registration card. Everyone else, it seemed, had cleared out soon after the shooting.

I was bone tired, but sleep was difficult. I tossed and turned and everything that had been happening tumbled about dizzily in my mind and kept sleep at bay. I thought about Allison Page. I thought a lot about her, and finally I went to sleep still thinking of her and of how little help I had been.

THIRTEEN

THE sound of people and traffic on the highway awoke me the following morning. I got out of bed, showered, put on the same clothes and wished I'd brought along a razor. Then I called the sheriff's office and spoke for nearly ten minutes with Phillips. What little information he had to convey was less than cheerful, but he did express every confidence of being able to assist in hanging the big one on Erle Donetti.

Outside a few newly arrived cars were parked on the concrete apron. At one a man was busy messing around in the engine, trying to control his language as he answered the questions of a woman in bell-bottom slacks who leaned over his shoulder. I walked up to the office and found Ann Newton in attendance. She still looked very tired and tense, and still amply attractive.

I put down a few dollars and told her I planned to leave within the hour.

"Please, Mr. Cameron," she said, pushing back the money, "there isn't any need for that. After what you did for us yesterday I couldn't think of charging you a cent."

"Nonsense. It all gets booked to expenses and the man footing the bill can afford it."

She began another protest, but I won out and waited while she prepared a receipt.

"Someone from L.A. may try to phone me," I told her. "If they do, can you get someone to give me a shout? I want to stretch my legs along the beach."

"Certainly," she said, passing over the receipt and change. "If he doesn't, will we see you again before you leave?"

"I'm sure of it, Mrs. Merrit."

I was watching the antics of the sea when I heard her coming up behind me fifteen minutes later. From the deep blue of the Pacific the waves swelled and rolled, flattening themselves in long creamy stretches along the sand, as if groping desperately for something that lay eternally beyond their reach. Up in the cloudless sky a gull screeched wildly before starting a dive that swept it from sight. I turned to meet her.

"What are you doing?" she asked.

"Watching the sea. Thinking. And waiting, I guess."

"For—me?"

I shrugged. "I was hoping you'd come."

"Why . . . ?"

I didn't answer. Behind her the sun made a soft, fiery halo of her red hair.

"You called me Mrs. Merrit," she said in her quiet voice.

"Uh-huh. It was your name before you married Mike, wasn't it?"

Her nod was hesitant and so slight I had to watch for it.

"What happened to Merrit?"

"Daryl's been dead for over three years." Folding her skirt demurely around her legs she sat down upon the sand. "He—he was drowned while out on a fishing trip."

"And then you married Newton?"

"More than a year later," she answered defensively, looking up with a hand shielding her eyes from the morning glare. "How did you know I was married before? Did—did you know Daryl?"

I sat down next to her. "No, I never knew him. A girl in Taywood told me you'd married a Daryl Merrit and later moved to San Francisco."

"I—still don't understand."

"Yesterday you learned what sort of business I'm engaged in, didn't you?"

"Yes—but . . ."

"It isn't the most pleasant job in the world, Mrs. Newton. Especially at times like right now. I wasn't deliberately prying into your past; it simply came up while I was working on something else. Someone told me about your marriage in Taywood and your move to San Francisco. It had no importance then. Not until I remembered your present husband telling me you were virtually newlyweds and that some time had been spent up in Frisco before coming here. Some of the things that have been happening these past few days began to make a little more sense after that. Last night I spent a long time thinking about it. But up until now I still wasn't sure."

The gray eyes that studied me were emotionless, but no longer tired. "Not until I responded to the name Merrit, you mean?"

"There were other ways I could have found out, but they would have taken too long. It was a dirty trick, but I can't apologize for it." I took out my cigarettes and offered them. She shook her head so I put them back without lighting any. "Felicity-Anne. Back in Taywood they called you Felicity, didn't they?"

"Mike didn't like the first part of my name," she said quietly, anticipating the rest of my question. "Ever since we've known each other he's called me Ann. There's nothing mysterious about it."

"He thinks a lot of you, doesn't he?"

"I—suppose so." Then she gave a tiny but clearly affirmative nod. "Yes, he does."

"The kind of man who'd do anything for you?"

She looked down at the sand, scooped up a handful and let it sift through her extended fingers without answering.

Above us a small group of circling gulls made low sounds that could have been quiet curses spat down upon the two people who had invaded their beach.

"So you discovered I was married before," she said, her voice still subdued. "What I don't understand is the purpose of your questions—or your interest in me."

"That developed later. After I learned about your father."

"My father?"

"Eugene Green."

She moved to rise, but I put a hand on her arm and gently restrained her. She said:

"Please . . . I don't want to talk about it. It—it's been so long and I've tried so hard to forget."

"Is that why Cugino came here?"

"Who?"

"Let's not play games with each other, Mrs. Newton. You know who I'm talking about." I slowed down, experiencing a little self-anger for having forced the shadows that shifted into her eyes. "He was a friend of yours in Taywood, I know that. That's why he came to you."

"I—I knew Frank." The admission was slow, reluctant. "But—but his arrival here was—was accidental."

I shook my head. "I wish I could believe that, but it isn't easy. You see we know that Cugino was being chased by Donetti. We know that Erle Donetti wanted him dead, but there was something else he wanted before he would order Cugino's execution. A package of dope that never existed. Donetti had chased Cugino from New York right down into California, yet when things got hot for him in L.A., Cugino headed straight for here—not to any other big town where he'd be harder to find. What did he want from you? Money?"

"Are you mad?" This time she got all the way up and I couldn't stop her.

I pushed myself up from the sand. "Phillips had a comparison test made on the bullet that killed Cugino and one taken from Leo Strode's gun," I told her. "I phoned him this morning and he let me know they didn't match."

She started to walk away, but I grabbed her arm and held. "Mike killed him, didn't he? That's why the body was set alight—so recognition would be difficult, if not impossible. That's the only reason why Cugino's killer would go to the trouble and risk of ditching his car in the sea and burning the body. Because he didn't want him identified."

"Leave me alone!" she cried, jerking out of my grasp. "You—you're insane!"

"Get your filthy hands off my wife!"

I came around slowly to find Mike Newton standing there. It seemed he always wore those blue jeans and T-shirts. Only this time a small .22

short barrel revolver had been added to the outfit. It pointed at my middle and would be effective at that short range.

"Seems like I walked into a trap," I said.

"It wasn't intended so, Cameron. Just wanted to find out what your game was, that's all."

"That the gun that killed Cugino?"

"Not that it's going to make any difference where you're going," he snapped back. "Now get clear of my wife!"

"Going to kill me also, Mike?"

"You brought it on yourself, didn't you," he said, coming closer, sweat beading his brow, thick shoulders making restless animal movements under his thin shirt. "I kind of liked you, Cameron, 'Specially after yesterday. But now I've got to do what's got to be done. Not even you're going to louse up things for me and Ann. Not you or anybody! You hear that? We worked too hard to get what we've got and nobody's going to make us lose it."

"I hear," I said. "Are you planning to burn me the same as you did Cugino? It won't look so good, Mike. Not two killings in the same fashion. Especially since there's no longer anyone like Leo Strode to point a finger at."

"I'll figure a way. I'll figure something."

"Why did you kill Cugino?" I asked. "Because he tried to blackmail your wife?" I looked at her. "Does he know what happened to your father?"

"Sure I know," Newton growled. "There ain't no secrets between me and Ann. Not anymore. That creep needed getaway money so he figured he could come here and take it off us. Annie knew he killed her old man, and I guess she was stupid to have kept quiet about it so long. Only Cugino had things a little twisted to suit himself. He was going to say how it was Annie that killed her father, not him. And after all this time how would we prove different?"

"Why did she keep quiet in the first place?"

"She was scared, that's why. After Cugino let her old man have it he said if she peeped to the cops he'd tell them it was her that did it."

"Didn't she?"

"What?" he bellowed. In the sky one of the gulls tried to match the cry. "What'd you just say?"

"Didn't she kill her father?"

"No!" Ann Newton cried. "No, Mike, it isn't true! He's trying to confuse you. Don't listen to him!"

"He killed once for you," I said. "How many times do you want him to go on doing it? Isn't it time you told at least him the truth? He's in the same boat as you now."

"Shut your stinking mouth!" he ordered. "Shut up and get moving. Annie wouldn't do a thing like that. Not my wife. Not to her own father."

"No? Yet if Cugino had done it he'd think nothing of coming back here and risking his neck again by once more involving himself with the woman whose father he's supposed to have butchered? She would be the one person who could prove it, but he was going to try and blackmail her by reversing the facts of her story? How old are you, Newton?"

"You bastard! I ought to kill you right now," he hissed, the sweat growing larger than pearls on his forehead and chin as doubt and uncertainty sifted into his mind, elbowing aside the convictions that had made him kill once.

"Then you'd better do it now," I told him, "because if you listen you'll hear the siren of the sheriff's car. When I spoke to him this morning I suggested he get here as soon as he could."

Newton turned his head to look up the road, providing all the time I needed to jump him. We rolled only a short distance before he bounced away and leapt to his feet. In panic he fired twice, wildly. I kept rolling and the slugs found only sand in which to lodge.

Far enough away I stopped, flattened against the warm sand, and dragged out my own gun, firing one shot over his head. He tried to aim the small gun, then deciding it would be a waste of time now that I was also armed, and probably afraid of what may be coming down the road, whirled around and took off down the beach.

Fists clenched at her mouth, his wife watched the rapidly diminishing figure that raced across the sand, the sea lapping hungrily at his speeding feet. "Mike! Mike!" she screamed, dropping her hands to start running after him.

I got up from the sand and ran, bringing her down in an easy tackle. She cursed and clawed and screamed things I'd been called before. Only never by a woman.

"There—there wasn't any siren," she said after I'd succeeded in pinning her to the ground. "You lied!"

"We're both liars. Me and you both, aren't we, Felicity?"

2

Hidden in between a cluster of wet rocks was the way they found Newton some four hours later. He left nothing to tell us about the kind of thoughts he'd been entertaining while hiding there with the sea whipping at his body, with no other place to go. But though nobody mentioned it then, there were a few of us who had a fair idea. It's never easy seeing everything you have loved, worked for and even killed for come to an abrupt end. Or perhaps it was simply that he had no wish to continue anymore, knowing he had been lied to and used by the one person who was important in his life. Whatever the thoughts had been he had ended them with one of the remaining bullets in the small revolver.

Only after they carried him out from the rocks and the woman saw him did she break down and tell us the entire story.

FOURTEEN

VERY late that Thursday night, with Ross Rigby sitting anxiously beside me, I drove across the county line into Imperial. Not until he had been quite sure every known fact had been recorded, that there was nothing more I could add to what I had already told him, did Under-sheriff Phillips permit me to leave Vadear Point.

"I can't help it," Rigby said, stirring. "But I'm still worried. Supposing she isn't here? Everything has been tidied up beautifully, but there's still a contract to be signed."

"We'll soon find out," I assured him. "Diane Riley told me that, though it was never mailed, she once wrote a letter to the McCords at El Centro. I've checked and there's only one family of that name in the city who have corresponding initials."

"Well, I only hope you're right, that they're it and that she's with them." Rigby sighed, staring out the dark side window.

"We'll see," I said.

Still later, I was parked in front of the modest house. Rigby was inside and, it seemed, he'd been in there a long time. I got out of the car and lit a cigarette, trying not to feel tired. In the drive a light blue Studebaker stood exposed to the night. The garage door was closed.

The front door of the house opened long before I was through with the cigarette, and then she was there, the light from inside silhouetting her small figure. For a few seconds she stood unmoving while her eyes adjusted to the dark, then she started out for the street. Nearing the sidewalk, she called softly:

"Mr. Cameron?"

I flicked away the cigarette. It hit the sidewalk in a shower of glowing sparks.

"Paul?" she said very softly before I could answer, and before I knew what was happening her arms were about my neck and there were things being said that sounded like expressions of thanks. But there was only one thing I was really aware of, and that was the closeness of Allison Page. My arms reached around her of their own accord, or perhaps because it was what they had been wanting to do since first I'd seen her in Rigby's study.

Simultaneously we become conscious of what was happening. I felt her hold loosen and let my arms fall away from her waist.

"Thank you, Paul." She took my hand, squeezing it tightly. "Won't you come inside? Mom and Dad they—they. . . ."

I went in and met the McCords, Stuart and Angela, and for the first time I could really appreciate why their daughter had been ready to throw away everything she had worked for rather than hurt them by being a part of something that would open old wounds. They were the kind of people no one in his right mind would think of hurting, and, strangely, they were very little different to the mental picture I had painted while listening to Sam Ettman talk about them. Stuart McCord was a tall, quiet man with thinning gray hair; his wife a frail woman in her mid-fifties who had the eyes of one who has lived a long time with a personal torture. But she was smiling now when I came into the living room, standing at her chair, hands clasped in front of her small breasts, waiting.

Allison made coffee after my hand had been gripped and shaken repeatedly, after I had been obliged to listen to her mother and father say things which were embarrassing. I had told Ann Newton that mine was not the most pleasant job in the world, and it wasn't. But there were times such as these, though few and far between, that made the whole business worth it. I no longer even felt bad about what I had done to her. Not now when it was obvious other people would have a chance of living again.

Seated, with hot black coffee warming my bones, my ears still burning, I told them everything they wanted to know. Everything we had learned from the Newton woman, filling in the gaps as best I could, for it was the only way anyone would ever be able to complete the entire scene of that day in Taywood twenty years ago.

I told them how, in spite of her father's ruling in the matter, Felicity-Anne Newton, then Green, had been continuing her friendship with Frankie Cugino.

"That afternoon when she was returning from school she met Cugino near her home. It appears he had been waiting for her, watching the house, for he knew the Green's housekeeper was in town shopping. The girl had a crush on Cugino. He was older than her and different to the boys she knew at school. Perhaps that was his basic appeal. I don't know. Whichever, it didn't take much for him to persuade her to take him into the house. In the kitchen she poured Cokes and they talked for a bit. Only a Coke wasn't exactly Cugino's idea of an afternoon's entertainment. It wasn't what he had been waiting for. Things got a bit out of hand there and the girl became a little jittery. She wasn't sure just when the housekeeper would return. But by then, unfortunately, Cugino was insistent about staying." I looked at the faces that watched me. "They left the kitchen," I said, "and went to the garage to finish what they'd started."

Allison rose and refilled my cup, raising eyebrows to ask the others if they wanted more. They didn't.

"Probably at the time all this started," I said, picking up the story again, "Eugene Green had already left his office. He'd been having trouble with an ulcer and decided to quit work after lunch. How he found them is uncertain. The house is the type that has the garage built behind it, so it isn't unreasonable to suggest that Green parked out front, entered the house, and was later attracted by a noise or something from the garage. Whichever way it was, his daughter swears she never heard him arrive. Their first knowledge of his early return was when he pushed open the garage door and found them in . . ." I drank the second cup of coffee, uncertain of how to finish the rest. "What happened then is a bit vague, even to the girl. She claims her father grabbed Cugino and started striking him. Afraid of what he might do to the boy, she went to his aid. All she remembers is hitting out at her father, not stopping until Cugino intervened. Only then, she told us, did she realize there had been an axe in her hands—apparently picked up from the garage floor when she went to her boy friend's defense."

Angela McCord lowered her face.

I said: "It isn't a pretty story. If you prefer, I'll skip the rest."

"No," said her husband, reaching for her hand, taking it tenderly in his own. "We've hoped so long to one day hear the truth . . . Please go on, Mr. Cameron."

"The girl was in a panic," I said, disposing of the coffee cup. "But Cugino kept his head. He made her go inside and change out of her blood-stained clothes. While she did that he cleaned the glasses they'd used in the kitchen and then went back to the garage and wiped away the fingerprints from the axe shaft. The axe was then thrown into the grass outside the garage. With those details taken care of the two of them left the house. Cugino went to mingle with his cronies while the girl went to the library and made sure she was seen there. On her way home she encountered their housekeeper and together they stumbled upon Eugene Green's body. Perhaps she arranged it that way, we don't know. She wouldn't add anything more to it when she told us what had happened."

"But Clark . . ." Stuart McCord said. "His prints were found on the axe—Green's blood was on his clothes . . . That's why everyone was so sure he had done that terrible thing."

I nodded. "We can only guess what happened there, sir. My own is that Clark took his delivery up to the house, and when no one answered the front door bell, walked around to the back. Remember Green's car was parked there where he could see it, so he'd be bound to think someone was home. If he went to the rear of the house he'd have seen the axe lying where it had been thrown. He must have picked it up, realizing too late what was on the blade. Probably in doing so is how he got the blood on his clothes. After that he must have made further investigations, ones that took him into the garage. It's easy to imagine the boy's reaction to the sight that greeted him."

"Then—then he must have been going for help," McCord said, unable to control his excitement. "He must have been going for help when he overturned the truck." Still holding his wife's hand he turned to her. "Did you hear that, honey? Our boy wasn't running from anything he did. He was . . . going for help."

"I'm sure he was," I said, standing up. "That's the reason he was speeding the truck in the first place. The investigating team found a packet of nails near the scene of the crime—an item your son probably dropped from the stuff he had come to deliver. That, the truck accident, the fingerprints on the axe and the blood-stains on Clark's clothes all helped to create a rather definite conclusion." I wanted to tell them that Sam Ettman could never be blamed because the facts had been misinterpreted, but I held back. It wasn't the time and they would come to realize it themselves later.

Leaving Allison's Corvette locked up in her father's garage, we drove back in my car. I let Rigby take the wheel. Allison went back with us because Rigby wanted her at Lynx's offices early in the morning. She sat on the front seat between us.

"What I still don't understand," Rigby said thoughtfully, "is how Cugino was able to find his old girl friend after all the time he'd spent away from California. You said he'd been working in New York, didn't you?"

"He was. But eight years ago he went back to Taywood to see his father. Presumably he found out then that Felicity had married and moved to San Francisco. When Donetti was chasing him one of the places he went to was Frisco. He needed money badly and Felicity seemed like a possibility. When he found she wasn't there he made it his business to find out where she had gone, later paying her a visit at the motel. The first time he called, on his way to L.A., she convinced him her and her new husband had no money. Every cent she'd collected from her first husband's insurance had been used to buy the motel. She gave him all she could manage and he left them. It was in L.A. that he discovered who Allison was, and there that he tried to blackmail her. When that backfired and he skipped out of town he went straight back to the motel, this time demanding that the Newtons raise enough for him to buy a long boat ride."

"But he contacted Allison again," Rigby reminded. "He phoned her from that motel."

"That was her idea—Felicity's. She talked to him, convinced him that Allison would pay if enough pressure was applied. In the meantime she let her husband in on what had happened in Taywood. Only the way she told it Cugino was the one who had used the axe, not her. Then Rose Lang upset matters by phoning and warning him about Donetti's men. After hearing from her he left the motel in a hurry, driving up to San Luis Obispo where he was to wait until Donetti's crew left and Allison showed up. Before he left the Newtons had been given two choices. Either they raised a lump of money themselves, or else they were to make the contact with Allison and get the money she was bringing with her. Cugino himself was too scared to venture back to the motel in case Donetti's boys were still lurking there. So the drill was that Newton would meet him somewhere along the coast road to deliver the money. It no longer seemed to matter whether it was Allison's money he got, or theirs, just as long as it was enough to help him get very far away from Erle Donetti. If Newton didn't play along, Cugino threatened to turn himself over to the police for protection, after which he'd spill everything about how Green was killed."

"Only Newton didn't play ball, did he?"

"No," I said. "He never had the money and he couldn't ever raise the kind that was wanted without selling the motel—something that was very precious to him. But even that would have taken time. On the other hand he had no wish to involve himself with Allison. According to his wife he saw her visit to the motel as some kind of trap planned for Cugino. Anyway, Newton phoned Cugino as planned, told him he had the money— Allison's money. When they met that night he got into Cugino's car, but instead of handing over any money he presented him instead with something from a gun. After ditching Cugino's car, he carried the body in his own car to where it was eventually found, and set it alight. I don't have to repeat the reason for that."

"She must have been an absolute bitch," Rigby muttered.

Allison said nothing.

"If you'd met her you wouldn't have thought so. I liked her at first. It took something that happened this morning to change my first impression."

"He—he must have loved her very much to do what he did for her," Allison said, her voice scarcely more than a whisper in the dark.

"He did. I guess she did, too." I didn't tell them how she had looked when they'd shown her her husband's body, nor what she had done. They were things I wanted to forget.

We drove on in speeding silence for most of the way, listening to the muted music from the car radio. Occasionally Rigby or Allison would say something, but after a while I stopped hearing a thing. When the car finally stopped it was Allison's voice that roused me. I sat up, lifting my head from her shoulder, thankful for the dark that concealed the color of my face.

2

Rigby never got his wish about avoiding publicity. Throughout the state, and probably the rest of the country, the newspapers were having themselves a ball. There wasn't a detail they didn't exploit. But it was the kind of publicity none of us had suspected could be achieved. Her willingness to forfeit the opportunity of a movie contract rather than cause her parents further anxiety or grief, made Allison Page the kind of girl everybody and his brother wanted to read about. Lynx got her name on to a contract without any delay, realizing perhaps that others would be after her now. And they weren't wrong. In this town the right kind of publicity is a valuable asset. It didn't do me any harm either.

The money Donetti had instructed Strode to stuff into my pocket that night above the florist setup was used to buy Rose Lang a decent funeral. The day they buried her I went along to say goodbye. There were only a few of us in the chapel that morning, but I never found out who the rest were.

In New York the narcotics boys had been busy trying to find out if there had been anything to Gino Donetti's story, satisfying themselves in the end that there had never been anything entrusted to Frank Cugino before his arrest.

Allison phoned me at the office two days after our arrival back in Los Angeles and I received an invitation to join her and Rigby for dinner. I went. There were two more invitations extended by Rigby, and I accepted them only because she would be there also. Later I thought about asking her out, but each time I talked myself out of it. Then she phoned one morning and asked if I would come to a party Rigby was throwing for her. I made up some excuse about being tied up with a case, and after that hung up, smoked a cigarette and went downstairs to buy a few drinks. Rigby called a few minutes after I returned to my desk. I was coming to the party, he insisted, even if he had to arrange for a police escort.

So I dragged my tux out of moth balls and had it cleaned and pressed.

The brawl was being held at Rigby's home. Cars jammed the drive and at the door there was a tuxedoed muscle to receive the guests and keep out the riff-raff. He must have been given my name for I got in without any trouble, working my way through bunches of people packing the large room, progressing eventually to the bar and a stool that was vacated when I got there. It was somewhat different to what I had expected. The glitter and the glamour, it was all there, but there were few faces I recognized—though there were bound to have been some of the big names who kept Lynx's shares and their own private incomes high in the top brackets. But from the conversations that surrounded me it appeared that many of the guests were columnists, publicity hacks, or agents who had nothing to talk about but the industry, the current Oscar nominations, and the headaches it was creating. At the opposite end of the room a band played softly for the benefit of those who wanted to dance. I looked for Allison and couldn't find her. But she found where I was. A talkative character who was convinced I was somebody from Metro had me cornered, telling me why he thought the movies still had much more to offer than TV when Allison came up behind and drew me away. The trouble was our privacy was quickly interrupted by others demanding her company. I crawled away back to the bar and let the white coat feed me more of the high priced Scotch that was being splashed about.

A sudden lull descended over the crowded room. Even the band stopped playing. From the opposite end a man said something I couldn't hear and everyone applauded loudly. I got up and found out the reason for everyone coming to attention. They had her up on the small dais, a member of the combo adjusting the microphone to her height. She started to sing. From the bar I listened, then gently pushed my way across the crowded floor until I was nearly up front. With everyone yelling for more she prepared to go into her second number. I went away. Back to the bar.

Although strings of lights had been strung across the Olympic size pool, tables and chairs set up conveniently around it, the music from the band—and now the singer—piped through concealed speakers, there wasn't a soul outside. I carried my drink to the pool edge and studied my reflection in the clear blue water. It told me nothing comforting, so I finished the drink, lit another cigarette and started off to find my way out of the place.

She was coming out of the house as I turned to go in.

"Paul—is something wrong?"

"No. Nothing's wrong."

"But there is, isn't there?"

"The party's great, Allison. Swell. I enjoyed it. I'm glad I came."

"But there's still something not right," she insisted.

"If it is," I said, "it's with me. This is the first time I've been to one of these things."

"Then that makes us even. It's my first also."

"Only you belong here."

"And you don't?"

"Like someone from *Confidential*," I said. "If that thing still exists."

"Will you let me be the judge of that?" she asked.

"Why?"

"Because you've been drinking and you sound depressed, that's why. Your judgment is bound to be lousy."

"I'm not drunk," I returned defensively.

"Aren't you?" she smiled, cocking her blonde head in a way that made my hands restless.

"Okay. I've had my limit. Another reason why it's time I left."

"Please, Paul, stay. For me?" Her head still angled, those blue eyes flashing, she said: "You never once phoned me. Do you know that?"

"I thought about it. Often."

"Then why didn't you?" She tried to make the question sound like a joking reprimand, but it didn't come off.

"I thought about it too long," I answered.

Her eyes asked the next question.

"Do you know where you're going from here, Allison? Straight up. You're starting to travel."

"I thought you would be happy for me, Paul. I thought you were a friend." And this time there was no trace of pretence in her voice.

"I am. Both. A happy friend."

"Then what's the problem?" Slim fingers deftly removed the cigarette from my hand before it had a chance of burning any closer to the flesh. She dropped it on the tiles, leaving it to die in its own time.

"This," I answered, reaching for her.

She came as if the movement had been rehearsed, as though we'd been around together for a long time and it was an expected thing. Her lips tasted sweet and warm and turned a moment into an eternity.

"And that's the problem?" she asked, her voice husky with surprise when I released her.

"Part of it."

"Because of where I'm supposed to be going?"

"Uh-huh."

"But what difference would that make?"

"A hell of a lot. I'm not Hollywood, Allison. Damnit, if anyone ever sneered I wouldn't even have a muscle or a bank balance that'd be worth shoving in their faces."

"Don't talk like that," she admonished softly. "Don't ever talk like that. I owe you too much for anything like that to be of importance."

"Nuts," I growled quietly. "Rigby paid me more than my usual fee."

"But still not nearly enough."

"Knock it off," I said harshly. "You don't owe me a thing."

For a little while she was silent, her face soft and expressionless under the colored lights, but still very vulnerable. Then she asked softly: "Don't you even want to try? Are you afraid to find out if it will make a difference—what tomorrow brings? I thought you—?"

"You're crazy." My voice matched hers.

"Yes," she said, and whether or not it was to prove her mental instability, leaned up against me, her head buried against my chest. I had to stoop again to kiss her, but that was something I could easily get accustomed to doing.

"Want to try?" Taking my arm she steered me back to the sound of activity. Rigby was at the door waiting for us, a smile pasted broadly across his tanned features. I felt like a sulking kid who'd been pacified.

It could never work out. Not in a million years. I knew this town. They'd never permit it—even if it was possible. But I was a little drunk and tomorrow was a distant thing that could go and take care of itself.

THE END

About the Author

Wade Wright left school at the age of 14, starting work as a laboratory assistant, storeman, nightclub photographer, and private investigator. Along the way he spent two years traveling around Africa the hard, but inexpensive way, before settling down to married life. Subsequently, he secured diplomas and further qualifications in marketing and other business functions while occupying various managerial posts, finally operating as a project specialist.

He has written a number of books, as well as numerous scripts for radio and articles relating to the movies and publications of yesteryear. Wade Wright died in South Africa in early 2009.

RAMBLE HOUSE's

HARRY STEPHEN KEELER WEBWORK MYSTERIES

(RH) indicates the title is available ONLY in the **RAMBLE HOUSE** edition

The Ace of Spades Murder
The Affair of the Bottled Deuce (RH)
The Amazing Web
The Barking Clock
Behind That Mask
The Book with the Orange Leaves
The Bottle with the Green Wax Seal
The Box from Japan
The Case of the Canny Killer
The Case of the Crazy Corpse (RH)
The Case of the Flying Hands (RH)
The Case of the Ivory Arrow
The Case of the Jeweled Ragpicker
The Case of the Lavender Gripsack
The Case of the Mysterious Moll
The Case of the 16 Beans
The Case of the Transparent Nude (RH)
The Case of the Transposed Legs
The Case of the Two-Headed Idiot (RH)
The Case of the Two Strange Ladies
The Circus Stealers (RH)
Cleopatra's Tears
A Copy of Beowulf (RH)
The Crimson Cube (RH)
The Face of the Man From Saturn
Find the Clock
The Five Silver Buddhas
The 4th King
The Gallows Waits, My Lord! (RH)
The Green Jade Hand
Finger! Finger!
Hangman's Nights (RH)
I, Chameleon (RH)
I Killed Lincoln at 10:13! (RH)
The Iron Ring
The Man Who Changed His Skin (RH)
The Man with the Crimson Box
The Man with the Magic Eardrums
The Man with the Wooden Spectacles
The Marceau Case
The Matilda Hunter Murder
The Monocled Monster

The Murder of London Lew
The Murdered Mathematician
The Mysterious Card (RH)
The Mysterious Ivory Ball of Wong Shing Li (RH)
The Mystery of the Fiddling Cracksman
The Peacock Fan
The Photo of Lady X (RH)
The Portrait of Jirjohn Cobb
Report on Vanessa Hewstone (RH)
Riddle of the Travelling Skull
Riddle of the Wooden Parrakeet (RH)
The Scarlet Mummy (RH)
The Search for X-Y-Z
The Sharkskin Book
Sing Sing Nights
The Six From Nowhere (RH)
The Skull of the Waltzing Clown
The Spectacles of Mr. Cagliostro
Stand By—London Calling!
The Steeltown Strangler
The Stolen Gravestone (RH)
Strange Journey (RH)
The Strange Will
The Straw Hat Murders (RH)
The Street of 1000 Eyes (RH)
Thieves' Nights
Three Novellos (RH)
The Tiger Snake
The Trap (RH)
Vagabond Nights (Defrauded Yeggman)
Vagabond Nights 2 (10 Hours)
The Vanishing Gold Truck
The Voice of the Seven Sparrows
The Washington Square Enigma
When Thief Meets Thief
The White Circle (RH)
The Wonderful Scheme of Mr. Christopher Thorne
X. Jones—of Scotland Yard
Y. Cheung, Business Detective

Keeler Related Works

A To Izzard: A Harry Stephen Keeler Companion by Fender Tucker—Articles and stories about Harry, by Harry, and in his style. Included is a compleat bibliography.

Wild About Harry: Reviews of Keeler Novels—Edited by Richard Polt & Fender Tucker—22 reviews of works by Harry Stephen Keeler from *Keeler News*. A perfect introduction to the author.

The Keeler Keyhole Collection: Annotated newsletter rants from Harry Stephen Keeler, edited by Francis M. Nevins. Over 400 pages of incredibly personal Keeleriana.

Fakealoo—Pastiches of the style of Harry Stephen Keeler by selected demented members of the HSK Society. Updated every year with the new winner.

RAMBLE HOUSE's OTHER LOONS

The Case of the Little Green Men—Mack Reynolds wrote this love song to sci-fi fans back in 1951 and it's now back in print.

Hell Fire—A new hard-boiled novel by Jack Moskovitz about an arsonist, an arson cop and a Nazi hooker. It isn't pretty.

Researching American-Made Toy Soldiers—A 276-page collection of a lifetime of articles by toy soldier expert Richard O'Brien

Strands of the Web: Short Stories of Harry Stephen Keeler—Edited and Introduced by Fred Cleaver

The Sam McCain Novels—Ed Gorman's terrific series includes *The Day the Music Died, Wake Up Little Susie* and *Will You Still Love Me Tomorrow?*

A Shot Rang Out—Three decades of reviews from Jon Breen

A Roland Daniel Double: The Signal and The Return of Wu Fang—Classic thrillers from the 30s

Murder in Shawnee—Two novels of the Alleghenies by John Douglas: *Shawnee Alley Fire* and *Haunts*.

Deep Space and other Stories—A collection of SF gems by Richard A. Lupoff

Blood Moon—The first of the Robert Payne series by Ed Gorman

The Time Armada—Fox B. Holden's 1953 SF gem.

Black River Falls—Suspense from the master, Ed Gorman

Sideslip—1968 SF masterpiece by Ted White and Dave Van Arnam

The Triune Man—Mindscrambling science fiction from Richard A. Lupoff

Detective Duff Unravels It—Episodic mysteries by Harvey O'Higgins

Mysterious Martin, the Master of Murder—Two versions of a strange 1912 novel by Tod Robbins about a man who writes books that can kill.

The Master of Mysteries—1912 novel of supernatural sleuthing by Gelett Burgess

Dago Red—22 tales of dark suspense by Bill Pronzini

The Night Remembers—A 1991 Jack Walsh mystery from Ed Gorman

Rough Cut & New, Improved Murder—Ed Gorman's first two novels

Hollywood Dreams—A novel of the Depression by Richard O'Brien

Six Gelett Burgess Novels—*The Master of Mysteries, The White Cat, Two O'Clock Courage, Ladies in Boxes, Find the Woman, The Heart Line*

The Organ Reader—A huge compilation of just about everything published in the 1971-1972 radical bay-area newspaper, *THE ORGAN*.

A Clear Path to Cross—Sharon Knowles short mystery stories by Ed Lynskey

Old Times' Sake—Short stories by James Reasoner from Mike Shayne Magazine

Freaks and Fantasies—Eerie tales by Tod Robbins, collaborator of Tod Browning on the film FREAKS.

Six Jim Harmon Double Novels—*Vixen Hollow/Celluloid Scandal, The Man Who Made Maniacs/Silent Siren, Ape Rape/Wanton Witch, Sex Burns Like Fire/Twist Session, Sudden Lust/Passion Strip, Sin Unlimited/Harlot Master, Twilight Girls/Sex Institution*. Written in the early 60s.

Marblehead: A Novel of H.P. Lovecraft—A long-lost masterpiece from Richard A. Lupoff. Published for the first time!

The Compleat Ova Hamlet—Parodies of SF authors by Richard A. Lupoff—A brand new edition with more stories and more illustrations by Trina Robbins.

The Secret Adventures of Sherlock Holmes—Three Sherlockian pastiches by the Brooklyn author/publisher, Gary Lovisi.

The Universal Holmes—Richard A. Lupoff's 2007 collection of five Holmesian pastiches and a recipe for giant rat stew.

Four Joel Townsley Rogers Novels—By the author of *The Red Right Hand: Once In a Red Moon, Lady With the Dice, The Stopped Clock, Never Leave My Bed*

Two Joel Townsley Rogers Story Collections—Night of Horror and Killing Time

Twenty Norman Berrow Novels—*The Bishop's Sword, Ghost House, Don't Go Out After Dark, Claws of the Cougar, The Smokers of Hashish, The Secret Dancer, Don't Jump Mr. Boland!, The Footprints of Satan, Fingers for Ransom, The Three Tiers of Fantasy, The Spaniard's Thumb, The Eleventh Plague, Words Have Wings, One Thrilling Night, The Lady's in Danger, It Howls at Night, The Terror in the Fog, Oil Under the Window, Murder in the Melody, The Singing Room*

The N. R. De Mexico Novels—Robert Bragg presents *Marijuana Girl, Madman on a Drum, Private Chauffeur* in one volume.

Four Chelsea Quinn Yarbro Novels featuring Charlie Moon—*Ogilvie, Tallant and Moon, Music When the Sweet Voice Dies, Poisonous Fruit* and *Dead Mice*

Five Walter S. Masterman Mysteries—*The Green Toad, The Flying Beast, The Yellow Mistletoe, The Wrong Verdict* and *The Perjured Alibi*. Fantastic impossible plots.

Two Hake Talbot Novels—*Rim of the Pit, The Hangman's Handyman*. Classic locked room mysteries.

Two Alexander Laing Novels—*The Motives of Nicholas Holtz* and *Dr. Scarlett*, stories of medical mayhem and intrigue from the 30s.

Four David Hume Novels—*Corpses Never Argue, Cemetery First Stop, Make Way for the Mourners, Eternity Here I Come*, and more to come.

Three Wade Wright Novels—*Echo of Fear, Death At Nostalgia Street* and *It Leads to Murder*, with more to come!

Six Rupert Penny Novels—*Policeman's Holiday, Policeman's Evidence, Lucky Policeman, Policeman in Armour, Sealed Room Murder, Sweet Poison*, classic mysteries.

Five Jack Mann Novels—Strange murder in the English countryside. *Gees' First Case, Nightmare Farm, Grey Shapes, The Ninth Life, The Glass Too Many*.

Seven Max Afford Novels—*Owl of Darkness, Death's Mannikins, Blood on His Hands, The Dead Are Blind, The Sheep and the Wolves, Sinners in Paradise* and *Two Locked Room Mysteries and a Ripping Yarn* by one of Australia's finest novelists.

Five Joseph Shallit Novels—*The Case of the Billion Dollar Body, Lady Don't Die on My Doorstep, Kiss the Killer, Yell Bloody Murder, Take Your Last Look*. One of America's best 50's authors.

Two Crimson Clown Novels—By Johnston McCulley, author of the Zorro novels, *The Crimson Clown* and *The Crimson Clown Again*.

The Best of 10-Story Book—edited by Chris Mikul, over 35 stories from the literary magazine Harry Stephen Keeler edited.

A Young Man's Heart—A forgotten early classic by Cornell Woolrich

The Anthony Boucher Chronicles—edited by Francis M. Nevins
Book reviews by Anthony Boucher written for the *San Francisco Chronicle*, 1942—1947. Essential and fascinating reading.

Muddled Mind: Complete Works of Ed Wood, Jr.—David Hayes and Hayden Davis deconstruct the life and works of a mad genius.

Gadsby—A lipogram (a novel without the letter E). Ernest Vincent Wright's last work, published in 1939 right before his death.

My First Time: The One Experience You Never Forget—Michael Birchwood—64 true first-person narratives of how they lost it.

Automaton—Brilliant treatise on robotics: 1928-style! By H. Stafford Hatfield

The Incredible Adventures of Rowland Hern—Rousing 1928 impossible crimes by Nicholas Olde.

Slammer Days—Two full-length prison memoirs: *Men into Beasts* (1952) by George Sylvester Viereck and *Home Away From Home* (1962) by Jack Woodford

Murder in Black and White—1931 classic tennis whodunit by Evelyn Elder

Killer's Caress—Cary Moran's 1936 hardboiled thriller

The Golden Dagger—1951 Scotland Yard yarn by E. R. Punshon

Beat Books #1—Two beatnik classics, *A Sea of Thighs* by Ray Kainen and *Village Hipster* by J.X. Williams

A Smell of Smoke—1951 English countryside thriller by Miles Burton

Ruled By Radio—1925 futuristic novel by Robert L. Hadfield & Frank E. Farncombe

Murder in Silk—A 1937 Yellow Peril novel of the silk trade by Ralph Trevor

The Case of the Withered Hand—1936 potboiler by John G. Brandon

Finger-prints Never Lie—A 1939 classic detective novel by John G. Brandon

Inclination to Murder—1966 thriller by New Zealand's Harriet Hunter

Invaders from the Dark—Classic werewolf tale from Greye La Spina

Fatal Accident—Murder by automobile, a 1936 mystery by Cecil M. Wills

The Devil Drives—A prison and lost treasure novel by Virgil Markham

Dr. Odin—Douglas Newton's 1933 potboiler comes back to life.

The Chinese Jar Mystery—Murder in the manor by John Stephen Strange, 1934

The Julius Caesar Murder Case—A classic 1935 re-telling of the assassination by Wallace Irwin that's much more fun than the Shakespeare version

West Texas War and Other Western Stories—by Gary Lovisi

The Contested Earth and Other SF Stories—A never-before published space opera and seven short stories by Jim Harmon.

Tales of the Macabre and Ordinary—Modern twisted horror by Chris Mikul, author of the *Bizarrism* series.

The Gold Star Line—Seaboard adventure from L.T. Reade and Robert Eustace.

The Werewolf vs the Vampire Woman—Hard to believe ultraviolence by either Arthur M. Scarm or Arthur M. Scram.

Black Hogan Strikes Again—Australia's Peter Renwick pens a tale of the outback.

Don Diablo: Book of a Lost Film—Two-volume treatment of a western by Paul Landres, with diagrams. Intro by Francis M. Nevins.

The Charlie Chaplin Murder Mystery—Movie hijinks by Wes D. Gehring

The Koky Comics—A collection of all of the 1978-1981 Sunday and daily comic strips by Richard O'Brien and Mort Gerberg, in two volumes.

Suzy—Another collection of comic strips from Richard O'Brien and Bob Vojtko.

Dime Novels: Ramble House's 10-Cent Books—*Knife in the Dark* by Robert Leslie Bellem, *Hot Lead* and *Song of Death* by Ed Earl Repp, *A Hashish House in New York* by H.H. Kane, and five more.

Blood in a Snap—The *Finnegan's Wake* of the 21st century, by Jim Weiler and Al Gorithm

Stakeout on Millennium Drive—Award-winning Indianapolis Noir—Ian Woollen.

Dope Tales #1—Two dope-riddled classics; *Dope Runners* by Gerald Grantham and *Death Takes the Joystick* by Phillip Condé.

Dope Tales #2—Two more narco-classics; *The Invisible Hand* by Rex Dark and *The Smokers of Hashish* by Norman Berrow.

Dope Tales #3—Two enchanting novels of opium by the master, Sax Rohmer. *Dope* and *The Yellow Claw*.

Tenebrae—Ernest G. Henham's 1898 horror tale brought back.

The Singular Problem of the Stygian House-Boat—Two classic tales by John Kendrick Bangs about the denizens of Hades.

Tiresias—Psychotic modern horror novel by Jonathan M. Sweet.

The One After Snelling—Kickass modern noir from Richard O'Brien.

The Sign of the Scorpion—1935 Edmund Snell tale of oriental evil.

The House of the Vampire—1907 poetic thriller by George S. Viereck.

An Angel in the Street—Modern hardboiled noir by Peter Genovese.

The Devil's Mistress—Scottish gothic tale by J. W. Brodie-Innes.

The Lord of Terror—1925 mystery with master-criminal, Fantômas.

The Lady of the Terraces—1925 adventure by E. Charles Vivian.

My Deadly Angel—1955 Cold War drama by John Chelton.

Prose Bowl—Futuristic satire—Bill Pronzini & Barry N. Malzberg .

Satan's Den Exposed—True crime in Truth or Consequences New Mexico—Award-winning journalism by the *Desert Journal*.

The Amorous Intrigues & Adventures of Aaron Burr—by Anonymous—Hot historical action.

I Stole $16,000,000—A true story by cracksman Herbert E. Wilson.

The Black Dark Murders—Vintage 50s college murder yarn by Milt Ozaki, writing as Robert O. Saber.

Sex Slave—Potboiler of lust in the days of Cleopatra—Dion Leclerq.

You'll Die Laughing—Bruce Elliott's 1945 novel of murder at a practical joker's English countryside manor.

The Private Journal & Diary of John H. Surratt—The memoirs of the man who conspired to assassinate President Lincoln.

Dead Man Talks Too Much—Hollywood boozer by Weed Dickenson

Red Light—History of legal prostitution in Shreveport Louisiana by Eric Brock. Includes wonderful photos of the houses and the ladies.

A Snark Selection—Lewis Carroll's *The Hunting of the Snark* with two Snarkian chapters by Harry Stephen Keeler—Illustrated by Gavin L. O'Keefe.

Ripped from the Headlines!—The Jack the Ripper story as told in the newspaper articles in the *New York* and *London Times*.

Geronimo—S. M. Barrett's 1905 autobiography of a noble American.

The White Peril in the Far East—Sidney Lewis Gulick's 1905 indictment of the West and assurance that Japan would never attack the U.S.

The Compleat Calhoon—All of Fender Tucker's works: Includes *Totah Six-Pack, Weed, Women and Song* and *Tales from the Tower,* plus a CD of all of his songs.

Totah Six-Pack—Just Fender Tucker's six tales about Farmington in one sleek volume.

RAMBLE HOUSE
Fender Tucker, Prop.

www.ramblehouse.com   fender@ramblehouse.com

228-826-1783   10329 Sheephead Drive, Vancleave MS 39565